DRIFTLESS

*"We don't see things as they are, we see things
as we are."*

Anaïs Nin (1903 – 1977)
American/French Writer

Ardys Brevig Richards

This is a work of historical fiction. Two Minnesota institutions named herein, the Rochester State Hospital (PKA Second Minnesota Hospital for the Insane) and the Owatonna orphanage (PKA the Minnesota State Public School for Neglected and Dependent Children) have long been shuttered. The author has researched their histories and some of the practices within, however some literary license has been taken in the finer details. The setting of this story is predominantly in Houston County, the southeasternmost corner of Minnesota. The county lies near the western edge of the Driftless Area. The Mississippi River forms its eastern boundary and Iowa forms its southern. Specifically, the story takes place in a neighborhood of dairy farms located north of Spring Grove and west o f Caledonia. Spring Grove was the first Norwegian settlement in Minnesota. The farm neighborhood of Hawk Ridge, however, is a fictional one. Other towns and place names used in the telling of this story do exist. However, any similarity found in this book to any real person, living or dead or any real business or historical event is accidental. Readers interested in learning more about the history of Minnesota and this area in particular are referred to the Minnesota Historical Society and to the Giants of the Earth Heritage Center based in Spring Grove, Minnesota.

Cover artwork and design by Deb Akey 2021

Dedication

Illustration 1: L to R, Four generations. Norwegian-American immigrant, Torine Frederiksdatter Eri Rosaaen Omodt, born July 19, 1865, emigrated from Sogn, Oppland, Norway c. 1885. Her son, Melvin O. Omodt (third of ten children) was born Sept 7, 1898 in Black Hammer, Minnesota. He is holding Torine's great granddaughter, Mavis Brevig Wallace, born Sept 21, 1942. Torine's granddaughter, born March 16, 1922 is Vivian Omodt Brevig.

In memory of my humble and tenacious immigrant ancestors that doggedly grubbed the wooded bluffs to make a Minnesota wilderness their home. Among them stand unsung heroes.

CONTENTS

Preface

The kind of family life on a small dairy farm that I knew as a child has all but vanished in the United States. Corporate farms now cover the landscape; fences are largely gone, and fields can be measured in square miles rather than acres. One rarely sees a herd of dairy cattle lazily grazing across a pasture.

Dairying before the time of automated milking parlors required dedication to an unrelenting routine every day of the year regardless of farmer illness, holidays, blizzards and family tragedies. Cows were milked twice each day at twelve hour intervals.

Field work was more time-intensive than it is today, using equipment that was much smaller. Fewer chemicals were used. Instead, the animals' own excrement provided rich fertilizer that was plowed into the soil each spring. Crops were rotated and grown primarily to feed the farm's dairy herd and other farm animals rather than to be sold.

Children raised on a dairy farm in the twentieth century had a vast playground to explore with a few dangerous exceptions. Children roamed the woods and played in the barns, their bare feet growing tough callouses throughout the summers. Like all children, farm kids first learned to walk and talk. And soon after, they began to learn about the farm animals and how to care for them.

Even small children could bring the cows home from the pasture, herd cows armed with only a switch, or open and close a gate for equipment to pass through. Children contributed to the work life of the farm by picking up many skills: they drove the horses or tractors, fed the farm animals, milked cows by hand or machine, put down bedding for the animals, cleaned the pens and gutters, put up fencing, cut firewood and carried it in to feed the wood stoves, baled and stacked hay, wielded paintbrushes, snow shovels and pitchforks, and too many more skills to name.

The milking schedule drove all other farm activities. Homegrown foods were served at breakfast after morning milking. Noontime dinner was the main meal of the day, and supper could be eaten before or after the evening milking. "A little-lunch" of an open-faced sandwich, piece of cake, cookie or bar was brought out to the field workers mid-afternoon to tide them over until supper-time.

Sunday was a day of rest for most. A casual Sunday afternoon drive was common and might bring visits from faraway cousins or nearby neighbors. When one family got an early start, they might meet their would-be visitors on the dusty road as they were leaving their farm. Friendly four-finger waves were exchanged between the two steering wheels, followed by a discussion within each car. "Looks like they're heading to our place. Should we turn around and go back home?" When farming guests came to visit, they always departed by five o'clock at the latest, in order to milk their own cows at home.

By necessity, successful dairy farming required families with strength of character, intelligence, patience, creativity, flexibility, appreciation for the earth, risk-taking despite drought or deluge, and the perseverance to forge on despite the difficulties bound to arise. It is the stalwart, yet gentle character of those farming families that I knew as a child that inspired me to write about them as they faced some of the hardest times.

For readers who may be unfamiliar with Scandinavian names:

Arvid –	AR'veed
Marit –	MAH'reet
Fjeld –	Fj is Pronounced like "fi" in "fiord." "fee-YELd"
Kjelle –	Kj sounds similar to a "Ch" sound. "CHEH'leh."
Trønby -	ø sounds a little like the "oo" in "crook."

Illustration 2: Brown Swiss dairy herd and four-year-old Ardys with a switch.

Acknowledgments

I am grateful to my six siblings for sharing their memories of life on our family farm before I was born. The seven of us were raised on the same dairy farm, however the eldest have memories that precede mine by eight to fourteen years and in those years there were several changes on our farm. I count myself fortunate to have heard new (to me) family stories in the process of writing this book. I mention below a few of them that didn't make it into the book. Several of my siblings' memories from the farm *did* find their way into the story.

From my eldest sister, Mavis Wallace (I call her Stacey) I heard something of what it was like to be the eldest in a large family and the responsibility she felt to look out for the younger ones at home and at school, whether appreciated by them or not.

From my next sister, BevAnn Brevig, I learned something about fieldwork with a team of horses, cutting down trees to heat the house, and about taking her 4-H pig, Pinky, to the Minnesota State Fair as a brave nine-year-old.

My sister, Lou (Mary Lou) Knight shared a very early Christmas memory of our young parents bundling up their six little ones under a horsehair robe for a sleigh ride to our grandparents' farm. By traveling cross-country, up and down forested bluffs and across Beaver Creek, the trip to Beaver Ridge was shortened by several miles.

From the fourth of my sisters, BJ (Betty Jean) Schmidt I heard stories about the effort to protect the dating teenagers' hair from smelling like a milk cow after milking by hand morning and night. Sharing a bathroom with five other teenagers was no small feat as well.

I have vague memories of some of my fifth sister's shenanigans. Vernice Klug introduced me to playing 'Annie I Over' the house and to the swimming hole in Beaver Creek. She demonstrated swinging from ropes and building forts in the haymow. She showed me how to catch a "ride" on a cow in the barn and how to look for adventure any and everywhere on the farm.

Lastly, my only brother Fordyce, also a farmer himself for many years, told me about the nuts and bolts business of farming: dehorning calves, castrating pigs, expected crop yields and how a cream separator worked. When I was small, he taught me how to trap gophers, how to shoot and skin a squirrel and to fish in Beaver

Creek. Thank you to all of you for your precious stories about farm life before it was my turn to be our father's last helper.

Thank you also to my writers' group in Memphis, the Literary Loons, Britt Shideler, Michael Greenleaf, Bill Runyan and Belinda Looney. They were the only non-family that I met with, socially distanced, of course, during the long months of the CoVID 19 pandemic. They slogged through each chapter of the book with me and provided helpful observations and suggestions.

A special thank you to my Norwegian language consultant, Brit Eddy, a native of Norway, now living in Spring Grove.

A very special thank you to my friend, and generous mentor, Deb Akey, a fellow sailor and author that I met while living aboard our sailboat. She is an incredible editor, formatting wizard, teacher, cheerleader and designer, who read and reread this book, offering invaluable insights and suggestions.

Lastly, I thank my husband, Carl, who has taken excellent care of me during the writing, ensuring that I had food to eat and the space and time to write. His patience has been a thing of beauty and the best gift he could have given.

Illustration 3: L to R: Mavis, BevAnn, Mary Lou, Betty Jean, Fordyce and Vernice Brevig. Teddy is the four-legged family member. His namesake in this book is based upon him.

ARDYS BREVIG RICHARDS

PART I

A HARD RAIN

"At the end, it means more than religion to have had a happy childhood. Memory of it serves to hold off pain and fear; it is an unfailing resource."

Helen Hoover Santmyer (1895 – 1986)
20th century American Writer

Prologue

Long Island, New York 1926

Mrs. Westerham, for once, chose to ignore her son's protestations of 'Mother, I–' She had already scrutinized the mettle of the distinguished gentleman standing in her receiving room and determined that money would not dissuade him from his intent. He would see his daughter's reputation saved, to the extent possible. She, therefore, ignored her son's interruption.

Grandchildren had been on her mind of late, but more importantly, she thought it was time that her son should cease his dalliances with young ladies outside of their social class. She had no intention of allowing her fine family name to become the subject of busybodies and rumormongers and she'd already finagled and finessed a few unpleasant situations in order to extricate her son from the grips of distraught girls. They were shameless flirts, all of them, no doubt gold-seekers.

No, this Mr. D' Bouvier was certainly not part of the moneyed Long Island society. He and his family did not move within the social circles that she and her family did, and yet, he was tastefully dressed, well-spoken and intelligent, probably an attorney, she surmised. There was no question that she absolutely could not, would not introduce someone of *obviously* low status into her social circle, of course, but there was something distinctive about this visitor. And she couldn't fault the father for coming to his daughter's defense, even if his daughter was a little tart.

Mrs. Westerham's line of reasoning on this matter was nearly instantaneous. She would rescue the Westerham name from potential social derision. At the same time, she'd get herself a grandchild. Two of the women at her Bridge Club had grandchildren already and they both seemed especially pleased with them. Surely, her own grandchild would be far superior to theirs.

"Does your daughter—what was her name...Vanessa? Does she already appear to be with child?" She eyed the gentleman shrewdly.

"My wife tells me that yes, in her undergarments, she is noticeably with child." Mr. D' Bouvier did not want to let his sorrow over the premature loss of his daughter's childhood interfere unduly with this critical discussion and so he held his emotions in check.

"Obviously, the formal marriage ceremony will take place after the birth of the child," Mrs. Westerham stated with authority.

She didn't bother to look at her son, nor Mr. D' Bouvier, for affirmation of that assertion.

Mr. D' Bouvier had not expected this response. The woman before him was dressed richly, despite the early hour of the day and she was dispensing with all pretense of astonishment or denial. She'd flown quickly toward decision-making and clearly intended to take charge of that. He'd been reluctant at first to have this discussion with the matron of the household, a household that was actually more like a castle than anything he'd ever seen. But when she said that her husband was not expected back in the country for several months, there was no alternative. The conversation had to take place without the elder Mr. Westerham present.

Mr. D' Bouvier drew himself to his full height. "What assurance do I have that the wedding will take place at all after the birth? The child is not at fault here and shall not be born without a legitimate surname. It is my grandchild's right."

"We will make arrangements for a civil marriage to take place immediately. Not here, of course. Poughkeepsie, perhaps. It's a reasonable distance for a daytrip and we have no social connections there. I trust that you don't either?" She gave her guest a brief glance. "Good. Then, after the child is born, we shall celebrate with a proper ceremony and all the festivities." She paused, her eyes drilling him. "Please tell me, Mr. D' Bouvier, that your daughter is a practicing Catholic."

Vanessa's father nodded his head, still reeling from the speed with which this woman took over, making plans for all of them.

"Alright then." She straightened her pearls and continued with authority. "So, your daughter will confine herself to your home throughout the pregnancy. The Westerham family has never been the subject of wagging tongues and will not subject ourselves to it now." She cleared her throat and started anew with plans. "Formal invitations to an event such as this, an event that will surely be the highlight of the season, must be delivered at least two months in advance. It would be improper to do otherwise. Don't you agree, Alistair?"

Her son, Alistair never looked quite so much like a sad pup that was turned away from his mother without a turn at the teat, than he did at that moment.

Without waiting for his response, Mrs. Westerham continued. "We shall take the Rolls, the Phantom. It's roomier than the other automobiles and we'll leave at first light. Your family and Alistair and myself. Alistair will drive. We'll come for your family in Brooklyn and deliver you all home again by nightfall. Your daughter will return to your house with you, naturally, and Alistair will return home with me, as usual."

"When are you proposing this trip, madam?"

"Why tomorrow, of course. What have I just been talking about?" Mrs. Westerham gave Mr. D' Bouvier a dismissive glance and sniffed.

Thus, within forty-eight hours of divulging her pregnancy, young Vanessa D' Bouvier, at a mere fifteen years and four months of age, was joined in marriage to Alistair Charlton Lincoln Westerham, III, twenty-eight years of age, in Poughkeepsie, New York. It was a private ceremony. No one aside from those five were ever to see or hear of it.

There could not have been a more uncomfortable journey to Poughkeepsie and back for the bride and groom. The two made only grudgingly brief eye contact during the exchange of the vows but beyond that, pointedly paid no attention to one another all day. At dinner they seated themselves at opposite ends of the table. The bride returned to Brooklyn in the same manner as she had made the journey; she was seated on the right side of the Phantom's backseat with her mother's shoulder shielding her from her father's view. Her shame was so great she could not bear to have him look at her.

Mrs. Westerham gave no indication that she was aware of the raw tension between the young couple. She alone felt some degree of control over the day's events. The other four wore funereal faces, stricken by a world spun out of their control.

Alistair, in particular, found it difficult to control his facial expressions and to keep his tone of voice in check. He had never been betrayed quite so thoroughly by his mother. The way she handled this whole debacle was mind-numbing. It was difficult for him to think. But then, he hadn't been asked to think about anything at all, once Vanessa's pregnancy was known.

It was Vanessa Westerham, therefore, rather than Vanessa D' Bouvier, that returned to her parents' home in Brooklyn that evening, wearing a small gold band as a temporary token of marriage, and with explicit instructions from her mother-in-law that she was not, under any circumstances, to show herself outside the home, indeed not to anyone at all, until well after the baby was born.

"You will be wise," she quietly instructed her new daughter-in-law, before she could escape the vehicle, "to let it be known immediately that you are going away to visit a relative somewhere, something like that...to keep your little friends from looking for you. Alright then," she looked past Vanessa and her parents at their tidy Victorian home and with one raised eyebrow concluded, "I'll be in contact with you by courier with further instructions. Alright." A pause while she looked straight ahead. "Drive on, Alistair."

Alistair couldn't be outwardly furious with his mother. She was his mother but so much more. She was his mentor, his financier, his judge and pardoner for all of his wrongdoing, as well as his biggest fan. It was clear to him that he would have to assign his rage to Vanessa. He would make certain that she was sorry she'd become pregnant. He promised himself he would have to teach her some lessons. Maybe multiple lessons would be needed.

By the very next day, a carefully created story was well underway. Mrs. Westerham had in mind nothing less than a fairy tale of a chaste romance between her son and young Vanessa D' Bouvier. When it was completely drafted, it was indeed a thing of beauty. Smugly, she told herself that she had quite outdone herself. She wrote out the entire fabricated story to examine it carefully for flaws. When she was satisfied that all the pieces fit, and before her son could get into any further mischief, she sent Alistair off to Europe on an extended holiday.

"You are pining away, waiting for your bride-to-be to turn sixteen, Alistair, thus your travel. To distract you." she said. While he was away, she leaked the fairytale story, subtly, of course. From there, Alistair's romance became the talk of Long Island society. The creatively crafted story spread swiftly at parties and other gatherings without her speaking of it again.

"Did you hear? Alistair Westerham is hopelessly smitten with a beautiful young girl, but he is a gentleman, of course. He'll wait until she's sixteen before formally courting and wedding her." Mrs. Westerham smiled a self-congratulatory smile to hear the excitement with which people spoke about the grand social event to come. Known only to her and the D' Bouvier family, the allotted timeframe conveniently coincided with a reasonable length of time following the birth of Vanessa's baby. She wanted to be certain that Vanessa's figure would once again be as lithe and slim as it had been before her pregnancy.

Those months also allowed time for Alistair Westerham, II to receive the letter from his wife telling him of the upcoming nuptials. He was in Japan at the time but would have plenty of time to make his way back to the East coast of America before the supposed "happy" occasion. Mr. Westerham, the elder, had become inured to the unpredictable actions of his wife, but this scenario was especially surprising. He suspected there was much more to the story than he was being told.

As the wedding drew closer, a second story was added to the first. This fairytale was tragically beautiful and told with great fervor and awe.

"A baby was born to the cousin of Alistair Westerham's fiancée, in Chicago. The poor young mother, however, died of pneumonia, leaving her baby an orphan."

"What? Orphaned?"

"Yes, you see, the baby's father died at sea before the baby's birth. He was a Great Lakes' mariner, lost in one of those nasty storms on Lake Superior. Such a dreadful thing! Oh, it is all just too horrible. But listen to this–Alistair and his fiancee are making plans to adopt the orphaned baby! Immediately after they are wed!"

"Oh, my heavens!"

When the ladies of Mrs. Westerham's bridge club learned that the baby's given name just happened to be the same as Mrs. Westerham's, she remarked sweetly, "Imagine that! Such a coincidence. Another Caroline in the family."

After the wedding, and before anyone else could point out the obvious, the grandmother said, "Isn't it just remarkable, how the baby favors Vanessa? Of course, her family has always said that the two cousins had an uncanny resemblance."

Mrs. Westerham knew how to make her wishes known to the world without having to do more than utter a few seemingly casual comments. During an afternoon bridge game she sighed deeply and said, "The death of Vanessa's cousin is so painful for her. Oh, I do hope that it doesn't become a topic of conversation in her presence."

Later, after Alistair and Vanessa were married and the baby was brought to live with them at the castle, Mrs. Westerham murmured to her closest confidantes, "You can see how Vanessa loves her cousin's baby. If you didn't know better, you'd almost think she gave birth to the child herself." She offered a poignant smile at the notion. "All I can say is that the baby is certainly fortunate to have a devoted young woman like Vanessa, step right in for her mother, isn't she?"

"Oh, indeed she is," one confidante leapt to agree.

"Yes, she certainly is," the group chimed in.

Mrs. Westerheim was that kind of woman; her influence and social power were iron-clad.

Not one of the Long Island society ladies would have ventured to disagree with her statement. Nor would any have dared to pose an alternative theory to explain the presence of a baby that so closely resembled her "adoptive" mother, not even within the privacy of their own homes.

Alistair's mother was quite pleased with herself. For her son to adopt the child of his bride's cousin, and so soon after marriage... why, it was beyond charitable. It was, indeed, a fairytale story, everyone said so. What a remarkable and generous family, those Westerhams!

1

SILENT

Caroline
Summer of 1948

Leah Marit Fjeld (fee-YELd) was born on a hot and breathless July afternoon in the bluff country of southeastern Minnesota. Before the newborn was discharged from the hospital, her young mother was convinced that the baby was evil. If not for that, this might have been Leah's story. I am her mother.

Leah's father and my husband, Arvid Fjeld is a dairy farmer. His family's third-generation farmland atop Hawk Ridge was borne out of a long and hard-won battle with steeply forested hills. From our first meeting, I have believed that Arvid is one of the best men and the best farmers there could be. Perhaps the latter is true but what would I have known of farms and farmers back then? I was raised a city girl and fortunate to have survived my desperate childhood.

The summer of 1948 is so hot and dry that the corn is "firing." That's how the farmers describe field corn parched for rain. Instead of being bright green and supple, the cornstalk leaves have dry brown edges and they point straight up, "firing" toward the sky, pleading for rain.

In my eighth month of pregnancy, Arvid mounts a gratuitously large bell on a post by the kitchen door. The day he comes home with it, I hear his pickup lumber down the long dirt driveway, and when I look out the kitchen window, I see a cloud of fine dust precede him into the farmyard. I can see that he is pleased about something by the way he launches himself out of the pickup. He's wearing an infectious grin when he yanks the kitchen screen door open, looking for me. Then he swings me around in a polka until I giggle like a little girl.

"I found just the thing," he sings out. He tosses his head back with a self-congratulatory "Hah hah!"

"What in the world is 'just the thing'?" I laugh, already breathless from the polka and the growing weight in front. When our two-year-old, Sophie, runs into the middle of the fray, Arvid scoops her up, wisely trading me for his daughter for the remainder of the dance.

"A bell," he answers triumphantly, tucking Sophie in the crook of his left arm and holding her extended hand as if she were an elegant dance partner. "Daddy bought us a great...big...bell!" He meters out each word and ends with a kiss on Sophie's flushed cheek. "It was sittin' there on a hay wagon at the farm auction this morning, pretty as you please, just waitin' for the auctioneer to open the bidding."

"Daddy got uth a big bell!" Sophie exclaims, thoroughly engaged in her daddy's excitement.

"I didn't know you were looking for a bell, Arvid." I can't help but join in his enthusiasm.

"I didn't know I was either, but when I saw it sittin' there, I knew right away. This is just what we need! When it comes time to deliver the baby, Caroline, you can just ring this bell to call me. Even if I'm way out in the field or inside the barn, for that matter, I'll hear this thing. Wait'll you see it and hear it. It's *big!*"

It's been four weeks since the bell was installed, and I am washing up dishes after dinner when my water breaks. I clean up the floor and myself, and then Sophie and I go out to ring the bell.

"Lemme ring the bell, Mommy?" Sophie is hopping from one foot to the other and her eyes glisten with excitement. I nod and she uses my hand to aid her climb onto an upside-down half-barrel so that she can reach the ringer. Bong...bong...bong...bong...Four times she pulls the rope while her eyes grow bigger and her grin even broader. Then she and I stand on the stoop, watching.

Arvid is far out in the hayfield with his team of horses, Bess and Babe, and our sometimes-hired man, Martin. From our vantage point on the kitchen stoop, they are all the size of stick-figure ants. Arvid is forking hay into place as it falls from the hay loader towering over the back of the wagon. The hay loader is pulled behind the wagon and both units are pulled by the horses, like a three-car train. The hay loader, wagon and horses all straddle a windrow of raked hay.

We see the rig come to a standstill only moments after the bell is rung. The stick-figure that I know is my husband, takes two strides to the front of the wagon, where Martin stands, holding the reins. Although I can't hear what he says, I know Arvid is explaining that they are done with haying for the day.

Martin is "slow," a term that his parents say is better than "mentally retarded" and I agree. Arvid says that Martin is as strong as an ox and that he eats like a horse. The important thing, however, is that Martin can be trusted with repetitive tasks as long as he has a little supervision to prevent him getting sidetracked.

"Go right on home to your folks' place, Martin," Arvid is likely saying. "Don't dawdle along the way now." Dawdling is something that Martin can do very well without any supervision.

Then Sophie and I see Arvid jump to the ground and he quickly unhitches the team from the wagon. He turns Babe and Bess toward the farmyard, and at a quickstep the three of them begin to close the gap between us. With a smirk, I note that Martin hasn't moved from the hay wagon. He intently watches Arvid and the team as they pull away from him. Dawdling.

Teddy, our white cattle dog with a single black patch over one eye and ear, proudly leads the team. He knows they're heading for the barn. I see Arvid snatch the straw hat off his head. It has threatened to fly off, no doubt. They've crossed a field that was previously hayed off and then they swing wide around the end of a field of firing corn that is chest-high at the end of July.

Arvid and the team disappear then from our viewing point on the stoop. They are heading downhill to the barn and the horse stalls. Sophie and I go inside to wait while Arvid unharnesses the horses and turns them out to pasture.

When he throws the kitchen screen door open, he is out of breath from running up the hill. His straw hat flies with ease onto a hook in the corner by the door and his leather choppers (mittens) land on the floor below the hat. He heads for me with a sweaty grin.

I am seated at the kitchen table now in my first sincere contraction. Sophie has leaned into me, one pudgy hand clutching a piece of my damp dress and the other hand holding her ragdoll, Louise, that Arvid's mother made for her.

Arvid kisses me on my damp forehead. "How are you doing, Caroline?"

"My water broke." My smile is weak, I'm sure. I've been drenched in sweat even before labor began. My mop of dark hair that I piled so neatly atop my head this morning has been trying to come undone ever since. Wisps of hair stick to my forehead and neck. I am in no mood to talk.

Arvid's presence suddenly feels odd to me. I can't explain it, but then, I've had unusual thoughts and feelings over the past few weeks. It might have started when Arvid mounted that enormous bell outside the kitchen door. Sometimes I think I hear whispering but when I look around, I don't find anyone. There are times when I see someone, just a glimpse of a face, out of the corner of my eye and I think I am being watched, but when I look squarely at that spot, no one is there. I am alone. I think.

Now is one of those odd times. Arvid has drifted away from me. Swallowed up in a fog that draws him away. The room telescopes and his voice echoes while he becomes smaller and smaller. I feel the contraction of a metal band twisting itself around my head. And my womb contracts while the baby tries to escape me. Both contract at the same time.

Arvid knows that I am ready to go to the hospital by the packed suitcase at my feet. As planned, Arvid now has his list of things-to-do before we can leave the house.

First, Arvid rings his mother to come. Though the telephone box is mounted nearby, I watch him ring her line as from a great distance. The earpiece in his left hand trembles like Babe and Bess' muscles in anticipation of the command to pull a heavy load.

His mother, Marit's line is two long rings and a short. Hers is one of ten households on our party line. Arvid is always concerned about eavesdroppers but, today, getting me to the hospital is clearly the only thing that concerns him.

Arvid goes to the wide porcelain kitchen sink to wash up. Ordinarily I might gently scold him with a reminder, "Use the bathroom sink, Arvid." But today I feel as if words will betray me and so I don't say anything. I can be glad at least about this small bit of kindness to him today, while my very being is unraveling.

Our brand new bathroom is close by, on the wall of the kitchen near the staircase door, but the kitchen sink is larger and, when he is in a hurry, Arvid prefers it over the small bathroom sink. We were married nearly two years before the Fjeld farmhouse had hot and cold running water but, as it turned out, I didn't mind much. I have always been happy married to Arvid. He plans to install an indoor water closet in the bathroom this fall, too. After that, there'll be no more need to trudge through the snow to the outhouse in the winter. And no more chamber pots kept under the bed to be emptied.

Arvid suddenly comes into focus. He takes off his shirt revealing a white, muscular back between two darkly tanned arms. He washes his hands and arms, then grabs a clean cloth and washes his face and then his chest. To inspect his beard, he goes to the tall, cracked mirror out on the screened-in porch. He comes right back, having decided it seems, that he looks good enough for the hospital.

When I close my eyes, I can see all that has happened so far today. But somehow I know that my memory will soon fail me. There's a twisting in my head, an awkward flip of reasoning, meaningless images and a sort of whispering or maybe humming that squeezes out memory. The pressure around my skull increases, my head is spinning. I am losing track of myself. Does Arvid see what is happening to me? Does he understand how I am changing, how our lives will change? I don't quite realize it myself. Not yet.

He flings open the door to the stairs and takes them two at a time. I hear him moving around overhead, individual floorboards squeaking to give away his position. He is in our bedroom, the largest of the four rooms upstairs. In the wardrobe hangs the freshly ironed button-down shirt, the one that I've told him makes his eyes so blue. The wardrobe door closes softly. He flies down the stairs again, where Sophie and I are waiting. Me...panting. Sophie studying her mommy's face...worried.

"I'm gonna start the car now. Gotta make sure Nellie is willing to go today," Arvid announces. With a gentle touch on my cheek, and a chuck under Sophie's chin, he is out the door, my suitcase with him.

Nellie is an old '39 Ford sedan parked in the shade of the ancient box elder tree out front. She is reluctant to turn over at first most days, and in the winter, she is especially obstinate. Finally, I hear her engine catch and then Arvid is back in the house to get me.

Arvid's father bought Nellie brand new, only months before his death late in the winter of 1940. With some tender loving care, Arvid is hopeful that Nellie might last another few years though I have my doubts. Nellie is asked to take us only to church and to get groceries in Spring Grove, ten miles away. And still she complains. I don't think her heart is in it anymore.

From our farm, it doesn't matter what direction we go, whether north or south, east or west; the first several miles are terribly uncomfortable. The gravel roads are either deeply rutted or they've become a washboard after a grader tried to "smooth" out the ruts. Because of the mud and gravel, Nellie wears a permanent layer of dust over her skin. Her paint color is a mystery most of the year.

I walk slowly on Arvid's arm out to the car with Sophie trailing behind, "Mommy? Mommy? Mommy? I come too? Wanna come too, Mommy, pleathe? Pleathe?"

"Oh, Sophie, not this time. Mommy is going to the hospital. You're going to have a new baby brother or sister. Remember? Won't that be exciting?"

"No," I hear the pouty little voice as the earth tips beneath me again.

Arvid helps me to settle into the front seat, as much as he is able, where I try to find the best position for breathing. "Are you comfortable now, Caroline?" Arvid asks me, his voice like a distant echo. Sound skids past me in waves.

11

"Well...no." His question strikes me as patently absurd. A chuckle might have been in order. "Not exactly. I am so huge...it's hard to breathe. And the car is so hot. But...it'll be okay." I lean back and exhale deeply while he recedes into the distance. I've got to find myself more air.

It's as if a tunnel has swallowed up my Arvid. The humming sound, or maybe it's whispering, seems to be within the car. Did it follow me outside? The tree limbs look black and treacherous overhead, like the arms of a monster.

Regardless, I pretend that all is as it should be. I parrot what I've said before. "You'll be a big sister, Sophie. Grandma will be here with you while I'm gone. Daddy will be back before you know it. We talked about this; do you remember?"

Sophie nods her head but frowns. "Wanna go to hothpital too." Sophie doesn't pronounce her "s's." Marit tells me that the lisp will likely work itself out. Not to worry. I find Sophie's lisp so sweet and dear when she says sentences with lots of "s's". Like this one, "Thing me a thong, Mommy, before I thleep." At this moment, however, I want only silence.

Although the car sits in the shade of the box elder tree, with the windows down and my door wide open, the heat inside the car is stifling. Smothering. I long for a cooling breeze. But even more than that, I long for that metal band to stop squeezing my skull. Maybe then the ground will stop shifting and twisting.

Arvid scoops up Sophie with her ragdoll and waves a buzzing mosquito away from Sophie's head. "Grandma's gonna make her special donuts one day, and your favorite chicken soup with dumplings." Sophie gives her daddy a face like she's been asked to eat worms while Teddy waits patiently at Arvid's feet.

After that, we wait in silence for Marit. Arvid's mother is as devoted to her only surviving son as any mother could be. I know that Marit would protect Sophie with her own life. Marit opened her heart to me from the moment we met. How does the woman have so much to give? A short while ago, while she and I sat on the front porch, shelling peas, she confided, "Before we were married, I told my Adolf dat God blessed me with a heart big enough to love lots of children. I wanted to fill up dis big house with dem."

She paused in shelling for a moment and sighed. "God doesn't answer all our prayers de way we want dem, of course, and so, I had to accept dat." She brightened then and held up her pointer finger. "But de day dat you, my daughter, have dis baby, I will have another little one to hold and God willing, I will get to watch *two* grandchildren grow up." She beamed at me and then resumed shelling peas.

Marit lives in a very old, but solid, log cabin at the eastern end of the Fjeld farmland. The family has been calling that end of the farm "the Second Place." But by the summer of 1948, it is called "Grandma's house," ever since Sophie learned to talk. Marit lives there from early spring until late fall each year.

In the winter months, Marit moves into the farmhouse with Arvid and me. Arvid says it's because it's a lot of work for him to plow out that extra quarter-mile lane back to her cabin every time it snows. But Marit told me, "Oh ya, it's dat, too, but what he's really afraid of...is dat if I fall down goin' out to de outhouse in de winter...well...a person could freeze to death before anybody would know." She shrugs as if that would be the only reasonable conclusion.

A plume of dust follows Marit's ancient car into the farmyard. I have a momentary sense of relief until that band twists even tighter around my head. Before the dust settles, she is moving quickly toward us. A hint of a smile makes her face glow. Arvid shifts Sophie into her grandma's arms. "Thank you so much, Mom. I'll call you when we have news."

"I'll be waiting. Don't drive too fast now den, down dat hill," she cautions, with both maternal concern and excitement playing on her face.

Arvid kisses Sophie goodbye. Marit gives me an encouraging smile and a squeeze of my hand. "I'll be waiting," she says again, more softly, only for my ears. Arvid shuts my car door and runs around to the driver's side. "Ha det," (goodbye) she says with a little wave.

Through my open car window, the last thing I see is Marit talking to Sophie. I can read her lips, "Come on den, little one. Come sit with bestemor (grandmother) and we'll read one of those little books of yours. How about de *Three Billy Goats Gruff*?"

"Can you thay the goat and troll voitheth, Grandma?" They've turned around to walk to the house, but I know what Marit answers.

"Oh ya. I will sure do dat."

The chalky, gray dust from the gravel road seeps into the old Ford as we go. It filters into the car through the floorboards and around ill-fitting door frames. Regardless of whether the windows are up or down, the car becomes a churn of fine dust. If we should meet another car on the road, we hurriedly crank the windows up, but it is only a weak attempt to minimize the constant dust storm.

The band encircling my skull tightens a little more. The incessant humming continues. So many things are wrong. It is too hot. It is too dusty. A person could choke to death on so much dust! Am I going to be that person? Arvid pulls out the large white hanky that he carries in his pocket when he goes to town and tells me to breathe through it.

The car makes the hairpin turn to the right within a few hundred yards of the mailbox at end of our driveway. Then Nellie descends into the narrow, densely wooded slash in the landscape that separates one bluff from the next. It is barely wide enough to accommodate the gravel road that's been carved into one of the steep hillsides. The hospital in Caledonia is only twelve miles away but those first miles are especially slow-going.

Today for some reason, the sound of crushed rock popping and skittering off the road and into the ravine below is especially irritating to me. It frightens me. Those ruts carved into the roadbed after a rain grab at our tires, jerking Arvid's steering wheel this way and that. One deep rut catches a front wheel and it grabs us back from the edge of the cliff just below my window. But in the next moment the car slips off another deep rut and that one slides us closer to the edge, threatening to heave us into the rocky ravine. Involuntarily, I gasp.

Arvid drives carefully and slowly and yet he dares to take his right hand from the wheel to gently rest it on my belly for a moment, "How are you now, my love? Are you in a great deal of pain?"

I desperately wish that he would not touch me, but I tell myself to remain silent, to collect myself. Breathing through the hanky is laborious and the swirling dust claws at my eyes, so I keep them closed. The humming seems a little louder. I try to place the sound without success.

"So far so good," I finally answer him evenly, in a measured breath through clenched teeth. Maybe he hears me, maybe not. How can I possibly tell him what I am feeling? I won't even try. I am careful, though, not to flinch from his touch.

I answer his question a second time, in part to reassure him, but more importantly, I don't want him to ask any more questions. "No, it...it is tolerable," I say over the sound of the crushed gravel beneath us. "But could you talk to me a little as we go ...you know, just something to help keep my mind off the labor. Can you do that for me?"

"You just want me to talk...about anything?" He cocks his head a little with this question.

14

"Yes, please."

"Okay." He purses his lips, thinking. "Okay, here goes. The summer when I was nine, Erik and I went with Mom and Dad on a car trip to Owatonna, to visit my mother's cousin." He smiles at me then, and offers this aside, "Little did I know that I would someday find my beautiful wife in Owatonna because of that same cousin."

I give my husband a thin smile. Maybe it is more of a grimace, but he can't see through the white hanky so it's alright. He breathes out a big sigh, as if he's relieved about something. He ought to be relieved. He won't be pushing this baby into the world. These unusual feelings I'm having persist. How is it that Arvid tolerates the dust? I puzzle over my very existence.

I see myself as from a great distance, deep within a darkening tunnel...like a small nervous animal shuddering in the dark. I am struck with that thought and I suddenly know...it is because of the burden I am carrying. That is the exact word, *"burden,* it's a *burden,* the baby's a *burden,"* that reverberates in my skull over and over, like a pounding spasm of light. I carry a burden!

Arvid continues. "Anyway, it wasn't until that car ride to Owatonna that I understood, much to my surprise, that the entire state of Minnesota does not look at all like our land around here. Only this corner of the state has these bluffs. Dad told us they call this the Driftless Area.[i] Y' see, all the places that I'd been to before that day were all within the bluff country. Y' know, like Decorah, Iowa...Winona, Minnesota and La Crosse, Wisconsin. That whole area, and more, too, is within the Driftless Area.

"Dad explained that most of our state is more or less flat, with lots of lakes and wetlands. Our schoolteacher had taught us that people call Minnesota the 'Land of 10,000 Lakes' but I'd never seen any lakes around here, so, I don't know what I thought but...I guess it just didn't make sense. In my little kid head, *this* is what Minnesota looks like right here." He waves a hand in a broad circle, to encompass the steep hills around us. "Wooded bluffs, cliffs, creek valleys. And sinkholes. Everybody everywhere has sinkholes, right? What would people do with trash that doesn't burn if they don't have sinkholes?" He aims his face toward me briefly, to convey his childhood quandary.

I am afraid to say anything to Arvid. A feeling of being somewhere outside myself pulls at me. It is so strong, like a giant magnet. My body rides in the dust-filled car to Caledonia, but the real me is pressed deep within that dark tunnel, weighted with this burden. And the humming? The humming burrows ever louder into my brain.

With a jolt, I suddenly realize that it's not humming at all. Rather, it's the sound of voices that I hear. One or maybe two men's voices are talking over each other. They tell me how bad I am!

15

"Shame! Shame on you, you little brat! Listen to me and listen good!" I must be still and silent now so that I can hear the voices. I don't dare move. I am silenced by terror.

Chuckling at himself, Arvid becomes more animated as he talks about the sinkholes in the Driftless Area.

"I loved the idea of sinkholes as a boy. They're like tunnels to the limestone world below us, to the caves. When I was a kid, know what I wanted more than anything else?" He pauses for only a moment before answering his own question. "I wanted to find a cave under our farm. I checked our two sinkholes every spring to see if I could find an opening to climb down inside the sinkhole, but I never found one." He gives an exaggerated sigh of disappointment and then grins at me.

We are crossing the valley floor now. The tiny burg of Sheldon with its scattered houses and a lone store with one gas pump is across a field on our left. My husband, ever courteous, removes his foot from the foot feed, no doubt attempting to minimize the whirlwind of gravel dust that follows in our wake. Even the cornfields in the valley have grayed; they've become desolate and parched things. The wrenching pain in my lower gut grows more intense, and now I think how peculiar it is. How peculiar everything is… off-kilter. Each contraction is an affront, an assault on me. The concept of labor is a horrible thing, a precarious road to hell, a rock teetering on the lip of a deep precipice. It threatens to heave me over the edge at any moment, and then it will crush my soul.

Arvid glances at me, "When my dad grubbed land, he'd fill the sinkholes with the stumps that he'd blasted out of the ground. And we've always piled the trash that won't burn onto the sinkholes too. You've seen that yourself; by the time summer comes 'round again, all that stuff we've thrown into the sinkhole the fall before has been swallowed up. It's gone!"

I am not listening to my husband. I can't. I've been assigned an impossible task, under threat of mortal harm. Something inside me pulls at my gut, twists and squeezes so that I can't breathe. My body will split apart like kindling, and when it has, then every part of me will be lost. An unseen thing with cruel hands twists that metal band around my skull tighter and tighter and tighter till my skull wants to explode, right then and there in the car. The pieces will shatter the windshield and my brain will plop and splatter like slop poured into the hog's trough.

Suddenly I understand. I am nothing but the bag of skin that carries this burden. Whatever I am is ruined and rotting from within. My insides are putrid dung.

While Arvid's voice hums in the background, the voice whispers in my ears. *"You are bad, worthless trash. You rotten thing. It's all your fault. All your fault. Shut up. Shut up. Shut up! It's your fault.*

Your mother is dead. You should have been quiet like I told you. Should have been silent. Your fault. All your fault!"

"I don't know if you've heard the story of the farmer that went looking for a missing pig or sheep?" Arvid gives me a quick glance with the question. "So, when the guy goes out to look for his animal, he hears the animal bleating, but it's *under* the ground! The farmer finds an opening through the sinkhole and he goes down into it with some ropes attached to a tree, to pull himself and the animal up again. And when he gets down there, he finds there's a cave under his farm! We'll have to go see the Niagara cave over by Harmony sometime."

Illustration 4: Pasture land. Spring Grove is on the horizon, ten miles distant.

Arvid would be terrified if he knew what I truly am. Arvid has always been kind and gentle to me, but now? Now that I'm this other thing? This bag of putrefied skin, a fetid, rank beast of burden? This thing inside of me is no baby. It's an evil thing, a demon. Once it has destroyed me, it will set about destroying my family too: my beloved husband, my dearest little Sophie and Marit, the most loving of mothers. It will dump us all into the darkest sinkhole like so much garbage.

What can I do? How can I fight a demon? A mere filthy child myself. It names me time and again, so I don't forget who I am. *"Nasty Caroline. Caroline, the brat. Caroline, the cunt. Dirty Caroline. Get her away from me before she spews her stink. You sicken me. Wretched thing,"* the man's voice says these things over and over in my ear. *"She's going into the cupboard where she belongs. There, I've locked it. The repulsive thing can't escape now. I'll throw away the key if you don't do as I say."*

"Remember my prayer words," I mutter to myself. "Pray very hard. Please God, do not abandon me. God, I am your humble servant. Please hear my prayer. I pray to you now in the hour of my certain death. Protect my family, please. Please protect them from this evil, this demon." I've prayed many times over the past weeks and have found no comfort in it. God is ignoring me. He's abandoned me. If He cares about me, why hasn't He removed this burden, this THING from me? I've tried so hard, so hard not to give in to it.

"Did you say something, sweetheart?" Arvid sounds worried.

"No, no, no. Praying," I mumble.

Momentarily I recall Sophie's birth. Relatively fast and easy for a first birth. Everyone told me so. Even the one neighbor that was no more than a child herself, even a whole year after Sophie was born told me. It was that girl, Inga, fifteen-years-old and hugely pregnant. She came right up to me outside after church one day. I knew who she was; she lived with her parents on a little farm in the narrow valley south of us.

That day, Inga grinned at me like we were old friends, and said, much too loudly, "Your hips must be just about right for havin' babies. Is that somethin' you get from your family, where you come from? Cuz I know you're not from around here." Me, with my hair so dark among all these blondes and brunettes.

The memory of that floods me now with embarrassment and dread. That loud-mouthed tomboy talking to me about my hips and speculating about who I come from? It's obvious to her and everyone, I suppose, that I'm not from around here. Have I done something to draw her attention? I turned as far away from Inga as I could that day. And now, riding in old Nellie, I turn as far away from Arvid as I can. Inga should have kept her thoughts to herself, just as I am keeping my thoughts to myself now. No one can know what I see, what I hear.

2

DEVIL BABY

Caroline

Arvid rambles on, like a swarm of mosquitoes buzzing in my ears. He drives us to the foot of another ridge upon which sits Caledonia. We rattle across a one-lane iron bridge with Beaver Creek below and Schech's Mill to our right. I hold tight onto my head for fear it will crack apart like a rotten egg. The road begins its winding ascent. At last we are nearing Caledonia and the small hospital that is the only one for twenty-five miles in any direction. I don't hear Arvid's words or even the sound of his voice anymore.

I hear only one Voice and it is the Voice that wants me to deliver this awful burden and then to disappear into the darkness of the underground. To die!

I see the old white-haired doc in the room near me. People say he has delivered almost every baby in two counties over the past thirty-five years. I know him. He delivered Sophie two years earlier. At my last doctor visit, I made the mistake of mentioning that I'm not feeling like myself.

I made light of it, "But I'm not sure who I *do* feel like." I forced a chuckle, but the doctor didn't think it was funny at all. He asked me if I've been seeing things or hearing things that aren't there. I told him that was ridiculous. I begged him not to tell Arvid about our conversation.

"I don't want to worry him unnecessarily," I said. He agreed, although I could tell he wasn't happy with me. He said that he wouldn't say anything to Arvid if everything continued going well for the baby and me.

Now in the hospital, as labor progresses. I become hysterical. The Man's Voice wants me to curse. It grows louder, more insistent.

"You are damned. You are Bad. Cunt. Nasty. Whore. Dirty. Slut."
The Voice spits out the words at me. I scream good and loud. Over and over. And I don't take the name of our Lord God in vain. Not once.

I scream to push the Voice away. It doesn't go, but I can't hear it so well. What else can I do to make it quiet? The Voice is talking, calling me names throughout labor. The band around my head is crackling, twisting, pulsing.

Movement continues. A deep and dark wooded tunnel. More Voices join in. Long, stretched-out faces blur, spinning faster and faster. Some smile, some grimace, but without teeth, they're all ghastly things with boney fingers. Spinning fast, and faster, they drill holes into the ground beneath.

The ghastly things perform an ancient dance, with me as the main attraction. Then I am the tunnel itself. I am the passage from the other world to this one—the tunnel, through which that burden comes. Suddenly, there It is, It comes all in a rush. The Voice becomes quieter then. My head feels bruised and battered. I am relieved to still be alive. I plead with God to send the Voice away. The cussing and swearing and the taunting.

"*You are damned. You are foul. Nasty. Trash.* **Bad.**" Little by little the Voice fades.

When Arvid comes in with a proud smile to see the Baby and me, he says, "It's a good thing we got here when we did! The baby wanted out!" *No more than I.* I can't talk about the burden with him, but that doesn't matter. For now, Arvid seems thrilled with what he sees.

It's a girl, so Arvid calls her "Leah" right off. It is the name that Arvid and I had agreed upon at home. Leah, for a girl and Josef, if it's a boy. Leah is a name from the Old Testament. For a middle name, we chose Marit, after Arvid's mother.

The doctor looks so proud of himself and announces that it was a "fine" delivery. I didn't see **his** bearded face during the worst of it. Where was he? He would have let me die. I'm certainly not going to say anything about the tunnel to him. He didn't give me enough drugs for this birth. Not like for Sophie. Was there a Voice in my ear when I came to the hospital to deliver Sophie? Maybe I just don't remember it because of the medicine?

Momentarily, I am presented with the pink bundle, and I want to ask, *how can this be mine?* Instead I just count her fingers and toes. I see that her hair is dark, almost black. Her eyes are deep, deep blue and I know they'll turn dark brown. Both her hair and eyes are like mine. But she was in the tunnel with the Voice!

Arvid takes It from me when I say that I am too tired. He walks around the halls with It and then tells me that he has shown her to everyone he saw. Later, after he's gone home to milk the cows, the nurse comes back to put that Burden to my breast.

It is then I notice with alarm that my arms are sticks. I no longer have skin. The sticks feel tight, *too* tight, and I have no fingers. Some sticks are shrinking while others protrude at sharp angles. Sticks! My head is brittle, metallic, fragile. I hear it crackle.

That Baby won't suckle although I know there is plenty of milk. It isn't my fault...I can feel how tight my breasts are, but she doesn't want to suck. She cries and cries. I don't really *want* her at my breast either, and I think, well, I gave her a chance. She didn't like it, so there.

The nurse is full of ideas about how I should comfort the Baby, and I think, *Well, you do it then.* The Burden still cries. I am so tired. I want everything to be over. Please, please, is my prayer. Have it all be over.

"Take It away," I say. At least I *think* I say that out loud; I'm not sure now. I want to be as quiet as possible. I am afraid to have the nurse touch me. And afraid for the screaming thing to touch me. I pushed It out of the tunnel. It doesn't have to be in there with the Voice anymore. Do I owe It anything more?

I come to dread seeing the nurse carry that pink bundle into my room. *It is just going to cry the whole time,* I want to say, but I don't dare. It has decided I am not good enough. Why does It have so much power? I don't want to hear It cry anymore. The Voice is coming back. What do I do?

I finally tell the nurse that the Baby should be bottle-fed. "This One is too fussy. Too difficult to please. Take It away. *You* feed It."

What I do not say out loud is that I am afraid of the way that It looks at me. It chills me to the bone. That Burden has the power to see through me. It alone knows about the Voices. It knows me as a fraud. God is not pleased with me. This Burden is how He shows me His displeasure.

Arvid, on the other hand, is elated. He visits every morning after milking and holds the One he calls Leah. He kisses me on the cheek, tells me that Sophie misses her mommy, and then he walks proudly up and down the hallway carrying Leah. The Burden is very innocent and Baby-like when he holds It. It doesn't even cry. He touches the little cheeks so gently and kisses the forehead. He stops to show that Baby to anyone who is even mildly interested, even to those who aren't, I'm certain.

Before he leaves each day, he says something like, "Why are you so quiet, Caroline?"

I try to smile for him, and I sigh deeply. "Tired, I guess."

"But what else are you feeling, Sweetheart? I can't wait to have our little family all together under one roof. Can you? Aren't you just *so* happy? We have a family."

I try to mirror his happy and concerned face. Don't I know how to appear as though I am happy? Of course, I do. I can act.

"Are you feeling...maybe a little...depressed, my love? I know that women sometimes have that problem after a birth." Arvid twists his face a little to get the word, "depressed" to leave his mouth. Obviously, it doesn't want to come out. "I wish you would talk to me," he says.

I just smile and nod or shake my head to answer. He doesn't notice that my arms are sticks. That's a relief, at least. But if I start to talk, I can't be sure what will come out. Maybe the Voice will come out. So, I am quiet. Very, very quiet.

I have my Bible with me, and I read every night for hours. I look for things I've missed before. I can't sleep. I'm on my second time through the Bible from front to back. I can hold off the Voice while I read, so I read with an intensity that shuts out the world. Sometimes I whisper a passage aloud, when it is especially meaningful and reread it over and over again. I am reading the book of 2 Thessalonians when I get to the following passage:

2 Thessalonians 3:3 "But the Lord is faithful,

and he will strengthen you and protect you

from the evil one." *The Evil One!*

My eyes narrow and I stare into the wall. I place my finger on the verse while I find a black pen and underline it over and over until the thin paper threatens to tear. I fall asleep for the first time in two days, comforted a little at last.

I hover over the tunnel that leads to the underground. That's how the dream begins. Every time. What's down there? I'm afraid. I want to stay above ground where there was someone that once told me that she loved me. It was a long, long time ago. "My Carolina Baby" she called me sweetly. From that juncture, the dream goes one of two ways.

I am flying above the tunnel. My heart fills with excitement, laughter. I am alive in every way. The possibilities are endless. All the bad things are left behind. I soar. I tremble with pleasure. When had that been my life? Think. Think. Think. Ah, yes, there it is. Not so long ago. Just there behind my eyes. It is magnificent and it began after the war.

It is 1945, and the Owatonna orphanage where I spent the last years of my childhood has closed for good. The men are returning from the war, filling up the town. My friend Eileen's fiancée is one of them. She'd been engaged since she was fifteen years old and he was eighteen. She has waited for him for four long years...throughout the war. I wonder whether the man who came back to her is anything like the boy that she sent off four years earlier.

I recognize some of the soldiers. They were boys in school with me. It hurts to see them again as wounded, scarred men. I'm glad they have survived, but I don't want to date them though I've been asked many times. I understand that the men don't want to remember what they've seen. I see that hollow place inside of them where everything good and innocent has been leeched away. I know that they want to crawl out of the dark hole where they were trapped, in faraway places.

I understand them because there's a dark hole in me too. When I try very hard, I can find some of the years that came before the orphanage. Some, at least, were good. But some were so frightening. I tell no one of them. Memories have the power to terrify me.

But this is my good dream. A dream come true.

At my friend, Eileen's wedding dance, I see a blond-bearded man standing alone on the far side of the dance floor. He is tapping his foot in time with the lively polka. I am attracted to him from the very first. Perhaps partly because I know that he's not from Owatonna. I've never seen him before. I can tell that he is not one of the men returning from the war. He doesn't wear that look of having just awoken from a nightmare.

I gamble that he will not have heard stories about me from my orphanage days. We can get acquainted like ordinary folks do. I can tell him just what I want him to know. I catch his eye and he crosses the dance floor. He asks me to dance. I wickedly make him wait until the next set begins, a waltz set. I intend to have all three waltzes with him, if I can. When he takes my hand on the dance floor, I have the sensation of walking through a wonderful shining doorway.

Arvid's smile comes easily and I like how his beard frames it in just the right way, rather than hiding it. His simple forthrightness and honesty make me feel safe in his company. His accent is Minnesotan, but something more than that. It is charming and maybe a little exotic. I am captivated by the melodic sound of his rich tenor voice.

Before the end of the first waltz, I have learned that Arvid is thirty years old and works his own farm. He immediately owns up to having inherited the land. His father died tragically several years ago. He and his mother manage the farm together. When I tell him I've never even visited a dairy farm, his eyes sparkle. He seems intrigued and is delighted to answer my questions about cows and barns and pigs. And I have many questions.

I feel exhilarated and daring. I suddenly want to hear this man call me by my real name, the one I was born with. It's been so very long. Years and years. So I introduce myself, "My name is Caroline, but you might hear people calling me Carol...sort of a nickname." I pause for a moment. "But that's a long story." I smile and wrinkle my nose while I look into his clear blue eyes. "I prefer Caroline," I say.

I tell Arvid that I am eighteen years old and live in a boarding house for women in Owatonna. I am two years out of high school, and I work at a dry goods store. In his eyes, I see genuine sadness when I tell him I was orphaned at age eleven. I explain that I know lots of people in town, of course, but that I am choosy about those that I call my friends. What I don't tell him right off, is that I've been asked out by several young men, none of whom have made me feel "safe." A few weeks later, Arvid asks me to marry him on bended knee. I say, "yes" without a moment's hesitation, knowing somehow that the life I am meant to have is about to begin.

Arvid is a kind man and has never pressed me to tell him about the orphanage, for which I am grateful. At the orphanage, I was told that I am "a very pretty girl" many times, even "beautiful" now and then. I heard it first from folks who mistakenly thought they wanted to adopt me, and later, by men who thought they would have their way with me, but I have been careful. I know how to look out for myself.

I always understood what an orphanage was and what it wasn't. An orphanage is not a place for a child to become who she's supposed to become. An orphanage is where they feed you and give you clothes to wear and a job to do. Then they tell you to be happy as they push you out the door. I can't even count the number of times I heard that fidgety headmistress tell me, "Oh, won't that be just so lovely, Carol, to be adopted by a nice family?"

But I already knew a thing or two about "nice families" and I wasn't buying any of her lies. I did a good job of preventing anyone from seriously wanting to adopt me. Safer to stick with what I already knew.

Arvid and I are married only two weeks after his proposal. It's mid-December and Arvid is afraid that when the first big winter blizzard hits, "We might be unable to see one another again for who knows how long? Feasibly," he said, "it could be for the duration of the winter."

That concern of his might have led me to consider just how far out in the hinterland his farm was located, but I didn't. My lack of exposure to rural Minnesota saved me from worrying in advance about things that I would have plenty of time to worry about later.

My friend Eileen loans me her wedding dress and veil. I am fortunate that we wear the same size. I find a pair of cream-colored satin slippers at the dry goods store where I work, and my boss gives them to me for an early wedding gift. Eileen will stand up for me and Arvid asks a good friend and neighbor named Bernt to be his Best Man.

I worry initially about the seating at our wedding, because I have no family to fill the pews on the bride's side of the church, but I needn't have worried. Arvid's immediate family is very small, too, only him and his mother. His father and his younger brother, sadly, have both passed. His second cousins and their families come from Winona, Red Wing and Owatonna. His mother's cousin in Owatonna is the very reason that Arvid was at Eileen's wedding dance where we met.

In addition to my Matron of Honor, Eileen and her husband, there are two other friends from high school that come from Owatonna, as well as three women who lived at the boarding house with me. Even my employer from the dry goods store and his wife come. He says he is sorry to see me leave his employment but happy for me, nonetheless.

"Having Carol's pretty face behind the counter boosted sales," my boss tells Arvid and me in the reception line. "Oh dear, excuse me—Caroline is what I meant to say," he interjects looking at me. "I never knew that was your full name." He goes on as he enthusiastically pumps Arvid's hand. "Especially with all the men coming back from the war needing new shoes and ties. You're a lucky man, Arvid. Take good care of her," he added with a final squeeze of Arvid's hand.

"I am a very lucky man, indeed." Arvid beams. "And I will do my very best, sir."

Arvid is so very handsome on our wedding day. He has had his hair cut in town especially for the occasion and his beard trimmed neatly. I notice, of course, that he looks especially polished that day, but I don't say it like that. Arvid is handsome every day, no matter where his hair has been cut, and I shyly tell him so.

Our wedding service takes place at eleven o'clock in the morning at Arvid's little Black Hammer Lutheran country church, surrounded by rolling farmland. Early that morning, Eileen and her husband deliver me to the portrait studio in Arvid's hometown, Spring Grove. We have our wedding portraits taken and from there I ride with Arvid out to the country church. A morning ceremony allows us time to celebrate with our guests before Arvid, as well as most of the other men, have to return home for evening chores.

Before we leave the church, my new mother-in-law, Marit does something extraordinary. As Arvid and I hold hands, she places her hands around both of ours. She looks up at us, "I do not want to interfere with your first night together in your new home, Caroline. Here is what we will do. You will drop me off at de Second Place tonight, Arvid, before you go home —"

"Mom, it's going to be really cold in that place. It hasn't been heated all day. Maybe you should come home with us first, give it a chance to warm up over there a lit —"

"Pffft...I can get dat cozy little cabin warmed up faster dan you will get de big farmhouse warmed up. Nei, nei, I will be yust fine. You can come get me tomorrow afternoon, Arvid. And I won't go out to de outhouse

tonight. So, no worries dere. I want you to have privacy on your first night together. Dat's for sure. Dat is only right. Now, though I will be riding home with you, in de backseat, I will be far away in my own memories of my wedding night and your father, Arvid. So you yust forget I'm back there." She stretches to kiss his cheek and mine as well.

"And Caroline, I left an egg and sausage hotdish for you to heat up in de morning for breakfast. Yust to make things a little bit easier for you de first day. It's a big house, Caroline. There is a lot to explore. I will leave you to it. If you need anything, you know where I am, Ya?"

It is then that I realize that Marit is giving up her own home for me, for the family Arvid and I will become. The selfless love she has for her son and the love she offers so freely to me makes my heart swell. Oh, the sweet love of a mother. Tears pool in my eyes with the memory.

We arrive home by five o'clock that afternoon. Darkness has fallen already by that time of day in December. A dusting of snow on the ground swirls and sparkles in the car's headlights before us.

An occasional kerosene light pinpoints the location of near and distant houses alike, on our way to Arvid's farm. Therefore, on my first trip there, I see only shadows of what will become my new community, my home, my life.

Marit climbs out at her cabin and we go on to my new home. I have never lived in a house that I could call my own. I shiver with excitement. Or maybe I shiver because I have never been with a man. Whichever it is, I am exhilarated.

But now I am no longer flying above the tunnel. I'm diving down, down, down. And the tunnel swirls around my head and everything goes black. My body slams against the walls of the tunnel until I fall out, bloodied and weak. I am terrified, and I scream.

Voices are calling to me from the great below. I hear crying. Who is it? It's...it is my own mother! Weeping. Screaming. Terrified. "Leave her alone," my mother screams. I can't speak. My throat chokes on my fear. She is running and I have to keep up. She pushes me into a cupboard suddenly. And shuts the door.

"Be quiet," she says, desperately. "You must be quiet, or he will find you. Shhh."

And then her feet move farther and farther away from me. But I can't be quiet. Not entirely. I am so frightened. I sob. Just the once, and then I hear the sounds of the heavy feet coming. Slowly, hunting for me. Hunting like I'm a scared rabbit. Then the cupboard door is unlatched, and I can't see anything. Nothing at all. I am in such pain and I can only scream, "Mommeeeee!"

And then I'm awakened by the nurse's voice, "Mrs. Fjeld?"

She lays the Devil Baby into my stick arms. I'm startled and I scream again. That Devil Baby screams right back, and the nurse finally has the good sense to take It away.

26

Of course, Leah looks like an ordinary baby while Arvid and the nurses are present, but when they leave me alone with It, her true self is revealed. Nobody else sees the way It looks at me when we two are alone. It has the Devil's eyes. She cries and cries when I hold her with my stick arms.

The baby is going to turn others against me. She's going to make others see that I am a bad person. Others will take Leah's side. It will be entirely up to me alone to deal with this matter. God expects it of me, my cross to bear.

That night, the Evil One sits on the wall above my bed, staring at me with gleaming and grinning eyes. It has unnatural powers to move objects with Its eyes. It can will things to happen just by thinking them. Evil Incarnate masquerades in the body of a newborn.

By the time of our discharge from the hospital, that Evil Thing has a plot to destroy me. Only one of us can win this battle. It will be the Evil One or me.

3

HOMECOMING

The August day was heavy with the kind of humidity that shrouds a bright blue sky. "That alfalfa I mowed yesterday won't dry out with this much moisture in the air," Arvid told his mother over breakfast. "We're gonna have thunder bumpers today, for sure. A good day for me to be away from the farm." He nodded his head, pleased. "It's a good day to bring Caroline and Leah home." He reached for his coffee mug with a satisfied grin.

"Oh, Arvid. I can't wait to hold dat little one. Will you be back by dinnertime, den, do you think?"

Arvid could all but see his mother working out in her head what she'd make for dinner at noon, the big meal of the day. He knew that she was always thinking two days ahead in her meal planning. He smiled at her, imagining the raft of lists she must keep in her head without writing any of it down on paper.

One list must be the jars of canned food she'll want to bring up from the cellar the next time she goes down, to prevent an unnecessary extra trip later. On another list, no doubt, she's tracking the ripening vegetables that should be eaten fresh from the garden. And of course, Marit always knows the contents of the ice box without looking. She's probably checking with herself now; is there enough cold milk in the ice box for dinner, enough cream for coffee or rømmegrøt (cream pudding)?

"Oh, I should think we'll be back well before noon. I can't imagine why it would take any longer than an hour or so, to discharge a mother and baby." A bubble of excitement was expanding in Arvid's chest that made him feel as if he might float. And yet, for some reason he thought to mention the following before he got up from the breakfast table.

"Caroline has been so quiet in the hospital, Mom. It's like she doesn't have much to say about the baby. 'Course I spend most of my time holding Leah while I'm there, just walking around with her, showing her off. She is such a beautiful baby, Mom. Wait'll you see her. I know I've said this several times already, but she is the spittin' image of Caroline." He paused, smiling. "But still, I woulda thought that Caroline would have enjoyed walking with us, but she never did. She always said she'd rather nap."

"Ya ya, den, well it probably feels good to have a little quiet time for herself." Arvid could see that his mother's excitement wouldn't be dimmed by a vague concern on his part, given the prospect of holding a new grandchild in only a few short hours.

Arvid drove out of the farmyard, predicting that as soon as Caroline was home with the baby, she'd return to her old self. He allowed himself a measure of pride in being able to bring his mother a second grandchild to love.

At the hospital, Arvid was surprised to be called out of Caroline's room in order to talk alone with her nurse before she and the baby were discharged. The nurse apologized first on behalf of the doctor.

"The doctor was called away suddenly this morning. A tragic farm accident involving a horse and mower. He intended to speak personally with you today, Mr. Fjeld." she said. "I assured him that I will talk to you in his stead. We have a lot of things to discuss."

The nurse was a well-fed, silver-haired woman in a white uniform and cap. "Well-fed" was how he'd have described a hog that was being fattened up for slaughter. Arvid chuckled to himself.

The nurse indeed had a lot to say. "Please have a seat." She sat down opposite Arvid. "Your wife's appetite is not recovering as we'd like to see. She isn't sleeping well either, and I am, naturally, very concerned. I pride myself on sending all my mothers home with good appetites and healthy sleep habits. "

"My night nurses tell me that Caroline is awake at all hours of the night, reading, reading, reading. It is not good for her, Mr. Fjeld, nor for the baby. She must get her sleep. And she must get more calories into her, Mr. Fjeld. Whatever she likes to eat, let her have it. Whatever will stimulate her appetite. If it's ice cream, so be it. Potatoes with gravy. Foods made with cream. You see what I mean? We want her to gain weight."

Arvid nodded his head, curious about the nurse's choice of words, "my mothers." He involuntarily raised his left eyebrow. "Yes, I understand," is what he said. He wished he'd been told about this concern before the day of discharge, and told himself that he would have at least encouraged her if he'd known. She's reading way into the night? He had no idea she was doing that. She's only got her Bible here with her, he thought. He knit his brows, thinking.

"There is another, bigger issue which must be addressed, and this is what worries the doctor and I the most. Caroline is isolating herself from others. She will not even talk to the nurses when they go in to check on her. And she seems...mmm...well, disinterested in the baby, Mr. Fjeld, which I hate to say, but it is the truth, nevertheless."

She paused for effect, it seemed to him. "Has your wife ever had problems with nerves?"

"Nerves!" It was an outburst that he hadn't intended. "I have never known her to be the nervous type."

This little chat wasn't going well, and he was not even going to respond to the nurse's claim that Caroline was disinterested in the baby. How ridiculous was that? He thought there was no point in getting into an argument with this chubby nurse. We'll be out of here soon enough, he thought.

"As I said, I like to send my mothers home at discharge with a healthy appetite and sound sleep habits," the nurse summarized. "Of course, since she's not breastfeeding, her appetite may be less vigorous than if she were. And there's a chance she'll sleep better too when she's in her own bed at home. I certainly hope so, anyway.

"You're going to want to keep a close eye on her," the nurse instructed. after clearing her throat. "She's not adjusting to motherhood. How was she with your first child?" She looked at Arvid over her glasses.

"Well, she was just fine." Arvid was taken aback, stunned by the nurse's report, especially the last bit. "She breastfed Sophie and devoted every waking moment to our daughter."

There was another different conversation, however, that was taking place in Arvid's head without any forethought. In that other conversation, Arvid was telling the nurse, *She adjusted to motherhood two years ago quite nicely, thank you, without any of your input.* And he would finish that with something like a sneer, although Arvid was not a man that sneered.

He discounted the nurse's despairing comment and chalked it up to hunger; *the nurse must be due for a feeding. It wouldn't have killed her to sound a little encouraging, but instead she sounds annoyed with Caroline.* He wanted to ask her if her own children had found her to be motherly and caring? He was leaning toward doubt on that count.

Arvid was certainly surprised by what the nurse had to say. He didn't know that Caroline wasn't breast-feeding. It had never been Leah's feeding time during his morning visits and Caroline had never said anything about deciding against breastfeeding to him. She'd breastfed Sophie and there hadn't been any problems, as far as he knew.

So, now he had a question he'd never had to ask before, "How soon can the baby drink cow's milk, because we certainly have a lot of that on the farm, y' know," and he smiled broadly at her, hoping she would warm up a little.

Apparently the nurse had no intention of warming up to him. He told himself that he had rarely met a more disagreeable woman in his life. The nurse cleared her throat again and adjusted her glasses before launching into what would become a lecture. The last time Arvid had been lectured in that manner was in high school, when he and Bear teamed up on a volcano project for Chemistry class. Their volcano performed *too* well for the height of the ceiling.

"Mr. Fjeld. I should say that your baby will not be drinking cow's milk for some time to come. A baby's stomach is unable to digest cow's milk for the first months. You can discuss when to switch over to cow's milk at the baby's doctor visit.

"I have a list of supplies written down here for you. These are things you will need to purchase on your way home today, baby formula and such. All of these items can be purchased at the IGA in town. If you don't already have enough bottles at home, those can be purchased at the dry goods store." Her voice droned on a bit longer. It was becoming somewhat painful to listen.

How embarrassing! Arvid shamed himself with a self-lecture. *I'm a thirty-three-year-old man, managing a dairy farm with fourteen milking cows, a hog house with four sows, a chicken coop with a dozen laying hens, and the best team of draft horses you could ask for, and yet, here I sit, like an idiot in front of this nurse.*

By the time Arvid drove Nellie down their long gravel driveway with Caroline and Leah alongside him in the front seat, there were towering thunderheads piled above them in thick clumps of silver and gray. Thunder was rumbling, growling. A spectacular lightning show danced between the darkest clouds as they drove. And then, when the car came to a stop in front of the house, there was a lightning strike with a nearly simultaneous ***boom-crack*** nearby.

Arvid heard Caroline whisper, "Oh. My. Lord." When he came around to open her door, she was gripping the handle so tightly that he had to wait a moment to open it. She seemed to have forgotten the baby lying by her side and quickly exited the car. Arvid carefully gathered up the baby and followed.

The dog owned the space between the car and the house. Teddy was, therefore, the first to welcome the new baby with a vigorous tail wag and an appreciative sniff of the air as the bundle in Arvid's arms approached him. On a day such as this, when the sky growled like mad dogs and bolts of lightning flashed all around, Teddy was known to make himself scarce. Today, however, was an exception. Arvid smiled at the dog's interest in the baby and scratched Teddy's head as he passed, saying, "You can go lay down now." The dog stood his ground, watching the humans scurry past to the house where Marit held the screen door open.

Marit urged them inside, "Hurry now, before de sky opens up and dumps all dat rain on us." Before she closed the screen door, however, she called out to the dog, "Gå legg deg" (go lay down) at which Teddy made a hasty retreat to his dry spot under the front porch. Marit suspected that the dog preferred Norwegian.

With the rumbling overhead and the kitchen growing darker, Arvid proudly carried his new baby daughter inside, ready to present her to his mother's waiting arms. Sophie, meanwhile, wrapped her arms around Caroline's legs and hugged them tightly, grinning and jumping.

"Mommy'th home!" Sophie squealed, over and over again. She was not interested in the bundle in Arvid's arms.

"Look who we have here, Mom. Leah Marit Fjeld. Isn't she beautiful? Sophie, do you want to come see your new sister?" he said smiling, as he handed the baby to his mother.

"No," Sophie proclaimed, and and raised her arms to be picked up by her mommy. Neither she nor Caroline made an effort to move toward the baby.

Marit enveloped the baby in her arms and leaned close to kiss her forehead and nuzzle her generous shock of black hair. "Oh, my my ya," she clucked her tongue, "there there, what a *beautiful* baby," she cooed. "Jeg er bestemor," (I'm grandma.) Lightning continued to flicker through the windows. Arvid lit the kerosene lamp over the kitchen table.

He looked over at Caroline, hoping to catch her eye. He felt so proud, so happy, but Caroline had taken Sophie onto her lap and her attention was only for Sophie. She was ignoring him and the baby. *Well, I guess that's to be expected*, Arvid thought. She hasn't seen her for ten days.

But in the next moment, he had an odd thought, she seems almost…indifferent. Like the nurse had said. It startled him to realize that he had no idea what her feelings were about returning home.

Caroline then did meet his gaze. It almost seemed as if she were waiting for something else to happen, but what else was there? Their new baby was home with them at last, the whole family under one roof.

Marit was radiant. With her mouth forming a perfect "O" she examined baby Leah. She was oblivious to everything but the baby in her arms for several moments. She assumed that back and forth rocking motion that a grandmother never forgets. She found Leah's fingers and her toes. Leah was wearing only a diaper and a thin cotton shift. The air was too clammy for anything more.

"She has so much hair, Arvid, yust like you did as a baby. But she looks like *you*, Caroline. Oh…you both must be yust *so* proud and happy." Leah's eyelids fluttered a few times. "Awww, look there, she's going to have brown eyes, too, I see. Oh, my, my," Marit closed her eyes, smiling. Arvid assumed she was relishing a vision she foresaw of the brown-eyed, dark-haired girl this baby would become. She was enthralled, just as Arvid knew she would be.

Grandma Marit wanted to bring Sophie into the excitement, too. "Of course, Sophie was a beautiful baby, too," she said, looking at Sophie, who was intent on finding the optimal grip for squeezing her mother's neck as she bounced. "Sophie looked like you, Arvid, of course, blue-eyed and fair-haired. But dis little beauty looks *yust* like *you*, Caroline," she said again. "Don't you think so?" Marit did not withdraw her gaze from the baby who yawned, producing a dimple in her right cheek.

Arvid agreed heartily. "She certainly does, doesn't she?"

Caroline glanced in Marit's direction. "Hmmm," she responded and returned her attention to Sophie.

"I've missed you so much, Sophie," Caroline said softly to her. "Did you miss Mommy?"

"Yes, I mithed you thith much." Sophie spread her arms as wide as she could, till she nearly fell off her mother's lap.

Marit had set up the white bassinet in the kitchen next to the table. It was the same bassinet that had been passed around between the neighbors for years, whenever there was a newborn. The Flagstads, Hedlands, Bjergums, Fjelds and the Kjelles, had all used it. He didn't know who claimed ownership but that hardly mattered.

Finally, Marit's trance was broken. "Oh, ya, I s'pose dat I should get our dinner on de table den. I'll have to put you down, little one," she breathed, and kissed Leah's rosy cheek. She gently laid the baby in the bassinet on her tummy, between Arvid's chair and her own at the table. "Ooh, there there, so sweet." She paused to gaze at the drowsy baby, easily settling back asleep. "Oh, I have been so looking forward to dis day. *Such* a happy day," she beamed, her hands clasped over her chest.

"It surely is," Arvid answered. "I am a lucky, lucky man and father."

"Yes, you surely are dat, and I am a lucky grandmother." Marit's entire face was a smile. "Well, I'll be right back, den. Sitte deg god. (Sit and get comfortable) Our dinner is waiting in de summer kitchen."

"Can I help you Mom?" Arvid offered.

"Nei, nei," (No, no.) "Yust wait right here. I'll be back in a yiffy."

Marit slipped out the screen door and made the dozen steps to the summer kitchen and back without getting noticeably wet. "I ran between de raindrops," she smirked, a phrase that she liked now and then.

While Arvid held the screen door open for her, Marit carried in a grand homecoming dinner on a large tray. There was a roasted pork loin with rosemary, four cobs of sweet corn and boiled potatoes with parsley. A bowl of her sliced cukes in her special tangy, vinegar sauce was already on the table along with Sophie's favorite—beet pickles served in the fancy glass bowl they usually saved for company.

As usual, a plate of sliced homemade bread was on the table, along with a bowl of butter and two jars of jam, strawberry and apricot, Caroline's favorites. Arvid's mother had outdone herself for the dinner. It was indeed a feast of celebration for Caroline and Leah's homecoming.

"Oh, Mom. What a feast you've made! Everything looks delicious!" Arvid fairly drooled in anticipation.

Arvid took stock of his family's good fortune as he looked around the table. The Fjelds had never known hunger. The basement shelves were heavily laden with canned goods. They had all the fresh milk they wanted, skimming the heavy cream off the top for coffee and desserts and cooking. And they had plenty of butter, churned right there in their own kitchen. Arvid smiled, realizing his family was blessed with good fortune, health and plenty of good food. What more could a man want?

The four of them had just bent their heads to pray as the gunmetal sky stalled overhead and lightning cracked as if to rip a hole in the sky. With it, a train of thunder made the floor vibrate beneath their feet and then the rain came down 'like a cow peein' on a flat rock,' an expression that Erik and Arvid laughed about when they were boys. He smiled with the memory of it and dug into the homecoming feast.

4

A CRACKED MIRROR

Caroline

Arvid holds out his hand to take mine and we begin to say the Table Prayer together. "Come Lord Jesus, be our Guest. May these Gifts to us be Bl—" CR—ACK!

It's a deafening sound, a whip striking the earth with a flash of lightning, illuminating the room. We, the four of us seated and holding hands, become in that instant the brightest of all things, lit up like the figures on a roll of negative film. Arvid's hair and beard glow. I leap off my chair and try to swallow an involuntary scream. The angry clouds I watched as we drove to the farm, unzip and dump a torrent of water on us.

The roar of the wind pushes against the house as well as the box elder tree limbs that scrape against the siding on the house, threatening to tear off pieces of clapboard. Arvid and Marit both jump up to close the windows on the west side of the kitchen where the curtains suddenly blow inward.

Marit excuses herself and runs upstairs to close other windows while Arvid joins her in the fray. I can hear window sashes being pulled closed, upstairs and down. Shwompp! Shwompp! Sophie and I remain at the table, she, covering her ears and me, trembling at the angry storm outside. I try to read into the meaning of such a storm erupting at the same time as our homecoming. And yet the Evil One doesn't wake up.

Arvid and Marit return to the table. The rain on the tin roof over the kitchen stoop beats like a Gatling gun. Deafening. The wind and driving rain prevent any attempts at conversation. In spite of all that racket, wouldn't you know that Devil baby has nothing to say about any of it! She sleeps soundly through it, there by Marit's knee. She's going to be a tough opponent; I can see that.

Marit finally gives up on waiting for the timpani of rain to dissipate. She calmly raises her voice to be heard across the table, as if such a wind and deluge were an ordinary occurrence. "How does it feel to be home again, den, Caroline?"

Marit is so pleased to have the baby in the house. Her face is flushed pink from the hot summer kitchen, from running upstairs and down to shut windows and the excitement of that baby lying in the bassinet only inches away from her knee.

I manage to respond in kind. "The doctor kept me in the hospital too long." I speak loudly to be heard over the din. Tipping my head toward the bassinet, "This one cries a lot."

Marit looks at me with a hand cupped by an ear. She can't hear me.

"She *cries* a lot." I say, more loudly, pointing at the bassinet. "We've had to put her on the bottle because she will not accept mother's milk. Not all babies can be as easy as this little one," I say, smiling at Sophie. The heavy pounding of the rain quits as abruptly as it began.

"Oh, so you're not breastfeeding, den." Marit glances at me quizzically, but not judgmentally. "Uff, ya, well, you know best. I'm sure you are tired, too, Caroline. I remember when I had Arvid. I remember telling his father dat I was *so* tired; I'd a liked to die yust to get enough sleep. Of course, I was only yoking. There is nothing like having a new baby in de house, is there? Arvid was an easy baby, too. And we got off to a fine start after de first few days at home. I'm sure you will too." Marit held her buttery cob of sweet corn between her fingers while offering that prophecy.

"Well, I am here to help you for as long as you want, of course. You yust tell me what you want me to do, if I'm not already doing it de way you like." She takes a series of quick gnawing bites off the corncob. The sound of her chewing is unpleasant to the Voice. I hear It complaining again...loudly.

After dinner, Marit wants to check on things at her own little cabin for a bit, so Arvid helps clear the table and Marit quickly cleans up the kitchen before she leaves.

"Takk for hjelpen (thanks for helping)," she says to Arvid.

Arvid responds with a smile, "And takk for maten (thanks for the food)."

Then, gathering a few items to bring with her to the cabin, Marit says, "Ya, ya, ha det, (goodbye)," and starts toward the screen door. She turns, "I'll be back in time to make supper before milking, den," she calls out, and she kisses Sophie and the Evil One before she's out the door.

After Marit drives away, I sit motionless for some minutes. My thoughts are muddled. I try to collect them, put them in order. It's so wonderful to be home with Sophie again and Arvid. And God bless Marit. But what do I do about the Evil One only a few short feet away? Something horrific is bound to happen, I can feel it. And without anyone in the room talking, I can hear the Voice again.

Telling me that I am garbage, nasty, and foul. I'm called one horrible name after another. Clearly, that One in the bassinet is dangerous.

Arvid says, "I gotta go check the cistern. I'll take care of that and a couple other little jobs in an hour or so. Do you want to lie down a little while, Caroline? I s'pose it's soon time to feed the baby?"

"Yes, I would like to rest." I answer him. Keep my answers short, I think. I remain in my chair, however.

"I think Sophie is ready for a nap, aren't you?" Arvid says in my direction. "And Leah is sleeping so deeply. Even loud noises don't wake her, do they?" Arvid smiles tenderly at me and the baby, apparently admiring the Evil One's ability to shut out the world by sleeping. Only *I* am not fooled by the Devil Baby.

"Sophie, let's go for a nap on the davenport in the front room," Arvid says. And with that, he leads Sophie into the front room and sits on his haunches at the head of the davenport, while Sophie snuggles with her favorite blanket. He talks quietly to her, helping her settle down for her nap.

I can't hear what Arvid says, over the noise of the Voice talking to me, ridiculing me. It isn't long before Arvid returns to the kitchen where I still sit at the kitchen table, looking out the window, transfixed. Leah sleeps, pretending to be an ordinary baby.

"Would you like to lie on the bed on the back porch, Caroline? I don't suppose you want to go upstairs to rest—being it's so far from the baby." Arvid is such a kind man. He deserves a baby that will not cause trouble, that will not harm me or anyone. "You are so quiet, Caroline. I've hardly heard a word out of you the last several days. You must be exhausted, hmm?" He touches my hair softly.

My gaze slowly returns to the kitchen and to my husband's eyes looking into mine. I can't help feeling distracted. I see into the future. Our future is dark. Darkness is coming. The Voice tells me how worthless I am. How I should be shut away, locked away for good. It is what the Evil One wants. It is what I deserve. How can I possibly fight that?

"Yes, that would be just the thing. Don't worry about us. We're fine here while you go outside for a while. No rush."

And so, very quietly, as if an obedient child, I allow him to guide me to the little bed that we keep downstairs on the screened back porch. It faces east and so the afternoon sun leaves it in the shade. In addition, oak and maple trees shade the back of the house. I remember days past when it has been a very pleasant spot for an afternoon nap.

Arvid goes out, quietly closing the screen door behind him. I immediately arise from the bed and go to the bassinet in the kitchen. I gather up that baby and carry her, still asleep, out to the back porch. I lay the One we are calling Leah on the bed where I had lain only moments before. I undress the Evil One, closely examining every square inch of her small body. I try not to awaken her. I don't want to have those Devil eyes looking at me any longer than necessary.

When the diaper comes off, the Devil Baby wakes up. She makes little mewing sounds, as if unsure whether she is contented or not. She waves her fists around and kicks out her pointed toes. She dribbles pee onto the bed. Now she decides that she is not contented and turns the corners of her mouth down and begins to cry, softly at first, and then louder and louder. Her face reddens as she screams that wavering newborn cry.

I pay the crying baby no mind. When in the company of Evil it is best to ignore Him if possible. I undress myself completely then, and roll my clothes into a ball, shoving them under the bed. There are words that seep through the walls and into my ears. They are clear and precise. *"Make thyself pure, in order to win the favor of the Lord. Make ready to do battle with the Evil One."*

I sit on the edge of the rattan chair and unpin my long hair. It falls below my waist and tickles the tops of my buttocks. I go to my bag from the hospital, still sitting on the kitchen floor and I find a hairbrush. I pick up my silver sewing shears on the way back to the porch. I brush out my hair and let it fall over my shoulders and breasts like a dark waist-length cape.

There might be another voice here. Perhaps it's Sophie's, but I can't hear what she says. She speaks from so far away. Maybe it's the future. I think she says "Mommy," but I can't answer to that name now. The Evil One is in charge now. Setting the stage. Plotting to do away with me. To expose me for the wretched thing that I am.

I am but a wraith. A mere vapor of something greater and unholy. Her little girl words are so faint, while the other Voice is so loud. A mere two-year-old cannot comprehend the reality of the Evil in the room with us.

A decrepit mirror hangs on the porch wall. It's a fragile, yellowed glass with a long crack that goes from one top corner to the opposite bottom corner. I see my reflection in it, there on the wall, with the crack splitting my body apart, shifting my proportions like I've been sawn in half and put back together haphazardly. I have seen myself in that mirror many times before, while cleaning the room or just walking past. This is the first time, however, that I see myself for who I truly am. It startles me until I tremble.

It is *Me* that is bad, after all. The mirror dislocates my features into jagged pieces. The eyes are no longer things of beauty. Rather the eyes are two holes into a black soul. My nose is broken and my mouth split down the middle. If I stick out my tongue, it will be forked. *I* am the Serpent. The mirror spits out the true story—*I am broken and sinful. The Devil Baby comes to claim me—to take me away to the dark place where I belong.*

I don't know how much time has passed. Time is meaningless. It is this Thing alone that I fear. How do I destroy the Evil, that pink, sweaty, screaming Thing on the bed?

Years later, I will try to envision what my husband sees when he finds me. By then I am someone else entirely. By then, I am beyond his reach.

5

NIGHT

Arvid was whistling when he left the house after their delicious homecoming dinner. His little family was all together for the first time. The farmhouse was a cocoon, sweet and warm, protecting those he loved.

The windmill had been free to run since he started milking that morning but without much wind until the thunderstorm passed over, the cistern still hadn't filled. He walked to the cistern and looked between the slats of the cover, down into it. He calculated it would likely be another hour or so before it would be full.

While he waited for the cistern to fill, he went to the machine shed to get a start on sharpening the blades of the hay sickle. He sat down at the whetstone wheel, put the shield over his eyes and began pumping the stone wheel.

When he stopped pumping, he heard a noise that was out-of-place, just outside the shed. He removed the shield to listen. That was when he saw Sophie standing outside the shed door, sobbing and pleading for him, "Daddeeeee."

Arvid jumped off the wheel and scooped her up in his arms. "What's wrong, Sophie?" He looked her over carefully, didn't see blood anywhere. Sophie's face was a mess of tears, sweat and snot. She'd been wiping her face with her dress. "Honey, what is it?"

"Mommy. Mommy," she howled when she could catch her breath. "Mommeeeeeeee." He ran with her in his arms up to the house and into the kitchen. When the screen door slapped shut behind him, he heard only the sound of Sophie's sniffles in his ear. The bassinet was empty.

"Caroline?" he called out. And then he heard it. The sound of a newborn expelling the last of her air, only to suck in enough breath to let loose with another quivering cry. The cry led him to Leah, where she lay on the iron bed on the back porch. The same bed where Caroline had laid down to rest just before he went outside. Leah was naked, her skin mottled, purplish, and hot. He saw no sign of Caroline.

"I'm going to put you down, Sophie, okay?" He put his mouth next to her ear so she could hear him over Leah's prolonged wail.

"No, Daddy," she sounded desperate and gripped him tighter.

"I need to pick up the baby and put a diaper on her," he said gently, as he undid Sophie's arms from his neck and put her down. Sophie ran away, back into the front room, beyond his reach.

The diaper Leah had been wearing was lying next to her, damp. The fresh diapers were likely stacked upstairs. His mother had washed them. He decided the damp one would do for now. *Where is Caroline?*

He picked up Leah, attempting to settle her by sheer will power, while Sophie clung to the door frame of the front room. *Leah is hungry, no doubt.* He called out again, "Caroline?" No answer.

He stood still, his brain ticking off possibilities. Did she go outside? He frowned with that thought. Why go outside? Why leave the baby crying, here alone?

His heart rate quickened further. His imagination hard at work. *Someone had come into the house and stolen Caroline away? A kidnapping?* No, no. He would have heard a car drive up.

Sleepwalking? Could she have walked herself outside and wandered off? Maybe that happens sometimes…maybe after having a baby? *Maybe she slipped and fell somewhere and is injured.*

Maybe she's injured so badly that she can't answer me!

Arvid carried Leah with him, calling Caroline's name and walking through the house with Sophie's hand clutching his pant leg. He climbed the stairs. Walked into each of the four bedrooms, afraid of what he might find. They were empty, all empty. Back downstairs he went.

Did she fall down the cellar? Why would she go to the cellar?

His hand trembled opening the cellar door, fearing he would see her broken body sprawled at the bottom. No, it was dark. *She wouldn't go to the cellar without lighting a lantern.* Yet, to be sure, he took the lantern that was used on trips to the cellar. "Sophie, wait here a moment." He descended the steep stairs a little way to check. He saw only shelves of canned goods in the cellar.

Back upstairs. *Why didn't I check the bathroom first?* He opened the bathroom door, expecting the worst. His heart was in his throat. It was empty.

Arvid with Sophie attached to his leg, went through the front room and vestibule and out onto the wide front porch. The porch swing was empty. He looked toward the barnyard, down the long, narrow driveway. There were no footprints anywhere. *With all that rain, she would have left footprints.* He looked in every direction and saw no sign of footsteps leaving the house by the front door.

Think...think...if she didn't go out the front door or the kitchen door, she must have gone down the back-porch steps. Maybe. So, onto the screened back-porch he went, passing in front of the tall cracked mirror and catching his reflection. *What's that on the floor?*

There was something under the bed behind him.. He turned, cradled the baby's head and bent down to have a closer look. Sophie backed away from him when he bent down, trembling, frightened. "Mommy," she whispered.

Arvid hardly recognized her. "Caroline?" It was but a mass of flesh and hair pressed against the wall beneath the bed. For a long moment he struggled to make sense of it. Hair and skin. Naked body. *Is she alive?* Then he saw an eye looking at him through the hair splayed across her head and torso. The eye blinked.

Arvid hadn't realized he wasn't breathing. He took a deep breath and laid Leah on the bed. He knelt so that he could peer under the bed. "Sweetheart," he tried to say it softly, "Are you hurt? What happened?" There was no answer. The eye stared back at him.

Rather than becoming calmer now that he'd located his wife, he became more frightened. "Caroline," His voice cracked. "Are you able to crawl out of there?" No response. Leah, who had calmed in his arms began to stir once again. Little sounds foretold her screams to come.

"My love, you are frightening me, and the children." He steadied his voice. "What's wrong? Can you come out so that I can see you?" He heard a keening from under the bed. It started so softly, as if it were wind through the trees. Then it grew louder.

"Please, let me help you out from under there. Please, my darling. Let me help you." He became aware of his own tears.

The keening became, "Nooooo-oooooo, nooooo-oooooo, NOOOOOO-OOOOO." Louder and louder. And then, "Take It away. Take It away. Take It AWAY."

"What are you talking about?" He pled with her. "Take what away? Come out so we can talk–"

"He hides in plain sight. He's tricked you. He wants to harm me. Don't look at It."

"Please, I don't understand. What are you afraid of? If you come out, I can help you. What do you mean by the trick—"

"It's there on the *bed*," she raised her voice, emphasizing each word. "*Beside* you. I hear It cry. It's *Evil*." Her words were nearly a chant. "I'll stay here until It's gone. Stay here. Stay here."

Then a sound from her that Arvid would remember forever. A crooning that was like an animal singing its death song, "Nhhaaaahhh." A ratchety drawing of breath and the eerie sound began again a little louder, "Nhhaaaahhh," while Leah screamed along with her mother in a haunting duet.

He sat upright, still kneeling. He looked at Leah, crying, and at Sophie, huddled in a ball just through the doorway, in the front room. *Sophie's afraid to be in the same room with us!* "My God. What is it? What's evil?" Then Arvid's body went cold in spite of the heat. *She's afraid of Leah!*

Arvid ran to the kitchen to ring his mother to come back. He had only to say, "We need you here right away." Marit had been away from the house less than two hours.

While he waited those few minutes for his mother's car to pull into the farmyard, he went out to his car to get the powdered formula and bottles, nipples and whatever else had been on that list that the nurse gave him that morning. *Was it only this morning?*

He sat Sophie down on a stool by the counter so that she would be closer to his eye level. He tried to read the directions on the can of powdered formula, but it was unsteady in his hand and the words blurred. *Leah probably should have been fed before now...Will Sophie remember seeing her mother like this?*

Arvid heard his mother's car coming fast over the rise, the sloppy road spitting behind her. Her car braked hard into the mud. He waited for her on the stoop, with the screaming baby in his arms. Sophie ran to the car, slamming herself into her grandma's legs and crying, "Grandma, Grandma...Mommy'th under the bed. Thee thcaring me."

"There, there, uff, nei, it can't be as bad as all dat, can it? We will figure it out." She picked her up, hugged her and kissed her wet cheek while hurrying to the house.

Arvid's eyes were red. "Mom, it *is* bad. *Real* bad. Something's wrong with Caroline. I don't think she's hurt, physically. I don't know for sure. I can't see all of her. She's hiding."

"What? What do you mean by dat? She's hiding? Where is she?" She walked into the kitchen, holding Sophie while Sophie buried her head in grandma's shoulder, arms wrapped so tightly around her neck that Marit had to loosen them a little so she could talk. So she could breathe.

Arvid followed his mother into the kitchen, and steered her to the outside far wall, away from the front room and back porch. The four of them huddled, facing the open window.

"All three of them laid down to nap," Arvid began as quietly as he could, his mouth to his mother's ear, to be heard over Leah's screams. "Then I went out to do some chores—*oh my god—the water! The cistern has been filling all this time.* I have to go shut off the windmill!" He jumped and without thinking started for the door with Leah in his arms.

"Wait, wait, tell me what happened?" Marit could barely hear him over the baby's howling. "Give de baby here."

43

He turned back and handed the baby to his mother. In a hurry, the story came out. "Sophie came out to find me. She was crying. We came back to the house and there was Leah naked on the bed on the porch, screaming. I looked all over the house for Caroline. Everywhere. And then, I found her. She's *under* the bed on the back porch. She won't come out. She doesn't make sense, talkin' about the devil and evil and take it away, and listen…"

Then Marit heard the sound from the back porch, like a tomcat crying in the night. An eerie high-pitched whine.

"Mom, Leah is hungry…"

Marit's face had turned white. "Ya, I'll feed her. Go lock de windmill."

Arvid was gone in a moment.

Marit put Sophie on the stool where she'd sat only minutes before. "Watch Grandma make de milk for de baby, okay?" she muttered, to herself more than Sophie. Leah wailed on.

"Okay, den little one. I'm gonna have to put you down for a little bit. Let's see, first, sterilize de bottles…den I'll get dis formula into your little tummy. Hmmm? Dat's the most important thing right now. Isn't it?"

Marit continued a monologue, as if the baby could understand her, but it was more to reassure Sophie that Grandma had things in hand.

"She sure can make a lot of noise for such a little thing, can't she, Sophie?" Marit tried to produce a comforting smile for Sophie's sake. "Oh my, my. Let's get at least *one* of us to settle down a little bit, den, how 'bout dat?"

Arvid was back in a few minutes with the news that the cistern had overflowed. In that amount of time, a new pond had formed in the barnyard and from it, a small stream meandered down the hillside to the woods. The keening like a tomcat with a high-pitched cry continued.

"I'm going to sit down and feed de baby now while we talk." Marit sat on the davenport with Leah. Sophie buried herself under her grandma's arm, the one that was holding the bottle. The sound like the dying animal stopped too, after Leah took the nipple in her mouth. The sudden silence felt peculiar. Arvid's ears were still buzzing.

Arvid sat on his haunches next to his mother. He whispered, "Mom, she's afraid of Leah," and his stomach lurched as he said it.

Marit shook her head. "Uff, nei nei…dat can't be, can it?"

"I'm going to try to get her to come out again. Now that you're here to look after the children."

"Ya, in a little bit we three will go upstairs. Maybe we will finish dat nap, okay den, Sophie?" Marit raised her eyebrows and turned the corners of her mouth up, hoping for Sophie's sake, that it looked something like a smile.

Arvid stood and straightened his back, as if preparing for battle. Marit took in his figure standing before her. "You are a good man, yust like your father, Arvid." It was the best blessing she could think to give him in that moment.

He returned to the porch where his wife remained, naked and pressed against the wall under the iron bed, frightened. He dragged a rag rug alongside the bed and lay on it next to her, his head pointing in the same direction as hers. He looked into the eye between the swaths of dark hair nearly covering her flesh.

Arvid talked quietly. Calmly. Talked of pleasant things. Anything but the bizarre reality of lying on the floor in order to see his wife as she lay hiding beneath the bed. He went from one meandering thought to the next, whatever came to mind. Talked about the dog, Pep, that they'd had when he was a boy, and all the tricks he could do.

He told her about how he and Erik would run full throttle and by planting their hands on the rumps of the Shetland ponies, they would leapfrog onto their backs. And told her about the barn cat that rode bareback with them, and never once dug her claws into the pony's back.

Caroline had not moved from her position against the wall under the bed, but she had been watching Arvid. He took that as a good sign, that she *was*, at least listening to him. With a chill, he made the rapid decision that he would give this...this situation they were in, until morning before he would call the Sheriff's Department for help. God forbid he would need that help. *Any time now, she will come out from under there*, he told himself.

"Sweetheart, I'm going to go to the barn and milk the cows. Mom is here and she'll take care of Sophie." He carefully avoided mention of the baby to her. "You are safe right where you are. I'll be back as soon as I can. Do you need anything before I go? Shall I get you some water or something to eat?"

A long moment passed and then the eye closed. "No," he heard her whisper, at last.

"Alright, then." he started to push himself off the floor, then paused. "I love you, Caroline, so very much."

He went upstairs to find his mother. "I'm going to the barn to start milking now. I think Caroline will stay where she is until I come back. I'm counting on it, I guess you'd say." Arvid's mind raced as he tried to think through whatever events could possibly take place while he was in the barn, four hundred yards away.

"I hate leaving you and the girls alone here in the house with her this way. But I don't dare leave *her* alone in the house either." He agonized over how to see that everyone was safe. A quandary like none that he'd ever considered before.

"But Mom, if she *should* come out from under there, I want you to take the girls with you and run to the barn for me."

"Ya, I will do dat. Don't worry..." He saw his mother's forehead knit together with worry.

"So...Mom, you can't be upstairs while I'm in the barn, you understand? Because you wouldn't know if she comes out from under there. And...what if she..." Arvid took a deep breath and swallowed hard, to get the rest of it out. "What if...you got trapped up there if she becomes...you know...difficult somehow? You wouldn't be able to come for me then."

"No, ya, we'll yust be in de kitchen. Leah will sleep now for a while I think. If she does wake up, I'll feed her right away den." Marit tipped her head in lieu of pointing a finger toward the back porch, "She won't hear a peep out of her."

"You and Sophie should eat whenever you get a chance. I don't want you to be distracted by messing with the stove, though, in case Caroline crawls out from under the bed." *And does what?* "Can you make me a sandwich to eat later...after chores? The dried beef or tongue, I don't care which it is."

"Nei, nei, we'll be fine here. Don't worry. You yust do what you have to do. I'll make something for you to eat when you come in from de barn." Arvid guessed that his mother was trying to look as if these sorts of requests were ordinary.

Milking seemed to take longer than ever. As usual in this heat, the barn doors were chocked open wide, to catch any breeze that might come along. Arvid listened closely to every sound. Of course there were the usual sounds: cows swishing their wet tails now and then, the stream of milk into the bucket, a cow shifting within her stanchion producing an occasional clank. But he was listening especially hard for any sounds that were out-of-the-ordinary, coming from the direction of the house, up on the hill.

The barn seemed oddly unfamiliar to him that night. As usual, he scooted his milk stool up close to the cow's right flank so he could reach the cow's udder, leaned his head in against her right hip and reached for the teats. But his head was still up at the house, lying next to the old iron bed on the back porch.

He frequently found himself puzzling over what he was doing. He'd milk one cow and after dumping her milk into the ten-gallon milk can, he'd turn around and stand with the empty bucket in his hand. He was frozen in place. *Which cow did I just milk?* A few times he had to return to look at the cow's udder, to be sure he had actually just milked her.

Without any forethought, he found himself sitting on a pile of straw at the bottom of the hay chute. *What do I do? What's happened to her? Why? We have two beautiful daughters and she has me. We have a good life together. Don't we?*

His tears flowed then. He slapped his face in frustration, demanding himself to stop crying. "I don't have time for this," he spoke aloud to the more reasonable, calmer version of himself that apparently had gone for a walk and forgotten to come back.

The sun was still well above the horizon when Arvid finished in the barn and headed toward the house. The night threatened to plod along as slowly as had the afternoon. In spite of his distraction, he remembered to carry the covered half-gallon of fresh milk along to the house with him. It would go into the icebox to be cold and ready for breakfast. Before entering the door, he made this childish wish, that when he entered the house, he would find everything to be as it usually was. His mother would be singing a hymn while she picked out the melody on the piano. Sophie would be chattering away, and Caroline would be laughing with her. Instead, the house was deathly silent.

He carried a plate of sandwiches with him to the back porch, along with a glass of cold water. He laid down again on the rag rug alongside the bed. He slid the plate of food toward his wife.

Caroline's eye, he thought, might be glad to see him. Maybe. He tried to smile as warmly as if she were smiling right back at him. Oddly, this scenario reminded him of a time when he tried to tame a wounded raccoon. So, that was the story he began to tell his wife hiding under the bed. It was with a gentle voice that he spoke to her, the same woman that he'd loved from the moment he first met her three years earlier, though she didn't resemble that woman now in any way he could have ever imagined.

Fall 1930

It was Saturday, a crisp fall morning in his sophomore year at Spring Grove High School. Picking his way down the steep bluff through the woods, he came upon a raccoon lying partially hidden under a hollow, rotting tree trunk. The raccoon must have been injured because she would surely have run away if she could. He figured she had to be thirsty. Probably hungry too. Since raccoons are nocturnal, he felt certain she'd been lying there since the night before.

Arvid decided that he would befriend her. Whatever it took. He would spend all day there with her, to earn her trust.

So, he walked back to the house and returned with a little pot of water and a shallow saucer. He also brought a bowl of fresh scraps from his mother's slop bucket. She put potato peelings, carrot and celery tops, leftover grease from cooking meat, and every sort of thing like that into the slop bucket to give to the hogs along with their slop. He told his mother that he would be gone until suppertime. On his way out the door, he grabbed a ratty old rag rug to lie on. Maybe he was lying on that very same rug now.

Arvid lay next to the raccoon all that afternoon. Slowly he moved the saucer of water closer to the raccoon's nose. She was thirsty. After lapping up the water, she rested for a while. She must have decided that Arvid would not harm her and closed her eyes to sleep. He fell asleep, too.

Later, the raccoon awoke, her nose twitching, sniffing the air, the bacon grease. Arvid slid bits of fat and anything with bacon grease on it, over to her on the saucer. He inched himself just a little closer. She watched him as she licked at the scraps.

After she'd eaten, he rested his head on his outstretched arm. It was the hand that smelled like bacon grease. He laid his closed fist only a couple feet from her nose. If she were to bite him, at least she wouldn't be able to bite off a finger.

When the shadows grew long, he knew that it was getting on toward milking time. He'd have to leave the raccoon. He left the pitcher of water, the saucer and the bowl that held the few remaining scraps where they were, not far from the raccoon's head.

Arvid returned to the woods after dark, wearing his warm barn jacket, carrying a lantern and with more scraps from the slop bucket. He also brought an old blanket to cover himself. As he got closer, several little pairs of eyes shone back at him in the glow of the lantern light. The raccoon's buddies had gathered round her. They predictably scattered as he walked closer, but after he lay still for a while, they came closer, watching.

The injured raccoon seemed a little perkier. He gave her more water and a few more tiny scraps of food. The other raccoons crept closer, interested in the scraps. He turned out the lantern and lay close to the raccoon. The night air turned quite cool, though it would likely be a couple of weeks before the first frost. He slept.

By dawn, the raccoon allowed him to touch her. She licked his fist. She put her little black "fingers" onto his hand. "She had a look of trust in her eyes," he'd told friends after his night in the woods.

Some of the guys chuckled and wanted to know what "trust" looked like on a raccoon's face. "It was just something that I saw, that's all I can say," he told them. At dawn he left to help with the morning milking. When he returned to the woods the next time, the raccoon was gone.

August 1948

Arvid lay next to Caroline all night long, occasionally talking softly to her. Later, during the night when she talked about the Devil and the Evil One, he accepted those things as her truth. By dawn, he knew that he could no more tame his wife's fears, than he could have talked that raccoon into following him home.

Arvid guessed it was about one o'clock in the morning when he heard Leah cry and the sound of his mother walking overhead by the occasional squeak of a floorboard. He heard her step carefully down the stairs and knew that she was getting the baby's bottle ready.

The moon was full and bright such that Arvid could see shadows under the bed. At some point, Caroline had pushed her hair aside and he could see both of her eyes in the silvery light of night. Her eyes showed fear. The baby was crying.

"The Evil One," she whispered. "He'll hurt me. My eyes have seen too much. I know what He looks like. I know who He is."

Arvid's heart went cold again. In a beam of moonlight that reached beneath the bed, a brief glint revealed something in Caroline's hand that he hadn't seen before. It was her large pair of silver sewing shears! They'd been hidden beneath a puddle of her hair the entire time she'd been under the bed. Arvid sucked in his breath. *Oh, my God, what if she had come out from under there with it while I was in the barn milking?*

"Caroline," he said, softly. "I am your husband, your protector. No one will hurt you in this house. *I* should be the one to hold those scissors. Let *me* be your protector."

She stared, unblinking. "These are *my* shears. The Evil One is out there now. Wait."

He returned her stare. "I'll stay here with you until the baby goes back to sleep. Is that what you want?" Arvid could feel the tears pricking his eyes again. His perfect baby daughter was now deemed evil by her own mother.

"Yes. Stay here," Caroline muttered through clenched teeth.

Eventually, Marit climbed the stairs again, taking Leah back to bed. After there were no more sounds from upstairs, he had another plan. "Caroline, I'm going to go to the kitchen now, to take care of some things."

"You're getting a knife."

A knife was the last thing he wanted, but since she saw that as a reason for him to go to the kitchen he choked out, "Yes."

Arvid went to the kitchen and found a candle. He hunted for paper and a pencil. He placed them on the counter beneath the candlelight and wrote a message to his mother. He tacked it onto the icebox.

If Leah's tummy could be counted on to act as an alarm, he guessed that his mother would be up again in about four hours. *Milking time. Those damn cows. They'll have to wait a little longer today. If they get mastitis, so be it.*

He lay back down next to his beautiful young wife and lied, saying he had a knife in his back pocket. There would be no more sleep for him that night.

When he heard Leah begin to make noises upstairs, his mother responded quickly, just as she had before. The sky was growing lighter. Again, Arvid heard his mother's footsteps descend the stairs and go to the icebox. A long pause. He imagined her face as she read his note. Then, she continued with the preparation of the bottle for Leah.

Marit carried Leah back upstairs with her, to feed her. After a while, the footsteps overhead went into Sophie's room and then the faint sound of Sophie's sleepy voice could be heard, although he couldn't hear what she was saying. Time passed.

There was the scuffling of feet overhead. Sophie was getting dressed, no doubt. The footsteps came downstairs and walked across the kitchen. Sophie's small voice, "—we—to—ouse—breakfast, Grandma?" Then the grandma and her two granddaughters were out the door just as the first rays of sunlight shot over the horizon.

When he heard his mother's ancient car pull away from the farmyard, Arvid asked Caroline again, "Can you come out now? The baby is gone. She's not coming back. I promise you. You must be very hungry. And thirsty." She had eaten nothing from the plate of food he brought to her the previous evening, nor the water.

Caroline squinted her eyes, as if thinking carefully. She pushed the scissors ahead of her and began to slide her body out from under the bed. "May I hold the sewing shears, Caroline?"

"For a little while," she answered hesitantly. At last she emerged from under the bed. Her long hair with dust motes falling over her breasts and to her waist.

"Let's go find some clothes to put on first, shall we?" She looked down at herself.

"He says I can put clothes on now." She nodded her assent.

Arvid thought better of asking *who* told her that it was okay to put clothes on. By then, he understood that Caroline was hearing voices that no one else heard. He took her by the hand and together they climbed the stairs.

She allowed him to choose a dress from those hanging on the hooks in the wardrobe. He handed her the undergarments and she allowed him to assist her in dressing, whenever she paused as if puzzled about what to do next. Or, maybe she was listening to a Voice other than his. He couldn't be sure about anything she was experiencing.

"Now, let's go get some breakfast," he said. Caroline said nothing but allowed him to lead her downstairs. He seated her at the kitchen table. "It's going to be another hot, muggy day," he said, trying to sound "normal."

He set out food for Caroline, some bread, butter and jam. He fried up a few eggs and a couple sausages. Poured two glasses of milk. She was ravenous. He ate beside her. All the while she was eating, he listened for the sound of car tires on the long driveway.

He thought about what he ordinarily would be doing at this time of day while he talked softly to Caroline. He would have called the cows in from the pasture by now. Teddy would have run out to the pasture to herd them home. Instead, Teddy was lying on one of the steps from the back porch, waiting patiently for his Master to begin his usual morning routine.

Without being milked, some of the cows would soon become very uncomfortable. They'd bawl, especially the one with a new calf only two days old. Without her calf to drain the milk from her udder, the skin on the teats would be shiny and tight. Regardless of his usual routine, he tried to talk about anything but that.

Caroline's eating slowed. She sat back in her chair at last. "I'm full," she said, with what might have been a smile. Or not.

"Would you like to put your hair up again?" he asked. "The way you usually do? I can get your brush."

"Yes," was all she said.

He took the stairs two at a time and found a hairbrush in a drawer and a handful of hairpins and returned with them. He led her to the bathroom to use the mirror there. She brushed her hair and the way she put it up seemed so natural, so ordinary that he thought that perhaps the past day had been nothing but a nightmare. When Caroline's hair was up, she looked almost like her old self again. In fact, something about her made it seem as if she had only just awoken from a deep sleep.

"Where's Sophie?" she asked him. "I haven't seen her for so long. I was away for a long time, wasn't I? I'm glad to be home now. But where is Sophie?"

Arvid's second lie was this. "She's upstairs sleeping. It's too early for her to get up yet." He did not want Caroline to be upstairs when they came. If she were, that would just make things that much harder. He was glad that she was dressed, and her hair done up.

"Oh," she said. "Well, I have dishes to do, don't I?" She spoke sweetly and simply, much like an innocent child might sound. Not like a woman that has been terrified by her own baby daughter.

51

"Yes, I'll help you. I hardly ever help you in the kitchen, anymore, do I? Remember when we were first married, I did a little? I'll dry while you wash."

That's where the two of them were, standing at the kitchen sink, as if there was nothing at all wrong in the world, when the three cars drove slowly down the driveway.

6

LIES AND SHAME

Arvid heard the sound of tires on the muddy lane before Caroline did, and he awaited her reaction. He wanted her to remain at the sink, washing dishes for as long as possible. The window over the sink did not face the driveway nor the lane which continued past the house and over the knoll to his mother's cabin, for which he was thankful. He heard the sound of car doors being cautiously closed before Caroline pulled her hands from the dishwater.

"Oh, who's here?" she asked.

Arvid had a lie ready to be spun out. He'd prepared it during the night as well as a string of others that might be needed.

Arvid forced cheerfulness into his voice. "Oh, Caroline. People have heard that you're home again and come to welcome you back. It's kind of like the chivaree[ii] on our wedding night. Isn't that nice?"

"Like the chivaree?" She repeated, puzzled. "But I'm not ready for company, Arvid. I have no food prepared. Nothing to *offer* them." Again, her lovely voice sounded so natural, though somewhat distracted.

"It's okay, they probably brought things with them, just like the night of the chivaree."

A knock on the kitchen screen door announced the first "guests." Arvid opened the door to welcome them.

"Well, hello. It's Rolf and Anna," he called over his shoulder to Caroline. "What a pleasant surprise." He smiled at them with wide eyes, as if saying, Play along here, okay? "Come on in. We were just saying how nice it is to have people come to welcome Caroline home after being gone so long. Kind of like when you came over for the chivaree on our wedding night. We are so happy to see you."

Rolf and Anna were their closest neighbors. Their land adjoined the Fjeld farm, but they did not farm it themselves. They leased out the land to Arvid while they continued to live in the original family farmhouse on the acreage. Anna was the young Spanish and French teacher in their hometown high school, Spring

Grove High and Rolf was a skilled fine woodworker. He made one-of-a-kind pieces of furniture using local walnut, cherry, and oak. His unique furniture designs went to customers in the Twin Cities, people with more money than the Spring Grove folks wanted to spend on a single item.

Both Rolf and Anna had grown up on dairy farms and so, were well acquainted with milking cows. To Arvid, their presence meant that they had agreed to take care of his barn chores all that day. That was the first request he'd written on the note to his mother before dawn.

Anna rearranged her expression, letting Arvid know that she'd caught on to the "story" Arvid was spinning for Caroline's benefit; she was ready to play along. Rolf followed suit. Anna went to Caroline and told her how glad she was to see her again. There was no mention of the new baby. Arvid breathed a sigh of relief.

Next to enter the kitchen was a neighbor from down in the Sheldon valley. Myron Bakken was the County Sheriff. Soon to retire and a widower, he lived alone in a new retirement home he'd built for himself alongside Beaver Creek. Sheriff Bakken came into the kitchen wearing civilian clothing and a wide smile. Caroline had seen him a few times since he'd moved to the valley. He was a likeable, grandfatherly fellow.

"Myron," Arvid greeted him with a smile. "It's good to see you. It's been a long time. You remember my wife, Caroline?"

"Of course, how are you Caroline? It's good to see you again." Following Myron was a young man with an uncanny resemblance to him, minus the receding hairline.

"I want to introduce you to my son, David. He's following in his old dad's footsteps. He's just finished training at the police academy and is visiting me for a bit before he goes off to start his new job out in St. Peter." Myron clapped his son on his back, grinning with fatherly pride. The presence of those two men told Arvid that they had made arrangements to be available to assist with transportation, if needed. He breathed an inaudible sigh of relief.

Lastly, the old white-haired doctor entered the kitchen. He came in his weekend clothes. No tie or white coat. He carried his doctor's bag, however. He had no time for the ruse referencing the wedding night chivaree.

He went directly to Caroline and took her hand between both of his, "How are you?" he asked Caroline with sincerity. Watching him, one might have thought, *so this is what he's like in the exam room.*

Arvid monitored Caroline's reactions to each of the three parties that entered their kitchen. She smiled and welcomed Rolf and Anna. She knew them well. She was calm with the entrance of Myron. She shook his hand and that of his son, David with a polite smile. When the doctor entered the kitchen, however, Caroline's face darkened. She did not extend her hand to the doctor. He took it in spite of her reluctance.

"Doctor?" she said. "What are *you* doing here?"

"I've been concerned about you, Caroline. We had a conversation near the end of your pregnancy that gave me pause. I put it aside at your request, but against my better judgment, I'm sorry to say. You reminded me that there are some women that, unfortunately, encounter special difficulties during pregnancy and in the weeks afterward.

"It's not a common problem but when it occurs, it is *very* serious indeed. Nothing to take lightly. I thought it was time to make a home visit to see how you are coming along."

"I am perfectly fine, Doctor. It was good of you to be interested, but, well, there's nothing to be concerned about." Caroline withdrew her hand brusquely. She clenched both hands into tight fists at her sides.

"And how is the baby, Caroline? And what did you name her?"

"Oh, no, you don't," she glowered at him, backing away. "That *Baby* you sent home with me does not fool me one bit. It wants to harm me. It *would* harm me, but I do not look at It. The eyes, Doctor. Its eyes would destroy me. It has others fooled. But I know what It's doing. Arvid had It sent away, didn't you, Arvid?"

The doctor said softly, but with intensity. "My dear Caroline. You gave birth to a beautiful baby daughter for you and your husband. Where is—?"

"Oooh no. I said NO!" Caroline's response was intense and rapid-fire. "The Devil has fooled you too. Infected you!" Caroline's face flamed red and the veins in her neck bulged. She spun on her heel and headed for the stairway.

"I'm going to get Sophie away from here. Before that Evil Thing finds its way back here. Arvid's mother took It away. She has to look out for *herself* now. There's nothing I can do for her." She looked at her husband. "I'll be right back with Sophie."

"Caroline," Arvid caught her hand. "Sophie's not here. She's at her grandma's house."

She spun on him, eyes wide. "She is with the Devil? That can't be true, Arvid. Sophie is just a little girl. She can't protect herself. Go after them. Save Sophie. Save her from the Devil!" Caroline raked at Arvid's arms in desperation, pushing him away. Her voice shrill, hysterical, eyes darting around the room. Arvid saw with dread that she had positioned herself in front of the knife drawer.

The doctor gave Caroline space, using only his voice to reach out to her. "That baby cannot, *will* not harm you in any way, nor anyone else," he tried to assure her.

As the doctor spoke, Myron and his son quietly, discreetly moved a little closer to Caroline.

Caroline turned to face them, angrily. "Why are you blocking my way? We have to get out of here, NOW."

Caroline quickly reached behind her and faced them again brandishing a large carving knife. A ray of early morning sunlight glinted off the long blade.

"Caroline," Arvid cried, "you don't need that knife. These people are here to help us. Trust me, please, Caroline. Put the knife down."

Myron grabbed a kitchen towel, wrapping it around his right arm to draw Caroline's attention. As she stepped toward him, David slipped behind her and grabbed the wrist of the hand wielding the knife. Arvid winced. He knew just how sharp that knife was; he'd recently honed it.

As David grasped her wrist, Myron reached to pry the knife from her fist. It was done in an instant. Caroline screamed. "No, you put us all in danger!" In the space of a few seconds, her face showed fury, then fright and switched back to fury again. Arvid could no longer read her face.

The nightmare was only beginning.

The doctor signed and placed the necessary paperwork in the front seat of the Sheriff's car without saying another word. He then backed down the long driveway to be out of the way of the Sheriff's car. Rolf and Anna disappeared discreetly, heading toward the barn to call the cows in for milking.

Caroline kicked and screamed at Myron and David to keep from being put into the cruiser. Arvid saw Myron give his son a nod, at which David more or less carried Caroline to the car while Myron opened the back door.

In the backseat, Arvid told himself that when she butted him with her head, it was an accident. She hadn't meant to give him a bloody nose. She pushed against Arvid to keep him at arms' length in the back of the car. Caroline scrabbled to unlock the door without success. Pounded with both fists on the glass. Her knuckles and the glass were soon bloodied.

"We can put her in handcuffs, Arvid," Myron said into the rearview mirror as he started the engine. "I don't want you injured."

"No, no, she's calming more now. She didn't mean to hurt me." Arvid was nearly certain.

Caroline screamed at the glass. Screamed at the man driving on the other side of the grate. Shrill, hysterical howls continued mile after mile. Ranted about the Devil finding her. Tricking all of them, but for herself. She alone was not fooled by the Devil. He would want her eyes, she said.

Arvid clenched his teeth and told her one of the lies he'd created during his long night on the floor alongside her. "The Devil can't follow where we are going, Caroline." What was one more lie?

"You will be safe there." He repeated it time and again, pretending a confidence he didn't feel. He told her that lie so *many* times that he nearly believed it himself. *How do I know she'll be safe from her own thoughts, anywhere? From voices that only she can hear?*

With an hour behind them, she finally quietened, but for a soft moaning as she made herself smaller, shrinking into the corner against the car door, and away from Arvid.

Finally, the massive grounds of Rochester State Hospital loomed ahead. Arvid caught a glimpse of the plaque by the front entrance. Rochester State Hospital was already 70 years old and looked every bit of that. He'd read *Frankenstein* in high school and when he saw the place, decided that the monster would have been created in a place like that.

His breath caught in his throat. What kind of man leaves his wife in such a place? And what kind of man would take his wife home knowing what she'd done and said. A mother who called her own baby "evil."

By the time the three men left Rochester that day, Arvid saw Myron as his champion. He had taken charge when Arvid was too dazed to speak. He answered the simplest questions about who, what, when and where for the hospital records. He presented the old doctor's statement for the emergency placement. And later, when Arvid's voice gave out in exhaustion, or perhaps defeat, Myron offered calm reassurances that the admission process was proceeding according to a protocol with which he was, unfortunately, too familiar. Sheriff Bakken had transported patients to Rochester State Hospital under commitment enough times in his long career, and that helped him to steer Arvid through the painfully foreign hours in that cavernous place.

Arvid sucked in his breath when the men in white forcibly removed Caroline from the Admitting office to bring her to her ward in Oak Hall.

Myron was by his side. Caroline panicked at the end, when she realized that her husband was leaving without her. Then, and only then, did she finally clutch at her husband. She wanted Arvid to hold her when it was too late for that, when the day was ending, and time was running out. It crushed him to see her pulled from the room, crying his name.

"Arvid, Arvid, Arvid. You're not leaving me here! Arvid, please. Please don't leave me here. I want to go with you. Arvid. Arvid. Arvid. Take me with you—"

Arvid struggled to hold himself in check within the walls of the hospital, but that resolve broke down upon getting into the privacy of the car. With Myron driving and his son, David, in the backseat, Arvid talked much of the way back to his farm and wept openly more than once.

"How could I have not seen this before, Myron? Am I blind? Stupid? I told myself that she would be back to her normal self once I got her home with the baby." Arvid chastised himself in every way he could. He tried to name the moment when Caroline's descent into madness should have been apparent to him, but he could not find it.

"You must be hungry, Arvid," Myron said during a long pause. "You haven't eaten anything all day. I know David and I need to get something in our bellies. Let's pull over here, at this diner. Get us a bite to eat."

Myron listened more than he talked, and by the end of that long day, Arvid was grateful for that. When Myron did speak, there was some comfort in his words. "I don't think we can really know what is in another person's mind, Arvid. Could the doctors in that hospital back there have predicted months ago that this would happen to Caroline at this time in her life? I don't think so."

"She didn't trust me, Myron. She didn't confide in me." The pressure of the tears pulsed behind his eyes again, making a headache that pounded.

"Maybe she knew, Arvid, but prayed and hoped that she would get through it...that everything would go back to normal after the baby was born. I think I would have hoped for that if I were in her shoes."

Arvid glanced at Myron, knowing that he understood that the hospital admission was so much more than Caroline's absence from their home and family for an undetermined length of time. Even if Caroline were discharged from the hospital next week with the hospital's blessings and assurances that she was entirely "cured," Arvid knew their lives would never return to what they had been before that day. He would always have room for a doubt, for a question about what might be waiting just around the corner.

Eventually, Arvid's anger at himself abated long enough to ask one painful question after another. The questions spun rapid-fire like tires digging deeper and deeper into the mud and getting nowhere. "What do I *say* to the children when they ask questions?" Arvid held his hands wide, palms up. "Will I ever see her come out of that hospital again? Tell me, truthfully. Do people get out of that place once they're admitted?"

Myron looked at him with gentle eyes. "I don't have the answers, Arvid. I wish I did. I *have* seen people leave that hospital and be much better than they were when they went in. And yes, I know of some that are still there after many years. Maybe they never *will* leave. I don't know." Myron looked at Arvid again. There was genuine sadness there.

Myron continued. "Why some people are able to get out of there while others don't, I don't even pretend to understand. But when the doctors have a conference with you in a couple of weeks, they'll have a better idea. Until then, you've gotta sit tight. Your job right now is to sit on a fence, isn't it?"

"I'm not good at sitting on fences." Arvid clenched his fists, looking out the window.

"Don't expect yourself to be good at that, Arvid. Nobody is."

Miles passed. The sky remained fairly bright for some time with the sun setting behind them. They had passed through Harmony and Mabel, Minnesota when the golden full moon rose over the roadway in a twilight sky.

"What will Leah's life be like? To be a child called Evil by her own mother?" Arvid heard himself ranting, the panic constricting his throat.

Myron listened, which gave Arvid the room he needed to talk. Before they drove down the gravel driveway to the Fjeld farm, Myron offered one thought which Arvid would refer back to many times over the following months.

"Today is the *only* day you can live, Arvid. You can't live tomorrow until it comes."

And then just before Arvid got out of the car, Myron's final words, "Leah will *not* be ruined by this. Believe me. She has what she needs most. You and Marit and her big sister. That is more than some children have."

Arvid watched Myron's cruiser pull away. Did Myron somehow know the way things would turn out? Or was this just Myron hoping, the same way he was.

As Arvid expected, Rolf and Anna had gone home for the night, the chores were long done. The barn was empty but for the calves. The milk cows were back in the pasture. Arvid found a note on the kitchen table telling him to "Call in the morning if you want help. No trouble at all. Rolf."

Marit was waiting at the kitchen table. Sophie and Leah were asleep upstairs. Arvid glanced toward the back porch where Caroline had lain hidden, naked, for some fifteen hours. The iron bed, that reminder, was gone. He was exhausted near to death.

Marit held her son as he stood, her shorter frame dwarfed. "It's the shame of it all now, Mom," he said to her.

Her only response was, "Shhh now. Shhh, Arvid. You are over-tired. Don't try to think any more today now. Shhh."

The dirty feeling of shame was a sharp, ugly thing by the time he tried in vain to sleep. Layers upon layers of shame. Shame that his wife was at that very moment, alone in a mental hospital. Hospitalized in a place whose very name caused people to cringe. He had left her there. He could not save her, nor protect her there. He felt utterly stupid, emasculated and stripped of self-worth. How could he have been caught so off-guard, blinded to what must have been right in front of him?

He felt shame at what he'd done to his family name. His father told him more than once in his slow, thoughtful brogue, "Ya, ya. My father came over from Norway with nothing more than his good name. But Arvid, you see dat was de most important thing to bring with him. Because no amount of money can buy a good name."

He'd never given much thought to his father's sayings while he was alive. Arvid was young and his father's gentle voice was a kind of background noise, like the birds singing while he went about his farm work; he didn't have to think about them. "There's a right way and a wrong way to do everything," and "If you're going to do a yob (job) you might as well do it well."

Suddenly, the background noise felt like a marching band. He had to think about his name, about what he'd lost for his father and for the Fjelds going forward. He would feel conspicuous wherever he went, as if he were using up more than his fair share of the air. When he walked into a meeting at the town hall or even the church council meeting, he'd have that nightmare feeling that he'd somehow forgotten to put on his pants before he left the house. A person can't unsee a thing like that.

Arvid envisioned the sign people would "see" painted across his chest. 'My wife lost her marbles.' The sign on his back would read, 'I am a Bad Husband.' Folks would register his arrival and they would look just a little too long. Perhaps they'd give him the obligatory head nod in greeting, a smile if he was lucky, or maybe they'd look away quickly, embarrassed to be caught looking.

Sophie and Leah would grow up lugging that Fjeld name along with them. Just out of earshot, people would say things like, "Those are the Fjeld girls. Their mother is in the insane asylum. Tsk tsk. What must that be like to have a mother that lives in the loony bin?"

He remembered what the kids said about crazy people when he was a boy. And then there were the horror stories. One particular story went around more than once, a deliciously frightening tale about an asylum escapee that went on a murderous rampage around the countryside, sneaking up on young lovers necking in a parked car.

Arvid was ashamed that he'd ever listened to those stories, that he'd ever participated in them without once thinking that they were taking pleasure in the misery of real men and women, with families and people who loved them. Oh for shame! Creepy ghost stories and tales from Rochester State Hospital for the Insane, both sources of deliciously scary stories that had made him afraid to sleep alone in his room at night.

Only yesterday, he'd promised Caroline he would protect her. "That's what husbands do," he'd said. Instead, he turned her over to become one of those people locked in that horrid place.

Myron would not tell anyone about the trip to Rochester, nor would his son. Arvid knew that. And he knew that the old doctor would certainly not talk about what he saw at the Fjeld house. Professional confidentiality and all of that. But Rolf and Anna?

Arvid could see how the news of Caroline's hospitalization would spread. One of the neighbors driving past would have noticed Rolf and Anna's car parked in his farmyard today. The neighbor might even have noticed that the car was parked there twice today, early in the day and again late in the day. Rolf and Anna certainly wouldn't have stopped in for a casual visit at either of those times.

The neighbor would wonder if there was something wrong at the Fjeld place. The next time that neighbor crossed paths with Rolf and Anna, naturally he'd ask, 'Say, I saw your car over there at Arvid's place. Is he havin' trouble with somethin'? Could he use a little help?' When the reason for Rolf and Anna's presence on the farm was known, then the truth about Caroline's whereabouts would be known as well. The news would spread rapidly from there.

"No such thing as privacy around here," he muttered aloud. Arvid lay fully-clothed on the bed he'd shared with Caroline for three years. One hand crept toward Caroline's pillow, noting the faint indentation that was there, the place where her head had always lain. And he wondered what the pillow was like where she now lay.

He felt ashamed of himself for even imagining how the story of this day would spread, when he should only be thinking about Caroline, alone in that place. But that didn't stop him. He felt as if his head were cleaved in two. One part was with Caroline, while the other was here, on Hawk Ridge, ashamed of what had happened to his wife. Of what he'd done; of what he'd had to do.

Neighbors would tell stories about what they'd heard, and they'd speculate about the rest. The news would travel around Spring Grove, Caledonia and beyond. People would gather out front after church to visit, or at the grocery store, or while sitting at the livestock sales barn. Some of the talk would be under the guise of Lutheran concern and kindness. Some of it would be purely conjecture, trying to fill in what wasn't known. It would be too juicy to keep quiet about. Arvid tossed and turned into the night. By tomorrow night, there wouldn't be a soul that hadn't heard something about what his beloved wife had said or done. And what he then did.

Arvid could "hear" the related conversations repeating themselves over and over in his head.

"Where'd you say Arvid met his wife?"

"Oh, she's from Owatonna. Grew up in that big orphanage over there, I hear. That's what they say, anyhow."

"Oh, ya, she's real pretty, but I don't think she's even a little bit Norwegian. As dark as she is. Her hair is almost black, y' know. Course, I s'pose dat maybe don't mean nothing, either, but den, you never know."

"Well, I s'pose he was real taken with her, ya. But when you don't know anything about the family either. Well, that would make a lot o' guys stop and think.

"No, those kids at de orphanage came from all over de country. She coulda come from yust about anywhere, but not from Norway, dat's for sure." There'd be a chuckle.

"Ya, I heard dat she had to be carried out of her own house kicking and screaming.

"God, I hope no one has heard that she thought Leah was the devil." Arvid found that there were still a few tears left, after all. At dawn, he wasn't sure if he'd slept at all.

PART II

SINKHOLES

*"Living never wore one out so much as
the effort not to live."*

Anais Win (1903 -1977)
American/French Writer

7

SISTERS

Caroline
Mid-August 1948

Memories are fuzzy. Was it yesterday, or was it the day before? Or the day before that? The Voice is talking and then I'm here. It's darkness, then light, then the grays between quickly fall away. Fragments twirl in my head. Are these memories? Nightmares? Something else?

I see Arvid in the backseat with me. The dark upholstery is crusty and dirty. I hug the door. The cornfields fly by. One little town, then another. "Who's there?" I ask, frightened. Arvid says the driver is Myron, the old Sheriff. A grate separates us from him. Arvid says the other man is Myron's son, David. I don't know him. Why can't I roll down the window?

I panic. The window must be opened. I'm going to break the window! I want to throw myself from the car, to roll into the ditch and disappear. I'm terrified, caged like an animal. I feel like trash being hauled to the dump, like a hog led to slaughter. I scream and I cry. I pound my head against the window until Arvid holds onto me so tightly, I can't move. He pins my head to his chest after I bunt his head with mine. I didn't mean to hurt him. He has a bloody nose. Now I feel wetness. His tears fall on my head.

"Are you able to handle her, Arvid," the deep voice in the front seat says. "I can stop the car and we'll restrain her together. I don't want you injured."

"But how would you do it?" Arvid's voice is brittle.

"I have handcuffs so she can't strike you. We'll move her to the middle of the seat, away from the window. David can sit back there with you, next to the window."

"No, no, that's alright. I've got her. She's settling down now, aren't you Caroline?" Arvid sounds scared. Pleading with me to do as he says.

I've frightened my Arvid. My dear sweet Arvid. I am so sorry. So sorry. Why did I hurt you? "Why why why..." I say over and over, and I cry.

Eventually, a row of enormous brick buildings appears. A nunnery! There is a man standing in front of the middle building, guarding it with a gun. "That man has a gun! A gun!" I whisper in terror.

"No, no, Sweetheart. He doesn't have a gun. He's just standing and waiting for someone," Arvid says firmly, but I do see a gun. I'm sure I do! The heavy front door latches loudly behind us.

"Are there more people with guns inside this building?" I whisper to Arvid terrified. Arvid does not answer me. Have I melted away? Become invisible? I hold my hand in front of my face to be sure I am still here.

Arvid doesn't *want* to leave me here; I know that. But I don't hear him bargain for my freedom either. It's his choice to leave me here, in this cold, walled nunnery. He says it is the old white-haired doctor's decision too. I don't know what the doctor could have to do with the nunnery.

The gray floors stretch out for as long as I can see. Corners are dark. Strange noises bounce off of dull-green walls with peeling paint. Distant screams echo, along with moans, ranting, pleading and songs sung off-key.

I cover my ears. With the sounds out there and the Voice in here, in my head, it is all too much. I beg for it to stop, "Stop it. Stop it. Stop, please!" I hold my head between my hands to keep it from cracking apart.

"Stop what, Caroline?" the silver-haired man in the nunnery asks me.

"Stop the Voice, the other sounds," I say in desperation and put my head between my knees. "I *know* what to do. I don't need Him to tell me."

The men in white trousers and smocks take me away. "Arvid, Arvid, Arvid. Take me with you. Don't leave me here. I'm sorry, Arvid. I'm sorry, I'm sorry. I'm sorry." I cry.

I don't hear him say anything but, "Goodbye, Caroline."

The smell assaults me...cleansers mixed with urine, feces and body odor. One person smells cleaner than the rest—Sister Alva. I hear her called "Big Alva," the big woman in white. She's in charge of me now. Does she own me?

I try to think of some other place to be. Anywhere other than the nunnery. But someone is talking to me. Talk talk talk tock tock tock tick tock tick tock, Think think think. I squeeze my head tight. They lead me to a narrow bed covered with a thin gray blanket and then tell me that it's mine. This bed can't be mine. I have a bed already, at the farm, the one where Arvid and I sleep.

Arvid. Arvid has left me here! Oh, please let me be somewhere else, anywhere other than this nunnery. Big Alva dislikes me. These nuns aren't nice. They're gruff and angry-looking. They stare. Without warning, I am held tight while one of them cuts my hair. I panic. I scream. I cannot be here. I cannot. Be somewhere else. Somewhere else. Someplace safer.

The orphanage maybe? Even though they asked me silly questions, I could mostly ignore their ridiculous ideas. The trim and stiff red-haired lady who worked in the office on my floor of the orphanage said to me many times, "Won't you be so happy, Carol, to be adopted by a nice family?"

I ignored her and after a while, she stopped talking nonsense. And nobody ever cut all my hair off.

"A nice family," Pfft. I was only a child but I knew a thing or two about "nice families" and I wasn't having any of it. "The devil you know is better than the one you don't," my mother once told me.

We were having a picnic under a tree by a lake. I threw breadcrumbs to the ducks. She thought for a moment and added carefully, "My mother, your grandmother told me that. But *we* know that's not always true, don't we, Caroline?" My mother looked into my eyes. "You have to decide that for yourself. Especially when the Devil you know is terrible."

I nodded my head. That was after we had gotten away. Far, far away.

At the orphanage, I was frightened whenever there was a potential adoptive couple coming to see the children. We were lined up like little soldiers in the parlor wearing our Sunday best. We were told to smile nicely at the couples and politely say our how do you do's and thank you's.

One of the caregivers, Sarah, understood my terror that someone would take me away, *pretending* they wanted a daughter. I would do whatever I had to, to stay at the orphanage.

I wasn't stupid. I saw those bigger boys at the orphanage taken to work on farms. I'd seen those boys back at school, when and if they were allowed to attend, that is. They were worn out boys with blistered, filthy hands and sometimes bruises, courtesy of their farm "fathers."[iii]

If a man and his wife wanted me, they were likely looking for someone to be their maid, or nanny or something much worse than that. I couldn't risk it. I'd learned what happened to some girls with no one to protect them.

During my six years at the orphanage, I used every trick I could imagine, all to avoid adoption. I played at being clumsy. I tripped when I walked, and I spilled a pitcher of lemonade over a man and his unkempt wife. That only worked once because I was never put in charge of carrying in the lemonade again. I "accidentally" tore the dress of a woman while helping with her coat to be hung up. But I quickly realized it was going to take more than clumsiness to put people off.

I twirled in circles until I was so dizzy, I fell down. Without even planning it, I managed to knock the man over, and he cut his head. That was a bonus as far as I was concerned. One time I refused to speak at all, and instead made grunting noises directly into the faces of the skinny little man and his fat wife. Sometimes I just screamed loud and long, over and over.

One time when the visitors came right after breakfast, I smeared jam on my face and fingers and then "fell" against them. I got jam on their clothing and I drooled, too. But I knew I could do better yet. I pounded my head with my fists and then rolled my eyes back and "fainted." Fainting was a good way to make a man and his wife lose interest in me, even after they'd said I was pretty.

Puberty brought more interested adoptive couples. Even the visitors who came looking for a boy to adopt, gave me a long hard look. It made me sick to my stomach. Finally, I made use of something that the grandmother had called "Caroline's nervous stomach." Back then, when my worries came at me hard and fast, they sometimes made me throw up or have diarrhea.

It became my most powerful weapon at the orphanage. To be able to empty my stomach onto an interested adoptive couple brought notoriety.

I had no reason to vomit or to be worried like that at school. School was the best part of my life. I was a model student. I would have lived at school, if they would have let me. Books were my savior. They took me far away, to places where I was safe.

But that was years ago. Now it's a nunnery that has me. Am I to stay here, forever? At the orphanage, I tricked people so I *could* stay. Do I trick them now so I can *leave*? Is it safe to stay here? Or just until the Devil finds me?

They call the women that sleep in the enormous dormitory with me my "sisters." Why, I don't know. The three "sisters" that sleep nearest me cannot be avoided. Every day, whether I want to or not, I must spend the bulk of the day in their company. I've tried to shake loose from them many times, without much success. Just once I'd like to eat by myself in peace and quiet.

And then one day, I meet Sally. It is a rare moment without my herd of "sisters" trailing me and in that moment, I hear whimpering behind a door in the hallway. I know I shouldn't, but I'm going to get in trouble with Alva anyway, so I open the door. In the darkness is the crumpled form of a person. I pull the string hanging from the ceiling and a bare lightbulb reveals a janitor's closet with a slender Negro woman surrounded by buckets, mops, rags and cleaning supplies. She gasps and scrambles to get her feet beneath her.

I quickly pull the door closed behind me. She slips, however, on something slick and she's back on the floor again. The young woman wears the gray uniform of a cleaning lady with a white scarf wrapped around her head. "I's sorry Miss. I...I get my things 'n get busy right away." She appears to be frightened of me. I cannot bear to see that look in her eyes. Not after seeing it in my Arvid's eyes.

"No, it's alright," I say to her. She reminds me of someone I used to know, someone else with skin just about that color who rarely spoke. "Are you hurt?" I crouch down and ask her.

"No, no, I's alright. Please Miss, if 'n you c'n see fit not t' mention finding me like this? To Miss Alva, I mean? She...she—" This young woman's voice is low and tender, and it makes me think of a lullaby.

"I won't tell anyone," I shake my head. "Certainly not Big Alva." I roll my eyes and put out a hand to help her up. She is of slight build and shorter than I am. She gets up by herself.

"Oh, Miss. You mustn' get dirty. It be my fault an' she already mad at me 'nough, ever' blessed day—"

I pat her shoulder. "Now, now. Shhh. Don't worry about that. But why are you crying?" I ask her. It strikes me then how odd it is that I've heard women crying many times since I arrived here, and never have I heard anyone ask, 'Why are you crying?' Her dark eyes are filled with deep sorrow.

"What's happened to you?" I ask her. "You're not a prisoner here, are you? You can leave if you don't like it here, can't you? I wish I could, but I don't know where I could go to be safe."

"It hard t' 'xplain," she answers softly. "If 'n I leave, be nobody here t' watch over her." She looks at me suddenly as if she realizes she's said too much.

"What do you mean?" I search her face. "To watch over who?"

The small woman doesn't answer my question. She only appears to be more anxious. So I speak. "My name is Caroline," I say finally, and I hold out my hand again to shake hers.

"Sally," she says and looks down. "You' a good person, Miss, t' on'y one 'n 'is whole place 'at I know of." But she doesn't take my hand.

"Am I." It's not a question. "I think there might have been a time when I was," I say to her, letting my hand drop to my side. Nobody that was truly good would be trapped inside this nunnery.

"C'n I ax why you here, Miss?" she asks me gently. "I don' mean in 'is 'ere closet, but 'ere in 'is place, I mean?"

I narrow my eyes and look around, as if the answer might be hidden among the mops and brooms. "The Devil found me. I had to get away." I chew the inside of my cheek a little.

Sally looks at me. "I seen Him, too," she says and shyly holds out her hand, in case I still want to shake it. I do. "An' he come t' visit my mama diff'rent times." I take her hand and hold it a little longer than a handshake needs to be.

"What happened to your mother, Sally? Where is she?"

Sally's gaze narrows now, as if deciding something. "Up two floors...'n 'is very buildin'. Ye won' tell no one on me, will you, Miss?"

"No, why should I tell? Of course not." Sally's story, at least part of it, seems clear to me. "You work here so you can be near your mother. But you're afraid that if they knew, they wouldn't let you work here? Is that right?"

"Please, Miss, I got t' see her ever' now 'n again. They's no one else c'n be here," her eyes plead with mine.

"I'm good at secrets, I promise you," I say. "And my name is Caroline, remember?" I try a timid smile. This woman has entrusted me with something valuable. I feel as if I can stand up straighter now, like a grown-up because of it.

"Car'line," she tries out my name. "You really call 'er 'Big Alva'?" And she manages a small smile.

"Yes, I do. Other sisters do too. She's not a good person," I answer with confidence.

"No. She not." Sally agrees by shaking her head and then sighs deeply. She smooths her apron, adjusts her headscarf.

"You never told me why you were crying. Is it something about your mother?"

She nods her head solemnly. "'Ts up there cleanin' early this mo'nin' an' I saw 'er. She chain t' the wall again, ankles 'n wrists, so's she can' hardly move. She a mess. Somebody shoulda taken her t' the water closet. It right there. But no. There she lay... up there in her own filth like that. Stinkin' somethin' fierce. I just had t' cry is all. Can' do nothin' else 'bout it sometime but cry for my poor mama."

A chill spread through me. "Why? Why would they chain a person like an animal?" I ask, and then I gasp. I have to wonder, is the Devil only two floors above me? Is He in charge up there?

"Well, y' see...she, my mama...she hurt 'erself. She chew on her mouth 'fore she come 'ere. Ate 'er own lips clean off. But she dudn' know what she doin', y' see. Dudn' know nothin' sometime. She use t' be a strong woman. So strong. Now, she bite 'erself an' anybody that get close 'nough fo' to catch hold o' 'em.

"A danger t' 'erself 'n others, they say. My li'l brother tol' me all o' what happen. My brother, Amos—he been tryin' t' keep 'er safe from 'erself, but 'e couldn'. He got bit real bad too. Still, 'e try 'n keep the po-lice from comin' in t' the house an' so they arrested him. Just tryin' t' take care o' his mama and they threw 'im in the jailhouse."

Sally looked at me. There was fire in her eyes. "He only seventeen years ol' then. When he get outta jail, he come lookin' for me. Foun' me in Mowaukee. Tol' me 'bout mama. Tol' me t' come to Min'sota. Figure since I's a woman, maybe I c'n get close t' her.

"So I come to Rochesta', an' I fin' out if I get a job as a cleanin' woman here, they lemme sleep in a room with some o' the other cleanin' women. An' I c'n catch a glimpse of her now 'n then." There was a catch in Sally's throat. "But this mornin', she don' even know me, Car'line. Dudn' know her firstborn chil'." She swallowed hard.

"When they can' control a body up there, they chain 'em up, like a dog mad with rabies." She pauses and I can think of nothing to say. This is more horrendous than I'd even imagined. Sally's face has emptied itself. Such dark emptiness.

"An' now you know...'bout everythin' they is t' know 'bout me."

I nod my head. "You can trust me. I won't let you down, Sally. I promise. I suppose we should get out of here before somebody comes looking for you. Are you okay to leave now?"

"Yes 'm, an' thank you, M'i—Car'line. Nex' time I see you I try t' give you a sign t' let you know I'm thinkin' o' you. An' how much I 'preciate you holdin' my secret safe 'etween us. I'm not s'posed t' 'ssociate with you sisters. But if 'n it ever happen that we alone again, an' you want to, an' it safe, maybe we c'n talk a little mo'."

"I'll keep an eye out for you, Sally. But I won't give anything away. I promise you." I put my hand over my heart as a pledge, something I haven't done since I was a child. "Should you leave first, or should I?"

"I go first," Sally says. "Nobody think t' look in 'ere once I's out there. Wait a bit, an' nen I knock on de door when de hallway safe for you t' come out. A'righ'?"

I see Sally nearly every day when she comes to mop and clean this cavernous floor. She is ignored by all but Alva, who seems to enjoy chastising her.

"Haven't you learned anything? I don't want you mopping the main hallway after nine o'clock. Why is that so hard for you to remember, Girl?" Alva stands below the giant clock high on the wall and adds, "Maybe nobody taught you how to tell time, is that it? When the little hand is on the number nine, it's too late to start mopping the main hallway. Got it?"

Sally stands straight , her eyes downward and answers, "Yes 'm."

I feel closer to Sally than to any of my "sisters." She is my one true friend here. Friends hold each other's secrets close and they trust one other. We share the secret of Sally's mother who lives upstairs in chains, and the secret of our friendship, Sally's and mine.

As Sally works on this floor, she takes stock of our surroundings, and when it's safe, she smiles and then I can smile back. We talk a little when we can sneak a few minutes here and there.

Sally moves around this place in plain sight with that old mop and bucket. It seems to me, however, that most people don't see her at all, like she's invisible. I want to be invisible too, like Sally. If I were invisible, I could just walk right out the door.

But as the days go by, I become more certain that nobody leaves here alive.

I would give anything to spend a day apart from my "sisters." I'd walk out these doors alongside Sally and we'd spend the day together. What a luxury that would be!

I tire of hearing the nuns patronizing twaddle. "Wait for your sisters, Caroline," or "Please help your sister when you can. Remember, helping one another makes the world a nicer place, doesn't it?" and "You must look out for one another. You are sisters here." I wonder if I can still make myself throw up.

The nuns all use that singsong voice. Do they practice it together like a choir practice? The truly important thing for me is to be certain that none of the sisters harbor the Devil, to be certain that He hasn't found me here. I evaluate each of my closest sisters carefully.

Estra is probably the closest in age to me, with a thick neck, thin beige hair and she could stand beneath my armpit. She weighs more than 400 pounds. Her eyes are too big for their sockets and sit close together below a short forehead. She is forever scanning the environment for whatever is edible. No unattended food is safe from her short, fat fingers. "Edible" to Estra includes things that are not food, too.[iv]

Estra likes to talk. "Took a while to weigh this much," she tells me cheerfully, as if it were a goal of hers, her ideal weight. "Eight or maybe twelve years for sure. I haven't gained any more since I got here." She seems unhappy about that. "Six years. Been here six years or is it nine? One o' those numbers. I'm nineteen. I think. I might be twenty now. How old 'er you?"

I choose not to answer. That doesn't matter because Estra talks even when no one is listening. "My family has a restaurant in St. Paul. Fancy. Mama made me dresses out of flour sacks." She nods to agree with herself. "Mmm-huh." Estra's flour sack dress is so wide that it fans out only a couple inches above the floor. When she walks, she resembles a giant bell tottering back and forth on two stubby feet.

Maybe Estra's restaurant story is true. Maybe it isn't. Sometimes I wonder how much the truth matters here. How can a person live a true life in a place like this?

Ruthie is the eldest of the four of us, I think, though I've never really talked to her, mostly because she spits when she talks and, clearly, she does not like to talk to the sisters. She is as skinny as Estra is fat. She has a narrow chin and broad nose with a crease down the middle. When she does speak, her voice is nasal and it wavers and cracks as if she is about to cry. Her eyes are too far apart, and she has a harelip.[v] "Ruthie" is an unfortunate name because she doesn't pronounce it well. Frankly, she doesn't pronounce many things very well.

Ruthie reminds me of a scrawny tomcat on the prowl. I feel sorry for her, because of her appearance, of course. She certainly had no choice in the matter of her harelip, but why didn't someone do something about it? I can't help but be repulsed by her lack of cleanliness and the sounds and sight of her eating. It's an awful thing that no one should have to witness.

Her favorite pastime is holding Dolly, a filthy ragdoll with stitched eyes and mouth. The doll goes everywhere with her under one arm. She rocks Dolly to sleep whenever she gets the chance, using one of only three rockers in the day room. No one challenges her for "her" rocker. When a new sister mistakenly sat in it, Ruthie summarily dumped her out and then sat in it with her dolly. "Go to thleep now, Dolly. Don't cry. That'th a good girl."

Ruthie has some favorite words, though they are few and incongruent with her "mothering" of Dolly. The words startled me at first. She pronounces them better than anything else she can say, however.

"Puthy fuckin' shitfathe," Ruthie says, issuing them forth in one rush, like it's somebody's name. Maybe it is.

"She's hard of hearing," Big Alva claims. "She doesn't know how loud she is when she talks." I don't believe that for one second, nor much of anything else that comes out of Alva's mouth.

I am embarrassed for Ruthie because of her ragdoll. I wouldn't say that Ruthie is "harmless" but that doesn't have anything to do with the Devil. He's not hiding within her. That I know because the Devil is cunning, and Ruthie is anything but.

The third sister is Lois. She is clumsy and has thick, straight, black hair that is cut so short and so sharply across her forehead that it appears to be a black-bristled brush atop her head. But her face is the color of softly polished copper. She shuffles around the other three of us, back and forth, back and forth she walks, around in circles, too. Where is she going? Plaintively she says something that sounds like, "*niin wanishin daga giiwewidoon nookomis.*"

"Where do you *think* you are going?" I finally ask her. She doesn't answer me. She rarely speaks. When she does, it's that long string of consonants again, "n's" that sound like humming, the guttural "g's, d's" and "w's."

It has to mean something. When I ask Big Alva if she knows what she's saying, she says, "She's talkin' Ojibwe.[vi] It's some kind of Indian tongue from northern Minnesota. Never mind her, if it bothers you."

"I'm not bothered, I just wond—" Big Alva puts her hand up and turns to go.

As Big Alva walks away, I hear her mutter under her breath, "She shouldn't even be here to begin with...hmph."

With all her shuffling, Lois falls sometimes. Her right foot turns under and trips her. She gets hurt when she falls against chairs and tables, especially. Dark bruises pepper her coppery-colored arms and head and she is missing two front teeth. Perhaps most of the sisters don't know that because she never smiles. Why should she? What would she have to smile about?

The worst thing of all for Lois is that she has convulsions.[vii] Really *hard* ones! Grand mal, is what the ladies in white call them. Her seizure or fit always comes just before dawn and afterward she is wiped out for another two hours at least. That's why she rarely has to eat breakfast with the three of us. She's out cold. Lois is completely harmless. There's no Devil in her. She is innocent and gentle. She is, however, the most likely of all the sisters on our ward to be harmed, by herself and by others. She cannot protect herself.

Estra, Ruthie and Lois have been together for some time, months at least, maybe years. The previous fourth "sister," the one that was here before I came, killed herself. It happened several days before my arrival. Rhonda, or Ronnie, they called her. When I arrived, I was assigned to the dead woman's bed.

I dread sleeping on dead Ronnie's bed. I lie in bed at night trying to remember everything about my family on Hawk Ridge, but it slides away from me. The earlier years are clearer. If only the Devil hadn't found me on Arvid's farm. Everything would be different now. Eventually I do fall into troubled sleep.

*T*he Devil visits me in my dreams. The Devil makes Himself comfortable, reclining on the wall above my bed, as if resting on an invisible bed. The dream is terrifying. The eyes of the Devil are gleaming, glowing, laughing at my horror.

A tunnel leads to the underground. It is the same way every dream begins. I feel like I am required to go there, but I don't want to go. I am afraid of it. I want to stay above ground where it is warm, where there was someone that once loved me. From there, the dream goes one of two ways.

In one of the ways, I am flying above the tunnel. My heart is filled with excitement, laughter. I'm alive in every possible way. All the bad things are left behind. I soar. I tremble with pleasure. When had that been my life? Think, think, think. Ah, yes, there it is. Not so long ago. Just there behind my eyes. It is magnificent.

It is our wedding night. I've fallen asleep in Arvid's arms after we were...intimate. It is the first time. He is gentle and I feel safe with him. I've found my home. Suddenly, we are awakened; I think it is around ten o'clock at night. There is an awful racket on the front porch and out in the yard. We hear pounding on the front door.

Shrill whistles and bells ringing...sleigh bells, cowbells, and who knows what all else. There are shouts and hoots and laughter and what sounds like wooden spoons banging on metal pots and pans.

I sit straight up in bed. "What in the world!" I whisper, trembling. "What's happening, Arvid? What's wrong?"

In the dark, Arvid kisses me on the tip of my nose and says with excitement in his voice. "It's a chivaree, Caroline." Arvid tosses off the covers. "Oh, my...I didn't think anyone would do that anymore. Not in this day and age. I mean, it's 1945, for goodness sake!"

I have no idea what a chivaree is. But it sounds frightening. "What's going to happen, Arvid?" I imagine being pulled from our bed and tortured.

He chuckles but looks into my eyes in the moonlight with tenderness. "It's nothing to be afraid of. A chivaree is a party, Caroline. Before the war, neighbors used to throw chivarees for newlyweds. The idea is to wait until they're sure that we're in bed and then to come over making lots of noise so that we have to go down in our nightclothes to make them stop. Then they demand food and drink, or they bring it with them. But to have a chivaree on a night such as this when it's so cold! I never imagined!" Arvid pulls on his pants and a wool pull-over.

"Come down with me, Caroline. Put on something warm over your nightgown and your shoes. Don't worry about how you look, just so you're warm." He takes my hand and pulls me from the warm bed. I quickly twist my hair into one long braid. "Come, we need to greet and welcome our guests into the house before they freeze to death out there."

We have no food or drink to offer but our guests provide enough for all of us. Hooting and loud, they come in through the kitchen door, rather than the front porch, where they've been making so much noise. They stomp the snow off their boots and then set them in the front room around the wood furnace to stay warm while they slip on their shoes. The floors are icy cold. Everyone carries in food and drink to share.

The Flagstads that live just east of us come in the door first, Rolf and Anna. Rolf, I learn, is an artist in woodworking and Anna is a schoolteacher. I admire them both. They are the only neighbors that do not farm their land but rent it out to Arvid.

The Hedlands, Ole and Orpha come too. Together with their sons, they own the largest farms on Hawk Ridge. The Hedlands' two grown sons, Paul and Peter are there with their wives. Both of them are pregnant! There's a little teasing about that, about Hawk Ridge being "known for its exceptional fertility."

The Hedlands bring packages of venison and blood sausage and smoked pork summer sausage along with a Norwegian cheese they call Primost (PREE-most) which I don't care for much. It's gritty and the color of caramel.

Three more couples come in. Trygve (TRIG-vee) and Olga Kjelle (CHEH-leh) come with Knut and Thorine Kapperud. They carry in a Norwegian wedding cake, a treat called kransekake (KRAHN-suh KAH-keh). It is a tower of increasingly smaller rings made of ground almonds, flour and butter and it's decorated with icing. I've never seen anything like it!

And lastly, the only elderly couple to come that evening, Nels and Mathilda Trønby, whom I later learn are Martin's parents. Nels carries in a huge pot of Norwegian fruit soup for his tiny wife. He sets it on the stovetop. Her eyes sparkle at me.

"What is fruit soup?" I ask Mathilda. "It's very dark, isn't it?" I am still astonished to find all these people milling around in my new home.

Mathilda, in her little sweet voice, fills me in over the din of women chatting away while finding room for all the foods on the counters and kitchen table. "Oh, it's cherries 'n raspberries, if you got 'em, 'n apples cooked with tapioca or barley, 'n den you have to have a little cinnamon in there, y' know 'n some nutmeg. Ya, it's something we have to remind us of warmer weather."

It's unusual but I can probably get used to it. And what a houseful of people!

In only minutes, there is food everywhere, it seems. There are jars of pickled herring, pans of bars made with chocolate, oatmeal, walnuts and coconut. There are delicate almond-flavored cookies shaped like wedding bells and pieces of lefse rolled up with butter and brown sugar inside. One of the women has made rosettes, sweet and light, crispy stars and circles that have been deep-fried and sprinkled with powdered sugar.

The last guest to walk in the door is Arvid's Best Man. He'd been introduced to me earlier of course, at the church. "This is Bernt Hauk, my best friend since country school." Arvid had looked so proud to introduce him to me that morning.

With Bernt comes the last bottle of whiskey brought by the men. There is so much laughter. The men good-naturedly challenge Bernt or Bear, they like to call him, to go outside to break off pieces of icicles that hang from the porch roof. "We should have a little ice for our whiskey, dontcha think, Bear?"

Bear grins in return. "You know, you coulda just left your bottles out in the snow for a few hours today. But, well, I s'pose since nobody thought to do that, I'll have to go out again." He pulls his boots back on and hangs his head in mock despair. "It's all of two degrees out there! If Arvid hadn't opened the door when he did, I was thinkin' of startin' a bonfire on the porch. To warm up my hands a little."

There are fits of laughter, guffaws, jeers and then Bear goes outside. He comes back in with a bucket full of broken icicles. He set the bucket back outside the door again to keep the ice frozen, as soon as all the men have taken a chunk of it for their glasses.

I learn that Hawk Ridge got its name from Bear's family name, Hauk, which means 'hawk' in Norwegian. He had to shout to explain it to me, in order to be heard over multiple conversations that jump-started at once.

"Some time back, when the Homesteading Act was passed, my grandfather was first in line to get his hundred and sixty acres on this ridge. So, people called it Hauk's Ridge. But before too long, bein' it was Minnesota, and not Norway, people got around to just callin' it Hawk Ridge, a hair faster 'n Hauk, I guess. If you listen for it though, you'll still hear an old guy now 'n then, call it Hauk's Ridge."

"Ya, old guys like me," Nels Trønby interjects with a chuckle and a nudge. Bear gives the slight white-haired man a nod and a grin.

"Nels, you're the youngest old guy I know."

"Mange tusen takk," (Many thousand thanks,) Nels replies with a grin.

Bear continues, "My grandfather didn't mind the name change to Hawk Ridge. He wasn't much for standin' out in a crowd anyway, so it was fine with him." Those that heard him say that laugh again.

I don't understand what the joke is. Arvid frowns in supposed sincerity. "Nope, I've never met a Hauk that was too showy," Arvid said. More laughter erupts from our side of the room.

"Are there more Hauks around?" I ask. There has to be more to this story.

Arvid explains to me. "O-oh ya! Seven of 'em. Nine, countin' the parents. Bear's eldest sister is Orpha Hedland over there. She's a close friend of my mother's." Orpha's ears perk up and she waves to me from across the room with a broad smile. "And there's another sister that lives in La Crosse. And then there's a brother that farms on the other side of Caledonia and another two brothers that farm together south of Spring Grove, just below the Iowa border." Arvid grins again.

"There's only one odd duck in the whole Hauk bunch, only one of 'em that actually likes to talk. That's Bear's brother that teaches Ag. and Shop at Spring Grove High School. Bear's parents live in town now, too." Town, I understand to mean, his hometown of Spring Grove. "But his father doesn't speak up if he can help it. Never has."

Much laughter again and someone raises a glass to toast Bear's father, Ivar. I'm told that Bear's parents raised their big family on the original Hauk farm where Bear now lives, so everyone knows him. Arvid raises his glass, "Skål (scol) to a man of few words, Ivar Hauk." Glasses clink during kindly chuckling.

Bernt (I've decided I like his given name, "Bernt" better than "Bear") takes ribbing so good-naturedly that I have the feeling that nobody could really be angry with him. Later, the men tease him about being the only remaining Norwegian bachelor farmer on Hawk Ridge but, again, he just laughs in turn.

"Well, there's gotta be one sensible man around here," he grins. When he raises his glass to toast bachelorhood, the men all raise theirs as well. "Skål," and the wives elbow their husbands, pretending annoyance. Bernt is so much fun to be around. It would be so wonderful if he finds a wife, someone that I can be friends with. The four of us would have such a good time together!

That chivaree is my real introduction to our neighbors. Foolishly, we all laugh and talk until one o'clock in the morning, before some reasonable woman, probably Orpha, looks at her husband and announces, "Ya, well I s'pose you still figure on gettin' up in de morning to milk those cows, den, dontcha?"

Everyone answers with a groan or an exaggerated sigh. The men go out to start the cars while the women gather up their pans and plates and whatnot. Without saying a word about it, each of them neatly wraps up the leftover food they've brought, of which there is a surprising amount, and it is all set aside for Arvid, Marit and I to have in the following days. Then, waiting for the cars to warm up, the men hurry back inside, blowing on their hands saying, "Uff, she's a cold one tonight."

Before taking their final leave of us, the men one by one warmly shake Arvid's hand and congratulate him on finding a good woman to marry. Bernt alters the message like this, "You're lucky you found a good woman willing to marry you, Arvid." He grins and gives Arvid a brief manly hug with a firm pat on his back. Arvid grins in return. Each of the women gives me a hug and whispers a few words of marital advice before walking out the door into the cold December night. When they've all gone, and we are alone once again, I decide that I've never belonged anywhere more than I do right here, in this farmhouse kitchen, warmed by our neighbors on Hawk Ridge.

When I awaken, it is to the sound of Lois seizing in her bed, her back bowed, straining like a rainbow over her bedclothes, sheets sliding beneath her feet, an occasional heel jamming into the iron railing at the foot of the bed and the knuckles of her hand scraping against the wall with each convulsion.

Estra stands over my bed, smiling at me, as she aimlessly toddles back and forth, from one foot to the other. *Go to the outhouse,* I want to tell her, but I don't.

There's the sound of Ruthie crooning to Dolly. "Ith Dolly hungry? Ith thee? Thall we go to breakfatht?"

The sounds from dozens of other women yawning, farting, stretching, hiccuping, moaning, bed springs squeaking, and feet shuffling are all around me. Occasionally a bed frame bangs against the wall, echoing through the long cavernous room.

Then Big Alva is there, telling us to get up and get dressed. I'm still a hostage in the nunnery.

It is many days later, when out of earshot from the nuns...or nurses, or whatever they are, Sally tells me, "My mama idn' gonna suffer much longer." She says it like it's a decision that belongs to her. With tears in her eyes, she says, "My mama gonna be a' peace a' last. When de Lord come 'n gathe'er up 'n His bosom an' 'e take her t' heaven, then she gonna have somethin' t' smile 'bout again."

She turns to go, as if she's said all that she wanted to say, but then pauses and slowly turns back to look me square in the eye. "Sometime Car'line, a person go on breathin' when they already dead 'nside. It be mo' 'n any person oughta be made t' bear. And I can' bear t' see my mama sufferin' no more."

"I understand," I nod my head solemnly. "There's a limit to how much a person can handle. Sometimes I think that being trapped here with these women is more than I can take. But how much more you must suffer, Sally, to see your mother so badly abused."

Sally's dark eyes go even darker and the set of her head is hard like a statue. "I never know before how much hurtin' one person c'n take. This idn' no way for a body t' live." I wonder for a moment if she's talking about herself or her mama, but that is all the time we have to talk.

8

STUNNED

Arvid's predictions about friends and neighbors finding out about Caroline's hospitalization were painfully accurate. The news of his wife's commitment at the State Hospital swept through Hawk Ridge and beyond like wildfire. It ripped through his hometown of Spring Grove before jumping to Decorah, Iowa, the other Norwegian-American community nearby.

By the time the news reached La Crosse, Wisconsin and Winona, Minnesota, all of Houston County was privy to the terrible news. Arvid Fjeld's beautiful young wife, Caroline, mother of two small children, had been taken to Rochester State Hospital under emergency commitment.

While in town, waiting for his corn and oats to be ground into feed, Trygve Kjelle caught sight of an out-of-towner...a guy that looked familiar and so he took him aside, "I s'pose maybe you heard already? About de terrible thing dat happened over on Hawk Ridge? My neighbor, Arvid Fjeld's wife was taken away to Rochester State Hospital." Trygve whispered while his voice trembled, "They say she got it in her head dat their second child, de new baby was de Devil himself! Herregud!" (Good God) He shook his head sadly.

Illustration 5: Spring Grove water tower and feed mill.

That man that Trygve took aside happened to be someone Arvid knew from a Farm Bureau committee they'd served on together. He ran into Arvid in town, later that same day.

"Is it true?" the man asked him gently.

"Yes, it's all true." Arvid sighed. He was relieved to have someone ask him straight out about Caroline rather than all the hushed talk that circled him without including him.

When the pastor at Black Hammer added Caroline's name to the list of hospitalized congregants and requested prayers on her behalf, Arvid listened for telltale gasps of surprise in the sanctuary. There weren't any. Clearly, everybody already knew.

After church, Bear came to him, as did a few other men, and in silence, each grasped his hand and held it firm and long. Some of the older women offered hugs to Marit.

Mathilda Trønby, Martin's frail and sweet mother didn't like to hear gossip about a family that was so good to her son. At Sewing Circle, when the talk swung toward Caroline's situation, which it quickly did, she redirected the conversation.

"Ya, you're too young to remember dat old guy dat used to live over west of us." Mathilda laid her sewing down. Her needle and thread remained aloft for emphasis as she spoke. "Back in de Thirties, it was, he started callin' people by de names of his dead folks, and family. He called me "Sarah," his dead wife's name. Whoa boy, *dat* felt pretty funny, let me tell you! He wasn't Norwegian, but he was a pretty nice guy anyway."

Marit was no longer attending Sewing Circle because she had Sophie and Leah to look after, but she heard the story word for word, from Orpha who was in Mathilda's Sewing Circle. That night, after the girls were asleep, she told Arvid about Mathilda shifting the focus of talk from Caroline to other people that had been taken to Rochester State Hospital.

Doc Knut, the veterinarian out of Spring Grove, drove by the Fjeld farm on a vet call now and then, and he waved if Arvid was working near the road. When he heard a conversation heading toward what Arvid's wife might have done or said that got her sent away to Rochester, he interrupted. "When I was a kid, there was this old guy that took off all his clothes down by the Mississippi, right there in downtown Winona." He shook his head. "He was talking politics to the birds."

"Were de birds more honest dan de politicians at dat time?" A few guys chuckled. Arvid heard that story, also, by way of his mother who talked with Knut's wife after church services.

Orpha Hedland's youngest daughter-in-law, only twenty-two, told about a distant relative she'd heard about. "She was an old maid living in Austin. She started wandering the town in winter without a coat and boots. Lost some fingers and toes to frostbite before she was sent to Rochester. She died there...she was pretty old, by then, though. I mean, I just can't believe this happened to Caroline, someone so young!"

Her words made their way back to Marit, too, by way of Orpha, and then that evening, to Arvid.

"Yust about everybody knows a story about someone dat went to Rochester. They talk about dem cause people are so sorry dis happened, Arvid."

"I notice that none o' the stories ever have the person leaving the hospital again." He paused. "And Caroline is always the youngest one, isn't she?"

"I think they hope dat will make her situation different. Better maybe, huh? Maybe it will."

Arvid gritted his teeth. "The doctors sure haven't said anything like that to me, Mom."

"No? Maybe not den. But I will keep on praying every night for her to come home again. We yust have to leave it in God's hands. Dat's de best thing we can do."

"Ya, Mom. That's about *all* I got, too." Arvid's voice was laced with sarcasm and louder than he intended. He saw the way his mother flinched at his words. He wasn't raised to speak rudely to his mother and had never made a practice of it. His mother, the kindest, most gentle woman he could imagine, would sacrifice anything for him. And now she was probably worried that he was losing his faith, likely the worst thing she could imagine.

"I'm sorry. I didn't mean to sound like that."

"No, I know. It's yust so hard when you're hurting so much."

"Ya." Arvid's voice broke. He looked down at his empty hands. "I don't wanna say anything to hurt you, Mom. I don't. Your faith is important and I'm glad for you." He swallowed hard. "But I just wanna say one thing and then I'll never say it to you again." He locked his eyes with his mother's. Tried not to look as harsh, as brittle as he felt.

"No, I want you to say whatever you need to say, Arvid. I'm de only one here for you to talk to." Marit braced herself against the kitchen counter.

Arvid stared at his mother for another long moment thinking that once things are said, they can't be unsaid.

Then the words steamrolled out of his mouth. "I am So... Damn...Mad...at God! Why did He let this happen? Why Caroline? Why did it have to be *our* family? Again? *My* wife? Hasn't our family had enough grief yet? Hasn't our family lost enough good people? Erik? And Dad? Why couldn't He just let us be happy parents of two healthy daughters?"

He swiped a tear in anger from his cheek. "What's wrong with that, huh? What did I do that was so damn bad...that my wife has to pay? Cause I know damn well, that *she* doesn't deserve this. Why God?" The tears spilled over then. "God dammit!"

A s is common practice in times of illness or sorrow, a few of the farm women on Hawk Ridge dropped by with food for the Fjelds. Naturally, Orpha Hedland was one of the first, seeing as she and Marit had been good friends since they were children in country school together. On top of that, her youngest brother, Bear, was Arvid's best friend.

Arvid nearly knocked the hotdish out of her hands when he pushed the screen door open after breakfast. He hadn't heard her car roll up. Orpha was just about to rap on the door. "Oh, hello dere, Arvid," she said. "Everybody knows dat your mother is de best cook around, but we yust want to let you know dat we are thinkin' of you over here."

"Thank you Orpha. That's very kind of you." Arvid gave her an awkward sideways hug, to avoid bumping that hotdish again.

Rather than follow her back inside, Arvid excused himself to tend to something in the barn. He wanted Orpha to have time alone with his mother anyway. Orpha would want to hold the new baby, play with Sophie for a bit and then, before she left, she and his mother would probably hug and cry together. He didn't want to be there for that. Before the door went shut, he heard Orpha ask his mother, "Hvordan har du det?" (How are you?)

After a few visitors came bearing gifts of food, Arvid was annoyed. "It's not like we can't feed ourselves," Arvid complained to his mother. "No one has died."

"Oh, Arvid, you know...they yust don't know what to say, so they bring a little something to let us know dat they are sorry for what you are going through. They don't know what else to do."

One visitor that was quite a surprise to both Marit and Arvid was Inga, the teen-aged mother of one-year old Matthias. She lived with her parents and worked alongside her father. "She must be yust about sixteen or so, now," Marit guessed after she'd gone.

"Ya, I guess. Cute little bugger, that Matthias, isn't he? I'm surprised she came by, though. Caroline told me she gave her the cold shoulder after church one day, back when Inga was pregnant. 'Inga is too forward, too personal.' That's what Caroline said about her after we got home that day. I figured Inga would steer clear o' her...of our family, after that."

"Well, she *is* forward. Dat's for sure. And she's full of de dickens, isn't she? A spunky girl. And a caring little mother to dat baby. I was surprised dat she said she would help you if you ever need it."

"I was too, but she's actually doing all o' that farm work now, with her father, at the same time as she's taking care o' Matt. She caught me outside again, just before she rode off. She came on horseback; did you know that, Mom?"

"Ya, I saw de horse standing out there." Marit allowed herself a smirk. "I knew it anyhow cause of de way she had de baby strapped on her chest. "It is so sad dat her mother won't help out with dat grandson yust a little bit anyway. What a shame! Her mother is willing enough to help with de other grandson of theirs...Rolf and Anna's boy, Yon (Jon)." Marit paused. "So, did you tell her anything diff'rent when you talked outside?"

"Oh, well, I said that I'm gettin' along alright and that I call on Martin when I need another pair of hands." Arvid gave his mother a sheepish grin. "I did suggest that she might wanna stop over at Bear's place...see if he could use her help. Seeing as he's all alone over there. And she lives so close by, when she cuts up through the woods anyhow like she does. It'd be handy for both of 'em."

"Uff da, nei." Marit found an unexpected grin on her lips. "Do you think Bear would care to hire dat young girl? When she comes with a baby, too?"

Marit put her hand over her mouth and chuckled a little. Bernt and Arvid had been playing little harmless pranks on one another since junior high.

Arvid knew what she was thinking. "It's not a prank, Mom. Inga is anxious to get away from workin' 'longside her dad. I can only imagine what he's like to work for. And Bear really could use somebody that knows somethin' about farmin'. Some of those teenage boys from town that he hires? They might be strong enough, but...they're not good at seein' what needs to be done. He's gotta tell 'em everything."

"Ya, dat is true." Marit cocked her head, tentatively nodding. "You got something there, alright."

Arvid nodded his head. Before he went back outside to work, he gave his Mom a peck on the cheek. It was the first time either of them had found cause to smile since Caroline was taken away.

September 22, 1948

A rvid was driving past Bear's farm on his way into town the following week when he noticed a horse grazing with Bear's heifers, far out in the pasture. It didn't look like either of Bear's dapple grays. Although he was in a bit of a hurry to get his errands done and get back home, (his mother was to serve at Ladies' Aide today) he decided he could spare just a few minutes to let Bear know about the stray horse in his pasture.

He pulled into Bear's driveway and looked toward the open barn door, expecting to find Bear still milking at that hour. As he started toward the barn, however, he was surprised to hear voices behind him, coming from the house. Bear's voice called, "Arvid...whatcha doin' out and about so early?"

Coming out of the house behind Bear was Inga with the baby, Matt, strapped to her chest. "I got us some coffee inside, if you want some," Inga called out, a proprietary note in her voice.

Arvid's tongue was somehow stuck to the inside of his mouth. His eyes opened wide. "Oh, good morning. I...ah...no. I'm...I'm good. Thank you though. I thought you'd still be in the barn," he finally managed to say.

Bear grinned. "Well, milkin' goes a little faster now with two pair of hands." Neither man said anything further for a moment. Arvid made himself nod. He shifted from one foot to the other. Trying to look natural.

Bear plucked a toothpick from between his smiling lips. "Can I help you with somethin', Arvid?"

Arvid sifted through his mind for any sort of reason that he might have stopped, anything other than to tell him that the horse he'd seen in his pasture was obviously Inga's. He felt like a dolt. "Ya, I wonder if I might borrow that big come-along of yours. It's a lot o' trouble to harness up one o' the horses just to move a concrete trough a few feet." Arvid hoped that Bear wouldn't remember that he already had a smaller come-along of his own that in all likelihood, would do that job just fine.

"Oh, sure. I'll run get it for you. It's right here in the shed." Bear took off for the shed with a spring in his step that Arvid hadn't noticed before.

His absence left Arvid standing alone with Inga, and baby Matt. Arvid wished he'd thought of a better excuse for stopping. An excuse that wouldn't have left him standing alone with a teenaged mother and baby.

Arvid stuck his hands in his pockets, wishing he was in his pickup and gone. The fact that Bear had not bothered to tell him that Inga was working for him, probably meant that he'd been waiting for Arvid to discover it by himself. Why? Why didn't he tell me he hired her? Then he chewed a corner of his lip. Well, but why didn't I tell him I was sending her over? Hmmm.

"How's Matt doin'?" Arvid finally asked.

"Oh, good. I think he likes his new bed over here. It's a little nicer 'n the one he was sleepin' on at my folks' place. Course, it's not a crib, but that don't matter. I sleep between him and the floor, so no trouble there."

Arvid tried to keep his eyebrows where they belonged. "Well, that's good, then."

"Here y' go, Arvid. One come-along. I don't have any use for it right now so don't worry about gettin' it back to me right away. I suppose it's a little bigger 'n that one o' yours, huh?"

"Ya. It is," Arvid looked down, hoping that a faint blush wasn't noticeable on his sun-browned face. He took a step toward his pickup truck. "Okay, thanks, Bear. Well, I better get goin' then. Thanks again." Arvid bounded up into his pickup and shut the door.

He backed up the pick-up and turned around. In his rear-view mirror, Bear and Inga were sharing a laugh. "Probably at the surprised look on my face." he voiced aloud to the vacant seat next to him. He shook his head and laughed at himself. "I think I did somethin' good."

Illustration 6: Arvid's pickup

9

SICK STOMACH

September 1948

The meeting scheduled two weeks after Caroline's admission to Rochester State Hospital was to allow the doctors time to observe her. Dr. Reynolds, the head or chief psychiatrist (Arvid wasn't even sure of his title) would oversee Caroline's care and Dr. Coughlin, a much younger doctor would see and talk to Caroline frequently. This was to be the first of many conferences.

The use of the word "observe" had been bothering Arvid for days. "He wants to observe her for a while. That's what Dr. Reynolds said." Arvid blurted it out the moment he came storming through the kitchen screen door. He was livid, trying not to shout.

"He didn't say that he wants to get to *know* her. Or to see how she settles in. No, he wants to *observe* her, like she's a bug under a microscope or a cow gettin' ready to calve." He was wearing a path across the kitchen floor while his mother stirred the pot on the stove.

"Oh, Arvid." Marit turned away from the stove, wiping her hands on her apron and watched her son pace.

Arvid had finally worked himself up into a lather over the past few days, so much so, that he finally was compelled to tell someone what he thought of Dr. Reynolds. His mother was the closest someone available.

"He said that Caroline would not be coming to the meeting unless she would happen to make a drastic turn-around and he *certainly*," exaggerating that last word in particular, "wasn't holding out any hope o' that, so we should just plan on meeting without her." He grunted. "That's what he said to me! And then he smiled, like this was something unimportant." Arvid exhaled in disgust.

"A family conference, they said. Ya, right." His words dripped with sarcasm. "What kind of *family* conference is that?" He'd managed to work himself up to an even higher pitch. "They're not even tellin' her there's a meeting and they told me I shouldn't tell her either."

Marit sat down at the kitchen table and Arvid saw that she was inviting him to join her by pulling out his chair for him. The chicken soup was already simmering on the stove. Dumplings would be made just before it was time to eat. "I'm so sorry dat you have all dis on your plate. Uff." Arvid saw the lines of worry drawn on her face.

"Dr. Reynolds said that we'll invite her to join us after she begins to show progress in the hospital...when she is able to participate *constructively*. Hah." Arvid spat out the word "constructively" like it tasted bad. Arvid put his elbows on the table and folded his hands for a place to rest his forehead, his head suddenly heavy.

"You don't want me to go along with you, do you, Arvid? I would, of course. I'm sure dat Orpha would take de girls for me. She's been so good to offer." She paused, when she saw that he hadn't moved a lick. "But I don't s'pose dat would really help anything, would it? I yust wish there was something I could do to help you."

Arvid lifted his head to see his mother's compassionate face. "Mom," he said tiredly, "you help every day, all day." He sighed. "No, thank you for offering, but it's better if I go alone. I'm going to meet with Caroline afterward for a while, my first visit and..." another deep sigh, "it might be hard for her to take seein' me there. And too... there might be things that come up that...that maybe I'd rather you don't hear."

"Oh ya, I understand dat. You got to have a little bit of privacy anyhow."

"Thank you, Mom. I just needed to say all this out loud. I've been thinkin' about this for days. It was makin' my head want to explode." He followed up with another deep sigh before getting up. Leah stirred in the white bassinet. "Oh, now I've woken the baby with my ranting." But he wasn't sorry he did.

Arvid picked Leah up and held her close. The baby sneezed. Arvid laughed a little, low in his throat. "She must be sneezing cuz of the chaff that I carried in on my clothes with me," he said over his shoulder, so his mother could hear. He carried the baby to the window to look out over the pastoral scene below.

"Let's see what we have here, shall we?" he murmured to Leah. "Let's see if we can see any animals down there in the barnyard."

The red barn, built by his grandfather, sat tidily on the hillside below the house, and beyond that his own wooded hillside fell out of sight. Opposite his farm, the familiar opposing wooded bluff, the one he'd looked at every day of his life, rose up so soon and so sharply that a stranger would never have guessed that a thin ribbon of road lay hidden in that narrow valley. The top of the bluff, however, was no longer forested. It had been grubbed clean for farmland years ago, and this year it happened to be a hayfield.

On that horizon, Arvid could make out the silhouettes of three men working there, with a tractor, a baling machine and hay wagon. At that distance, he could only guess at which shape belonged to the elder Hedland and which were his sons. The three men were all lean and moved easily. They made working together look like child's play.

Arvid was seized with an unfamiliar sense of dread. It was the vivid contrast of those three men on the distant hilltop, working together, while here he was, alone, working his farm. Now, more alone than ever, without his wife. The farm was like a millstone around his neck. He'd never before had that feeling of weight threatening to crush him. The mere fact of that was frightening.

He was certainly not going to say anything about that to his mother. She'd be even more distressed than she already was and there wasn't a damn thing she could do about it.

Instead he nuzzled his nose against Leah's soft cheek. "Oh, what will you be when you grow up, hmm, my little one? Will you be a farmer? Will you be a teacher? Or a nurse? I'm sure you would be a much better nurse than that one at the Caledonia hospital."

Arvid gave his shoulders a pretend shiver of fright and made a noise with his lips like a pony's nicker, a humorous sound for Leah's benefit. He knew his mother could hear him talking to Leah and he wanted her to see that he was managing alright. He was just a dad talking to his baby daughter.

Arvid was told to arrive in Rochester before noon. "Be sure to have a bite to eat first and then go to Dr. Reynolds' office in Administration. We'll start the meeting at twelve-thirty," the Head Nurse had told him.

He could not ferret out the reasoning behind the nurse's specific request to eat before the meeting. "Of course, it'll be dinnertime by then, but why do they care so much whether I eat before the meeting?" He posed the question to his mother as he finished combing his hair in front of the bathroom mirror.

Marit handed him a paper bag with his noon meal packed inside. Smørbrød, two thick slices of her Houston County purple ribbon bread slathered in butter, and each covered with a slice of salty dried beef. A small container wrapped tightly in layers of newspaper held left-over green Jell-O salad with shredded carrots. For Arvid's dessert, Marit had cut him a large oatmeal chocolate-chip and walnut bar that she wrapped in cellophane. Lastly, was a thermos of orange Kool-Aid, the same thermos Marit used when she brought a little-lunch out to the field in the mid-afternoon to tide him over until suppertime.

"Ya, I'd have sent dinner along with you anyway. Well, I s'pose you'll find dat out after you get there, den."

"I guess." Arvid left the house with a shrug and a sigh, shaking his head.

Arvid was excited about the prospect of seeing Caroline and so, upon his arrival he immediately talked to the Head Nurse to ask her to show him to Caroline's building and to her ward right after their family conference. He told her he hoped to have two hours to spend with his wife before he had to begin the drive back to the farm for milking.

Doctors Reynolds and Coughlin, the Head Nurse, Alva and Arvid reintroduced themselves to each other. It was cordial, unhurried. Arvid vaguely remembered meeting them the day he brought Caroline to the State Hospital. Dr. Reynolds waved his hand for him to be seated, and asked, "Would you care for a cup of coffee, Mr. Fjeld? It's no trouble."

"Oh, no thank you. I don't drink coffee in the afternoon."

"Alright then. I believe I'll have a cup, if you don't mind." Reynolds paused for a beat. "Alva?"

"Oh yes, of course." The way Alva jumped up reminded Arvid of a calf getting bitten by a horse fly. "I'll be right back." She looked back. "Dr. Coughlin?" And she waited for his answer which was given with a shake of his head.

Arvid thought it seemed a bit contrived, rehearsed. How many of these family conferences have the three of them done together, he wondered, with other sad husbands or wives, mothers or fathers?

"How was the drive in to Rochester this morning?" Dr. Reynolds inquired with a smile. "I hope it was uneventful."

"Oh, yes, it was fine," Arvid answered.

"It must be, what...three hours or so from Spring Grove to Rochester?"

"Oh, it's more like two and a bit. Some roads aren't so good. Have you ever been down that way?" Arvid was aware that they were marking time until the Head Nurse returned with the coffee.

"No, no I haven't, I'm afraid. It's very pretty, I hear," he said with a polite smile.

"I'd say so, yes." Arvid offered. "My fields are on top of the bluffs, surrounded by forest."

When the large-framed nurse was seated again, Dr. Reynolds began. "Alva, would you begin by telling us how Caroline is doing on the ward and with her sisters?"

Arvid interrupted without thinking, puzzled. "Sisters? I admit that I don't know much about my wife's early years, but I do know that she doesn't have any sisters, or brothers either. She's told me that much." He offered a lop-sided smile so as not to offend the good doctor and to indicate his puzzlement, even before they'd begun.

"Oh, no, Mr. Fjeld." The Head Nurse had a gravelly voice to go with a smile that hid her teeth. "We encourage the women on the ward to develop relationships with those that are physically closest to them, the ones that they have meals with. We refer to them as "sisters" to one another. To promote a feeling of belonging." She seemed pleased with her explanation to Arvid.

Arvid was less pleased. The idea seemed artificial and maybe provocative when he knew that Caroline hadn't trusted anybody to be truthful two weeks ago, when she was brought here. It was hard to imagine she'd been tricked into believing she belonged here.

"I see," he said, raising his left eyebrow. "How does Caroline react to that? I ask because she didn't seem to want others to tell her what was truth and what was fiction when we brought her here. She became very upset when the doctor at home told her that her thinking was...off." He looked at his hands in his lap, ashamed to have to say such a thing about his wife.

"That is the way we've structured things for some time now on the ward, and it seems to have been helpful for many of the women." Alva adjusted the skirt of her white dress beneath her ample thighs, cleared her throat and launched into her report on her observations of Caroline.

"Caroline avoids conversation with her sisters. Of course, one of them speaks Ojibwe and so she wouldn't be able to talk with that one anyhow, but she has shown about the same lack of interest in talking with the other two. Regardless, one of them has taken a shine to Caroline and she attempts to engage her many times throughout the day. That is her sister, Estra.

"Caroline's caloric intake has been poor. She eats approximately forty percent of her food at any meal. Some potato and vegetables, maybe, sometimes her bread, but only rarely does she touch her protein. Had this been her pattern at home, Mr. Fjeld?"

"I'd say that she was eating well up until she delivered the baby. But the nurse in the hospital in Caledonia said, too, that she wasn't eating much. She can't afford to get much thinner, can she?" Arvid turned a worried face to the two doctors to answer his question.

"Nutritionally, she eats enough to get by, Mr. Fjeld. We will not allow her to starve herself, but I doubt it'll come to that," Dr. Reynolds offered.

Arvid wanted to ask another question about that but Alva, or Elva pressed on with her report.

"She is timid and skittish. She avoids eye contact with her sisters. We've seen no signs of aggression toward the other women or nurses. We watch for that, of course. There is always an attendant of some kind in the same room with any of the women. Even throughout the night, all of the women are observed for any unexpected behaviors.

"To date, she has not shown any interest in the Crafts Room, but she does seem to look with something like interest at the sewing machines when we go to the Sewing Building. Does she know how to sew, Mr. Fjeld?"

"Yes, she's quite a good seamstress. Do you think she'll sew again?" Arvid was struck with a new question he was afraid to ask. *Would this thing that was happening to Caroline change everything about her...even change what she likes to do? Make her a whole different kind of person?*

"Well, let's not get ahead of ourselves," the nurse responded with another thin-lipped smile. "She'll have plenty of opportunities to do things like sew and other crafts. She'll let us know what she wants to do, hopefully. Until then we'll expose her to different activities."

After Alva's contribution, it was apparently Dr. Reynolds' turn to carry the show forward. He was a fit, late middle-aged man, with silver hair and receding hairline. His face was the kind that would be right for the movies with a silvery mustache that reached his chin. Arvid thought it was past time for the doctor to get a haircut. Probably no one had mentioned this to him. He must not be married, Arvid concluded. Caroline had been good at reminding him when his own hair was getting too scruffy around the neck and ears.

"I wonder if you might be able to fill us in on your wife's upbringing, Mr. Fjeld," Dr. Reynolds began. "Her childhood. Since she's not been given to converse much, we've learned very little about her pre-morbid condition. Perhaps in time, with Estra–the sister that seems to be quite fond of her–perhaps we'll eventually learn more from Caroline's own lips. But until then, might we have you fill in some of the blank spaces?" Dr. Reynolds' mustache widened a little suggesting a smile. Arvid could see that the doctor was trying to make him feel more at ease.

"Well," Arvid cleared his throat, "I'm afraid I don't know a lot, actually. My wife has never wanted to talk about her childhood. She lived in that big orphanage over in Owatonna from the age of eleven, after her mother died. And then she moved to a boarding house the year before we married." Arvid warded off the question he knew was coming next. "And no, I don't know *how* her mother died."

"I wonder if you know anything about how it happened that she wasn't adopted." Dr. Reynolds asked gently. "It would seem to me that there would have been families that would have been happy to raise such an attractive girl as their own."

"Well, you have to understand. Caroline was terrified of being adopted. She went out of her way, I think, to be...mmm...unpleasant, you might say? When potential adoptive families came, she...she refused to talk to them, or she'd act clumsy around them. Things like that. Nothing truly terrible, but just enough to put people off."

Arvid continued. "She told me that she always thought it was safer to stay where she was. At least she already knew what the caretakers at the orphanage were like. But she couldn't know what a new adoptive family was really like until it was too late. But she didn't behave like that at school at all. She liked school a lot. She got really good grades. Caroline is a very smart woman." Arvid made eye contact proudly with each of the three listeners with a hint of a smile. "She's read a lot more books in her twenty-two years than I have in my thirty-three. She was just afraid to be adopted. There was one caretaker at the orphanage that she liked especially, and she was pretty sure that the caretaker liked her, too. She trusted her."

"That's important information. Thank you. Anything you can offer may be helpful. Any specific traumatic events in childhood? Losses? Abuse? Her father and her mother? Is she from Owatonna originally? I know that there was a time when orphans from some distance away were sent to the Owatonna orphanage."

Arvid took a deep breath and blew it out again. "I do know that she loved her mother very much. She looks just like her, too." Arvid glanced down and smiled to remember the portrait.

"Oh?"

"Ya, um, she has a formal portrait, from a studio, that was taken of her with her mother when Caroline was about seven, or that's what she thinks she was at the time. The portrait is precious to her. The only one she has. In the picture, she and her mother are dressed very elegantly, wearing fancy winter coats with fur collars and hats and gloves. Caroline has a muff and hat made of white rabbit fur. Her mother looks to be very young. I guess they must have had money back then, even in the middle of the Depression."

Arvid squinted his eyes thoughtfully. "She's never said anything about her father to me. I always figured we had plenty of time to talk about these things when she was ready. And I thought that, well, if there were things that she *never* wanted to talk about, that I would respect her wishes about that, too."

"I understand. I think we can safely assume that Caroline's childhood had significant unhappiness. Do you happen to know her mother's name? And her surname?"

"Yes, her mother's name was Vanessa. The last name was D' Bouvier." He pronounced it out slowly, exaggerating each syllable.

"Is that a maiden name or a married name?" Dr. Reynolds reached for a fountain pen and a notepad.

"I'm sorry, I don't even know if her parents were married. But I did see her birth certificate once, kind of by accident. I don't think she intended to show me."

"Oh, why do you say that?"

"Well, you see, we were getting dressed for church one Sunday morning, and I caught a glimpse of a very small box in her top dresser drawer. I'd never noticed it before, so I commented on the delicate engraving. She said that's where she kept the picture of her with her mother. "She said it was the only thing she kept private from all the grownups that suddenly became involved in her life after she was orphaned. She told me, 'When you're an orphan, people think they have the right to look through all your things.'

"She opened the box to show me. Beneath the picture was an old, official-looking paper, all folded up. 'My birth certificate,' she said. She seemed a little, I don't know, a little embarrassed about it. After I looked at it, it was time for us to get on the road to church."

Arvid thought then for a moment. "Excuse me, but I don't understand how this information could be of any help."

"Well, it may not be, but then again, it might. What did the birth certificate say?" Arvid thought the doctor seemed intrigued by this topic, though he had no idea why.

"Oh...yes. Well, after 'father's name,' it read something like 'Alistair Charlton'...something...Wester-something, and then the Roman numeral, III." He paused. "I remember that only because it struck me as unusual. Imagine giving a baby boy a big handle like that! I read the name out loud and I chuckled, and that's when Caroline tucked it away again. I wish I hadn't done that."

"Well, it is indeed quite a title for a little one, isn't it?" Dr. Reynolds nodded and agreed thoughtfully. "Do you remember any more?"

"Well, Caroline's name was written 'Caroline Celeste...Wester...something.' I can't quite remember." Arvid squinted, trying to "see" the correct name in the air, somewhere up and to his left.

"So, Caroline's last name, then, was Wester–something."

"Oh. Well, she said that she never *used* that name, not in her memory anyway. She went by her mother's maiden name, D'

Bouvier. That's her name on our marriage license." Almost as an afterthought, Arvid added, "When we were dating, I heard her called "Bovary," too, but she said that was like a nickname from childhood or something."

"I have one other question for you, though, about that portrait, if you don't mind."

Arvid shook his head slightly, "No, go ahead."

"Do you happen to remember the name of the portrait studio imprinted on the folder? Usually in the lower right cor–"

"I do, yes." Arvid brightened to hear a question for which he had a definite answer. "It was a French name, too. It was 'Doucette.' Why? Is that important for some reason?" Arvid cocked his head, questioning the doctor.

"I had a thought that it might tell us where Caroline was living with her mother. A portrait studio owned by a man or a family in one city, would most likely have a different name from a studio that was located in any other city. Maybe she didn't live in Owatonna as a child."

"I don't know why I never thought about that. Caroline doesn't talk like we do in Spring Grove, but of course, I figured, Owatonna is a much bigger town than Spring Grove, and that was enough to explain that. Fewer old Norwegians over there in Owatonna, maybe, you know?" Arvid offered a shy smile and flushed. He was acutely aware of how naive he must look to these two well-educated men. An unfamiliar feeling, to be embarrassed about being a small-time farmer of Norwegian ancestry.

"But again, is that important to know, in order to help Caroline?" Arvid couldn't work out what relevance there could be in this.

"Here is the thing, Mr. Fjeld. People can inherit mental illnesses from their parents. If we knew, for example, that one of Caroline's parents was mentally ill, then that would tell us a great deal. Do you see?"

"So, if one of her parents was like...like Caroline is now, then that could help you know how to help her get better?" Arvid felt a glimmer of hope at this thought.

"Well, let's not get ahead of ourselves." Dr. Reynolds cleared his throat. Arvid recognized that same trite phrase that the nurse had used. He concentrated on not rolling his eyes. "It would tell us that your wife should not have any more children," Dr. Reynolds said with quiet authority. "It would be cruel, and unnecessary to pass mental illness on to children...on to another generation."

Arvid's jaw dropped, "We have two daughters already, Doctor. Two beautiful little girls. Are you telling me that they will have this same thing happen to them when they get older?" Arvid's imagination produced an image of him as an old man visiting both of his daughters there, at the Rochester State Hospital. He felt nauseous.

"I cannot say that with certainty, of course, that they will have the very same mental illness, but it is possible." The doctor captured Arvid's gaze before continuing. "We do not perform sterilizations here, but an excision of her ovaries may be indicated, if, or maybe I should say, when, she goes home to you again, Mr. Fjeld. Defective genes pass from one generation to the next. That we know."

Arvid turned to stone. Unable to speak immediately. "I...I don't know what to say. I just can't believe that this is what my daughters have to look forward to." He felt himself go white. The other three people in the room waited for him to find his voice. "Am I ever going to get my wife home again? Please tell me the truth." Arvid's voice cracked with this question.

"It is true that many of our patients remain here with us for many years. Some, yes, will live out their lives here. There are those who will never be safe to re-enter society. Either because they are a danger to others or to themselves. Some of our patients have attempted suicide more than once. It is our duty to keep them safe, Mr. Fjeld. We can only do that by keeping them here, under close watch where they are protected from themselves."

"As for Caroline specifically, she is early in her illness, it would seem, although I do question the behavior that she exhibited in the orphanage. That might suggest something that was brewing earlier than the second pregnancy and birth of your daughter."

"And what *is* this illness? I have never been told what this *is*." Arvid's tongue was like parchment.

"Schizophrenia, Mr. Fjeld. Caroline hears things that are not there...sees things that are not there. Those are markers of psychosis. The particular type that your wife has is what we would characterize as a *paranoid* schizophrenia. Paranoia, meaning...fear. It is a very challenging illness in that the patient's fear of something, of someone or of some imagined being can spawn a drive to aggression. The aggression is to protect themselves from that perceived threat, but even so...it makes the patient potentially dangerous, as you saw that day before you brought Caroline to us."

Arvid's stomach was twisting in knots. He'd recognized that Leah had been frighteningly vulnerable alone with her mother. He'd even admitted that he himself, had been afraid of her when Caroline wielded the carving knife that day. But to hear the doctor, in a very matter of fact way, describe Caroline as having "a drive to aggression" and as "potentially dangerous" suddenly made his wife a stranger.

Abruptly, and off-topic, Head Nurse Alva interjected a question about Caroline's nightmares. "She sometimes wakes up her sisters with them. Do you have any idea what her nightmares might be about, Mr. Fjeld?"

"No, I have no idea." Arvid looked back to the nurse as if seeing her for the first time. "She didn't have them at home. After she had the baby, while in the hospital at Caledonia, they said that she was sleeping very little. She barely slept the night before we brought her here, as well."

Arvid looked up at the two empathetic doctors. And the Head Nurse. He pleaded. "I want you to know that Caroline has been a loving wife and a good mother to Sophie, right up until the day that she had to be hospitalized here." Dr. Reynolds and Alva raised their eyebrows at that.

"Well, alright then, I mean, up until the day she went to the hospital to deliver the baby, at least." Arvid paused and was allowed to hold the floor. "I probably missed signs that she wasn't quite herself after the baby was born. I was just so happy about our daughter's birth. I never imagined there was anything really wrong... I'm sorry," he told them, though as he said it, knew it wasn't for them that the apology was meant.

Arvid thought back to Caroline's prolonged quiet in the Caledonia hospital. "She hardly spoke after the baby was born. I thought she was tired. She was quite silent on the ride home from the hospital, too. She seemed so terribly afraid of thunder and lightning that day. Obviously, I wasn't paying attention the way I should have."

He tossed everything out then, in a frightened rush. "She didn't want to hold Leah. She didn't breast-feed her. But of course, I thought she was holding the baby when I wasn't there. Wasn't she? And I was so eager to hold the baby myself that I never questioned it." He wanted to chastise himself unmercifully. He breathed hard as if he'd been running.

Dr. Coughlin finally spoke, softly. He leaned forward in his chair. "Arvid, how could you have had any idea what was happening to her? Listen...I know that you want to help your wife and it doesn't help her to kick yourself now about clues that might have been missed leading up to this. You cannot, *could* not reasonably expect that of yourself."

Dr. Coughlin waited while Arvid's breathing returned to a more normal rate. "I can see that you love your wife, and your daughters very much. That is what only you can give her. Let us be the mental health professionals, alright? And you be the husband."

Arvid looked into his eyes and gave Dr. Coughlin a faint nod of his head, swallowing the lump in his throat.

Dr. Coughlin continued, but gently, "I see Caroline every day for at least a little while. When Caroline talks, it is almost exclusively about whether the devil is in the nunnery and how he'd tried to trick her, by appearing in the form of the small baby. 'Don't look at the eyes', she mutters to herself. She talks about the devil wanting her eyes because they've seen too much."

"My wife thinks she's in a nunnery?" Arvid asked, surprised once again, after he had decided that nothing more could surprise him.

"Yes, your wife was raised in the Catholic tradition, correct?" Dr. Coughlin asked, to confirm his assumption.

"No, I mean, I don't think so. She never said anything about that. I would think that she would surely have told me that before we were married." But as he thought more about it, it occurred to him that she'd asked him questions about h i s Lutheran upbringing without really giving away anything about hers.

"She never *said* she was Lutheran, but she never said she *wasn't* either. So, I guess I just assumed, and she let me." To say it aloud made pressure build behind his eyes.

Arvid switched gears. "There has to be a perfectly understandable reason that this has happened to her. Right? She'll come back good as new one day, won't she? She just needs some time, right?" He looked back and forth between the two doctors.

"You can be assured that we will do everything within our power," Dr. Reynolds said solemnly, "to send your wife back to you as healthy as is humanly possible."

Arvid was aware that his question hadn't been answered.

Dr. Reynolds explained the treatment options. "There are three of them. The first to try is Hydrotherapy.[viii] The second is Insulin Therapy.[ix] If we find that neither of them is successful, the third is Electric Convulsive Therapy or ECT."[x] Each of them was explained and Arvid thought that all of them sounded like horrible ways to treat his wife.

"Wouldn't those be the sorts of things that a cruel devil would do?" he asked in a dead voice.

Only silence followed for a long beat.

However, before the end of this first conference, Arvid had given his permission, "Alright...do what you have to do to help her." *God help us both.*

As if it was an afterthought, Nurse Alva added as she stood, "Oh...don't be surprised when you see her. She will look different."

"What do you mean, *different*?" he asked, another bolt of apprehension shooting through his veins.

"Naturally, the patients on the ward are not allowed to have sharp objects. Such things as hairpins and barrettes...hair clasps are all sharp. So, the women that come to us with long hair are scheduled for a haircut first thing."

Arvid steeled himself to see his wife with a changed appearance. Steeled himself to the thought that she could be in danger from other patients within the hospital. Other women may be paranoid as well and aggressive. But he only asked, "Was she terribly upset when her hair was cut? She always enjoyed brushing her long hair before bed."

The meeting ended with a plan to meet again when the doctors thought Caroline was showing progress, or at least, a change of some kind. Arvid politely extended his hand to shake the two doctor's hands. *Am I supposed to thank them?* He didn't.

Alva escorted him across the hospital grounds to the second of the five brick behemoths along the drive. "Caroline is on the second floor of Oak Hall. Her ward houses the younger of the women patients, those that are more easily controlled," the nurse explained to Arvid as they ascended the stairs. "Have a seat here in the solarium. Make yourself comfortable. I'll bring Caroline out to you."

Arvid tried to make himself comfortable. "Easier said than done," he muttered as he took in the environment where his wife was forced to live. Dull greenish walls. Sterile furniture. Linoleum floors and overhead lights in cages hanging from a ceiling that was at least fourteen feet high. The place echoed. The windows were too high to reach and there were bars on the inside. Nothing adorned the room but a single cross hanging high on the wall.

For the briefest moment, Arvid pictured himself stealing Caroline away from there. But where could he take her?

Time passed. Arvid checked his pocket watch. It was already going on 2:30 in the afternoon.

He gave up on trying to be comfortable and paced from one side of the building to the other just outside the solarium. At last, when he'd nearly given up on her ever coming out, he saw Nurse Alva coming down the hall with Caroline alongside her. Caroline with a short pixie cut.

Caroline had been crying; that was obvious. Her eyes were pink and puffy, her nose red. As they approached Arvid, Caroline looked him up and down. She appeared to be surprised, then puzzled and frightened. "What are you doing here?" she asked, her eyes darting around the room.

"Caroline, I've missed you *so* much. I wanted to see you. I couldn't *wait* to see you." Arvid arms ached to hold her close and put his hand on that head, now shorn of its long hair. He wanted to see her smile, to make the tears melt away. His hands remained at his side.

"It's not safe here," she whispered in his direction.

Nurse Alva backed away. "I'll leave you two to visit then. I'll escort Caroline back to the ward in about forty-five minutes." She looked up at the clock, pivoted on her heel and walked away.

Caroline continued to look around the room as if afraid of what she would see there.

"I was afraid that you were angry with me, that you weren't going to come out to see me," Arvid said to her, relief in his voice.

He invited her to sit beside him on the divan, but she declined, "It's better to keep moving," she whispered, as she paced in the same pattern that Arvid had made while he waited for her.

So, he followed along beside her as she paced from the south window to the north window and back again. "Your birthday will be in another three months, Caroline. I wish...I wish..." but Arvid couldn't figure out what wish he should make out loud, so he finally gave up on finishing the sentence. Caroline didn't seem to notice.

"You'll be twenty-two years old on your birthday. Can you believe it? And we'll have been married three years in December."

Caroline didn't react to his statement about her birthday, nor their anniversary approaching in December. She continued to pace as she had been, pausing briefly now and then to look behind her. "Just checking..." she whispered, to no one.

Arvid reached out for her hand as she paced, but she pulled it away after only a few seconds. "Look, look back there. What do you see?" she said. It wasn't like she was talking to him.

"I don't see anything back there, Caroline. It's just the two of us here. You're safe here."

He barely managed to graze her cheek with his lips before Alva led her away again. He watched Alva's sturdy, almost masculine figure guiding his wife down the hall, back toward the far end of the building and the women's ward there. She turned around just once to look behind her as they went. In doing so, she looked through her husband rather than at him. He could read her lips.

"Look, look back there. What do you see? Just checking...checking..."

Arvid climbed into the car to head home; instead, he laid his head against the back of the seat and closed his eyes, his stomach roiling. He released a long sigh. "So, this is why they wanted me to eat before coming in." The next sound to escape his lips might have been a wry laugh or a helpless sob.

10

HOT WATER

Caroline
September 29, 1948

There is some rhythm to the days within these brick walls. A new day starts just after midnight with Estra's cries. Her nightmares wake her, and me.

"Give it back. Give it back!" She screams. "That's mine. Mine. Give it back." She claws at her bedclothes. In the harsh glow of a yard light that illuminates the grounds of this prison-like place through the night, Estra jams a wad of her blanket into her mouth and bites down, hard.

Much later, I wake to a nightmare of my own that keeps me awake and vigilant until dawn. The nightmare is about that woman, Ronnie, again. The dead woman whose bed I sleep on. Some nightmares paint her as a gray-haired witch. In others, she's a buxom black-haired vixen. This time, she's the witch, a faceless witch.

Dawn comes, and with it, Lois with her grand mal seizure. If I had a watch, I think I could set the time by it. The seizure begins with a low growling kind of sound, deep down in her throat. Lois' head turns hard to her right, facing me, and her whole body stiffens. Eyes open wide, unblinking, unseeing, teeth clenched, lips pulled back. I hear teeth grinding as she drools.

Lois' back arcs. Her hands are fists and her elbows curl tightly, nearly touching her shoulders. Her feet jam into the end of the bed. Immediately after, it's as if her muscles turn to jelly and she collapses back onto the mattress only to repeat the sequence again and again. The nuns put pillows on the floor next to her after she goes to sleep, in case she throws herself out of bed during the seizure. I watch to see if that happens. It does. Her head misses the pillow. Clunk, onto the concrete floor. She'll have a good-sized bruise there by the time she wakes, later this morning.

There is always one uniformed woman, usually it's Winnie, that is charged with watching over us during the night. She sits in a chair at the entrance to our dormitory. One woman to watch more than sixty of us. Even I have to wonder if that's wise. She's to make sure no one wanders off after using the water closet or gets into mischief.

Winnie tells Alva that 'No one gets into mischief on my watch." Are we naughty children, apt to start playing games and tricks on each other in the dark?

After Lois' seizure, I get up to relieve myself and I see Winnie. She's asleep. I can barely contain myself. I creep up close. Barefoot, of course. And then it's "Boo" right in her ear and she jerks awake. I keep on walking. Like nothing at all has happened. I giggle. Oh, that felt good to be mischievous.

"Winnie, the night watch woman, wears a wee, white watch cap when she wakes us." Estra loves to repeat sentences with repetitive consonants and that one, in particular. When I told her yesterday that the sentence was an example of alliteration, she was so proud of herself. She begged me to say it with her. I finally agreed. But only once each day. I wonder what Estra might have learned, if only she'd been sent to school. But I suppose she'd have escaped into the kitchen every chance she got.

Shortly after I return from the W.C., Winnie stands and rings the little bell she carries on a string around her waist.

"Sisters, it is time to wake up. It's a new day."

Half of the room is awake already. Estra, Ruthie and I get up from our thin beds that squeak. We dress and make our beds. We wait for permission to head down the long hallway to breakfast. The two of them are clearly interested in the food whereas I am just too sleepy to protest the trip.

Many of us are not moved by the promise of food. Two more women in white uniforms enter our long dormitory, going from bed to bed toward the far end of the room. I'm beginning to wonder, are they really nuns? Could they be nurses instead? I'd rather they be nuns. As nurses I doubt they're much good.

"Get up now, Alice. Get up, Charmaine." Then sharply, "Trudy? Why are you hiding under your pillow?"

"Get up. Come on...Eleanor? We went through this same thing yesterday. Have you learned nothing? Stand up. Up up up! Undress now. Here's your dress. Quickly. Your breakfast is waiting."

From farther away, "Could you help me over here? Mildred has crawled under her bed again. She doesn't like to come out for me. There, there, Millie...here's your favorite nurse to help you up." Much muttering follows, none of which I can understand, but now I have confirmation...there's at least one nurse among the women in white.

The voices at the far end echo. "Susie...Loretta. That's enough chatter for one morning. Out of bed with you both." The voices of the women in white uniforms recede as they travel down the length of the long room until they blend with the muttering of all the sisters, being roused from their beds.

The breakfast menu is no surprise. Oatmeal mush and a piece of dry, burnt toast. We are some of the first in line. At the table, Estra sits too close to me. If any food drops from my plate, her pudgy hand is there before the food can touch the table or floor.

"I got it," she says gleefully. Estra moves quickly on the plank bench beside me. She does not fit in the dining hall chairs. Like a baby elephant that I saw when the circus came to town, she sways from side to side, her hand acting as the nimble trunk, plucking food from wherever it lands. She is an incredible thing. Hungry day and night, or so it seems.

Ruthie has trouble eating with her harelip, of course, and so she and Estra are not allowed to sit next to one another. Too many opportunities for Estra to grab extra food. They put me in between them. I am not enough of a barrier in my opinion.

Ruthie brings that awful, filthy ragdoll to the table with her and even tries to feed it. I know that Ruthie can talk, or at least, she understands everything that is said around her. I think she often chooses not to talk, so people won't laugh at her pronunciation. Some of the sisters do, actually. I don't laugh at her. I hope I never do. It's enough to turn my back to her when she eats.

When Lois eats with us...never at breakfast, of course, but at dinnertime and supper, she and I both sit between Estra and Ruthie. I get to the table first because I can walk faster than Lois. I prefer sitting next to Estra, rather than Ruthie, even though Estra watches my food like a hawk watches her prey. At least Estra's food always makes it into her mouth. I just have to be careful that my food makes it into mine.

Lois is slow, there's no doubt about that. She's "slow" as in mentally retarded, like Martin. Martin! Why is Martin able to live with his parents while Lois has to live here? Thinking of Martin makes me think about Arvid. How good Arvid is to Martin. He is patient and kind. Remembering that, I want to be patient and kind to Lois. She can't help it that she is slow. Mentally and physically.

Arvid visited me, was it only yesterday? I was so afraid when I saw him here. That Devil Baby may have followed him. He should have been more observant, and I told him so. Reminded him of the danger.

He seemed glad to see me, though, and I was kind of glad to see him too, if only I didn't have to worry about the Devil following him here. I felt relieved when he finally left.

At last the great dining hall fills with the sisters in drab garments, faded after months or years of washings. Arvid brought me two extra dresses and undergarments at his visit. I have more clothing than some.

A woman that talks incessantly sits across from me. Bertha is her name. Someone places a tray in front of her. Bertha is cross-eyed and she rocks too much to carry a tray from the food line to the table by herself. Once seated, she continues to rock, not so much moving from side to side as rocking from sitting upright to reaching forward with her shoulders and neck, straining out over the table.

Bertha reminds me of a horse stretching her neck through a fence to eat what is on the other side, and for no good reason. The grass is the same on both sides. Bertha's chin thrusts forward. Again, and again. If I were to time it just right, our foreheads could touch when I lean over the table for a spoonful of mush. I time it so that that will not happen.

I know you," Bertha says, her short phrases come in time with her rocking. "I know you. You're in Ronnie's bed. Ronnie's bed. Ronnie's dead. She's dead. She's dead. Dead. Dead. Dead. They say Ronnie killed herself. You wanna know how? You wanna know why? I can tell you. If you wanna know. If you wanna know."

Sister Alva is coming closer, walking between the long tables, looking over our shoulders. "Shhh," I try to hush Bertha. "Sister Alva is coming."

"Ladies, that's enough talking. It's time to eat. Are you working on your oatmeal there, Bertha? No? Well, it will be cold soon enough. That's what happens when you are too busy talking to eat." Sister Alva walks on to the next table.

I want to know what Bertha knows. Maybe I can get her to be quiet about it. "How did she do it?" I whisper with my eyes on my food. Trying to look disinterested in talking. "Quick, tell me how she did it!"

"I have a good memory. Very good! Photographic! Yes, I do. I can tell you everything. Everything!"

"Yes, alright, but be quiet then. Shhh," I whisper.

Bertha continues talking quietly, but I stop listening because I see Sally.

Sally is coming slowly down the hall that continues on past the dining hall to the washroom and solarium. She's different today. Sally is never one to meander, but it seems that's what she is doing. And she's not carrying her bucket and mop. I've never seen her go anywhere without her janitorial tools.

It's been a couple of days since I talked to Sally, when she told me about her mama, that she doesn't have long to suffer now. The poor woman must be very ill for Sally to have recognized that she is near the end. How horrible for Sally to have to go through this, so alone, except for our brief talks. I hope for both Sally and her mama's sakes that Sally is right. I wish I could go to her and talk right now.

There's another thing that's different about her. She looks ill, washed out Her warm-chocolatey skin looks gray. And then I feel certain that her mother must have died since we talked. That must be it. That's why she looks haunted.

But this isn't the right time of day for Sally to clean the washroom, nor the solarium, and those are the only other rooms down this way. There's a chance that Alva might catch sight of her over here when her schedule tells her to be upstairs. She risks another dressing-down from Big Alva for being found where she is not supposed to be at this time of day.

I notice that Sally carries an oddly-shaped flat brown package tied with jute. She stops and looks at me over the rows of other sisters eating breakfast.

The corners of Sally's mouth turn up when she sees me, but it's not the kind of smile that extends to her eyes. She risks being fired for disobeying Alva. Alva is mean-spirited anyway, but even more so to people like Sally and Lois, as if their darker skin makes them less than human. Arvid talks much nicer to the dog, Teddy, than Alva ever does to those two.

Perhaps we are safe for the moment. So, I smile boldly in return at my one true friend in this nunnery. She nods her head toward me slowly, as if to say, "How do you do?" or "There you are, my friend," or "See you later," or "Goodbye." I nod back to her.

"They's things worse 'n dyin'," Sally had said. She made death sound simple. "Ever'body dies, Car'line. Death is just part o' life. When you can' bear t' see the sun rise on 'nother mis'rable day, a woman's gotta right to take control o' her life. It's *her* life. It don' b'long to nobody else."

When Sally talks, it means something. She's the most trustworthy person here. I lean on her because she understands that I have to keep an eye out for the Devil, and she's promised to keep an eye out for Him, too. Sally trusts me with her secret, and she's the only one I can trust with mine, although mine isn't much of a secret. I'm quite sure that all the sisters know I am always on the lookout. They see me stare at them. Checking.

Sally resumes her walk past the dining hall and I look back to Bertha.

"Okay, how did she do it?" I say to Bertha, discreetly after Sally has walked past.

"But you wanna know why? Don't you? Know why first? Wanna know why? Why is the best part." Bertha rocks and somehow manages to get a spoonful of mush into her mouth. Nothing short of a miracle.

"Alright, tell me why. But hurry."

"It was the letters. She got the letters. Got 'em on a Wednesday. You know about Wednesday? Wednesday? Wednesday's child is full of woe? So much woe. Too much woe. She read me the letters. Just two short letters. Very short. So much woe."

"Tell me then. You must be quick, though."

"Ronnie never got mail. I never do either, but no matter. No matter. Ronnie never got mail. But that one day, she got two letters.

Two! Jackpot! Ronnie grew an inch taller with those two letters. She did. She really did. I saw it happen."

"Okay, I believe you." Though I didn't. "What did they say?"

"The first letter was postmarked 1947. Last year! Must have been lost. Somewhere. She opened that one first. That one was first, so she opened it first. First comes first. This is what it said. It said:

'I regret to inform you of the death of your son, Lucas D. Kaufman on November 20, 1947. You can be proud that he died bravely in the line of duty, serving the country that he loved. My sincerest sympathies go to you, his mother, and to his entire family. His sacrifice will not be forgotten.

Signed, J. Edgar Hoover.'

"Ronnie cried. She cried and cried all through the night. He was her only son. 'Mr. Hoover didn't need to tell me his name was Lucas,' she said. 'He was *my* son. I named him. I knew his name.' And then she cried some more."

"What about the second letter?" I whisper.

"Oh, that was even worse," Bertha said, rocking, her crossed eyes looking somewhere over my head. "Even worse than the first. Worse than the first. Well, maybe. I can't be sure. Can never be entirely sure. But she waited until the next morning...to open that one. That letter said this. This is what it said:

'In the matter of Rhonda H. Kaufman vs. Duane T. Kaufman. Rhonda Kaufman declines representation by failure to respond. Therefore, be it known that on this day August 7, 1948, the marital union between these two parties, being irrevocably damaged, is hereby dissolved.

The Honorable
Judge William Proust, Third District, Minnesota.'

I am stunned. Goosebumps spread over my body. To think that a husband might divorce his wife while she's in this place. It hadn't occurred to me that such a thing could happen. In my mind's eye, I see Arvid's face. He is laughing. Dressed in his wedding suit. Another woman would be a better match for him. He would soon forget me here.

Bertha isn't done yet. "Ronnie didn't know. She didn't know. That her husband filed for divorce. Not until it was all over. It was all over and then she knew. She knew she would never leave here. Never. Not after those letters. First letters she ever got and that's what they had to say." Bertha pauses in her rocking. "Never had a single visitor either. All the years she was here. Not one visitor. She told me, 'I'll never leave here now. Nowhere to go anyway. No home to go back to.'"

"Ronnie asked me, 'What's the point of it all?' You see? She asked me! Me! But *I* didn't know what the point was. I don't know even now. I never knew. Do you know? Do you? She could have asked someone who knew. Someone who knew the answer. Not me." Bertha's face is flat, vacant. No...not vacant. More like shell-shock is what I heard it called. Like those men who came back from the war with changed faces, empty eyes. The ones whose wounds are hidden inside.

The nuns or whatever they are, walk among the tables now, taking away the plates of those who are too clumsy or slow to clear their place settings for themselves. "So...how did she do it?" I whisper as softly as I can.

"Ooh, so sad. Sad for me. Too tired. She was too tired. To care anymore. But for one thing. Only one thing mattered. To be buried on sacred ground. Ronnie was Catholic. 'I want to lie next to my mother,' she said. 'On sacred ground.' But suicide is the Ultimate Sin. The worst of the sins. Worse than being sent here. No forgiveness for suicide. She wouldn't get into heaven. And not the Catholic cemetery. She would suffer for all eternity. Suffer in torment. That is why she had to get someone else. Someone else had to kill her. Someone else had to do it."

A pang of fear pierces me. "Ronnie got someone else to murder her?" I mumble aloud, incredulous. Is it hard to find a person willing to do murder? I glance at those I know the best. Estra doesn't have a murderous bone in her body. Ruthie? No. I narrow my eyes to examine everyone around me. The nuns...or the nurses, if that's what they are. The doctors, cooks, janitors, others that I cannot find any reason for being here. Which one's a murderer?

"Who killed her?" I whisper finally. My throat feels tight.

"That's the thing. We don't know. We don't know who it was. Nobody knows, I guess. 'Cept for the murderer. The gardener found Ronnie. Mmmm hmmm. Found her in the caves, he did. Where the harvest gets stored over in that side of the bluff over there." She hooked a thumb over her shoulder. "You probably never seen it over there. Them caves are carved from the sandstone. Same temperature all year round in there. Fill it with the apple harvest and all the vegetables we're growin'. The vegetables that we'll eat at dinnertime...they all get stored in the caves. At first...this is what I heard now. At first he said he thought that somebody had smashed a pile of tomatoes there. Ruined a lot of tomatoes, is what he thought. But no, it was Ronnie's head that was smashed. A bloody rock. Her brains on the ground. But..."

Bertha looks right at me for the first time. With at least one of her crossed eyes. "But she should have got into sacred ground anyway. That would have been one good thing. That was her last wish, to be buried in sacred ground. She was going to be happy that her flesh would rot in sacred ground."

I grow more anxious by the moment. "But she didn't?"

"No. No one came to claim the body. I watched out the window all day. She shoulda left here in a Coroner's hearse, but she didn't. They took her inside this very building and down into the subway tunnels. Once they take a dead body down there, they don't leave these grounds, ya know. No, they woulda taken her out to bury in the hospital cemetery. Over yonder," Bertha pointed behind her. "The unmarked pauper's graves. That's where they took her, no doubt."

"But how do you know this?" How could Bertha know everything?

"Honey, when you been here 's long as I have, you know how things 'r done. If you go down to the subway tunnels when you're sick, you're going to the sick ward, the infirmary. If you die down there, one of two things happens: One, your body comes up and goes out the front door into a hearse to be buried by the family, or two, your body doesn't come up. It's taken all the way through the subway and up and out the far end and then loaded into a wagon. I overheard one of the grave diggers talkin' once. He said it was a shame that it was raining that day; he didn't like diggin' in the mud, 'but paupers gotta be buried right away, before they start to smell.' That's what he said."

"But she was murdered! Wasn't anyone charged with her murder?" I feel panicked. This place is all wrong. Too much is wrong. There are layers of lies around us. Graves are filled with lies. Secrets.

"No, no investigation. The hospital has a good record to keep. Only one murder has ever taken place here, that's what they claim. If it weren't for the suicides, what a good record it would be! Suicides are better, I suppose, than homicides." I am speechless, frozen.

Estra listens to this entire exchange with mouth and eyes open wide. She leans in to confide with a pleased grin, "Know what?"

Just then, there's a shrill scream. Strangely, it sounds like Alva although she isn't given to emotion except for anger. It's coming from down the hallway, maybe the solarium or the women's washroom.

"What was that?" Estra interrupts herself, looking toward the broad hall.

Immediately after the scream, the women in white are running out of the dining hall. Then Sister Alva comes from that end of the hallway to meet the women that are headed her direction. "Bring the crash cart!" She shouts at them. She spins around and runs back down toward the solarium or the washroom. One woman-in-white runs one direction, the other ones run after Alva. I've never seen them move so quickly.

A man in a suit and shiny shoes enters the dining hall at a fast pace. Clack, clack, clack, clack. His are not the kind of shoes to wear on hard linoleum. Every single footfall is like a gunshot.

He calls into the kitchen, "Mrs. Fenster? We're going to need you and your kitchen staff out here on the floor for a while." The cook and her three helpers emerge from the kitchen, flustered, as if they're in trouble. The suited man uses hand signals while he talks to them, like he's directing traffic in Owatonna. Then Shiny-Shoes clacks hurriedly back toward whatever office he must usually hide within.

The cook and helpers position themselves around the dining hall. Bertha, Estra, Ruthie and I look at each other.

"What are they doing out here?" I say softly. "I've never seen Fenster without a spoon in her hand."

"Don't know, don't know. But somethin's happening down there." Bertha cocks her head toward the solarium end of the hallway, where we sit or play games sometimes. "Somethin' big. Big! Very big."

Estra has a fairly good memory, at least for things she understands. She returns to her previous thought and fills the silence with an aplomb that only Estra can produce. "Know what? My mother sent me here so I wouldn't die from overeating. That's what she told the doctor. The family's last hope, they said. Uh huh." Estra nods her head.

She seems delighted to have contributed something pertinent to the conversation about suicide. "They tried but they couldn't watch me every minute of the day. I've been here now...oh, about six years, or maybe ten, one or the other," she adds importantly. She screws up her eyes, approximating something like deep thought. I register that Estra doesn't count, doesn't understand numbers.

"But I have visitors sometimes. *My* family likes *me*." She folds her hands across her broad chest and grins at her own good fortune. "Mmm-huh."

I turn back to Bertha and softly ask, "If Ronnie got someone else to kill her, isn't that suicide all the same? She arranged for her own death." I am puzzled, and frightened.

Bertha shrugs her shoulders as she rocks backward, forward, backward. "Not for me to decide. Not for me."

I look around the hall. It seems that all the women from the dormitory are still here at their tables. Laughter erupts from the other end of the large room. There's more chatter now. More laughter. Some groans. The cook and helpers finish clearing away all the plates and remind us repeatedly to remain seated.

There seems to be no one present in the dining hall that will bother to tell us to stop talking about Ronnie's death, or about suicide in general, for that matter. Perfect opportunity. Arvid has an expression, "You gotta make hay while the sun shines." Well, the "sun is shining" right now in the dining hall. No ladies-in-white to be seen. Time to "make hay."

Ruthie apparently notices this at the same time I do. For her, this is a rare opportunity to talk without spraying masticated food at her tablemates. Her plate is gone. Most of the food that went into her mouth has made its way down her throat. She is as safe to talk now, as she likely ever will be.

"What about the man that killed hithelf latht month? Whaddayou know about him, Bertha?"

"I know this much," Bertha began. "He claimed he never succeeded. At anything. Not at anything. Ever. In his whole life. Imagine that. A failure at everything. Well, he was successful that time," she says with the merest hint of a wry smirk.

"I heard the doctor thay one time that when thomeone taketh her own life, that perthon taketh the eathy way out. 'Damn her,' he thaid." Ruthie's eyes look up and down our table, hoping for a reaction from someone other than me, perhaps?

Bertha nods, "You're right. Right you are. That's how they think. That we should let them try everything. Every crazy thing. Crazy things they call treatment. Hydrotherapy like you're prob'ly gonna get." She looks at me with, is it pity? "Insulin Shock. ECT. I've had 'em all. Just plain crazy is what I call 'em." Bertha gives a derisive snort. She's angry now. She doesn't repeat herself when she's angry. "Painful. Inhuman. They try 'em all out on us. Keep trying 'em until we die. And we *will* die. Of natural causes, they'll say. Natural causes! My ass! What's natural about 'em?" Bertha stops rocking long enough to spit on the floor.

Sister Alva's soft-soled shoes are padding toward us from the direction of the solarium. Her face is dark. The time for making hay is over. She stops at the head of the dining room. She is definitely upset, but in a different kind of way than usual. She rearranges her features and settles on her "important announcement" face.

"Sisters, we've had a tragic accident. For that reason, we will not be returning to the east end of the building after breakfast. We will continue on with our morning activities from here." She pulls a folded paper from her pocket and refers to it.

"Tables One and Two are scheduled to go to the Crafts Building. Your trustee will escort you. Where is she?" A pause while Alva cranes her neck to find the trustee at the back of the long room.

"There you are, Miss Edna. You are new as a trustee, and so you can be forgiven this time, but you should always stand immediately when I refer to the trustee for your group. You know who you are, don't you?" A burst of laughter from Table One. "That's enough of that," Alva growls. "Alright then. Miss Edna, you may leave now with your charges."

Quite predictably, this direction by Alva is followed by various noises. The scraping of benches and chairs as they're pushed back from the tables. Someone's chair tips over backwards. There's laughter that's quickly cut short. Chatter.

"Ouch!" from someone.

"I don't need your help," from someone else. At last the group shambles past our table, the outermost table of the dining hall.

Alva continues, "Some of you are scheduled to help in the laundry this morning. Table Three? I believe it's your turn today. Your trustee will take the group there." The trustee for Table Three pops up like she's on springs. Doesn't need to be told twice to get a move on.

I've figured out the trustees at last. They're prisoners here, like me, but they've done something to earn the trust of Alva and the other women dressed in white. They're helpers. Comparable noises of chairs and voices ensue at Table Three. Big Alva moves on to assign tasks to all the tables.

"The rest of you will be remaining here for just a little longer. Except for you, and you," she points, "and Caroline? You too. The three of you will follow me, now."

So, we do. She takes us down a long flight of concrete stairs, to the basement where one tunnel goes off to the right and one to the left. The one to the right is a shortcut to the Infirmary under the Administration Building and to the Laundry. I know because I've been to both. But the tunnel going to the left? I've never seen what's down there before. Entering the tunnel, there is a different kind of smell. Something like bleach, but sweeter.

Big Alva says, "You three are going to have special baths today. You will like them." She advises us of this so confidently. "The water will be very hot to begin with but not so hot that you can't stand it. It will be good for you." We follow her through a door with a sign above it that reads "Hydrotherapy."

I am greeted by steamy and moist air. It smells even more like bleach in here than out in the tunnel. The large room has two rows of enormous rectangular bathtubs, each encased in black and white tiles. One row of them butts up to the wall on my left and the other row lines up to the wall on my right. A taut, sturdy covering is stretched over each tub, hooked on somehow. And this is especially surprising. There is already a woman sleeping in all but three of the tubs, older women that I've never seen before. Each of the taut covers has just one small opening which encircles the woman's neck, keeping only her head above the water. Alongside each tub sits a narrow bed on wheels.

There are small windows near the ceiling, and I see grass outside. Sunlight casts an early morning swath of light across the room.

Big Alva directs us, "Get undressed for your bath. You may fold your clothing and leave it on the gurney by your tub. It will be a nice long bath," she says. "If you want to sleep, you are free to do so. It will be very relaxing."

Alva approximates a smile. Frankly, her attempt is a little frightening. I think she is so unused to smiling that she doesn't know how. I will try to be positive about this bath. It would be nice to relax. And I haven't slept well in days. Maybe the bath is a privilege that only a few women have earned. Maybe this may help me to become a trustee. I do attempt to be helpful to other sisters when I can. I'm surprised, though, that Alva would have noticed. I undress quickly.

Big Alva points at a cross on the wall in the tub room. "The room was blessed this morning. Nothing to be afraid of here," she says looking directly at me.

"Well, I will be the judge of that," I mutter under my breath. I climb into the big tub. The water is hot, definitely very hot, but I decide that I can tolerate it. I sit down slowly, into the water. It comes up over my shoulders. Sister Alva hands me a sweet-smelling pad to use for bathing while she and another attendant begin to attach the covering around me. She refers to the covering and says, "This apron will keep the water in the tub warm longer." The smell of the pad is sort of sweetly pleasant, and then...

I am so drowsy. My eyelids are weighted. I can't stay awake no matter *how hard I...*

11

COLD FEET

Caroline
September 30, 1948

*A*rvid's smile is beautiful in the dashboard lights of the '39 Ford. "At last, I'm taking you to our home. My wife. What a nice word that is," he says softly.

"I like the sound of it, too." Shyness makes me whisper.

Arvid and I are finally alone in the car. It is December, our wedding night. Cold! We have delivered Marit to her cabin at the end of the lane. Arvid stops the car at the top of the rise in the field between her cabin and the big farmhouse and there he kisses me, "on the highest point of land in any direction," he says. Of course, we had kissed before that, but this kiss is memorable because my head is full of the wedding vows we made to each other this morning, "to love and to cherish until death do us part." We are joined as One! The pastor said so.

He carries me across the threshold of the farmhouse kitchen, me in my wedding dress, thick winter coat, hat, boots and all, and into our new lives together. It is my first time inside any farmhouse, ever. And it is cold! I can see my breath! Without anyone in the house most of the day to add wood to the furnace, it has gone to coals.

Arvid changes out of his wedding suit upstairs and lights a kerosene lantern to take through the house and out to the barn with him. Before he goes out to milk the cows, though, he carries in armloads of wood from an enormous box of firewood on the back porch. The smaller chunks of wood go into the kitchen stove. The larger chunks go into the wood furnace in the front room. He stokes each fire to bring it back to life.

"And this is the flue, over here, and when it's open, like this, it will draw air in and that will feed the flames," he explains to me. "There, that should get things going again nicely." He readjusts the topmost chunk of wood with a long poker and sparks spurt within the furnace box.

"I've never tended a fire to heat an entire house before," I say, feeling especially young and inexperienced.

Arvid only smiles at me. "You'll get the hang of it." It's the first time I've seen him in his farm clothes. I find him very handsome, in a rugged kind of way.

"You remind me a little of Paul Bunyan[xi]*"* I tell him coyly as he bundles up to go out the door. *"He wore that same red and black plaid coat and the cap with earflaps in the story we read in grade school."*

I might have predicted Arvid would laugh. I have many things to learn about my husband, but I know that he likes to laugh. *"Are you quite sure that you want to be married to a Paul Bunyan look-alike until we are old and gray?"* He feigns seriousness.

I frown and tap my forefinger against my lips thoughtfully. *"Hmmm, let me think..."* I make him wait just a few seconds before answering, *"YES! I would love to be married to a Paul Bunyan look-alike but only if his name is Arvid Fjeld. I think that I would be quite a happy wife."*

Arvid sets the kerosene lantern on the floor to spin me around, he in his heavy wool barn coat and boots and me still in my wedding dress, clutching my black winter coat closed around me.

"I am glad to hear that. I couldn't bear to have my beautiful Caroline become an unhappy wife," he nuzzles my neck, smiles and kisses my cheek.

What a sight we must be! I giggle and he catches me for a proper kiss before he heads out to the barn.

"I'll be back," he says in a dramatically deep voice, with a broad smile and a wink. I hadn't known that I could feel so happy, so utterly delighted.

Left alone, the farmhouse intrigues me. I explore the entire first floor while Arvid is outside milking. There are three large rooms.

A round oak pedestal table sits at the center of the kitchen along with the kerosene lamp suspended above it. An icebox hugs an outside wall. Painted cupboards reach to the ceiling and a walk-in pantry holds more open shelving. The gray and black speckled stove has not one, but two oven doors and a can of lard sits on the right at the back of the stovetop. I picture myself ironing Arvid's shirts with the trio of irons sitting on the far left.

The calendar advertises Land O' Lakes butter. Someone has drawn a big red heart around today's date, probably Marit. It makes me smile. On the floor below it sits a pair of thirty-gallon Red Wing crocks with wooden covers. Hats, jackets, gloves and five-buckle boots fill one corner of the room.

The summer kitchen through the west window is dark and silent, abandoned for the winter.

With my lighted lantern I creep through the French doors into a dining room, trimmed in dark wood with a wall of built-in hutches with glass doors. There I find a glossy table and six chairs that match! I feel as though this room is in a museum, in some other lifetime.

Lastly, I go to what Arvid calls the *"front room,"* the room that I would call the living room. There is a well-worn davenport and three upholstered chairs gathered around a tall, crank phonograph and a battery operated radio. In the flickering light of the wood furnace, I shed my heavy coat and change out of my borrowed wedding gown into a simple dress and sweater to welcome my husband in from the barn. The house is on its way to warming up by the time he finishes with the milking.

"I've come back," he sings out with an impish grin and a kiss. His cheek brings the cold air in with him. "Have you checked out the upstairs yet?"

I shake my head and smile shyly, "No, not yet. There was so much to see down here." I glance around the kitchen.

"Well, let's see what's upstairs, shall we?" He opens the door to the stairway, takes a lantern in one hand and my hand in the other. He leads me up the narrow stairs and into the largest of the four bedrooms. "It might be starting to warm up a little in here." He looks at me hopefully. Then looks down at the floor registers.

"I left these registers closed before I went to the barn, to get the first floor nice and warm first. But I'll open this register now, let a little more warmth up here." He sets the lantern down and bends to slide the iron notch around on the round register. I can feel warm air from the front room below us, pushing its way into the bedroom around my feet.

"No wonder I couldn't tell," I say. Then, "Look." With a grin, I blow out a breath that produces a puff of steam in the cold air of the bedroom. I feel so shy at that moment. I am shivering from the cold, and maybe from nerves.

Arvid notices my shivering. He takes my hands. "Maybe we should wait for the upstairs to warm up a little more before we come up here again."

I hesitate before answering and look up at him. "Yes, maybe we should."

I think I know what he is thinking by the way he looks into my eyes. I hope that he knows that I want to be with him in that intimate way, and yet I also want us to start all over again, too. Have time alone together first, in this unfamiliar place, so far from where we'd courted. This cold farmhouse is a whole different world to me, another country, when compared to the town where I've lived since I was orphaned.

"Are you wishing you'd seen this place before we married?" he asks me.

"Oh, no. I'm happy with my decision." I'd explained my feelings about traveling to Hawk Ridge the same weekend that Arvid proposed to me. I told him then, "I love that you would spend an entire weekend driving, to bring me to meet your mother and to see your farm before we marry but —"

"It will be our farm, Caroline. As soon as you are my wife. Our farm, our home together."

"Oh yes...of course," I smiled, willing him to understand why I wouldn't allow him to drive six hours one day and six hours the next only to show me where I'll be living. "And of course, I am eager to meet your mother," I'd told him. "You know I am, don't you? But Arvid. I will be there soon enough." I paused, hoping for him to see that I was being *practical. I was being considerate. But, no. I didn't see it on his face. Not yet anyway.*

I was exquisitely aware that I was going to be a bride without a dowry. My bridal shower consisted of a luncheon with two girlfriends from high school and two from the boarding house. I had no hope chest. I had no parent to bless me and send me off with a wedding gift, nor a benefactor to pay any part of the expense of feeding our wedding guests. All I would bring to the marriage was what little I could earn at my job at the dry goods store. And so, I chose to forego a weekend long trip from Owatonna to Hawk Ridge before our wedding day.

Arvid holds the lantern higher and searches my eyes. He looks worried. He quietly asks me, "Caroline, do you have cold feet?"

I take a deep breath. I clear my throat. "Actually, I do have cold feet," I say. "I'm afraid that...well, I'm afraid —"

"I understand," he says quickly. He clearly wants to put me at ease, which I appreciate. He sets the lantern down again. "I don't want to pressure you. We have our whole lives together." He holds me close, so gently.

Arvid holds me by my shoulders then, so that he can stand back and see my face. "You're young and I pushed you to marry me so quickly. I didn't tell you, but I was afraid that you might find someone else during the long winter, when it would be harder for me to see you."

"Oh, Arvid. Pfft. You did not push me to marry you. I said yes immediately, did I not?"

"I love you, Caroline. I want to be close to you, but not until you are ready. I would never forgive myself if I frightened you. I would never force myself upon you, Caroline. I want you to know that. I could never be that kind of man. Please believe me." He looks at me so tenderly.

I want to reassure him that my poor circulatory system in the winter can be remedied by exercise, that I really can take care of the problem. It will be just fine. At least I hope so.

"I should have mentioned this before," I say. "Today while you were outside, I was so distracted with the novelty of the house and everything. I just...well, I didn't..." I make a hasty decision. "If you would wait right here, please. It won't take me long." I run down the stairs as quickly as I can.

I hurry into the dark front room, stop in front of the big wood furnace and peel off my warm sweater. There is just enough light from the fire coming through the small panes of mica to ensure that I won't kick any furniture.

"Caroline, what are you doing?" Arvid's voice startles me. His figure is a silhouette, blocking light from the kitchen behind him. I can't see his expression, but his tone is perplexed.

Stunned and embarrassed, I stop abruptly. "It's just...my feet —" breathing heavily now, "doing some —" big exhalation, "jumping jacks. To warm up my hands and fee —"

Laughter explodes from my husband's silhouette. The silhouette doubles over and falls against the doorframe without which I think he would have fallen to the floor in a puddle. Unable to speak. Gasping for breath between each jag of laughter.

"The orphanage was so drafty and so we used to..." But then, watching him convulse with laughter, I can't help but laugh myself.

He crosses the floor to me and kisses me soundly for a moment, before he has to stop in order to finish laughing. He wipes tears of laughter from his eyes in the flickering light from the wood furnace. I wipe tears of laughter from my own.

"I thought that you...you weren't ready to crawl into bed with me. Cold. Feet!" He blows out an exaggerated sigh of relief. "Haaaaa..."

The evening works out fine, just fine. Our marital bed is thick with heavy, warm quilts. It is a cocoon of warmth and safety.

*H*eavy quilts. Warm bed. Thick and so soft are the quilts, pressing down on me, holding me fast. I see my breath in the air.

The bed covers have become so very heavy, it's hard to move. No, that's not it. I can't move at all! Wet, the bed is wet. I am wet. Where am I? I am cold, so cold. So, so cold!

I awake with a start. I'm now lying on that narrow bed on wheels in the basement. I am wrapped tightly with something wet, perhaps a sheet, and covered with wool blankets. I cannot move. They have made me into a mummy! I cannot sit or stand. I panic.

"Help. Help me. Help me, somebody. Help me please," I scream, as loudly as I can. But I sound weak. Why am I so weak? I must get out of here. Before I freeze to death. Why am I wrapped like this? There once was light from the morning sun coming through that high window. The room is now in silvery tones of late afternoon, at least what little I can see.

"Oh God, help me. Oh, please, please, please. Whatever I did, I'm sorry. I'll never do it again," I plead. "Please get me out of this. I am so...so...cold." My teeth chatter.

My hands and feet are especially cold, like in the winter when my hands and feet become like cold stones. The aching of them thrums through my body. But it was summer only this morning, wasn't it? Do I have frostbite? Will I lose fingers and toes? I've heard of people losing them to frostbite, even whole hands and feet. I try to scream louder, but it is not any louder than before.

"Help. Help. Help me, please. I'm going to die in here. I'm freezing. I must get out of here now. Oh, please somebody. Help me." Time passes. Is it moments or is it hours? I can't think anymore. Too cold to think. I hurt so much. My entire body shrieks in pain.

And then, oddly, I become giddy. "I don't know what's wrong with me," I mumble. "Am I drunk? What did you give me?"

I hear a door opening. Two sets of feet come in and two pairs of hands are feeling around me. The weight of the wool blankets is suddenly gone. I am being unwrapped from the sheets, but not gently. I tumble back and forth on the hard bed as the ends of the sheet are pulled out. Now I am lifted and laid on a towel on the concrete floor. Hands rub me with towels. My arms, my legs, my breasts, my private parts.

"I can do that myself," I say. But it is shattered speech. I am shivering too much to be understood. The four hands pull me to stand and then dress me quickly. My body continues to tremble and I am unable to stand on my own. The hands pull me or carry me along through the door and the tunnel, up the stairs and down the hall to my bed. Then they cover me with warmed blankets.

No, they're not just warm, they're *hot* blankets, blankets heated in an oven. Oh my God! My hands and feet, especially, now scream in pain. The dramatic change in temperature is like a thousand needles piercing through my hands and feet, my legs, breasts. Everyone knows that you have to warm up frozen limbs slowly. Don't they? Don't they know that it's excruciating to warm too quickly? How could they not know this? I hurt so much. Everywhere. I can't go on like this.

I call out as loudly as I can, "You're killing me." But there is no one close by to save me.

Later, I see Estra's face peering down at me, my face wet with tears. "You're back," she says, and grins close to my face. "I just had supper. Meatloaf, boiled potatoes, butter and green beans. It was good." She pauses then, while she watches my face and breathes loudly.

"You prob'ly didn't know Sally. She was the Negro girl with the mop 'n bucket. I thought you'd wanna know anyhow, what happened. I woulda told you before but you were in the tub all day. She killed herself this morning, out there in the washroom," she says innocently, matter-of-factly, pointing out through the door. "She brought a piece of broken glass in with her. She pushed a pointy piece right up in here. That's what I heard. I heard." She pushed one chubby finger upwards into the soft folds underneath her chin.

"That's why we stayed in the dining hall so long this morning, y' see. I bet you wondered. I bet you did." Estra goes on.

"How'd you like the tub? Do you get to go again? I'm too short for the tub. That's what they said. Do you think that's true? Cuz I wanna go, too. I'd like a hot bath. Sounds nice."

Estra continues to chatter while I think about the way Sally smiled at me that morning. She *was* saying 'goodbye' to me after all. Only to me. That's why she ended her life on this floor. So I'd know that it was her decision to leave. She chose me. Sally was smart and true. She looked me right in the eyes and that's a rare thing here. And now I'll never be able to talk to her again. I close my eyes to see her again, as she was when she smiled at me. My one true friend.

When I am warm at last, Winnie brings me to the dining hall, along with the other two sisters that were sent down to the tubs with me today. I don't know what happened to those older women that were in the tubs. We are served a late supper. The other two sisters are quiet. "Have you been in those tubs before?"

Both of them nod. One of them, the one with pretty, gray eyes that look so sad says, "It'll get easier once you're used to it."

The other one stares at her and says tiredly, "You really think so, Marilyn? That it's easier after the seventh or eighth time? How many times does it take, 'cuz I'm still waiting."

I don't want them to argue. We are too haggard to argue. "Do you know where the older women went? I've never seen them before."

"You're new, aren't you," the second speaker with the curly, flaming red hair says.

I nod. "I'm Caroline."

"And I'm Celia. This is Marilyn. The older ones are from the old women's floor. Another whole unit with just as many up there as here. Some of those old women are pretty frail. Can't do anything for themselves. Some of 'em have been here for years and years. They'll die here. I'm glad I don't have to be up there with them. Smells like pee up there. And shit. And old people."

I stare at her. "Will they bring me to the tub again tomorrow, do you think?" I dread the answer.

"Probably," the first speaker named Marilyn answers me. "Once they start with hydrotherapy, they like to keep it going for weeks. Are you claustrophobic?"

"I don't think so...what's that?" I ask her with my eyebrows knitted.

"No, I don't think you are." Celia takes over. "You were calm enough while they were attaching the tub apron around you. Claustrophobia is when you go berserk in a small space." She takes a bite of food and chews as if it's hard work.

"Yes, that's claustrophobia, you're lucky you don't have that." Marilyn offers, "But I'll tell you what. The best thing you can do is to pretend that you like the tub."

"Like it?" I lean forward to whisper quietly, incredulous. "I hated waking up with those wet blankets around me. Why did they do that? Why torture me? What should I pretend?"

Marilyn explains. "It's like this. Those that fight going to the tub? They continue sending them there. They'll keep on putting you in there until you get used to it, or until you break. If you act like it's the most helpful thing in the world, sometimes they stop sending you down there sooner. I've heard that more than once from other women." Her gray eyes are soothing somehow. I feel as though I might be able to trust her.

Celia sighs and nods her head in agreement. "I've heard that too. I'm tryin', but it's hard."

"But what is it supposed to help with?" I feel panicky. This makes no sense.

"Whatever it was that got you in here, honey?" Marilyn looks at me kindly.

"But I don't know how I got here. Why am I here? I don't remember."

Marilyn smiles sadly, "Well, that's what you gotta figure out, then hon. Can you ask your doctor?"

"You mean, the priest?"

Celia takes a deep breath, "Sweetie, you are daft. There's no priests here. I saw Dr. Coughlin talk to you the other day. Ask him."

"See you tomorrow in the tub, most likely," both of them say to me as they leave the table. They sleep in beds that are close together at the far end of the dormitory.

I think about Sally before I go to sleep. I toss and turn, dreading tomorrow morning and the tub. At last, I fall into a horrible dream. Sally is giving me her small sly smile. And while she smiles, she pushes that long, pointy piece of glass up through her throat and into her mouth. She can still talk even with the glass piercing her tongue. She says, "I was ready to be done. Are you ready to come? I'm saving you a place."

How easily Sally slipped from this life to the next. There was no sign of terror or hopelessness in her eyes when she looked at me. She was at peace. And then I wake, screaming into the darkness.

And in the next moment, the screams of hundreds of my sisters join in.

At breakfast, Bertha is full of news once again. She waits until everyone around her is seated before she speaks. "Listen. If you wanna know somethin', you gotta listen up. If you wanna hear, you gotta shush." One by one, most of the women stop eating temporarily, while Bertha rocks back and forward, back and forward. Estra doesn't stop eating of course, but then, I doubt anybody that knows her would expect that she would.

Bertha continues. "There was another death in this very building yesterday. It was murder. There's no doubt about that. The second murder in a month, in this one building countin' Ronnie. Course Ronnie wasn't murdered IN this building. We all know that, but still, she was *from* this building.

"You're gonna wanna know who it was that got murdered. Pretty sure none of you knew her anyway but you're gonna wanna know. Right? Just to know. The second violent death in this building. In just two days. That's a record." Bertha's eyes are huge. She glances around the dining room as she rocks. Her words somehow coincide loosely with the rhythm of her back and forth.

"Death, Death, We've got deaths right here at Oak Hall." Quietly, Bertha mimics the style of a carnival hawker. Lois, alone, still chases a lump of lukewarm oatmeal around her bowl with a spoon, uninterested in any news that Bertha is about to share.

"It was another Negro woman. Lived upstairs, she did. Two floors up. Somebody held a pillow over her face till she stopped breathin'. That's what they figured anyway. That's what I heard. She could not ha' done that to herself, chained to the wall like she was. Don't that beat all? Two Negroes dead on the same day. The Negroes are dyin'. Can't say why that'd be, but they are."

The bottom drops out of my stomach and now it lies quivering on the floor. Oh my poor dear Sally! Sacrificing her life to release her mother from misery. That must be the deepest kind of love.

"My mama ain' gon' suffe' much longer," she told me. Her words echo in my head. "My mama gonna be a' peace a' last. When de Lord come 'n gathe'er up 'n 'is bosom an' 'e take her t' heaven, then she gonna have somethin' t' smile about."

I can't stomach the thought of food right now, and so I offer Estra as much of mine as she can sneak down her throat. And I weep silently at the table, hopeful that Sally and her mother are together at last, and that they're both smiling today.

12

COUGHLIN

October 29, 1948

On a golden October day, Arvid came home for dinner at 11:30 leading the pair of Belgians, Bess and Babe in their harness. He took them through the gate into the empty barnyard and told his two helpers to head on into the house for dinner. Arvid disconnected the driving reins and hooked them onto the back of the barnyard fence where Babe wouldn't be tempted to nip at the leather. He trusted that the pair of workhorses would not roll in the dirt while in harness.

Babe and Bess were the same team of horses trained by his father more than fifteen years ago. A steady, calm pair of animals. He could see the day coming when he'd probably have a tractor, but he'd sure miss these sweet-natured horses.

As was only proper, Arvid's helpers came home with him for dinner. Martin of course, but on this day, Martin's father, Nels, as well. Nels must be going on eighty years old, Arvid guessed.

Nels had told him, "Oh ya, I'm glad to back up my son's employer. It's good to see dat Martin gets a chance to work, earn a little money you know, like other men." Arvid knew what he meant. Because Martin was "slow," a lot of farmers wouldn't hire him. Plus, he couldn't drive so whoever hired him would likely have to go get him. Fortunately, Martin lived close by, so he could walk to and from Arvid's. Not withstanding the dawdling issue, it was a good arrangement.

Martin and Nels were already seated at the table with full plates, when Arvid opened the screen door. Before the door slammed shut behind him, his mother said, "You're going to get a phone call from Dr. Coughlin." So Arvid hurriedly fixed himself a plate of hotdish, green beans, Jell-O fruit salad and a slice of bread and butter. Dr. Coughlin hadn't called him before. It had to be important.

As he ate, Marit relayed the conversation she'd had with Dr. Coughlin that morning.

"In case there was something important dat he told me; I'll tell you everything."

"Okay, Mom."

"He asked me if you were t' home and I said, 'Well, has something happened? Should I run out to get him? I know right where he is in de field," I said. But den he said, 'No, no. It's not an emeryency. Nothing bad has happened.' He yust wanted to catch you before you went outside to work at...'whatever farmers do in October,' he said." She smiled. "And den, he said dat we'd prob'ly already figured out dat he doesn't know too much about what dairy farmers do outside. So, I said, 'Well, dat's okay, den. We will stick with de farming if you will take good care of our Caroline.' And he said that, ya, he thought dat was a good idea to do it dat way, too."

Arvid smiled at his plate as he chewed.

"He has a nice laugh, I think. So, den he wants to know do I have any idea when he might catch you at home? And I told him he should call at noon. 'He won't be inside for long, though,' I said. Course I knew very well dat you would wait here all afternoon for de phone call if it was something important about Caroline."

"That was good of you, Mom. Thanks." Arvid swallowed the last of his milk and sat back in his chair to wait. He folded his hands, twiddling his thumbs.

The phone rang at twelve o' clock. Arvid picked up the receiver on the first ring.

"Mr. Fjeld, hello, it's Dr. Coughlin in Rochester."

"Yes Doctor. What is it? How is Caroline?"

"Well, her hydrotherapy is coming along. Responding as well as we could hope. Nothing to be concerned about there." Dr. Coughlin took a deep breath. "No, the reason for my call is something else entirely."

"Excuse me doctor. Would you hold on for just a moment." Arvid's tone of voice changed, then. Became deeper, more authoritative.

"Mrs. Bjergum, would you hang up your phone, please? I'd like to have a private conversation." There was a click on the line. Arvid muttered, "Nosey woman."

"Okay, what is it?" Arvid returned to the doctor again and shared a look with his mother that said, "Eavesdroppers, ugh." Meanwhile Martin helped himself to another couple of spoonsful of hotdish.

"I found Caroline's family. Her grandparents, I mean. This may come as a bit of a surprise to you, Mr. Fjeld. Are you ready to hear the details? Do you have a chair nearby?"

"No but go ahead. I'm ready."

"I found the Doucette Portrait Studio. It's in Brooklyn, New York! Still in operation by the son of the original owner, who is living as well. I described the portrait as you described it to me, the very young woman and her daughter, dressed in their fine winter coats and hats, taken somewhere around 1933 or thereabouts."

Arvid belatedly uttered a response, "Really?" His face grew hot. Eyes Wide. "Brooklyn?"

"The man said that the number of people requesting portraits had dwindled in those years. It was the Depression, of course and well, it turns out the old man actually remembers the request to take the portrait of the young mother and daughter in their 'best winter finery.'"

"Good Lord," he burst out. Arvid's brain finally caught up with the surprising news that as a child, Caroline had been in New York!

"I asked whether the studio kept record of payments from back then. Was it possible that they might be able to identify the woman in the portrait for us? And the son said, 'Oh, my father was a fastidious record-keeper, but I don't need the records to tell you who it was.' He said that his father knows the young woman's father personally. They are acquaintances. And then, without me asking anything further, this man volunteered the story that his father told him. Are you doing alright so far, Mr. Fjeld?"

"Yes, just a moment." Arvid dropped his earpiece so that he could take the few steps he needed to grab a stool away from the counter. He returned to the phone. "I'm listening," he said, sitting down.

"He told me that Vanessa D' Bouvier, Caroline's mother, was married when she was only sixteen years old to a man from one of the wealthiest families on Long Island, New York. Alistair Charlton Lincoln Westerham III, the name you already know.

"Soon after the marriage, there was a baby, a few months old already, that was presented as being the child of Vanessa's cousin who had died of pneumonia in Ohio. And Vanessa and her husband announced shortly after marriage that they were adopting her cousin's orphaned baby. Now, Mr. Doucette said that as far as he knew, anyhow, no one actually believed that story. They were very polite about it, though. The D' Bouviers were well-respected people. Vanessa's father did a lot of pro bono legal work and well, it seems that nobody wanted to embarrass him or his family." Dr. Coughlin cleared his throat.

"He told me that Vanessa disappeared with her little girl, just the two of them. He thought it was soon after that portrait was taken so, somewhere around 1933. Some years later, Vanessa's father confided in the elder Mr. Doucette, who'd become a friend, by then. He told him that he sorely regretted having forced his daughter to marry the man.

"He said that when his daughter turned up pregnant at fifteen, that was what people did back then. He realized later that his daughter was very unhappy in the marriage, though. In fact, she told him before the wedding that she didn't want to marry him, that he wasn't a good man. But he was devastated knowing that his beloved daughter would not be able to live the life they'd dreamed she would enjoy. She'd wanted to go to college, pretty unusual for a woman in those days. He confessed that he wasn't really listening to what Vanessa was telling him until it was too late. And regretted it ever since. Are you still doing okay, Mr. Fjeld?"

"Yes...yes...go ahead...continue." Arvid could see his mother trying to read his face.

"Well, Vanessa and her child were rarely allowed to visit Vanessa's parents in Brooklyn, where she grew up. Her parents had to travel out to Long Island, to the Westerham 'castle'—that's what people called it—to see their daughter and granddaughter. Vanessa's father said that it felt kind of like his daughter and granddaughter were prisoners in that huge place.

"After Vanessa disappeared, the Westerhams hired a team of private investigators to look for Vanessa and Caroline. They had Missing Person posters distributed throughout the state of New York and New England, but there were no leads. When the two of them weren't found, Mr. D' Bouvier began to wonder if there wasn't a lot more to the story. Something sinister." Dr. Coughlin's voice lowered a little. "He feared that his daughter may have met with foul play.

"So, Mr. D' Bouvier went to see the Chief of Police for that part of Long Island where the Westerhams lived. He told him that there was something suspicious about his daughter's disappearance, and he was all but laughed out of the Department Chief's office. The Police Chief had a smirk on his face when he told him that he'd have a detective make a visit to the Westerham castle and have a conversation with Alistair III but to not expect much.

"When Mr. D' Bouvier returned later to follow up with the Police Chief, he was told that the Westerhams had waged a very comprehensive search and that he, the Police Chief, had no reason to suspect foul play. To mollify Vanessa's father, the Chief said, 'Look, if she had been afraid of her husband and had gotten away safely, then she was better off staying where she was, hidden from the Westerhams.' He wasn't going to authorize any man hours to look for a woman that didn't want to be found. And he told Vanessa's father that he would be wise to do the same.

"Her father asked, 'why do you say that?' The Police Chief told him that 'Alistair is suspicious of you, Mr. D' Bouvier. About what you might have done with her.' He told him, 'Look, Alistair has enough resources to throw at looking for his wife and daughter until hell freezes over.' He's not going to stand idly by while you send investigators to look for her. He told me that he has a tail on you right now and will have his people tail anyone you send out looking for her.

"The Police Chief supposedly then told him, 'if you truly believe that Alistair would harm your daughter, then isn't she safer to stay wherever she is now? Because if you find her, Alistair finds her, too.'

"So Mr. D' Bouvier resolved that he would have to live, just hoping that Vanessa and her daughter were safe and free and happy somewhere. They were never heard from again."

There was a substantial pause before Arvid spoke. "I am stunned. I...I don't know what to say."

Dr. Coughlin said, "It's an astonishing story to say the least. Of course, we won't say anything to Caroline about any of this. The purpose in seeking her family was only to learn whether there is a family history of mental illness."

The doctor's voice softened again. "Dr. Reynolds requests that I urge you to explore further. To learn, if possible, whether there is mental illness on either side. I don't know if there's—"

"Dr. Coughlin, I wouldn't have any idea how to go about something like that, and even if I did, I don't think I'd want to do it." Arvid surprised himself with his rudeness, but then decided that since it was entirely the truth, he was right to put it out there, frankly. No apologies.

Both men allowed a long pause to follow. Arvid broke the silence. "If I were to find out that there was mental illness on either side of the family, would that help you? Would it help you to understand Caroline? To do something different than what you are doing now?"

"Well, I can't say that it would, Mr. Fjeld." Dr. Coughlin sounded tentative. "Here is what I think. I think maybe...that if she would only talk...talk to me, perhaps we can learn what frightens her so. You see, I come from a line of thought that says that at least some mental illness may develop in response to real fears or trauma. If that is so, then the schizophrenia may serve a purpose. It may be shielding her from memories that are too horrible, too painful to face. Hearing this about Caroline's history makes me wonder now, even more, about this possibility.

"I believe that, in at least some cases, if those memories can be pulled out from the shadows, then the patient has a chance to combat the fears, the illness that is fueled by those memories. Do you see what I am saying?"

"Excuse me, but what you are saying now doesn't sound like what Dr. Reynolds was talking about in our conference. Do you disagree with his way of thinking?"

"You are very perceptive, Mr. Fjeld." Arvid could hear Dr. Coughlin take a deep breath. "In fact, not all doctors think alike about mental illness. But whether he is more correct, or whether I am, or whether neither of us are, I contend that no one can say with absolute certainty.

"Look, I wish that I could tell you everything about how the mind works...definitively. But I can't. We don't know everything. I would like her to talk with me." He paused for several seconds. "I hope that you are not upset with my being the one to have found out all this personal information."

"No, not about that. I don't even know what I am feeling at this moment." Arvid's head was spinning. "I'm not sure I can even think right now. Please forgive me, but my workers are here with me, waiting to get back out in the field. I'm gonna have to say goodbye for now. Thank you for calling. For telling me all of this... and not Caroline." He hung up without waiting for a goodbye.

"What was it, Arvid?" his mother asked, concern etched on her face.

"It's...it's...um...we'll talk about it later this evening, okay Mom?" Arvid gathered his helpers and the three men returned to the field with Babe and Bess.

Later that evening, after the milking was done and the girls were both asleep, Arvid began. "Alright, I wanna tell you what the doctor told me today."

"When your voice sounds like dat, I think I oughta sit down," Marit said, drying her hands on her apron.

"Ya, we probably should sit down for this."

They sat at the kitchen table in the pool of light from the kerosene lamp overhead. Arvid took a long, deep breath and began. He repeated what he'd learned that morning. As he spoke, it occurred to him that perhaps he'd been wrong in his thinking all along.

He'd always told himself that he was respecting Caroline's privacy, but now? The reality that his wife was probably holding back large pieces of her past...secrets that must be painful, with no one to share the weight of them? Privacy was one thing, but for his wife to have had to suffer alone with her memories, and with his blessing? Suddenly he felt ashamed of himself.

As the startling story unspooled from Arvid's mouth, his mother's face rearranged itself. Her eyes grew larger, her jaw became slack and her eyebrows frowned, then raised, and frowned again. As Arvid approached the story's conclusion, Marit at last found her voice. "Her mother yust disappeared with little Caroline?" She worked to catch up. "Nobody knew where they went?"

"No. Her mother *escaped* with Caroline. And the grandfather feared foul play." Arvid's voice dropped a few decibels and he leaned in closer to his mother. "Somethin' bad must have been goin' on there, Mom. And Caroline *must* have memories of that. She must! A seven or eight-year-old would remember things."

"Oh, mercy...ya, she would have to remember things at dat age."

"Dr. Coughlin asked me to find out more about the family. Well, it was actually Dr. Reynolds' request to find out if there's mental illness on either side of her family." He looked intently into his mother's eyes. "Well, I guess you heard me tell him that I'm not a detective...if Caroline's mother wanted nothin' to do with them, then what right do I have now, to go find them? I can't do somethin' like that behind Caroline's back. You wanna know what he said?"

Marit nodded her head slowly, as if she wasn't certain she did want to know.

"He said that even if we found out that there *was* mental illness, it wouldn't change anything about Caroline's treatment. But he did say that he thought it might be helpful if she would only talk to him about her past."

"Oh, my! Well, den, what's de use of looking for dirt about de family?"

Arvid shook his head at what he was about to say. "Plus," he took a deep breath, "I didn't tell you this before, but at the first conference, Dr. Reynolds said that it wouldn't be right for Caroline to have any more children." Arvid paused while his mother absorbed that statement. "I think that if we found out that there was somebody in Caroline's family that was mentally ill...I think that Dr. Reynolds would say that Caroline should be...sterilized!"

"Oh, no! No, dat can't be right, can it? They can't make a person do dat, can dey?" Marit's whisper conveyed horror. As well as anger.

"I don't know." He heard the timbre of his own voice waver, betraying the feelings that arose in him. He realized with his next four words just how panicked he was. "God I hope not!" Arvid bit his lip and worried his hands...letting them tell the story of the foreign world he'd fallen into. A world where the rules were mysterious if there were any rules at all.

"Dat yust can't be. I never heard such nonsense." Marit shook her head sternly, as if chastising a naughty child.

Arvid took another deep breath and let it out slowly. "Alright. I'm glad you agree with me. I'm closing the book on it."

"Ya, dat book is closed." Marit took a deep breath, matching Arvid's sigh of relief. "It's time for bed now. Let's yust put dat whole thing out of our minds." She stood and took Arvid's gaze with her. With uncharacteristic fearlessness, her arms akimbo, she announced. "Arvid, dat is *never* going to happen to *my* daughter-in-law. Not while I live and breathe."

Arvid followed his mother up the staircase in semi-darkness. She turned into her bedroom on the left and he turned to the right. As he expected, Sophie was sprawled across the large crib against the wall. One arm hung out between the slats on one side of the crib and a foot stuck out on the other. She slept as if she'd spent all of her energy to get it just right.

Arvid pulled the blanket over his daughter's sleeping form. His mother's words replayed in his head. 'Dat is *never* going to happen to my daughter-in-law. Not while I live and breathe.' His mother, ever the selfless, stalwart woman with gentle edges and a forgiving nature. But threaten one of her family? She became a brick wall. She'd stand nose to nose with Dr. Reynolds if it ever came to that. The image of his mother challenging the great doctor's authority was like an unexpected pillow of comfort as he lay his head down to sleep.

13

DOLLY

Caroline
November 18, 1948

I've tried to pretend I like the tub, like Marilyn said, and though I've pretended lots of things in my life, I'm not good at pretending that. Celia and Marilyn have done better than me. They're not brought down to the tubs anymore. I miss them desperately. I'd become accustomed to eating supper with them after each day of the hot and cold and hot. It was at least something to hold onto, just a little bit of time to talk together. The three of us. That was all I had to look forward to. But now, there's nothing. Sally is gone forever and now I don't have Celia and Marilyn either.

I smell deeply of the sweet-smelling pad each time when I'm put in the tub; I want to sleep for as long as possible. But when I awaken trussed up like a cold, wet mummy, each moment is an eternity. And then the hot, steaming blankets that make my body cry out, score and slice my body with knives of pain. I envision that when the blankets are removed, my hands and feet will have turned to bloody stumps. And without having even a little time with Marilyn and Celia afterward, there is only the interminable torture.

The next time that witch Big Alva comes for me, I'll be ready. I can't go into that hot tub and cook even one more time. I don't know how to escape it, but I have to, somehow. I wake up earlier now to be fully awake when she comes in to get me. Alva and the brawny man in white that carries me down to the tub if need be. The only thing I am certain about is that Alva wants to kill me. So I wake early to be alert.

I watch Lois having her grand mal seizure again just before dawn. The seizure looks just the same as it did yesterday and the day before that and every day since I've been here. It starts with the guttural groan, the clamp of her teeth and jaw rigid. Her head cranks hard to the right. Every vein in her neck straining. The eyes are open but unseeing. Her back is an arc over the sheets. She doesn't know that she is doing any of this, I am certain. She is someplace far away. I wonder if I might like it there.

I'm so lonely, I've taken to talking to her while she seizes. "Does it hurt a great deal, Lois?" I pause. I've also taken up chewing my nails on my red, chapped hands.

"Will you try to remember later, Lois? Afterward, I mean, will you remember that I talked to you? Can you try please?" Pause.

"Do you know the seizure's coming before it begins?" I pause to think about this. I am worrying away the cuticle on my left forefinger. It'll bleed soon, but I can't leave it alone.

"Is there anything inside you during the seizure? Or someone? Is it the Devil that's in there with you?" Pause. I think about the fact that I don't speak Ojibwe. Even if she could answer my questions, I wouldn't understand her answers. I sigh deeply, bereft. I want to be able to talk with Lois. I've looked into her eyes. There's someone in there.

Regardless of my inability to speak Ojibwe, I have one more question. "Lois, I want to know. Is God in there?"

I look away then and when I look back, the seizure has ended. Drool slips from between her lips. She is spent. I know that she won't be awake for another two hours at least. This time when she wakes up, maybe she'll talk to me. I wish. Maybe she knows something important. How I wish I could speak her language.

I try to recall what day of the week it is and uncover an unexpected jolt of relief. If I'm right, today is not a hydrotherapy day. Oh, thank you, God.

I sit between Estra and Ruthie at breakfast, as usual, while Lois sleeps off the grand mal. I hate my assigned place at the table. Estra is always too close, snugged against me, eyeing my food. Sometimes I do sneak food to her plate as I ask her to slide over a little. If she doesn't want to move away though, it's no use. It's like trying to make a dead cow stand up and walk. If the nurse catches me slipping her my food, she scolds me.

Estra is always done eating before anyone else. Estra is the efficient eating machine. I can't look at Ruthie, but I know she has not finished eating. She's always the last to finish, even when Lois eats with us at dinnertime or supper. Lois is clumsy with a spoon...and still it is Ruthie that is the last to finish eating.

I can hear the sound of Ruthie mashing the over-cooked creamed cereal, occasionally lumpy, into her mouth and when the sound becomes more like pulling a boot from the mud, it tells me that some of it has squeezed back out between her teeth and hare lip. I cannot bear the sound of her torturing her food any longer. The squishing, sucking, smacking sounds of masticated food being pushed in and out between widely spaced teeth.

Then, instead of getting her eating over and done with, she talks to Dolly, as if that filthy rag doll will suddenly be gifted with speech. She asks her, "Dolly, are you thtill hungry?" As usual, Dolly

131

has nothing to say for herself. If she would answer Ruthie just once, I would be so thrilled. I would be so much happier to sit beside her. Maybe I could tolerate the sounds of her eating. If only Dolly were a conversationalist.

At that moment, I have the best idea I've had in a while. Maybe ever! *Dolly will talk to me.* I feel twitchy. The fingers on both of my hands are tapping in rapid synchrony as my plate is removed. I will introduce myself to Dolly. Maybe I can get Ruthie to eat faster.

"Dolly," I begin, tilting my head in her direction without looking directly at her. "I notice that you are unusually quiet today. Is something bothering you?" Silence, of course. Ruthie stops with the smacking, squishing sounds that go along with her eating and I can tell she is looking at me. She moves Dolly over to her other arm, farther away from me.

"Oh, is that so?" I say, sympathetically to Dolly. "Well, I am sorry to hear that. It's very unpleasant to be under the weather, isn't it? And to be in need of a good, hot bath as well. Have you had one recently?" I allow a reasonable interlude before continuing. Nodding my head, I try to look thoughtful, carefully considering her situation.

"No? Well, I am not surprised to hear it. I hope I do not offend you by saying that your face is quite dirty. Yes, quite dirty indeed." From the corner of my eye, I glean that Ruthie's mouth is hanging open. That can only make the sight of her eating even worse than before, were I to take a good, hard look, which I do not intend to do.

Ruthie finally speaks. "Thee'th not talking to you."

"But she *does* talk to me. If it weren't for her, I would have no one to talk to at the table. Well, Estra talks to me of course, but I find Dolly's thoughts to be so...different and refreshing! How good of you to bring her to the table with you so that we can talk."

"Thee'th not talking to you. Thee only talkth to me." Ruthie spits when she talks.

"I am sorry, Ruthie, but I have to disagree. She was telling me just last night at supper how boring it is for her to sit at the table while you take so long to eat. What did you say, Dolly?" I cup my hand by my ear so that I can "hear" Dolly better.

"Oh, certainly. I am sure that you *do* know Ruthie better than anyone else. And if she says that she can't eat without you here at the table with us, well...I guess that's the way it has to be. It's too bad it's become so dull and tedious for you. Some things a person just has to endure, don't they?"

"You thtop talking to Dolly right now!" Bits of masticated food spray my left shoulder. I pretend to not notice. "Thee doethn't wanna talk to you. Thee thayth you're boring. *Thut Up.*" Ruthie's voice is loud, shrill.

"Excuse me, but I can't help it if she wants to talk to me. It would be rude of me not to answer." I put on my most sincere face while looking across the room. Two of the nurses in white are hurrying over and one signals to the male attendant to come as well.

Ruthie puts Dolly behind her on a chair. "*Thtop It Right Now. THUT UP!*" Ruthie screams. She stands up, knocking her chair over as she does. I ignore her growing tantrum.

"Ruthie, what seems to be the problem here?" Big Alva is closing in. She has a knack for being first on the scene for any brouhaha. Estra has scooted her bench farther away from Ruthie and me, her round eyes twinkling and a hint of a smile on her lips. The air is charged with tension as I skid my chair away from Ruthie as well.

Ruthie has reached the height of her tolerance. She strikes. She hammers food encrusted fists onto my head and torso. It's all I can do to keep from responding in kind. I put my arms up over my head and take only a few punches before Ruthie is restrained by the male attendant who surprises her from behind.

"Thee'th talking to Dolly. Thee'th not thuppothed to. Dolly would *never* thay bad thtuff about me. *Thee'th Lying. LIAR! LEAVE MY DOLLY ALONE!*" She is removed by the attendant.

Bertha, across the table is rocking as usual. She gives a look toward Estra with one eye that focuses on her and then the eye rolls in its socket. I resume eating, in peace.

"My, my, my. Ruthie really doesn't like you talking to Dolly," Estra says wide-eyed. "Know what? I thought it was funny!" She launches into giggles. Estra can talk all she likes. At least there are none of those squishing, sucking sounds of food squeezing in and out between her teeth. Whatever gets past Estra's lips is swallowed immediately.

I should feel guilty rather than pleased. But I *am* pleased that I've learned how to handle something so annoying. "You're smiling. Why 'r you smilin'?" Estra asks me. "Is it somethin' funny? Is it a joke? Will I like it?"

I pat her hand on the table. "No, I'm just thinking about how quiet it is at the breakfast table now. Quieter than usual, I mean. I like it this way."

"Hmmm." Estra looks puzzled. Then she grins at me, which makes her round cheeks expand even more. She reminds me of a chipmunk with cheeks stuffed full of nuts. "I know why. Cuz Dolly's not talking to you." Estra laughs and laughs. "She's not talking." She covers her mouth with her short stubby fingers and laughs even harder. Then she licks her fingers.

After breakfast, Estra and I and several others are herded to the Grand Hall. "Why do they call it a grand hall," I ask her on the way. "There's nothing grand about it."

She shrugs. "Maybe it's the staircase. Going up through the ceiling? Must be the staircase. Uh huh. Bet that's it. The staircase."

"But the stairs that go down underneath the staircase, down into the tunnels? Those are the opposite of grand. What if we were down there and Alva turned the lights off in the tunnels? We'd be in a black hole." I lean toward her to whisper the question.

"Why would Alva do that?" Estra shrinks from me. Her eyebrows rise nearly to her hairline, which to be quite frank, isn't all that far. Estra has a low forehead. Or maybe it's just that her face is exceptionally wide? Whatever. She's not bothered by it. I should probably try not to worry about her low forehead either.

"I wouldn't put it past her," I whisper back to her. "I think she enjoys frightening me."

In another minute, I hear. "Well, why will one wicked witch wanna watch women wail?" Estra grins at me and says it again. "Well, why will one wicked witch wanna watch women wail?" She likes the "w" words. There's a question mark on her face, waiting for my response.

I give it to her. "Yes, that's another example of alliteration. Good for you. But I'm serious. Alva hates me. I can feel it right here, over my eyes." I rub my forehead. Trying not to think about Estra's limited forehead. "I wouldn't be surprised if Alva was the murderer Ronnie found to kill her in the garden."

Estra's eyes go wide again and there are those eyebrows reaching for her hairline again.

Most days I'm assigned to one of the work buildings for a part of the day. There are big and small ones scattered across the grounds behind the five halls. The best thing about being assigned to one of them, though, is that Big Alva doesn't go out there.

The Grand Hall is an open area without furniture of any kind. It's in the center of Oak Hall between the East Wing and the West Wing. The other four brick behemoths, I am told, are all arranged in the same way.

When we reach the Grand Hall, Estra and I are assigned to fold the laundry from one of the huge laundry bins on wheels. Estra can't reach over the top so I have to pluck everything out of the bin for us to fold. While we work, I hear her mumble. She's trying to come up with another alliteration. It keeps her busy so I can think.

I think that Alva could be Ronnie's murderer. She looks the part. If I had to pick one person out of a crowd to be a murderer, I'd pick her. She doesn't smile and she shouldn't bother. Smiling doesn't suit her. Her eyes are steely holes beneath eyebrows that are two long caterpillars creeping across her head. She has dark hair sprouting on her chin and a little on her upper lip, too. I do worry about her. Is she actually a man? Hiding in a white dress? She has breasts but, really, how hard would it be to stuff the front of her dress with something? Maybe they're rags from the Rag Shop?

For a moment I'm distracted by the heavy snow coming down. Through the tall windows in the Grand Hall I can see that it is blowing sideways and drifting against the work buildings. Fields of frozen corn stubble and acres of vegetable gardens lie covered, asleep for the winter.

Dr. Coughlin walks by twice while we fold laundry. He acknowledges the women with a nod as he goes past, East Wing to West and later, from the West Wing to East. He's stopped to talk to me several times since I came here. He has a nice enough face. And he has all of his hair on his head. Somehow I find that comforting. One less thing to worry about.

While Estra mumbles, now trying out words beginning with "P" sounds, I work out a way to expose Alva for who she truly is. Or at the very least, a way to get her in trouble with the doctors, or that man in the suit, Shiny Shoes from the Administration Office.

I have the details worked out before we've finished folding laundry. I've been talking quietly to myself. Nobody's listening. I'm only one of many mumblers folding laundry. "Someone will need to fall down the stairs to the tunnel. That would be the most dramatic." I pick up a towel. Fold it the long way, then in half and fold it in half again. Grab another towel. "Or at the very least, maybe dump a pile of clean laundry down the stairs to the tunnels." I scan the women around me. "Vera! Vera will be the best one."

Vera is one of my sisters folding laundry too. She and her partner are working a bin by the stairs that lead to the tunnels. I've seen Vera when she's upset. She becomes a head-banger. She's tall and strong and easily riled. She doesn't adapt to changes in routine. I know this about her because I watch people, carefully. It's a benefit of paranoia. Vera also has a dent in her right forehead and a swath across her scalp where the hair grows askew. Estra says she had brain surgery long ago.

My plan is to do something to mess up Vera's routine, get her upset. Folding a sheet now. I have to get her so mad that she'll bang her head on the floor. But it's gotta be Alva's fault because she doesn't prevent it. We have to create some sort of commotion, so Alva has to come down to Grand Hall.

I stack the last of the sheets on top of a pile of towels. Estra and I are finished. We've emptied our laundry bin. "Now is my chance," I say quietly. I square my shoulders, stand tall and head toward Vera, toward the stairs to the tunnels. "Here we go," I whisper.

"Where you goin'?" Estra's voice is behind me.

"Never mind," I answer.

"Hi Vera," I begin. "Want me to help you with the rest of this laundry?" I can see my plan playing out before my eyes. I'll reach to grab a sheet away from Vera and I'll fold it badly and throw it back at her. She'll cuss and stamp her feet. She'll be mad and she'll scream. She'll bang her head. Alva will come running. I reach out to grab th–

"Hello, Caroline." Dr. Coughlin is at my elbow.

My hand drops to my side. "Hello Doctor." I turn to look at him. My plan to expose Alva dissolves into floating dust motes.

"I wonder if we might talk for a bit. The schedule has you going to the Rag Shop from here. Mind if I pull you away from that?"

I pause to think out loud. "The Rag Shop is good because Alva is not there...where would we talk? If it's close to Alva, I'd rather not, thank you."

Dr. Coughlin's expression doesn't change. "I was thinking we'd talk in the Sunny Room, off the solarium. It should be quiet there at this time of day. How does that sound to you? We'll leave the pair of doors wide open, if you like."

I weigh out everything. I've already asked him at least three times, how I came to be here, and he told me each time that when I remember it for myself, that's time enough for me to know. So that is no use. It's nice of him to not ask me about Alva, though. "I suppose that would be alright," I finally say.

"Very good, then." He actually smiles at me. "Let's walk there together."

"Okay." We walk back to the far end of the East Wing, the dining room on our right, dormitory on the left. Solarium straight ahead. The Sunny Room takes up the far-right corner of the East Wing. Dr. Coughlin hums quietly as we walk.

"What is that melody?" I finally ask.

"It's a Scott Joplin rag." He smiles and shakes his head at himself. Is he embarrassed? "I got the melody stuck in my head this morning and it's been there ever since." He's not humming anymore. "Does that happen to you sometimes?" He asks me with a brief glance. "Where you get something stuck in your head and it just doesn't want to move on out and live its life somewhere else?"

Is this a trick, I wonder? Trying to get inside my head again. Alva has told him things about me. I'll play along, but I'm no dummy. "I guess that has happened a few times."

I choose the chair closest to the door. It's the best one if I have to leave quickly. But then I have to ask, "But where are you going to sit?" I'll move if he wants this chair. I should have let him sit first. So that I can sit far away. There are enough chairs for eight people in here.

"I think I'll sit over here in the corner. I like being close to the windows. The snow is so beautiful coming down," he still looks pleasant.

"Yes." I agree. I scan the room carefully.

"The weatherman is predicting that the blizzard will continue until tomorrow for this and the surrounding counties. Early in the season for it, isn't it?"

"Yes," I agree again.

"May I ask how you are feeling about being with the other women, Caroline?"

"Fine. I've been in a nunnery before," I tell him.

He nods his head. "Yes...I understand that you see this place as a nunnery. I can see where there are similarities. It's a large brick structure as are many convents. And there are lots of people here that are dressed alike. In a convent, the nuns are all wearing habits, usually black, but sometimes white. And here the nurses are all wearing a sort of "uniform" too. The white dress and hat and shoes.." He paused. "What was the name of the nunnery where you stayed?"

"I don't remember. I was little." I bite the nails on my left hand.

"Were you alone there? Aside from the nuns, I mean. Was there a grown-up with you?"

"My mother was with me." I glance at him and quickly away.

"Ah, of course." He smiles warmly, as if I've given the correct answer.

"Is there anything else you can remember about the nunnery where you went with your mother? Like, where it was? What city it was in?"

"No, I'm not sure."

"Do you think that it was a large city? Did you see anything from the windows there?"

"Streets...sidewalks. A few trees. A golden dome...cars." I remember something else then. "There were streetcars!" I am surprised at myself. I don't think the nunnery would have been in Owatonna. I find a new hangnail on my thumb.

"Excellent." He clasps his hands and rests them on his knee. He waits for me to speak.

Instead I look out the windows. "It's coming down heavier now and it's blowing hard."

I dare to cross in front of Dr. Coughlin, to stand at the window so that I can see the blizzard's handiwork. I hug my shoulders. I feel the cold through the glass. "The snow is so thick that I can't even see the hills that are just over there," I say, more to myself than to the doctor. I pause. "Everything is shrouded in white. It's like a veil buffeted by the wind out there." I murmur to myself.

"Hmm. That is a lovely description," the doctor says quietly. "If I had to guess, I would say that you are someone that has enjoyed reading since childhood. Am I right, Caroline?"

I turn then to look at him. My eyes widen. "Yes, I had a whole library of books that I–" I interrupt myself. I frown. "But whatever happened to them? Where are they now? I haven't seen them in many years." I look back out at the snow coming down. I can feel a fat tear pooling in each eye. "Why did they take away my books? They were mine. I loved my books." I feel panicky. "They wanted to hurt me," I finish. "But..."

He waits for me. There's only the sound of the wind now, and the biting snow sweeping against the glass, in sideways gusts and swirls.

I feel stiff. I turn to look at the wall above the doctor's head. "No, they didn't take my books away from me." My words taste bitter in my mouth. I clench and unclench my fists.

"What happened to them, Caroline?"

"It was *me* that was taken away from *them*. Taken away from everything." I back away from the window then. Turning my head from side to side. Too bright. Too white. The snow is hiding things. I have to let it be. Leave it alone.

"What happened...that led to you being taken away from your books?"

"I have to go now, before it's too late." I run from the Sunny Room. I duck into the dormitory and crawl under the covers on my bed. In that enormous room of beds...only Lois and I lie here. Lois will soon awaken after her exhausting seizure while I hide from myself.

Rochester State H Pt:FJELD, Caroline DOB: 2/02/1926 Adm: 08/14/1948	
11/18/48 0930	Notified by RN that pt taunted her tablemate (R w/ harelip) at brkfst by pretending that (R's) doll talked to her. (R) physically attacked pt. No significant injury to this pt. Observed pt on laundry duty. Pt praised another pt for her use of alliteration! Pt agreed to meet alone with me in Sunny Room, door open. Pt believes she is in a nunnery. She stayed in one with her mother as a child for an unk period. Pt became distraught to recall being "taken away" from all her books as a child. Unable to talk about circumstances that led to that. Pt ran from room back to dormitory bed.
Impressions:	Pt is exceptionally bright. Afraid of her memories. She cleverly manipulated her situation at brkfst to get away from (R). Pt was apprehensive with me. Runs from her memories. Following————————HCghln, MD

Caroline
Sunday, November 21, 1948

It's Sunday morning. One of the nuns comes to find me in the solarium. There's a phone call for me. I am teaching Estra how to play backgammon. I don't know how I know this game, but I do. We've signed it out together. Apparently there's some question about whether Estra would attempt to eat the pieces, so, before I can go take the phone call, I have to return the game. I instinctively worry about the expense of the phone call.

"I have to bring the game back, Estra. I can't take my phone call until I do."

"But I can watch it. I will. Won't touch a thing. We can start where we left off."

The Games Closet Lady comes over. "I'll help you, Caroline. We have to put the game away if you're going to the phone."

"No, I can take care of it. I don't cheat." Estra declares with something like a pout.

"Estra, you know that's not allowed. Let go of the board." Games Closet Lady says tiredly. They've had this conversation before a time or two. With other games. Other game partners before me.

"Estra, please. I need to get to the phone. Calls are expensive," I plead.

"Big deal. What is money for?" she says. I shake my head.

I have learned that Estra really does not understand money. If I were to lay a five-dollar bill and a silver dollar in front of Estra, she can't tell me how much money is there. If she could choose between them, she would rather have the silver dollar. It's prettier. She would choose a quarter over a dime because it's bigger. She would choose a nickel over a dime for the same reason.

"They can just get some more from the bank," she adds, clutching the game board.

"Okay, Caroline. I'll let you go to take your phone call. Estra and I will work this out," Game Closet Lady says. Then more quietly, "Don't tell Alva I let you go before it's put away. I don't need the hassle."

I nod my head.

The other problem with telephone calls is that the phone is in Alva's office. Just past the kitchen. It's bad enough to be in Alva's office. Worse yet, if she remains in the room with me while I talk. I can't say anything with her there, listening. Arvid had a talk with her about that the last time he was here. He told me that he explained to her that I am a private person. Begged her to give me space to talk with him without her listening.

Alva holds the phone out to me when I get to her office. "It's your husband, Caroline." I shrink away from her touch. She does a 'tut-tut,' shakes her head and lays the phone down again and walks out. Only then do I pick up the phone.

"Hello?" I say cautiously.

"Caroline, my darling. How are you? I miss you so." It sounds like Arvid.

Where are you calling from?" I ask him.

"Where?" A long pause. "The farm. I'm calling from home." It still sounds like Arvid. He sounds sad. "Do you recognize my voice, Caroline?"

"I think so. It's Arvid?"

"Yes! Yes, it's me." I hear him draw a long, deep breath. "We aren't going to go to church this morning because the snow is still coming down. What a blizzard, huh? Reminds me of that winter when we were married. We had so much snow that winter. And it was so cold too, like now. Do you remember your first winter on the farm?"

My memory is foggy on the details, but I do remember that winter. "Yes, I remember."

"Well, since we're not going to church, I can talk a little longer. How about that?"

I can't think of anything to say. How about going to church? I haven't seen the inside of a church in a long time, it seems. That worries me. What will happen to me if I never go to church again?

Ever? That's where damnation comes in, I think. I'll think about that more later.

"Caroline, are you there?"

"Yes. I'm here." I hum a little, nothing musical. "I was playing backgammon."

"Really? I didn't know that you knew how to play backgammon."

"I do. I don't know how I know, but I do."

"Are you sleeping alright, Caroline?" Arvid's voice asks me.

"That's hard to say. Nights are...long." I decide that's enough of an answer.

Another deep breath through the phone. "Mine feel awfully long too. I miss you so much. I lie awake and think about you there, much of the night. Wishing you were home here with us."

There's a lot I could say. "I listen to the sisters breathing. A lot of them snore. Estra has nightmares. Others do, too. There's screaming sometimes. Ruthie whistles...when she sleeps, I mean. Lois' seizure comes before dawn. Nights are long...and busy."

Arvid makes a throat-clearing sound. A long pause. "My mother sends her love to you. She is taking good care of the chil—of Sophie. Sophie misses you. Do you want to talk to Sophie?"

I can hear a little child's voice in the background. "Ith it Mommy? Ith that Mommy? Daddy? Daddy? Ith it Mommy?" The voice moves farther away. "Grandma, Grandma...ith that Mommy? When'th Mommy coming home? Daddy let me talk to Mommy? How come?"

A soft woman's voice responds to her. A soothing voice. It's Marit, Sophie's grandma.

"What would I say to her?" I feel frightened suddenly, to speak to my own daughter. It feels like she is so far away. She belongs to another life. I'll never see her again. If I talk to her, I won't be able to bear it. I can't even think about her. "I can't talk to her. She should forget about me."

It sounds like a gasp through the phone line. "Oh, Caroline. No. She'll never forget about you. None of us will. We all love you so much." He sounds a little emotional. There's another long pause, while I chew my lip.

Alva stands at a station behind glass across the hallway. She's kept her eye on me this whole time. She left her office door wedged wide open so she can make sure that I'm not touching any of her things in here. As if I'd want to touch anything that belongs to her.

"Caroline, I have something to tell you. I've been hoping we'd have a winter without much snow. But you remember that first winter we were married? How I had so much snow to clear away just so I could get to the barn. So I could get the cattle out for water? Remember how that was?"

There's a good long pause. What can I say?

"It's starting out to be that kind of winter again. I am so sorry, but I can see that I'm not going to be able to come to see you this week like I'd planned."

Illustration 7: Arvid remembers winters with lots of snow.

"Oh," I say. He waits for me to say more so I oblige. "Yes, everything is covered with snow here, the animal barns, fields, the oak trees, the work buildings." I can't even think about the farm or what happens there. It's too far away from me. I'll never see it again. "So that's the way it is." I take a deep breath. "That's just the way it is now. Now and forever more. Amen." I feel disoriented.

I hear throat-clearing through the phone. A pause. I wait.

"I'll call you every Sunday, though," he says.

"Okay," I answer. I worry about the way that Alva is staring at me now. I have to get out of her office before she comes back. I hang up the phone without saying goodbye.

Rochester State H Pt:FJELD, Caroline DOB: 12/02/1926 Adm: 08/14/1948	
11/26/48 1130	Pt offered many reasons for hsb's failure to come visit last Sunday. "He called. It's going to be a bad winter." "I won't ever go back to the farm again." Pt having increase in nightmares. Affect flat today. Increased depression. Succumbing to hopelessness.
ORDER:	Encouraging pt to write. Provided her with notebook and dull pencil. Nursing to provide pt with her pencil during Solarium breaks.————————*HCghln MD*

Rochester State H Pt:FJELD, Caroline DOB: 12/02/1926 Adm: 08/14/1948	
12/01/48 0930	Pt declines to meet with me in Sunny Room today. "No, I'm tired. I want to lie down now." Managed to get pt to talk a few minutes in hallway. Asked pt for her thoughts on Hydro Rx. "It's okay." Asked what part she liked, if any? "Oh, I thought it was punishment. I've been bad so many times." Pt walked away. Pt's affect remains flat. Eyes dull. Face is drawn. Dress appears loose. Depression.
ORDER:	Nursing to weigh pt 1/wk. Ensure pt is seated at a reasonable distance from (R). Monitor quantity of food eaten. Cater to pt's food preference to extent possible. i.e. If she likes potatoes, but not the beans, offer extra potatoes———— *HCghln, MD*

14

CUTTIN' THINGS CLOSE

November 1948

From her first night on the farm, Leah slept in a cradle beside her grandma's bed. "It's de only reasonable thing to do, Arvid," Marit had said to him. "I should be de one to get up with de baby in de night. You ought to sleep, if you can. You work so hard during de day."

Arvid convinced his mother that Sophie's crib, at the very least, should be moved into his bedroom, in case she called out for her mommy in the night. "No sense in waking you or the baby when I can just as well get up with her. You can't do it all, Mom."

Rarely did Sophie wake from bad dreams, but when she did, Arvid slipped out of bed quickly to comfort her. He was often lying awake anyhow, listening to her breathe. The quiet of nighttime was when it was the hardest not to think about Caroline, and that he had left her alone in that cold, grim place in Rochester. He lay awake wondering how she was. Was she frightened? Did she think he'd abandoned her? Would she forgive him?

Without Caroline, it had been left to Marit to harvest the huge vegetable garden behind the farmhouse, as well as the smaller garden she had planted at Marit's Place, back when she'd assumed she'd be living there until late fall. Instead, she'd been saddled with two gardens to harvest, and enough vegetables to feed a bigger family than the one that now lived under the Fjeld roof.

The summer kitchen was the center of the hubbub from August into November. Marit canned quart after quart of tomatoes and green beans day after day, and then pints of peas, carrots, beets and turnips. Arvid picked the sweet corn and his mother spent hours slicing the corn off the cobs so that she could can what couldn't be eaten fresh. She picked acorn and Hubbard squash. Arvid dug up the onions and garlic and Marit stored those in a cool dry place in the cellar. She butchered the hens that weren't good egg layers anymore and cooked them until the meat fell off the bones. She canned the chicken meat in quart jars as well.

Bread baking was on Mondays and Thursdays and laundry on Tuesdays. Marit used the same hand wringer washing system on the back porch that she had used all the years that she was the lady of the farmhouse. While he was walking up to the house from the barn, Arvid saw his mother lugging the heavy baskets of wet clothes down the back steps and out to hang on the clothesline. As the weather grew colder, he knew that job was becoming more and more miserable.

Arvid's eyes grew wide when he took a good look at his mother's hands over breakfast.

"Mom! Look at those hands of yours! How rough and red they've become! Are you using that Corn Huskers Lotion before you go to bed?"

"Oh ya, I do dat. I don't want 'em to get too greasy though when it's time to feed Leah."

"Well, you can't skimp on it. I'll get a bigger bottle next time I go to town. Jeez, I wish the power lines had come out this far last summer. It would be so much easier now, if we had an electric washing machine and a dryer like the people in Spring Grove." Arvid was on a roll. "And Mom, you should lay down and rest when Sophie and Leah nap. Why don't you do that, okay?"

"Oh ya, I do sometimes," she said, but Arvid was skeptical. He worried too, that she would strain her back with all the heavy lifting. Even carrying the stacks of dry clothes from the clothesline back into the house was a chore. She scattered the stiff and cold diapers and garments around the front room to let them warm up near the heat of the wood stove. Afterward, when she didn't know he saw her, she stood and stretched carefully with a hand on one hip. He heard a small 'ngggh' sound as she did so, as if it hurt to stand up straight.

He worried deeply about his mother's health. And he agonized about Caroline. Was Caroline warming her cold hands and feet in Rochester? Arvid imagined what she might be doing at that precise moment a dozen times each day. Were all of the sisters doing jumping jacks together? The notion was almost...poignant.

A rvid's emotions felt raw and he chastised himself repeatedly. He felt his days spiraling downward with worry. He felt angry, helpless, and yet here was his mother who didn't bother to worry enough about her own health, so he had to worry for both of them. She worked long days, just as long as his own, maybe longer since she was up in the night with Leah, too. She tended two small children while at the same time, cooking, cleaning, doing laundry, baking bread and canning.

Arvid saw how his mother smoothly performed four tasks at the same time. She would go from stirring a pot on the stove, to changing Leah's diaper while teaching Sophie her colors using vegetables or whatever was at hand. Then she'd fold a few clothes before returning to the stove to stir the pot again. Meanwhile he saw himself accomplishing only one laborious task at a time, barn cleaning or milking or tending the horses or hogs.

More and more Arvid was questioning himself, questioning who he was and what was truly important. Why was he doing all that he did every day? When his father died, leaving him to work the farm, he was twenty-five, a single man devoted to carrying on the kind of farming that his father would have done himself. Back then, when he did a good day's work, he could feel his father's praises resting lightly on his shoulders.

But now, things were changed. Now he was thirty-three, married with a wife that may never return home again to share his future. Would he be living the life of a widower the rest of his days? A widower but with a wife that still lived? He had their two children to raise to adulthood, with or without their mother. His thrill and pride at fatherhood now bordered on something like hysteria.

Was he just as committed to the farm now as he'd been at twenty-five? Was it the same love for the land that got him out of bed every morning at five-thirty? Or was it panic? Decisions were feeling awkward, tenuous. Should he decrease his dairy herd? Or increase it? Should he raise more hogs? He confronted feelings of dread with any thoughts of farm improvement. Something that had before always been part of his thinking, his passion, his dream.

He lay in bed at night awake and feeling anxious. He worried about being worried. Worried about it showing. If he was wavering or growing uncertain, he certainly couldn't voice it aloud. He couldn't afford for his mother to hear that from him, for fear that it would undo her; the burden of this farm and his own little family would then be pushed onto her shoulders. A decent man would never do that to his mother.

'I am not a child,' he told himself over and over. He saw it as arrogance to believe that his life was not unfurling as it was supposed to. As if he'd been promised something different? A life that was better than this? Was he above suffering? God had certainly made no such promises to him. No, the depth of his anxiety had to be hidden away for fear that it might take on a life of its own. Become uncontrollable and devastate him beyond recovery.

And in all that anxiety, he recognized how entirely helpless he would be without his mother to help him. The knowledge of such neediness stirred an anger within him.

One day, the incessant worrying led Arvid to unexpectedly pull into Bear's driveway. He didn't know he was going to stop until he did. Inga made them coffee and then wisely busied herself in another part of the house. Arvid finally confided in Bear about at least one of things that was eating at him.

"A woman my mother's age shouldn't have to work so damn hard, Bear. But my mother gets no rest. And it boils down to who I chose for my wife, doesn't it? My mother will work herself into an early grave and it's because of me." He could feel his eyes squinting to slits.

"Let's take a walk," Bear said. They walked in silence down to the tall board fence by the barn. Bear's team of dapple grays sauntered over to collect some scratches behind their ears. Bear sighed deeply. "Arvid, you're not being fair to you or to your mother. And you know it."

"No, it is *not* fair to my mother. She's exhausted. She does everything Caroline was doing plus more, now with her gone."

"That's not what I meant, Arvid. Your mother is doing exactly what she wants to do. She would not have it any other way. You know that! And you," he produced a wry laugh, "you had the audacity to marry a woman that you love? Arvid!" Bear shook his head. "How can you fault yourself for that, for God's sake?"

"For God's sake? Ya, let's talk about God, shall we? Where is God in this? Here's my mother, prayin' every day...about everything!" Arvid clenched his mouth shut and shook his head. "What good is that? I can't do it, Bear! I don't see God in any of this. Is He up there laughin' at me? Punishing the people I love the most? Why? I don't know *this* God." He kicked the bottom board with his foot, hard. It didn't give.

Bear took a deep breath. "Look, I'm no pastor. You're angry at God. I'm sure not gonna tell you not to be. I don't know what all God is doin'. But I, myself, do not believe for one minute that He's laughing at you. Or punishing people. But there are some things that I *do* know for sure.

"I've known your mother since we were little. Your mother loves you, Arvid. The sun rose and set on you and your little brother. She couldn't give up doin' everything she's doin' for you and your girls any more 'n she could sprout wings and fly. You can't do anything to change that. And I also know that your mother gets comfort from God."

Bear paused and rested his hands on his hips. "Jeez, Arvid. If she can find comfort in the middle of all this, that's gotta be a good thing. I sure as hell don't understand why this had to happen to Caroline. I surely don't. It's a cryin' shame, is what it is. But loving Caroline can't have been a bad thing."

Arvid grabbed the top board of the fence, resting his forehead against the rough wood.

Bear continued cautiously. "I'm gonna say something that may sound brutal, but...here it is. I know that you're afraid she'll never come back. That she'll never be your wife again, like things were before. Well, what if you *are* right about that? Would you wish you'd never had those years together?" Bear stopped short when Arvid's head snapped upright.

"She was...IS the best thing I've ever done in my whole life." Arvid's eyes were red. From the headache behind them. From tears he was tired of holding back.

Bear thought carefully before adding quietly, "Well, that's the way it looks from where I'm standin' too."

In early November, as was his routine, Arvid slaughtered a hog and hung the carcass from a pulley suspended from one of the box elder tree limbs next to the summer kitchen. Each fall he'd sold at least a quarter of the butchered hog to a neighbor. A 275-pound hog was more meat than his family needed, considering they'd also have beef.

Last year he bagged a white-tail doe on the first day that deer-season opened. He didn't even have to walk far to do it. He just crawled up into the crotch of an ancient, sprawling box elder tree on the edge of the woods below the barn and waited for the deer to walk by. Within an hour he had his doe. It felt like cheating.

When he put the word out that he was selling a quarter hog, Bear was first to say he wanted to buy it. He'd never bought meat from Arvid before, but now with his hired help, Inga and her baby sharing the house with him, he wanted more food on hand.

After the blood was drained from the carcass, Arvid and Bernt cut the animal into pieces of manageable size and carried them into the summer kitchen. The pieces that would become hams and sausage and smoked bacon were taken to a man in Brownsville that had his own smokehouse, down by the Mississippi. Arvid bought smoked fish from the guy, too. As the dozens of jars of pork were canned, Arvid and Bear returned to the summer kitchen to carry them away. Some went to Bear's house, but more of them went into the Fjeld's cellar through the pair of outside cellar doors.

Canning was the women's domain. Or in this instance, the domain of a grandmother and one slip of a girl who'd never canned before that day. Together they minded the three children while they worked, although Sophie went along with her daddy to Brownsville to see the Mississippi River one day. Marit spent days in that summer kitchen with Inga, grinding meat, cooking the pork and canning it. Arvid yearned for the promised power lines to be installed out to the Ridge.

"How luxurious it will be to have meat for the winter, without all that cooking and canning," he remembered Caroline saying with longing just last spring. "And we can have pork ribs, too!" She'd been so excited to hear that the highline poles and electricity would finally come to Hawk Ridge within the next year. Would she be around to see it?

Hog butchering was the first opportunity that Marit and Arvid had to really get acquainted with Bear's helper, Inga, one-on-one. "She certainly is spunky," they both said that first evening after Marit had been working alongside her all day.

Arvid nodded his head and grinned to remember things she'd said.

"Did you hear her talking about de size of de hog and figuring how many pounds of meat we ought to be able to get from it? I never heard a young girl figure out something like dat." Marit shook her head with something close to awe.

"She's a worker, that's for sure. And she's smart. Listening to Bear talk, I don't think there's anything she doesn't know how to do outside on the farm. Her father must really miss her help." Arvid washed his hands and stood with his hands on his chair, while his mother spread the leftovers out on the table.

"No, I think you're right about dat. I don't think she knows quite so much about doin' housework, but den, she can learn dat, too." Marit filled their milk glasses.

"What do you think about her livin' in Bear's house, Mom? What do you hear people sayin'?"

Marit paused for a moment. "Oh, there's always some people dat are better yakkers dan thinkers. But...I know dat Bear is a good man. He's not going to take advantage of a young girl living under his roof. Anybody who knows Bear knows dat much. He's fair. She does a man's day of work; she'll get paid a man's wages. It sure is a different way for a young mother to live, but she's gotta take care of herself and her son, so..." Marit shrugged and left the rest hanging.

"And what do you think of *her*, Mom? Of Inga, as a person?" This was more pointed than just making conversation.

Marit looked at Arvid like she was searching for what was behind his eyes. "She looks to be happier dan I've ever seen dat girl, to tell de truth. I don't think she's had a very good life with those parents of hers." Marit shook her head. "I was glad dat her sister Anna, got away from dem by going to college. But Inga? She found a different way to get away. She's got gumption. There's more to dat girl dan meets de eye, Arvid. Dat's what I think."

Arvid spoke softly next, so as not to be overheard by Sophie in the dining room, playing "fort" under the big table. "I watched them together today, Bear and Inga. He teases her, kinda like she's a kid sister, but it's more tender than that. She smiles up at him, like they've got some special secret or somethin'...oh God, it made me miss Caroline so much. Some days, it's all I can do to stand up straight and walk.

"I'm afraid I've lost Caroline forever, Mom." He gripped the back of his chair and leaned hard over it, combatting the pressure that pulsed behind his eyes. This was no time for tears. Not with supper on the table and cows waiting to be milked.

"Oh now, Arvid." Marit took a deep breath and gently lay her hand on his bent back. "I know, Arvid. I know dat you miss her yust awful. But we can't think dat she's gone forever. We yust can't think like dat. I pray many times a day dat she'll be back here with us again. She'll come back to us. She will."

Marit scooped Leah up in one arm, "Until den, we yust have to keep going and take good care of dese little ones for her. Don't we? Ya?" Marit waited for her son to nod in agreement before calling Sophie to supper.

November 1948 to March 1949

The roads were closed for days after the first major blizzard dumped ten inches of snow on Hawk Ridge in late November. Arvid hadn't visited Caroline since then. Just before Christmas, a cold front moved down from Canada bringing another blizzard with it. That time, it came with less snow but high winds that kept the whole area in a total white-out for days.

Mid-January was dangerously cold. The weatherman advised against unnecessary travel for a week. On top of all that cold and snow, the heater in old Nellie finally gave up once and for all. If the heater in the pickup had worked better, Arvid might have driven that to Rochester to see Caroline but he certainly couldn't afford to freeze his hands and feet driving the pickup. And if he slid off the road, he'd freeze to death in short order.

Several folks on the Ridge were depending upon their horses again, those that still had them. Arvid pulled the old cutter out of the shed and put it into service for trips to church, when and if they occurred. The cutter held two adults and two small children comfortably. It would have been a tight squeeze with Caroline there, too. Arvid hated himself for that thought, as if it was a good thing she wasn't there, crowding them in the cutter.

Managing that amount of snow was a challenge for the county plows as well. Sometimes there was but a one-lane road all across Hawk Ridge. Cars or trucks meeting one another had to negotiate which vehicle would back up to the last driveway, to let the other car pass. When a vehicle met a horse-drawn rig, though, the horse always won out. There were a few instances of uncharacteristic testiness on the Ridge, followed by discussions between the men about the art of road negotiation. Discussions were brief because it was cold outside the church after Sunday services. The men seemed to be especially diplomatic, too, standing on church property.

Shoveling snow became an eternally exhausting nightmare. Arvid needed to maintain a path between the house and the barn, the barn and the stock tank and hog house. The stock tank was the only source of water for all the livestock through the winter. It was encased in a wooden shell of a hut lined with straw bales and sawdust to keep the water in the tank from freezing solid. He protected it like gold.

He didn't shovel paths down to the ground, just far enough to get down to where the snow was packed hard enough for walking. Hours of back-breaking work provided way too much time to wonder what Caroline was doing at any given moment. Was she thinking of him? Did she miss him? He remembered their last phone call. She'd sounded so small. So unlike the Caroline he knew.

"Is that you Arvid?" she'd said in a dull voice. It chilled him to the marrow.

Every job became harder than it would have been without several feet of snow on the ground. Cattle had to be watered twice each day. When it was warm enough, freezing or just above, they could be turned out of the barn to drink from the stock tank. Half of the herd at a time. While the first half were walking to the stock tank and butting heads, anxious to get their turn at the water, he'd clean out the first gutter and put down a bedding of fresh straw for the cows.

The hogs weren't as much work as the cows, but anytime there were young piglets, the hog house had to be kept heated, something which he never had to worry about in the cattle barn. Arvid stoked the brick oven in the hog house at least three times each day. He hauled wood from the woodshed down the hill on a sled and then stacked it all just inside the hog house door. He hauled enough wood to keep the oven going for the next twenty-four hours. Day after day. Then he'd slop the hogs, put down fresh straw and clean the one corner where the pigs defecated. Pigs were tidy in that way, at least one small thing to be thankful for.

In bitterly cold temperatures, however, he didn't dare turn the cows outside to drink. The fear was that their teats might become frostbitten. That had never happened on the Fjeld farm, but a couple farmers on the Ridge claimed that had happened to some of their cattle. So, instead of turning the cows out, he carried buckets of water to the barn from the stock tank. Trip after trip he made with his two five-gallon buckets. In spite of dangerously cold weather, he worked drenched in sweat. And after that, he still had the gutters to clean. Falling into bed at night, he was utterly exhausted with aching muscles on every part of his body. He would think about how Caroline would have massaged his sore muscles before they went to sleep, and how that would often lead to other intimacy. Sweet Caroline.

Without Caroline there to share life on the farm with him, to raise their daughters with him, he sometimes questioned his resolve. Was this all that life had to offer going forward?

By the first of March, traditionally the month with the heaviest snowfall, it was the sheer amount of snow that piled up in those wide ditches along the roadways that was remarkable. Arvid came back from taking Bess and the cutter to town and reported to his mother. "There's people stoppin' out on the road close to town, where the highline poles are. And they're havin' their pictures taken!"

"What?" Marit gave him a look that was a mixture of sweet remembrance and poignancy. Following a big blizzard in March of 1940, Arvid and his father had come home reporting the very same story. In a very old picture album was the grainy photograph from that day. It was that blizzard that spurred Adolf to buy a new car, Nellie. And it was shortly after that photograph that Adolf was dead.

"Ya, they're parkin' their car or their horse and sleigh on the plowed road, and then they climb way up onto the snowbank that's piled up in the ditch. It's like they're standin' on the edge of a snow canyon lookin' down at the horse or car down below."

"Well, den you oughta get someone to take your picture, too, next time you go to town."

"I s'pose I should, huh? Caroline would sure be surprised to see that much snow!"

Illustration 8: North of Spring Grove, March 1940

Arvid had established an easy way to let his mother know when he was going to be late for the noon meal. He'd step out of the barn, facing the house uphill, and wave his red hat. She'd be looking out the kitchen window by about a quarter to twelve and she'd wave back. The message conveyed was, "I'm fine but I'll be late. Please keep my dinner warm and don't worry."

There was one day in March, however, when things went wrong. Arvid was cleaning the gutters in the barn when a cow delivered her calf more quickly than expected. He finagled that slippery newborn to get him out in front of his mother so she could clean him up. Then, because of his slimy hands, he didn't want to reach into his coat to look at his pocket watch. Instead, he worked fast, and he guessed at the time. He guessed wrong.

When he finally approached the house, he saw his mother's back to him, pulling the kitchen storm door shut behind her. She was all bundled up. She wore her five-buckle boots, Adolf's old barn coat, a red paisley skaut (scarf), and a worn pair of lined leather choppers.

Sophie was there too, waiting. She'd outgrown her aqua snowsuit and with her warm clothes underneath it, the snowsuit looked ready to burst at the seams. With a red and white skaut tied over her nose and mouth, she apparently couldn't see her daddy approaching. She probably couldn't see anything at all, was what Arvid thought, and he started to smirk.

When Marit turned around, he saw that she also had Leah in her arms, all wrapped up like a Christmas package. For an instant, the three of them, unrecognizable by anyone but himself, brought a genuine smile to his lips. He started to snicker outright.

Though his boots squeaked on the hard-packed snow, he'd taken them by surprise. "Mom, what are you guys doin' out here?" Arvid's jovial voice met them just as she turned. And then he realized. "Oh, Mom, oh no...I am so sorry. You must have been so worried. I should have waved to tell you I would be late. I got my hands real dirty; I didn't want to put them in my coat to look at my watch...ooh Mom, I am *so* sorry." His voice pleaded for forgiveness.

A single tear escaped Marit's eye. "Arvid..." Before she said any more, she shook her head, straightened her face and found a wobbly smile. "We yust thought we'd come to see how Daddy was doing in de barn. Well, let's go in again, den. Are you hungry, Arvid?" Arvid knew what she had been imagining. It was impossible to think the same thing could happen twice, but still...

Arvid and his mother had reviewed every moment, every detail of that other time when it was Arvid's father that didn't come in from the barn at dinnertime. They'd shed tears together many times. The whole event played out in his head, like a grim silent movie. It was agonizingly slow, frame by frame. The silent movie even played the parts that he hadn't seen first-hand.

Some eight years ago it was, on a winter day much like this one. It was a Monday and there'd been a heavy snowfall the night before. Monday was Sales Barn Day in Spring Grove. The Sales Barn auctioned animals once each week come rain or shine or blizzard. The Fjelds had a bull calf to sell. Once Arvid and his father got the pickup free of a snowdrift and the bull calf inside the pickup box, Arvid's father sent him off to town.

After breakfast and after Arvid left, Adolf dressed to go back out to the barn again to water the cows and horses, and to clean the gutters before dinnertime. His mother had tried to talk Adolf into waiting until Arvid came back from town. It had been a comparatively warm day when the snow fell yesterday, and so it was heavy, wet and densely compacted snow.

"Oh, why don't you wait, Adolf," his mother had wheedled. "Sit and have another cup of coffee with me, why don't you? Arvid will be home in a few hours and den he can help you. There's an awful lot of heavy snow out there to shovel." Arvid knew what his father would have said. Once Adolf decided it was time to get a job done, he was anxious to get at it.

"Augh, a little bit of work never hurt anybody," he said to her, adding a shoulder shrug and a twinkle in his eye. It was a well-worn phrase that he'd used over the years. "I'll be back inside before dinnertime," he told her.

He didn't always do this, but that day, he gave Marit a peck on her cheek and a loving pat on her behind before heading out the door. His mother told Arvid every last detail of the morning, even that one. "He must have been feeling a little bit lovey-dovey," she'd told Arvid later with a tearful smile.

"You worry about me too much, Marit." Adolf winked at her. "Dat's how I know dat you still love dis old man." He opened the door, letting in a blast of cold air before he slipped through quickly and closed the door tightly behind him.

"Yust like I know you love me too, you silly man." she'd called after him. She wanted to believe that her words had escaped out the door with him, in time to be heard.

After a heavy snowfall, Arvid and his father usually waded together through the barnyard around to the back of the barn, carrying their snow shovels with them. Once they cleared away enough snow from the Dutch doors so that the cows and horses could exit the barn, then they cleaned the gutters in the barn together.

Arvid's mother went about her business in the house that morning, filling the wood stoves and cooking dinner. She looked out the window when Adolf wasn't in for dinner by noon. She thought it odd that she'd never caught sight of the cows walking back and forth between the stock tank and the barn, their heads bobbing agreeably. Maybe the snow had drifted so high now that they wouldn't have been visible from her window anymore. Only the deep imprints of booted feet heading toward the barn interrupted the blinding white of fresh snow at mid-day.

At twelve-thirty, she bundled up in her warm barn clothes and went out to check on her husband. Entering the barn, she was startled to see all the cows standing in their stanchions and the gutters were still full. That is when Marit found her husband lying on the concrete floor of the barn, "on dat dirty cattle walkway, as cold as ice."

Marit knelt by her husband's body. She stayed there next to him, tears leaking from her eyes, and asking him questions for which there were no answers. "What should I do now, without you, my Adolf?" Later she found that her shins were frostbitten.

Arvid found his mother there on the concrete walkway, kneeling beside his father after he came home from the sales barn sometime after one o'clock that afternoon.

Marit heard her son's footsteps entering the barn. She heard him call out before he saw her. "Mom? Oh my God, no. *Nooo.. Dad? Dad.* Oh, Dad why didn't you wait for me? *I* could have cleaned the barn. Oh God. No." Arvid cried and knelt beside his only living parent. He pulled off his leather choppers, and with his bare hands held them on his father's back.

Arvid's mother told him later that she'd wanted so badly to say something important and memorable to him as they kneeled over his father's body. What Arvid heard her say was, "Your father would not have wanted you to be left with dis memory of him in your head." Arvid remembered how the emotion caught in her throat then, so that she couldn't speak at all for a bit.

"He was only fifty-three years old, Arvid. He should have been around for you for many years yet. He loved you so much, Arvid. He was so proud of you. So proud of both his sons." Though the other son had been in the ground for twenty years, she'd included him in summing up her beloved husband's life. When she patted Arvid on his back as he lay over his father's cold body, he felt that he was receiving the blessing for both him and his younger brother, Erik, forever ten-years old.

Arvid at last rose on his knees. "Help me roll him over, Mom?"

Together they rolled him onto his back. They saw that he had unbuttoned his coat and reached inside. In unison, Arvid and his mother gasped to see the look of shock on Adolf's face, the bloody gash on the side of his head and the muck covering the front of his face and body. It was something that could not be forgotten.

That day that Arvid had been late for dinner, Marit waited for Sophie to run off to play before confessing, "I feel yust a little bit silly to have panicked so and dressed up de children to go to de barn with me. You are a young, strong, healthy man. Not a fifty-three-year-old man. There is no reason I should think dat is going to happen to you, Arvid."

"Things we're afraid of aren't always reasonable, are they?" Arvid reached across the table and felt oddly shy about patting her hand. His mother had always been first to offer comfort. Today it was the other way around.

Then Marit said something which Arvid had heard her say before when reflecting on the tragedies in her lifetime. "De Bible says dat God will not give you more dan you can handle, but I think He was cuttin' things pretty close for me a couple times."

The Fjelds often had more eggs than they could eat, so they sold a couple dozen each Sunday after church. That winter however, church was cancelled so many times that the surplus eggs were piling up.

"I'm sorry we're havin' eggs again, Arvid." His mother said apologetically when he came in for breakfast one morning.

"It's fine, Mom. I don't much care what I eat these days."

"Oh, Arvid, don't say dat. You got to eat a good breakfast. Whatever you want, I'll make dat for you."

"Mom!" He surprised himself with how sternly his voice came out. "I'm not complaining. Whatever you wanna make is just fine with me."

"Well, I'm yust trying to be helpful. You know dat, don't you?"

"Of course, I know that. It's just that it really doesn't matter to me. So, you don't need to apologize about it, alright?"

"Uff...I'll make whatever comes to mind, den, or whatever Sophie wants to eat."

Marit and Arvid ate breakfast in silence while Sophie chattered about her ragdoll that she thought would look nice wearing a winter coat. "Then she can go outside to play," Sophie reasoned.

Arvid responded as if he'd just been startled awake and he fairly boomed. "Sophie, Grandma doesn't have time for One. More. Thing. in her day." He immediately wished he'd have thought longer before speaking. Sophie's little face looked stunned. Her lower lip quivered.

"Oh, say now, Arvid." Marit frowned at him. Then she looked to Sophie, "we'll yust have to see what Grandma can do, Sophie. A coat makes sense in dis weather, doesn't it?"

Sophie sucked on her lower lip and looked carefully between her daddy and her grandma. She slid down off her chair and went to play in the little closet under the stairs.

When Arvid had finished his breakfast, he went to find Sophie and told her he was sorry he was crabby at breakfast. "Daddy is awful tired, I guess." He pulled Sophie onto his lap as he sat on the floor and asked her about what her dolly wants to play when she goes outside. He had hours of work ahead of him though before dinnertime and so he soon started to get up to go. But then he heard Leah cooing in the playpen and he just couldn't resist picking her up to play with her a little first, too.

Already six months old, Leah was a smiley and happy baby with thick dark curls. When he blew air out between his lips like a horse blowing chaff from his nose, he made a comical sound that he knew would make Leah laugh. And that in turn, made Arvid laugh. Then Leah blew bubbles between her lips and kicked excitedly, and the rest of the family giggled together. It was the highlight of the day as far as Arvid was concerned.

"I have the best two little girls a daddy could ever have, you know that, Sophie?" he chucked Sophie under the chin while he was holding Leah, bouncing her on his knee.

"You're funny, Daddy. You thaid that yethterday already. But I am pretty good for you, Grandma, aren't I?" Sophie looked earnestly, hopefully at her grandma's face.

"Uff ya, you sure are. Dat is de truth." She cupped Sophie's little cheeks in her hands. "Sophie is a big help to me. She runs upstairs for me to get clean diapers for Leah, don't you?" Marit looked at Arvid intently then, as if this one point was the very reason they were speaking to one another. "She is a very good helper. What would Grandma do without her?"

"And what would Daddy do without his girls?" Arvid put Leah back down again in the playpen and kissed the top of Sophie's head. He brushed his mother's cheek with a gentle kiss, then dressed for the barn and headed outside to care for the livestock, yet again.

15

AWAKE

Caroline

I know what she does, what she says. Big Alva sidles up to Dr. Coughlin. She whispers in his ear. "I'm on the lookout for evidence of paranoia." She stares at me. Inspecting me. Trying to probe inside my brain with her thick fingers. She's trying to get in. With her curled lip, she glares at me and says to him, "Caroline is sick. Sick. Sick. Sick." That's what she says when I'm not present. I see it on her face.

Dr. Coughlin talks to me. I ask him again why I'm in this prison; why can't I walk out the door? He says it's because the illness has a hold on me. The illness makes me afraid. But what illness? The illness that I'm afraid of people? I'm only afraid of the Evil in them. Evil isn't in all of them. How can that be illness? When there are people that want to hurt me, destroy me, I'm right to fear them. I can't give in. Dr. Coughlin tries but he doesn't understand.

Karla's bed sits empty a good long time before she comes. Things are better before she comes. Before Karla, I know how many of us are trapped here together. I count the beds. Beds on the inside wall. On the outside wall. Beds down the middle. Sixty-four of us. In one enormous, sickly-green room. Green paint that nobody else wanted. Give it to the crazies, the paint man must have said.

Six empty beds in the middle. That's what I counted before Karla. Somehow I can't count beds anymore. Because Karla sleeps in one of them. And all night, there's one foul-mouthed nurse, Winnie, that keeps her eyes on us. The nurse gets paid to be foul, but Karla does it without payment.

The first time I meet Karla, she walks by my bed and out of the blue, she stops to sneer at me. Never seen her before in my life and she sneers! She has bandages wrapped around her wrists. She carries them in front of her like she's proud of her suffering. And of her power. As if to say, "Look what I did. I'm not afraid to die. Not afraid of anything. Or anyone."

"Get out of my fuckin' way," she says to me with a growl. I'm not in her way. I take a step back anyway. I size her up. She sizes me up. Karla wants me to watch her. Watch *out* for her. To stay out of her way. Rage is the only thing that holds her together. Anger feeds her. If it fell away, she'd be nothing but dust. Things would fly out of her.

The sneer. A declaration of war. It's the Devil inside her. I hadn't seen the Devil in a while. Aside from Alva, of course. Now, here He is. He's found me. I don't want to feel afraid of Karla, but Karla is Evil. I *should* be paranoid about her, a skinny woman from a little town near Sioux Falls, South Dakota. Karla has hair the color of straw that'll go white in the sun, but she hasn't seen the sun in a while. Her skin is white, and her piercing blue eyes remind me of a snake, a rattler.

I'm at war with a rattler. I know because I've met one before.

Summer 1947

Arvid caught a rattler in a pitchfork. He stuck the pitchfork into a stack of straw and one of the three tines pierced a rattlesnake. He told me he dropped the fork and jumped back, then laughed at himself. The rattler was already trapped. When he came in for dinner, he told me about it. "I'm gonna bring a hatchet with me when I go back down to the barnyard, in case he's still alive. Do you care to see a rattler up close, Caroline?"

I did. "You think it's dead by now, though?"

"Maybe. But he can't move much regardless." I'd never seen a rattler, but now, living on the farm, I wanted to learn what they were all about. So, the three of us went, Arvid, Sophie and me. Four, if we count Teddy, the mutt with a Border Collie brain, as Arvid calls him.

"If you carry my hatchet," Arvid suggested, "I'll hoist Sophie up on my shoulders for a ride down there." We walked down to the stack of straw in the barnyard with the dog, Teddy at Arvid's heels. With Sophie on Arvid's shoulders, I didn't have to worry about her stepping in the cow pies.

The rattler was still alive. Acting as if the fork tine holding his body to the ground was meaningless. He hissed when he saw us and his rattles stood up, shaking, warning us away from him. He didn't know he was done for already.

Just like Karla doesn't know.

After Arvid cut off the snake's head and pulled out the pitchfork, the dog looked up at him, waiting for permission. Arvid just said, "Yep," and then Teddy took over.

Teddy shook that headless rattler for all he was worth, and suddenly, tiny snakes were flying through the air. I shrieked, grabbed Sophie and we headed toward the house. "Well, it was a mommy snake, after all," I tried to say as calmly as I could.

"Mommy thnake," Sophie repeated. "Teddy thook her." She made me laugh.

Later in the day, Teddy allowed Sophie to put her arms around his neck and hug him through that thick white fur.

Sophie likes her daddy to tell her Teddy stories. In them, Arvid speaks in Teddy's "voice" so that she can hear what Teddy is thinking. Teddy is always the hero because of his good behavior. He is polite when accepting treats, he stays close to home so that he doesn't get lost in the woods, and he leaves our bull alone because the bull is unpredictable; he can get crabby and dangerous very quickly. These are, of course, all the same lessons we teach Sophie.

I heard the first of the Teddy stories on the day I gave birth to Sophie. The story made me cry. Arvid had returned to the house mid-afternoon to check on me. He found me sitting listlessly at the table, with a dishpan full of clean water and a pile of dirty carrots from the garden waiting to be cleaned and cut.

He announced, "My darling wife, I'll tell you what. There's a bit of a breeze outside. Let's go sit in the shade and you can put your feet up. On me," he added. "I'll carry the pitcher of Kool-Aid and glasses. And you, hmmm..." and he looked me up and down with mock seriousness and shook his head a little. "You just carry yourself." He grinned sweetly at me.

"You don't dare stray too far from the house these days, do you," I said to him as I carefully maneuvered down the steps from the back porch, one at a time. I waddled across the grass and aimed my backside into a chair under the oak tree. I took a deep breath and melted into the chair.

"I am fortunate to have such an attentive husband." I gave him my hand and the best smile I could conjure on short notice. Smiling was a little challenging when I was so enormous.

Teddy was lying on the ground at Arvid's feet, resting. But when Teddy rested, he was still on high alert. His eyes were watching Arvid, so attentive. Waiting to be called to action.

"You know what?" I mused. "You and Teddy have an awful lot in common, you know that? I never noticed just how much before."

"What?" Arvid laughed. "I mean, Teddy's a good dog, but really?"

"Well, look how attentive he is." I explained. "He's just waiting to be needed. He's watching you all the time. Ready at a moments' notice. Like my husband." I smirked.

That preamble led to the first story. Arvid said, "Teddy's mother was a wild dog. One day, I heard an awful racket from down in the woods. Barking, growling, until suddenly...it was quiet. Well, I was curious, of course, so I walked down there to check things out. And there she was, Teddy's mother...lying dead. And nearby, a coyote, with a rip in his throat.

"Only this one pup was still alive, Caroline. His dead mother lay between him and the coyote. Guarded him with her life to the very end. That darn coyote must have had his eye on those pups. Probably just waitin' until the mother had to go look for food. When she came back...the poor thing. Finds all but one of her pups gone. And I almost didn't see this one. She'd pushed him as far back under the roots of a downed tree as she could."

"Ohhh...that is too horrible, Arvid. Please don't tell me such sad things when I'm pregnant. I just want to weep for the poor thing." And I did have tears coursing down my cheeks. "I'm emotional about everything these days."

March 7, 1949

When I next see Karla, she meets me as I carry my metal tray of food toward my table. Karla walks to intersect with my path, though it's out of her way to get to her assigned seat. I should have suspected. She sticks out her foot to trip me and I go down, my tray clattering to the floor and the food flying off the tray. I shriek. Creamed peas, mashed potatoes and gravy with something like meat in it, splatters across the floor.

Like dominoes, it goes. Another of the sisters slips in the slimy mess with her tray and falls backward. She screams. Her head hits the floor. Then another of the sisters trips over me. She screams and goes down on her hands and knees...her tray of food flying ahead of her.

I push myself up from the floor, in spite of a painful left wrist. On the floor somewhere, I've left behind a piece of my front tooth that broke off when it struck the raised edge of the tray. The pointed stump pierced my lower lip and my mouth has filled with blood. Between the three of us on the floor there is plenty of blood: from my mouth, from one of my sisters' heads and from the other's knees.

The last domino is Estra. She throws herself down in the middle of the food spatter to reach for the mashed potatoes, gravy and creamed peas.

I straighten my dress and aim my feet toward Karla. She is seated and innocently turns her head like she hasn't a clue what all the fuss is about. I might be the only one who knows what she's done, but that makes it even more important that I pick up the gauntlet she's thrown down.

When the Devil finds me, it is no use to try to hide. No time to withdraw. I have to confront Him. He cannot hide within that woman's body. And so, I walk to her, clutching the only piece of silverware we are allowed in this place, my spoon.

She sees me approach, but she doesn't see the spoon. I could have done so much more than I did if it was sharper. I want to destroy her. I want to cut her heart out. I have to settle for jamming that spoon into the soft space just above her collar bone at the base of her neck. Screaming at her, "EVIL!" With all the strength I can find, I push that spoon downward until the skin splits and the blood runs free.

Alva and another couple of the nurses in white come running. Momentarily confused, probably. Where to go first. Three sisters lying in blood on the floor. Two of them crying. Estra shoving food into her mouth. And me...jamming that spoon into Karla with rage. I draw the short straw.

Before anyone can stop us, Karla leaps up and strikes my hand away, dislodging the spoon from its nasty gouge. She wraps those slender white fingers of hers around my neck and squeezes. I wouldn't have guessed that skinny thing was that strong. It's the Evil One in her. She must not have lost much blood when she slit her wrists, is my fleeting thought.

Just as quickly, we are separated. A male attendant has rushed over from another ward. He drags me away from her, while Karla spits at me, and misses. I gloat over that. I've bested the Devil. I drew His blood and the next time we meet, *if* we meet again, the Devil will have more respect for me. I can be fearless, too.

The attendant holds me fast while Karla and the other two injured sisters on the floor are scooped up. They head for the tunnel. To go to the Medical Ward under the Administration Building. When they are well out of sight, the attendant holding onto me, steers me along with him in the same direction. Down the stairs to the tunnel. Surely he won't bring me to the same place where Karla was taken. Idiot.

"I'd have killed Karla if I could. Don't you know that?" But he is silent in return. When we get to the bottom of the stairs, to the tunnel, we turn left, not toward the infirmary. We walk past the Hydrotherapy Room. I smile about that. I hate that room, but I can't let on. And we go into a room with the sign that says, "Insulin Therapy."

I am propelled into the Insulin Therapy room and "invited", hah, to lie on the bed. To be certain that I accept the "invitation," the attendant places restraints on my wrists and attaches them to the bed on wheels.

"These are so that you don't harm yourself," he says, rather kindly. My eyes go wide.

Within minutes, that silver-haired one, Dr. Reynolds comes in, followed by a nurse I've never seen before, in a starched nurse's cap. So trim and proper. Her name tag says "Connie." The three of them confer in the corner. This looks very suspicious. Are they plotting something? Are they in on something with Karla? Wait. Is that what's going on? I listen carefully.

Dr. Reynolds is talking. "Who has the report on this patient? Did you see what happened, Fred?" So, the idiot's name is Fred. The doctor listens while Fred tries to piece the story together about what happened in the dining hall.

I wonder, does the doctor know that they've been putting me in one of those big tubs in that room next door? And that they wrap me up like a mummy so that I can't move. For hours? Using wet blankets? And then torture me with burning blankets?

Connie asks, "Do you want me to run for her records, Doctor?" Does Connie have designs on the doctor's affections? She seems more than ready to run.

"Yes, but you could wait a few minutes. I'd like you here while I talk with her first."

At last he approaches me. "We haven't seen you behave in this way before today, Caroline. That's your name, isn't it?" I glare at him.

Let him figure out my name. Or let Connie, since she's so smart. Behind the doctor I watch Connie to see if she is looking longingly at the doctor when his back is turned. Maybe she's one of those kinds of women. Loose. Wanton. You can dress her up in a starched hat, but you can't camouflage the character of a slut.

"What can you tell me about what happened upstairs, Caroline?"

My lips are sealed. I could tell you a lot, I'm thinking, but I don't think I will. There is something going on between you and that nurse. You're both wearing wedding rings, but that doesn't stop some people from cavorting. Oh, shameless! She's smitten with you. You pretend not to notice. You're having an affair, aren't you? I glare at him. He's reading my thoughts! How dare he!

Oh, my! Wait till I tell Estra about this. But if they're in cahoots over a secret love affair, what else might they be plotting together? Something to do with Karla? Karla was just at the infirmary with her slit wrists. They both know her. Why would they think that Karla is lily white in what happened today? "Oooh, Karla is a spy."

I didn't realize I'd blurted it out.

Dr. Reynolds looks like the Cheshire cat. "You believe that Karla is a spy? What makes you think that, Caroline? Did she say something to you of that nature today?"

Yes, I know all about *Alice in Wonderland* and the Cheshire cat. For all I know, he probably *is* the Cheshire cat when he's not here at the nunnery prison. And Connie might very well be Alice. They're playing a game together. "You want me to be the rabbit. To go down the tunnel so you can follow me. Capture...punish me. I know what's going on with you two," I hiss. "Shameless. And in a nunnery, too. May God forgive you your sins."

"What do you think is going on with us, Caroline?" Dr. Reynolds says, as if he is innocent and pure. Oh, butter won't melt in your mouth, will it? Shame. Shame. Shame on you.

Rochester State H Pt :FJELD, Caroline DOB: 2/02/1926 Adm: 08/14/1948	
3/07/49 1300	Nursing reports that pt had "violent outburst" in dining hall at noon. Genesis of event unclear. Pt fell prone to floor on brkfst tray, sprained L wrist, chipped front tooth with resulting laceration to lower lip. Pt then went to a seated pt, KM and stabbed her with spoon. Pt was in turn, briefly strangled by KM. Event concluded by intervention of nurse and attendant. Pt brought to Insulin Therapy Rm immediately after. No explanation of event was recovered from pt. This MD offered to assist with pt management in Insulin Therapy Room. Offer was declined by Dr. Reynolds. Pt is reported to have n e w paranoias. 'Hospital staff are plotting with KM' to harm her. Pt was restrained, placed in straitjacket and insulin administered per Dr. Reynolds Rx orders.
ORDER:	A marked decline in pt's mental/emotional status. Family notification of Injury/ Invasive Rx:Remains ON HOLD per Reynolds————*HCghln, MD*

Your secret is out. And I have nothing to say. Thinking, thinking. Something putrid is here, and my mouth tastes horrid. Did they bring cow manure in here? Is it the devil that stinks? Oh, it's the Evil inside her, isn't it? He was so bold. I see more than you think I do. My mouth is forced to blurt it out. "I see what it's all about. Karla and you and you," I lift my head in an attempt to nod in the direction of the doctor and the nurse. "I'm not fooled by you. Any of you. I'm watching you."

"Caroline, you seem distressed about whatever you think is happening here. I assure you there is nothing untoward going on. No attempts to trick you. I am concerned though about your state of mind. And I believe that we can help you. I'd like you just to relax here, and we will take good care of you."

"Relax?" I scream at him. He ignores me.

Dr. Reynolds becomes full of orders. "Connie, you may go pull her record now. Thank you." And he gets the other nurse's attention. "Peggy, prepare the standard insulin dosage for a 105-pound female, please. Fred let's get that straitjacket on. Then you can get going."

Dr. Reynolds turns back to me with a hint of a smile on his face. Oh, he is so self-satisfied, so smug, so licentious. And the nurse! Pretending that she stands before God blameless. "Shame on you, shame on all of you. You can't hide from God what you are."

I've been talking to myself, mostly, but some of the words slip out unbidden, in monotone. "Out with the chaff." And then, "Into the gutter where you belong. Out with the chaff." In another minute, I am driven to say, "Dirty. Dirty. Sly and Evil Cheshire cat."

"We are going to be treating you with Insulin Shock Therapy, Caroline. It's really quite a simple therapy. We know that when patients with diabetes don't have enough insulin in their systems, they have lots of problems with their thinking. They become confused and—"

"Evil," I burst out. "Dirty, dirty bastard," I shout at him. "Trickery!"

"—irrational, but when given insulin, things turn around quite nicely for them in short order. The same principle applies to schizophrenia. You are fortunate that we have the latest means to—" Fred released the wrist restraint and caught my hand to put that thing on me, the jacket with extra-long arms, even my painful arm, "to treat you in your current state of mind. Tomorrow—"

"Trickery. Sly cat," I spit out at him. "Shame, shame on you."

The doctor is not deterred, "—you will find that things are much clearer. You will be so much calmer. Your thinking will be more reasonable, and you will not feel like harming anyone. Won't that be a relief from all this anxiety and agitation?"

"Into the gutter..." Fred struggles to catch my hand to put into one of those sleeves. I'm not about to help. "Out with the chaff..." I pull my hand back out. "Trickery, it's trickery. Trickery trickery dock." Connie holds one hand firmly behind my back. "The mouse ran up—" Fred grabs the other hand again. Shoves it into the long sleeve. "—the clock. The clock struck down. Shame all around..." Fred and Connie conclude their work with my arms and the jacket with the long sleeves, and then tie something behind my back.

"We feel that this is the most appropriate treatment at this juncture. No worries. We will be watching very closely and taking good care of you. Fred, do you have the straitjacket secured? Then, you may go, and thank you for your help."

I scream, "No you don't. YOU...Licentious, evil, sinful," I hiss the words. "God sees you." I use my threatening voice.

166

But despite that, the doctor's face comes too close to me. There's something in his hand. Why is he so close? I feel a squeezing on my upper arm. "Get away from me!" I scream as loudly as I can. "Get away. Get *away* from me!" I strain against the restraints, the tendons in my neck stretching taut.

The doctor is pleased with himself, ignoring my pleas, as if I'm nothing more troubling than a fly to be swatted away. It's a glass vial with a needle in the doctor's hand. A second later there's a prick in my arm and he pushes the plunger down. "What are you doing to me?" I cry out. But he only massages my arm for a moment and walks out of my sight.

I see the frame on the wall around the picture of a man who thinks he's important. His name is in large letters, "Manfred Sakel" and below that it reads:

"Austrian-American Psychiatrist and Developer of Insulin Shock Therapy in 1927. Manfred Sakel discovered that insulin-induced coma and convulsions produce changes in the mental state of schizophrenics and opium addicts."

"What has he done to me?" I call out to the nurse that remains standing nearby. "Has he killed me?" She's watching me intently, but she doesn't answer me. Yet, she has soft eyes. Rather sad eyes. Maybe she will help me. Suddenly, I go wet and clammy. I can't catch my breath.

Tears pulse from my brain. "This is wrong. You know this is wrong. He can't just put something into my body. Is it poison? Can you save me?" Then I whisper to her although the doctor may very well still be in the room with us. "Tell somebody." I whisper. "Please, please. Tell somebody right away what he's done to me. He's murdered me."

Just before the room goes dark around me and I slip into the void, I hear the doctor's voice again. "I'm going to put the next two new patients into coma and then I've got a critical meeting with the Department of Hea...should inform me...out of the ordinary...I don't want...interrupted unless...emergency. You...three can handle eight... one time. Alright then." The voice moves a little away. "...this...will respond nicely..."

Every muscle of my body is flayed, pummeled by wild psychedelic horses with flaming nostrils to escape my fragile head. Each hair on my head screeches, twists around my bones. I am squeezed into a tattered ball of severed limbs. I drown in a black and stinking swamp. Before I am spit out into the deepest hole, every color that exists explodes in a halo around my brain and crushes me, takes my breath. The air is thin. I cannot breathe. Is this rebirth?

Is this what Bertha was talking about? And Sally? Things worse than death? Or is this my own death? Is it this doctor that murdered Ronnie in the garden?

Rochester State H Pt: FJELD, Caroline DOB: 12/02/1926 Adm: 08/14/1948	
3/07/49 1730	Checking on pt status at Insulin Therapy. Pt's breathing is rapid, shallow. BP depressed. Oxygenation lower than allowed per protocol per Nurse Mgr. She (Peggy) has called in additional staffing to ensure 1:1 nursing with this pt. Pt displays no sign of emerging from coma. Coma duration now 5 1/2 hours. Anoxia?
Impressions:	Heightened risk of cognition loss.
ORDER:	**Nursing to notify Reynolds of continuing coma. STAT.** ————*HCghln, MD*
3/07/49 1920	Pt remains in coma with 1:1 nursing. Respirations and BP remain depressed. Reynolds has entered orders attempting to improve vitals. Unsuccessful as of this writing. Family not yet notified of pt's status. This MD has requested permission to notify pt's hsb of Injury and Intervention. However, Reynolds', Chief of Psychiatry has ordered, *Family is not to be notified until pt emerges from coma OR the patient has expired.*
ORDER:	**Nursing to notify this MD when pt regains consciousness.** ————*HCghln, MD*

Caroline
Tuesday March 8, 1949

Time means nothing. I wait in a dark room that stands between waking and death. Perhaps I am alive, perhaps in limbo, and God is pondering my fate. My eyes won't open but my ears are open...the sound of women talking quietly.

"She's been under far too long. Have you had any patients that came back after this long, Peggy?"

"Yes, but only one that was ever right again. Scared the hell out of me, all three of them, just like this one. I don't know why that one made it back and was normal again. The other two...and these happened a while back now...the others were, you know, simpletons afterward. I'll never forget them. They didn't talk right. Uncoordinated. Couldn't remember how to dress or hold a spoon. Drooled. They both died within the year of pneumonia. They were aspirating their food."

The woman's voice goes quieter. "This is not to go beyond these walls, but I knew that the doctor shouldn't have put her into a coma with that dose. I had a feeling we should have played it safe and gone with a meagre dose her first time, but you can't tell doctors anything."

"No, you can't. And that's a fact." I hear a sound like two or three women going "tsk tsk." Someone has put something around my arm. It goes tight and tighter. They're checking my blood pressure. "Her BP is coming up! Oh, thank god."

"What is it now, Connie?"

"It's up to 85 over 50. Oh, thank you thank you God!" Someone is leaning over my body, her head and arms resting on my torso, quivering. She's crying!

Sometime later, my eyelids flutter open and the sun is shining brightly through the same window as if no time at all has passed. Or is it an entire day that has passed while I was...gone?

"She's waking up," I hear a woman say. She's sounds happy, excited.

There are two nurses in the room with me, Connie and another, older nurse that I don't think I know. They have starched white caps. Business-like. They look worried or maybe they're tired, with dark circles under their eyes when I can focus long enough to clearly see the one that hovers over me.

My eyes roll in their sockets; they don't want to work as a pair. Things look and feel strange. Out of focus? Blurry along the edges? I lick my lips. They're so dry. I'm parched. My mouth has been open for a long time.

One nurse touches my damp forehead. One reads off my blood pressure numbers and the other writes it down. They sigh together. They think aloud with each other, it seems. I have an IV in my left arm, that arm having been removed from the strait jacket at some point. My arm isn't free, however. My wrist is tied to the bed.

"Okay, you can go to breakfast now. I'll stay with her," the nurse I don't know says.

"Thanks Peggy, I'm famished. And I could use a little sleep." Connie sounds relieved. The door latches behind her.

Rochester State H Pt: FJELD, Caroline DOB: 12/02/1926 Adm: 08/14/1948	
03/08/49 0745	Pt slowly emerging from coma per Peggy, Nurse Mgr. Pt attempting to speak.
ORDER:	**Nurse Mgr. to notify this MD when pt is lucid.**
	Family Notification of Injury/Invasive Rx still ON HOLD, per Reynolds.————*HCghln,MD*

Caroline
Tuesday afternoon, March 8, 1949

My head is heavy, stuffed with wet cotton. It's so thick inside. My thoughts stick like honey. My muscles need to stretch, but I can't because of the restraints on one arm and both legs. I am certain about only one thing—I have not moved from this same spot for a long time because my tailbone is tender, and my heels feel sore. Even my shoulder blades. For having been asleep, or maybe dead for a long time, I'm not rested. I'm exhausted. Can I go back to sleep again? Maybe I'll feel better next time I wake up.

Despite my fatigue, I can't sleep. My stomach is roiling. Am I going to throw up? But I can't move enough to vomit away from myself. A gurgling sound as well. Maybe I need to use the water closet? What do I need? It's hard to tell. Something. I need something. What is it?

I'm wet beneath my bottom. Wet? Urine? Oh my God. I can feel it. I'm wearing a diaper! Like a baby, they've diapered me! A diaper! I am incensed. Humiliated. Angry. How could they have done this to me? Why did they do this to me? I'm going to talk, to tell them they can't treat me like this. Arvid will not allow it. Will he? Where is Arvid? I haven't seen him for so long.

"Ahhhh...eee..." is what I say. That's not right. That's not what I mean to say. "Ahhhh...eee..." That's maybe a little better. One word. "I". Next word. "doooonnnn..." I have to try harder. That didn't sound right. "dooooonnnmmm..." Keep going. I'm not even sure that the woman is listening. "waaaaaaahhhnn..." There. Three words. Is she paying attention to me? "dddddth...shhh."

"Good morning, Caroline. I'm Nurse Peggy. Do you remember me?"

I squint and then raise my eyebrows at her.

"How are you feeling? Can you tell me?" Peggy hasn't understood that I said, 'I don't want this.'

Gotta try harder. "Leeeh...maah...gooo." My tongue won't work right. I turn my head.

"You have been in a coma for some time now. Since yesterday morning. Do you understand the word, 'coma,' Caroline?"

"Yeeeeeehh..." Does she think I'm an imbecile? Of course, I know the word 'coma.'

"You've had us nurses quite worried through the night." I think that's a smile on her face. "You are coming out of the coma now. You probably feel rather peculiar yet, but that will pass. When you're able to talk better we'll talk. For now, just know that we're taking good care of you. We've been keeping you hydrated through an IV, this tube right here, in your arm. And we've diapered you, of course, because you weren't able to get up to use the restroom, but we'll take that off when you're entirely awake."

She goes on, "We've been monitoring your vital signs since yesterday afternoon to make sure you don't stop breathing. And we've kept an eye on your heart rate and your blood pressure. Nothing to worry about now though, Caroline. We're so glad to see you waking up." Peggy pats my leg and smiles at me like I'm a frightened child that she wants to comfort.

I'm not a frightened child, I scream at her in my head, but my tongue is thick. I'm a frightened grown woman. Will she take pity on me? Can she protect me from Doctor Reynolds? What has he done to me for a whole day? Why would I have stopped breathing? That needle he put in my arm? It's Dr. Reynolds that wants to hurt me. Ronnie's murderer. Murderer! I want to go home!

"Ho-o-o-o-o!" I scream as loudly as I can. "A-a-a-vi-i-i-i. HE-E-E-EP MEEE!

Rochester State H Pt: FJELD, Caroline DOB: 12/02/1926 Adm: 08/14/1948	
3/08/49 1500	Met pt at bedside. Reports KM purposely tripped her. "Devil uses KM to try to kill me. The doctor, too." Pt tearful. Pt's thinking is generally organized and goal-oriented, but for her belief that the devil is trying to kill her. "I want to go home. Can I talk to Arvid?" Pt is aware that she was in coma >24 hrs.
Impressions:	No obvious indications of anoxia, however we have no objective testing of pt's cognition prior to coma. Per spouse report, Pt is "very smart." Pt's fear of Reynolds is not unreasonable given the circumstances preceding the restraints and injection.
ORDER:	**Nursing to monitor pt and report to this MD re: any apparent changes in cognition or behavior since coma.** ————————*HCghln, MD*
3/09/49 0930	Per Reynolds' Treatment plan, pt to continue insulin coma Rx 5 days/week at full dose, 1 day at 1/2 dose and pt to rest on 7th day. KM remaining in Medical Unit for Rx of wound. Will assess whether pt and KM can safely cohabit dormitory. Following both this pt and KM.
ORDER:	**Nursing to notify this MD if there is exacerbation of pt distress.** **Family Notification of Pt Injury Pt status. Reynolds advises he will contact family today** ————————*HCghln, MD*

PART III

CREEKS RISIN'

"It is far harder to kill a phantom than a reality."

Virginia Woolf (1982 – 1941)
Modernist 20th Century English novelist

16

PHONE CALLS

Wednesday, March 9, 1949

A rvid told Bear that the weekly phone call to Rochester State Hospital to talk with Caroline was his Sunday morning "treat." When she sounded more or less like herself, it was indeed. But the truth was that she frequently was distracted and vague and then those minutes on the phone with her were like vinegar on a cut finger.

The telephone operator in Spring Grove was Elvina, and it was she that made the connections for Arvid to talk to his wife. Arvid knew that Elvina was keeping her friends and family in town informed about his Sunday morning phone calls. She had a well-deserved reputation for passing along interesting tidbits picked up on the job. Arvid didn't like it one bit, but he wasn't about to get on Elvina's bad side. She also had a reputation for turning spiteful if called to task. God forbid that one Sunday morning, the phone connections to the hospital were "somehow" jammed.

When the phone rang one morning in March, Arvid figured it was Bear. They'd talked about riding together to a farm sale over by Eitzen on Saturday. When he heard Dr. Reynold's voice on the line, however, his stomach dropped to his knees. It could only be bad news.

"It was time to initiate a more invasive method of treatment, Mr. Fjeld. Your wife's behavior warranted this change in treatment quite urgently. I am calling to notify you of the change and to answer any questions you might have." Dr. Reynolds' voice was clipped.

"What's happened? What behavior are you talking about?"

"Caroline had an acceleration of her psychosis two days ago." Dr. Reynolds briefly summarized the events surrounding Caroline's fall and the stabbing of another patient.

The horrible image of Caroline actually stabbing someone took his feet out from under him, stole his breath away. "I'd convinced myself that she'd never actually harm..." he began, when he interrupted himself. "Wait a minute, doctor. Please stand by."

Arvid switched to his gruffest voice. "I know there are people listening on this line. I will *not* continue until you hang up. All of you...And you should all be ashamed of yourselves." Click...click was heard on the line.

He waited another few seconds. Then...click.

Finally, Arvid was satisfied that he and the doctor were alone on the phone. He pulled himself to his feet. His mother had taken Sophie and Leah and gone upstairs.

"Caroline was injured too, you said?" Arvid questioned.

"Yes, she has bruising around her neck, a sprained wrist and she chipped one of her front teeth. The pointed tooth lacerated her lower lip. That should heal nicely. I wouldn't worry about that. But what you and I need to talk about now is the course of treatment we have instituted. We talked about Insulin Shock Therapy or Insulin Coma Therapy, when we met together in, what was it, early September? But you may have forgotten the details, or at any rate, have more questions now that we have gone forward with this method of treatment."

"Wait...wait...you said Insulin 'Shock' therapy? I don't remember you calling it that. It was just called Insulin Therapy. I made notes for myself, so I'd remember. We talked about so much, I had to write things down."

"I'm glad you did. Well, you might hear it called by any of those names. At any rate, "shock" refers to the physiologic shock caused by inducing a hypoglycemic coma. In short, we administer a large dose of insulin which lowers the patient's blood glucose enough to put the patient into a coma, producing a 'shock' if you will, to the patient's system."

Without waiting for Arvid to ask questions, he continued. "Dr. Coughlin and I have been reviewing Caroline's response to hydrotherapy. The hydrotherapy has been marginally helpful. But, now we are here, five months later, and your wife fits the criteria of patients that have been shown to be the best candidates for Insulin Coma Therapy. Just before this violent outburst, we had agreed in our weekly consultation that we should soon move ahead with the insulin treatment. Then, coincidentally, this event occurred two days ago, and so we went forward with it immediately. It IS the best option for her now."

Arvid's voice crawled through the muck to find some solid ground, "I'm confused. If she's such a good candidate, why didn't we do that in the first place? I don't understand."

"Well, there are some higher risks associated with insulin coma than with hydrotherapy, and so I made a calculated decision that it was safer to pursue hydrotherapy first."

"*What* risks with insulin shock...er...coma therapy?" Arvid's heart rate jumped.

"Risks include collapsed veins and after-shocks." Through the buzzing in Arvid's head he heard words here and there..."the possibility...aspiration...her own saliva...and...pneumonia... depression in breathing...blood pressure...irreversible coma... potential anoxia...brain injury...death...rest assured...we are...skilled professionals...not to worry."

"Oh. My. God!" he cried. "This is too much all at once. Doctor, I don't even really understand all that you've said." Arvid's throat tightened up. If the doctor had talked more slowly, Arvid might have understood it more readily, and if only he weren't so distracted by his own panic.

"Are you with me so far, Mr. Fjeld?" In spite of the question, Arvid could hear the eagerness in the doctor's voice to finish up the phone call.

"I don't know. My head is spinning. I'm not a doctor. I don't know how to think about all of this. What would you do if it was your wife? Would you put her in a coma?"

"If my wife fit the criteria, I would." It sounded as though the doctor was smiling, as if he'd heard Arvid say something silly. "My wife is actually older than the group with the best outcomes, so I probably wouldn't, but with Caroline? First of all, she's under thirty-years-old. She's had the psychosis for less than two years. Her symptoms came on quite suddenly as opposed to subtly developing over a long period of time.

"She's otherwise in good physical health. And from what I learned of her cognition and personality prior to the schizophrenia, from talking to you, she was a highly functioning young woman. She's the perfect candidate, Mr. Fjeld."

"So, how is this supposed to help her?"

"With insulin coma therapy, patients become less argumentative, less hostile, less aggressive. And I have high hopes that your wife's paranoia, her fears about the devil will dissipate. I would expect we'll see those...in time." Dr. Reynolds sounded so confident.

"What does 'in time' mean?" Arvid asked weakly.

"A course of treatment can be expected to be upwards of sixty treatments."

"Sixty? Over what period of time?" Arvid asked.

"Around two months give or take. Some patients respond more quickly than that."

"So, every single day, she's going to be put in a coma?" He could feel his heart pounding to escape his ribcage.

"The recommended course is five days per week at full dosage, the sixth day at half dosage. On the seventh day, she rests from the treatment. The actual period of coma will range from half an hour and up to two and one-half hours, with some variation, of course.

"We begin with insulin therapy early in the morning, no breakfast. Nurses monitor closely throughout." The doctor was back to rushing along with his explanation.

"I'm sorry, but I have to ask, why didn't you call me the day before yesterday, after this happened...after her first treatment? I mean, she's had *two* treatments by now, right? Or is it three?"

Dr. Reynolds allowed a few beats before answering. "Actually, only one treatment. Her first coma was longer, but all went well, after that. She came out of the coma yesterday afternoon. No ill aftereffects whatsoever. We'll resume treatments tomorrow morning."

"What?" Arvid screamed. He wanted to reach through the phone to shake the doctor. "In her first treatment she was in a coma for over a *day?"* His voice shook as he bellowed louder yet. "That seems like a pretty damn big problem to me! Oh my God, and you're just going to continue doing this for sixty days? Is that what you're telling me?"

Without waiting for a response, he continued, "So it didn't go very well the first time, but you'll figure it out eventually. You're just hoping she doesn't die in the meantime. Is that what you're saying to me? You didn't call yesterday because you didn't know if she'd come out of the coma alright or not!" Arvid's voice was a panicked howl before it broke. He gulped for a breath.

"Well, I wouldn't put it that way. We knew she would. Eventually." The doctor's voice was nauseatingly unruffled. "There was no point in worrying you unnecessarily; there was nothing you could have done to help. We wanted to be able to give you a good report and now we have. I urge you not to worry overly much. That same situation will not happen again, I assure you. We have learned her tolerance now. We can move forward with more confidence than before. I actually think you might allow yourself to be pleased at this point, Mr. Fjeld."

"Pleased? What if I tell you to stop? To not do this to her anymore?" Arvid shrieked into the phone just as he heard another 'click' indicating someone else on the party line had picked up their phone.

"Get off the line!" he roared. Click.

"Mr. Fjeld, I strongly urge you to resign yourself to this course of treatment. There is really no other option. It would be impossible to discharge your wife to your care without seeing the kind of improvement that this treatment can help to achieve. You asked me once if your wife would ever get out of the hospital. And I told you that I was hopeful that she would.

"My hope for her recovery, Mr. Fjeld, is born out of my experience with treating patients using all of the available reasonable treatments. Without pursuing this avenue, I cannot offer any hope of her returning home." Dr. Reynolds stopped talking. Allowed the silence between them to hang heavy on the line.

"What else can I do? I don't really have a choice, do I?" Arvid's voice lost its energy. "Alright," he acquiesced. With that, Arvid hung the earpiece back on the cradle and turned to an empty kitchen.

Arvid fell into his chair with his head in his hands. He didn't have a name for what he was experiencing...the hyperventilation and panic that flooded him. As the minutes passed, he worked at calming himself, slowing his pulse, his breathing. Tried to think about getting back outside to take care of the cattle, something familiar. Something he knew how to do.

Humiliation, helplessness and embarrassment filled his very being. His inability to protect his own wife had been illuminated and proven yet once again. And yet, for one clear moment, he envisioned a different, better world. In that world, he would swoop in to rescue Caroline and the world would make sense again. They were in love and happy to spend their days working to build their family and home together. Their lives in tandem shot out before them like the final rays of a sunset kissing the highest clouds, turning them golden and warm.

But there was no such world. In this, the real world, he had two little girls that depended upon him to keep them fed and safe, and they had a mother who believed their youngest was Evil itself, and he had cows to milk. If he neglected that, then all would be lost.

Friday, March 11, 1949

Arvid made the next phone call, and it was to the younger psychiatrist, Dr. Coughlin. He'd seemed kinder than Reynolds at that first conference. Still, Arvid fretted for two days before making the call. The change in routine must have startled the operator because Elvina felt compelled to comment to Arvid, "Oh my! It's only Friday. I hope there's nothing de matter."

Arvid simply cleared his throat and waited for Elvina to work on the connections as requested. Of course the doctor wasn't at his desk when the call went through, and so Arvid waited around in the kitchen for his return call.

"Yes, hello, Dr. Coughlin," Arvid said after the first ring.

"Oh, Mr. Fjeld, I do apologize. I should have called to tell you as soon as I knew." Dr. Coughlin must have rushed to the phone. He seemed out of breath. "You must be worried about how we're going to handle the situation between Caroline and the young woman that she had, ahh—shall we say, that difficult encounter with. You needn't worry. The young woman came to us from the far western part of Minnesota. When she needed placement, the hospital nearest her, St. Peter State Hospital, had no female beds available, so she came here. St. Peter now does have a bed for her, so she'll be transferred to St. Peter directly from our infirmary tomorrow."

"That *is* a relief. So, it's a relatively easy solution, then, to keep the two of them apart. And that other young woman will be closer to her own family now." Arvid's sense of responsibility about the woman's injury lessened a little then. He'd been experiencing what he thought of as Lutheran guilt by association, his association with his own wife. He allowed himself a sigh of relief.

"That's good then. Ummm...actually Doctor, that wasn't the reason for my call. It's something else."

"Oh? What is it?"

"Well, I can't stop thinking about what Dr. Reynolds told me. There are so many risks with the Insulin Shock Therapy but yet *he* says it's the only reasonable thing to do now. It weighs on me pretty hard. Every minute of the day. How am I supposed to get through two months of worry like this, every day? Will she still be herself... more or less, I mean, when she wakes up the next time? I need to know what you think. Please." Arvid thought he sounded like he was begging the young doctor and decided, 'I don't know any other way to say it.'

Arvid heard a deep sigh on the other end. "The risks are all real. That's true. But Dr. Reynolds is the expert on this treatment. I can't tell you more than he can. I just don't know—"

"But the problem is I don't believe he cares that much about Caroline, you see? How can I trust him?" The agony in Arvid's voice was palpable. "But it seems to matter to you."

"Yes, it does matter!" Coughlin waited a beat longer than was necessary to gather his thoughts, it seemed to Arvid. "I want her to go home to you again. To you and your babies. Where she belongs. And I think she can, someday."

"But not if she doesn't have the insulin therapy? Is that what you think, too?"

"I don't know. I don't pretend to know for certain. That is Dr. Reynolds' area of expertise; I can't contradict him."

"So what should I do? Should I let this go on day after day? Tell me, do you know of people that have had bad things happen to them in the coma?"

"Not personally, no. I've read accounts, case studies. I can't tell you just how high a risk it is for the bad things to happen. Look, I know you're scared, probably scared to death. I would be too, if it were my wife. I won't try to talk you into thinking one way or the other about this, except to say again that Dr. Reynolds is the expert in this area. But here's what I will do. I will check in with Caroline every day after the therapy. Some days I will sit and talk with her. That's what I really want, is for her to be able to talk about what's in her head. I will of course, tell you immediately, if I see something that gives me pause, and I will intervene with Dr. Reynolds."

"Then you will be my eyes and ears there. Do you give me your word?"

"Yes. Yes, I will." Coughlin spoke soberly.

"Alright then. We continue on. I am putting my trust in you, Doctor."

"I know. And I do not accept such an honor lightly, Mr. Fjeld." Both men allowed a few moments to pass to absorb the enormity of this unexpected bond between them.

"I am glad that you called because," and the doctor took a deep breath, "I have what *may* be a positive avenue to pursue. But I'll need your help." Arvid heard a hint of optimism in the doctor's voice.

"In that case, please call me Arvid," he said to the doctor with a bit of relief. "I've wished since the first day for some way to be helpful."

"Then, Arvid it is." Dr. Coughlin responded with warmth. "Okay, here it is. I've been combing the literature on schizophrenia, particularly with rapid onset of symptoms, as your wife had. I've found anecdotal reports of patients with extremely poor memory, amnesia you might say, for the period immediately before and during a rapid onset of the psychosis. Perhaps it is a self-protective mechanism. I mean, why should anyone *want* to remember those frightening visions and voices?" The doctor paused a moment to allow Arvid time to consider this avenue of thinking.

"O—kay?"

"Arvid, I think I know the answer to this question, but to be sure, have you ever talked to your wife about Leah since her hospitalization?"

"No, I haven't dared. I don't want to get her all worked up."

"Nor have I, of course, for the same reason. But here is the thing, then. I have been gently exploring Caroline's memories of home. She most definitely remembers her early pregnancy. As far as I can tell, the last clear memory she has of home may be of the day that you came home with a large bell that you said you were going to mount on a post outside your house. She described a little dance that you all had in the kitchen that day. But after that? It's as if the memory-making part of her brain went to sleep and "woke up" months later, here in the hospital.

"Perhaps Caroline truly doesn't remember those last days before her hospitalization because in a sense, she, herself, the real Caroline was not "awake" or experiencing that period of time." The doctor halted for a moment, "Arvid, *this* Caroline...the Caroline we have today, I doubt that she remembers having the baby. I have no reason to believe that she is aware of another child at home. She has not said anything about the devil coming to her in the form of the baby for months. Do you understand what I'm saying, Arvid?"

A long pause while Arvid felt the blood drain from his face. Then, "Oh!"

"Yes. Oh, indeed!" The doctor let Arvid consider this.

"Well, what..." Arvid struggled between astonishment and flummox, "So what does she think happened to the baby from her pregnancy? But, wait a minute, if she doesn't remember all those awful feelings she had about the baby, that's good, right?"

"Well, that is what I want to find out. And I think we will need to be patient. Give her time to stitch together memories that are real. The critical issue, of course, is that when she is reintroduced to the reality of the second child, will her fear of the baby be resurrected along with it? He sighed. "I think, Arvid, that we should be prepared for whatever may happen if or when she does remember more."

Illustration 9: Roads passable despite spring snowfall

"Uh...have we gotten to the hopeful part yet? 'Cuz I'm afraid I can't tell." Arvid felt oddly disoriented. Envisioning a horrible replay of the scene he witnessed when Caroline called their infant daughter "the Evil One."

"No, well, here's what I need your help with. We will be having a family conference soon...assuming the roads are more passable for you down there, and I want you to bring photographs with you. Photos of you and Caroline and of Marit and Sophie when she was a baby. And bring pictures of Leah. She'll be eight months old the end of March, right? " Dr. Coughlin waited for Arvid's response.

"Yes."

"Even if Caroline does have a vague memory of giving birth, she may confuse it with one of the hallucinations. It's possible she doesn't associate that memory with a real, living baby."

Arvid exhaled a long, slow breath. "Heaven help us. O...kay. bring pictures," he repeated to himself.

"Wonderful. After our conference, you and I can spend just a few minutes together so that you can tell me a little about each of them. I'll use them to attempt to spur Caroline's memories AND to see how she reacts to photos of the baby. It may be a slow process."

After this phone call, Arvid approached his mother. "I need photos to bring with me to our next conference. Caroline was always the one to take pictures. And she put them in an album. But I haven't been taking photos of Leah, Mom."

"Oh ya, dat's no problem. I've been taking one now and den, for Caroline to have when she comes home. We'll mail de film off to be developed right away."

"Oh, thank God!" He paused a moment, considering his words. Hmph! As if God had been any help to him at all.

Wednesday, March 23, 1949

So it was in the fourth family conference of Caroline's hospitalization that Dr. Reynolds transferred the responsibility of facilitating the conferences into Dr. Coughlin's hands. Reynolds had been lead in the first three, but now that Dr. Coughlin was spending more time talking with Caroline at least a few times each week, Arvid thought it made perfect sense when Reynolds explained the change.

Arvid thought there was a trace of something on Dr. Reynolds' face, however, something that said that he wasn't very pleased about it.

"Thank you, Dr. Reynolds," Dr. Coughlin said after the leadership role change was explained by Reynolds. Also present at the conference was Big Alva, who was there to address any questions about Caroline's interactions on the ward, and the Nurse Manager from Insulin Therapy, Peggy. Caroline was included in this family conference, the first time ever.

Dr. Coughlin directed his next comments directly to his patient and her husband. "Talking therapy, or psychotherapy is a mode of treatment that is gathering more traction of late. As you and I discussed on the phone recently, Arvid, I've recommended that we pursue the talking therapy further. And I have already been spending more time talking with Caroline over the past two weeks. But it is not obligatory, and I want to be sure that we are all onboard with this. Arvid, how do you feel about us continuing to focus more energy on talking therapy?"

Arvid nodded whole-heartedly and said, "I'm all for it, as long as Caroline agrees."

"And so, Caroline," the young doctor said with a smile, "is this agreeable to you as well? It will mean meeting with me two or three times each week like we've done recently instead of once a week as we've done in the past."

"Whatever Arvid thinks is best," Caroline answered softly, twisting her hands in her lap.

After the conference, Arvid showed Dr. Coughlin the photos he'd brought, with a few words about each. "Most of these are self-explanatory. Caroline, me, some with Sophie and this is my mother, Marit. This guy, Bear, was my Best Man and Caroline is quite fond of him. Some of our farm buildings in the background here. Arvid took a deep breath and shook his head, "And all of these are of Leah."

Dr. Coughlin set his jaw. "Yes, alright then. It's time for us to find out if Leah looks like an ordinary baby to her mother."

Rochester State H Pt: FJELD, Caroline DOB: 12/02/1926 Adm:08/14/1948	
03/31/49 1720	Pt viewed family photos with exception of baby Leah. When she saw photo of herself holding Sophie, while pregnant, significant startle response was elicited. Pt blanched, sharp intake of breath. Pt volunteers: "I had another baby, didn't I? I must have." MD nodded affirmatively. Pt: "Is it...alive?" MD: "Yes, she is." Pt: "So it was a girl, then." Pt sat silently for a time, looking out the window. Chewing on her nails. "Where is that baby?" MD: "At home with your husband and Marit and Sophie." Pt declined to see photographs of baby. "I have to talk to Arvid." Assisted pt with telephone call to patient's family.
Impressions:	Pt in turmoil about the baby. Following.————HCghln, MD

17

TOGETHER

Caroline
Saturday, April 1, 1949

This morning I wake to Lois' seizure as usual. Predictable and rhythmic, the seizures have been oddly comforting. Comforting because I've known to expect them and that's what I need. Surprises terrify me. Surprises take me away to be tortured, then to disappear from myself, my senses floating away like so much chaff and then I'm gone. Gone to a place I cannot breathe. Cannot think. Left to claw myself back from the edge.

Yesterday, I was extremely surprised. A couple of days earlier, I'd seen a picture of myself pregnant. Sophie was in the picture too, so I wasn't pregnant with her. In that instant, I was falling away. Struggling to breathe. It seemed as though I had had another baby after Sophie! But it was only the vaguest sense of a baby. Not as if I gave it birth. A baby that had nothing to do with me, but as if it came in a fog and remained there, nameless, without form. I left Dr. Coughlin puzzled and frightened, but I said nothing about my suspicion. When we met yesterday, I was ready to tell him what I suspected was the truth.

Dr. Coughlin helped me to place a phone call to Arvid.

"Arvid?" I said, ready to weep.

"Yes, Caroline. I'm here. What is it, my darling?"

"We have a second child, don't we? Is she there with you and Marit?"

I hear Arvid gasp. "Yes, she is."

"So we named her Leah, didn't we?"

"Yes, she's a beautiful little girl, who looks so much like her mother." I can hear Arvid's voice change, become tremulous.

"Why didn't you tell me? Why didn't anyone tell me?" This was a monstrous trick played behind my back. Somehow a baby had been born without my knowledge and nobody wanted me to know. How could a thing like a baby be kept hidden from me? It had to be a collusion between them all. And I don't know why.

"Caroline, we, Dr. Coughlin and I, agreed that it would be best if you were allowed to remember this on your own, when you were ready."

"But why don't I remember such a thing? What's wrong with the baby, Arvid? There must be something wrong with her." I envisioned a baby without limbs, or with no ears, or deaf, or with a harelip, like Ruth. I cringe at the images in my mind. Terrified.

"No, no, Caroline. She's perfect. You can trust me. A perfect little eight-month old baby girl. And she looks like you, my love. I can't wait for you to see her."

"But how can I trust you? That you would keep such a thing from me?" I felt as though nails were driving me into a wall. I could not move. "Don't you love me anymore? That's it, isn't it? You're keeping the baby instead of me." I bawl aloud then. Unabashed bawling.

"No, that's not it at all. I want you home here with us. All of us together. I long for that day. We have two perfectly healthy daughters. I love you so much, Caroline. Don't ever doubt that."

This exhausted me beyond my comprehension. I was allowed to go to bed early last night.

So now I lie here listening for other sounds. Ones that don't belong. The hairs on the back of my neck standing up, on alert, electrified. Every bump in the dark during the night was Karla, coming back for me. Or the doctor with the needle. I am drenched in sweat, afraid to make a sound, afraid to make a move that might be wrong. Afraid that needle will pierce my skin again and again until I'm gone for good.

There is no place to hide here. I pray that God will take me. I've made my peace with Ruth and she with me. At mealtime, I will no longer listen for the squishing sounds of her food going in and out between her teeth. I pay no mind to Dolly. Instead, I encourage Estra to talk throughout the meal. That's easy enough to do.

Estra was never taught her nursery rhymes. The poor thing, she's hungry for them. Hungry for food and for rhyming words. She's especially fond of "Jack Sprat could eat no fat. His wife could eat no lean. And so betwixt them both, you see, they licked the platter clean." She giggles and adds, "Jack Sprat's wife is fat. Fat like me." And she beams with each new rhyme she's taught. What will I do when I've run out of nursery rhymes?

I think of the two young women lying near me when I awoke in that Insulin Therapy room for the first time, just two weeks ago. They were the same women I'd met during hydrotherapy, Marilyn with the sad gray eyes and Celia with the stunning, curly, red hair. We saw each other from our gurneys. If only my tongue had worked, I'd have spoken sooner.

I'd have said, "Marilyn, yours are the saddest gray eyes I've ever seen, but so beautiful. Let me disappear inside them. Let me hide there, in a place where there are no needles. No hot, hot baths. No ice water. I would not be wrapped like a mummy in icy cloths. No insulin comas." But my tongue wasn't working and so I told Marilyn all of this with my eyes. I think she understood. She was able to hold her gaze on me for a very long time without blinking. If only I could talk with her for real, I thought.

The other young woman, Celia, lay beyond Marilyn and she could see me as well. How I've missed Celia's sassy nature! If only I could make my mouth smile, I would, because I am so happy to see her. I imagine her as a skinny little girl with wildly glorious hair, telling jokes and playing tricks on the boys. I lie there waiting for my tongue to be manageable. For so long, I've been certain I'd never get close enough to talk to either of them again. And there they are, enduring this same insulin torture. Have they missed me, like I've missed them?

Big Alva's face appears in the half-light over my bed. "It's time to get up now, Missy. They have plans for you downstairs."

Alarmed! Now I'm very much awake. I stumble over my tongue to defend myself. "I haven't hurt anyone for a long time. I haven't even seen that Karla. Why am I being punished again? Please leave me be." I hear myself whine. I clutch my blanket to my chin.

"Oh, Missy, it's not my call. Dr. Reynolds wants you down there in ten minutes. Up with you. Up up up. Do you need help to put your dress on, Missy?"

"No I don't. Why do you call me Missy? My name is Caroline. Remember? It's Caroline."

"Alright then, Car-o-line." I detest the way she exaggerates each syllable. "Get up right now, or I will have to dress you myself." She stares into my face and pulls away my blanket revealing my skinny bare legs. I sit up automatically. Alva should not see my pale, thin legs.

I begin to dress myself. Big Alva watches, arms akimbo. "I can do it," I say without looking at her.

"I'm staying here till we go downstairs, Missy—Car-o-line, is what I mean to say."

I expect Alva will go to check on Lois, still seizing. She doesn't. "Lois has been seizing for a long time already," I tell her. "It's been too long. Her seizures don't go this long. Can't you do something?" I can't take my eyes from Lois. Something is wrong. Very wrong.

"Mind your own business Missy Caroline. I've seen her seize a thousand times. Now finish dressing."

"But it's not stopping. Don't you see? This time it's different." I button my dress and put on my socks and shoes. Still she seizes. I don't really know how long, but it seems much longer than usual.

"Lois, you must stop this," I go to her. Touch her forehead. It's burning up. Her skin is too pink, her hair plastered to her head with sweat.

"Let's go," Alva says. She takes my shoulder and pulls me away from Lois.

"She's terribly hot. She's feverish...see? Touch her. This isn't right."

"It's not your concern Missy. We'll check on her when we get everyone else up for breakfast. Get going. I've got more to do than chaperone you around. Now stop here for just a moment," she says when we approach the door, grabbing my arm. She turns back to call in a loud whisper over the long row of beds. "Winnie? Do you have Marilyn and Celia ready?" A muffled sound. "Come on then. Let's go. I don't have all day."

Then they are suddenly beside me, both of them, as they have been for the past two weeks. Marilyn with the soulful gray eyes and Celia with her flaming red hair and bright blue eyes remind me of me, terrified. We stare at one another, as if pleading for one of us to do something about the indignity that is coming but there is nothing to be done. Alva prods us into a procession toward the stairs and the tunnel.

The cavernous tunnel echoes with only our four pairs of feet. Marilyn, Celia and I drag our feet. Celia takes my hand. "Help me," she says to my eyes, pleading, but I don't know how to help her or anyone. I couldn't even help Lois.

"Celia, there's no help for it," Marilyn whispers softly to her and takes her other hand. The three of us walk together hand in hand, our shoulders rubbing. Theirs were the first hands I had touched in so very long; such a long winter without seeing Arvid. I tightly squeeze Celia's hand. I don't want to frighten her more than she already is. I don't want to let go of her hand.

187

"It'll be okay," I say once again, though we all know it's a lie. "We'll be together." Together. Such a lovely word. Have I never used it before? My eyes pulse with tears that want to come. But if I cry, I will make it harder for Marilyn and Celia. We are three friends. We must look out for each other.

"Yes, we are together," Marilyn nods her head slowly. Gives Celia her sad gray eyes. The door that says "Insulin Therapy" opens and we are ushered inside.

Late morning

The nurse, Connie is talking to me. "There you are, Caroline. Nicely done. How do you feel, my dear?" She looks into my eyes that struggle to focus. My tongue feels thick. Frightened again by my loss of speech, my fuzzy thinking, incoordination.

"Nnnnnnh..." is all I can say.

I hear another nurse talking. "Well, Celia, you should be ready to go back upstairs pretty soon. Your vitals are all good. Everything looks normal," the nurse actually has a smile in her voice.

"I'd like to wait for Caroline and Marilyn if that's okay. Then we could go up and eat together." Celia's words warm me. Her words are meant for me to hear, and for Marilyn. The three of us. Together.

Marilyn is the last of us to emerge entirely from the coma. When Connie tells me that I am good to go, I follow Celia's lead. "I don't mind waiting for Marilyn. Then the three of us can go up together." I offer Connie a timid smile and she nods her agreement.

By the time Alva sends a young woman in white to escort us from the Insulin "Hole" (which is how I now think of this place,) all of our fellow sisters have finished with their dinners and are off to their assigned places. Marilyn, Celia and I have the enormous dining hall to ourselves. A plump kitchen helper hands us bowls of potato soup with an ear of corn and then returns to the kitchen, rattling around just enough to remind us that we are under her supervision. A feeling of shyness still slides over me when I sit close to these two women, that I can openly call my friends.

There is a moment where we all hold back. We have just survived another day of torture together. "Again, we are lucky to be alive," I say.

"We can still walk and talk and feed ourselves," Marilyn whispers.

"Come ladies, our table awaits," Celia says with a wink. And without another word, Marilyn and I follow Celia to a table and once seated, consider our situation. The relative silence wrapped around us somehow pushes back against all that we have endured over the last several hours.

"I like the quiet here," I say, just before someone down the hall shouts out an obscenity. The helper in the kitchen drops a pan on the floor and in the distance someone is crying.

"I do, too," Marilyn and Celia say together. We stare at one another and the three of us laugh until we cry.

Illustration 10: Potato soup with corn.

In the eyes of Marilyn and Celia I see my own tortured soul reflected. It is the reflection of each new day's traumas. Today it was Lois' unending seizure, Alva's rush to be rid of me, the tight restraints on my arms and legs before the prick of the needle and the drop into the black abyss from which I may or may not emerge. Then, barely alive, I do return, but unable to corral a scrambled brain, unable to move, recognizing the cold fear that I will remain forever locked in this body that cannot speak for itself. Only my wild eyes will communicate my private horror. The three of us, we were all there, together.

Marilyn looks into our eyes. She looks down at her lukewarm potato soup. Her hand finds mine and then Celia's. She speaks in a voice that reminds me of Marit's sweet oatmeal, "For what we are about to receive may the Lord make us truly grateful. Amen."

18

UNPREDICTABLE

Caroline
Late afternoon, April 1, 1949

I know how important the memories are, at least to Dr. Coughlin, and he's the one person here that wants me to get home. So my job is to tell him about every memory that I can. Sometimes things would be easier for me if I would keep them to myself.

"I remember something, Dr. Coughlin. About my mother," I offer the next time I see him.

"I'd love to hear about your mother, Caroline. When you're ready," he says, kindly.

"Well, I was quite little, maybe seven or so? I think it was the middle of the night, very dark, and my mother and I were all dressed for traveling."

I whisper now, to convey the feeling of that moment as I recall it. "She told me to come quickly and to be careful not to slip in my stocking feet. I followed my mother on tiptoes. I remember the house from the top of the staircase. There were tall stained-glass windows behind us. In the mornings when the sun rose over the ocean, I used to play within the colors that danced down the stairs."

Suddenly, I remember something else that's new. "Oh, it might have been April at that time because I remember this. My mother's mother, my grandmama taught me this not long before that day. She said, "March comes in like a lion and goes out like a lamb." She had lots of sayings like that." I am astonished that I remember her.

"My mother opened the door at the back of the house, and it made a click sound. We stopped to listen, but we didn't hear any movement in the house. Even Cook wasn't up yet at that hour. I remember wondering what she would say when she found us gone.

"Cook was so good to me. When I made her laugh, tears rolled down her cheeks and her apron jiggled. She made me special treats, like Red Velvet Cake. That was my favorite thing. Red Velvet Cake on a plate with a big glass of milk. Mmmm!" I smile to remember this.

"I remember there was a time when I decided I would cut my own piece of Red Velvet Cake. I thought I was so grown-up. I was alone in the kitchen when Cook went to the water closet. I poured myself a big glass of milk first, because that's what Cook always did. But then I bumped it over and the milk went everywhere. The glass broke on the floor and I cut my foot on it. I was barefoot. The whole cake was drowning in milk and I was so upset. I cried because I'd ruined the cake. There was the blood on the floor, too, but I felt the worst about spoiling the cake.

Grandmother was angry with me. Grandmother was angry with my mother too. She said that I should be taught a lesson. My mother said I'd already learned my lesson. That she knew I wouldn't do that again."

I close my eyes now to better remember that night of our leaving. "The air was so cool and fresh outside. I could smell the ocean. I followed my mother through the gardens. I remember my mother looking behind us and up to see if anyone was watching from the windows. I didn't see anyone." I pause. "There must not have been a moon because it was so black." I add thoughtfully.

"I wanted to walk where there were streetlights, but my mother said we shouldn't. She kept turning to look behind us, but I really don't know how she could have seen anything in that darkness. I was so hot because I was wearing several dresses and my nicest winter coat. Mother wouldn't let me take them off. She reminded me of how Heidi went up the mountain to live with her old grandfather. You know the story of *Heidi*? She wore several dresses, too, so that she wouldn't have to carry them." I pause for a moment. I'd loved the story of *Heidi* as a child.

"So, we walked, and we walked. My mother turned to look behind us every little while. I was carrying my doll, Cynthia Lee. I wouldn't have left her behind!" When I close my eyes now I can remember her long reddish blonde curls and how her eyes closed when I laid her down to sleep. I thought she was the most beautiful thing in the world.

"I must have complained some, I don't remember what I said, but I was hot, and I'm sure I wanted to rest. My mother told me that Cynthia Lee would have to walk a little farther before we stopped." I smile to remember how sweet my mother was to me that night in the darkness.

"There was a railroad depot. I'd seen it before. We met Grandmother there once, when she got off the train from Cleveland." I smile to remember her words that day. "Grandmother... Grandmother said that people in Cleveland were wild Indians. I thought that Cleveland was a wild west show." I chuckle at myself.

"The train's whistle was so loud, and that bright light coming down the tracks from out of the darkness." My eyes grow wider to remember. "It was exciting. I'd never been on a train before.

"We changed trains in Manhattan. Oh, my, it was *so* noisy there." I shake my head to recall. "I remember going through the mountains. They were beautiful. We ate in a dining car. You know what I remember the best of all? The waiter. My mother nudged me under the table and told me to close my mouth. The waiter's skin was as black as could be. And his teeth were so white! He was nice to me and he bowed a little before he left our table.

"One of the maids at Grandmother's house was Negro too, but her skin wasn't nearly so dark as his. The maid hardly ever talked or smiled." I remember her with fondness, and suddenly it's as if there are blinders being removed from my eyes and I can remember so many little things.

"My mother told me we should be extra nice to her because she had to travel a long way to get to Grandmother's house each morning." I cock my head to one side, "But you know? Grandmother *expected* the other servants to live in the house, up in the top floor attic rooms, but she said, 'It's enough that I give one of them a job; I see no point in housing a Negro, too. Separate water closets and all of that nonsense.'" I pause to remember the grandmother's sharp voice and unkind words.

"My mother said it would have to be a very hard life working for grandmother because she was so picky. Nobody could do a good enough job to please her. Well, I didn't care much for Grandmother myself."

I feel strangely concerned now but I don't know why or about what. I cock my head suddenly; it is becoming easier to remember. And more frightening. I look at Dr. Coughlin and then at the floor. I continue, "My mother told me once that she tried to be nice to everyone. She said that being nice cost nothing at all, and didn't everyone deserve some good things in their day? And I decided that I would try to be like my mother. But I asked her if that included...him." I feel my skin go cold at this. I make myself continue soberly.

"She said that we should be especially nice to him because he's plenty grouchy without us adding to his bad mood." I shake my head, straining to push the image of the grouchy man from my head.

"After we ate, we walked from train car to train car, to stretch our legs. I remember asking my mother why the men on the train were arguing about the alphabet." I snicker at myself. "I realized later that they were talking about the CCC and WPA and TVA." I want Dr. Coughlin to see how I can laugh at myself as a little girl.

"We came upon another little girl just about my age with her parents. I was fascinated with her because I'd never gotten to play with many other children my age. She had long blonde hair tied with blue bows. I don't remember her name, but her mother introduced her and invited us to sit for a while so that we could play. The woman complimented my mother and me on our beautiful dark hair, so I did like my mother taught me. I thanked her and I curtsied a little. Nobody curtsies anymore, do they?" I ask Dr. Coughlin. This seems poignant to me.

"The girl let me play with one of the dolls she'd brought on the train. Mine was in the sleeper car, of course. While we played, my mother visited with the lady. The lady told my mother that they got on the train in Boston. She asked where we got on the train and my mother said 'Philadelphia,' which I knew wasn't right, but I didn't say anything because she'd told me that if I heard her say something that wasn't quite the truth while we were on the train, I should just let it go.

"You see, my mother had told me that we were pretending like we were like Sherlock Holmes and Watson. Lady detectives! Well, that sounded like fun to me.

"The girl and her parents were getting off the train in Pittsburgh. My mother told her that we were going to Cleveland, but I didn't say anything about that either. I knew we were going to Minnesota and I was going to show her that I could be a good detective.

"It wasn't long after that that we did something very odd, but I didn't know at the time just how odd it was. I figured it out much later, after we were in Minnesota, when I was probably in fourth grade. We were learning about the Oregon Trail west. I really liked maps and I knew that my mother and I had traveled west. But it was that day that I realized that when we changed trains in Chicago, we got on a train going back east again for a while. Away from Minnesota!

"Of course, when I was seven, I didn't know that Gary, Indiana was east of Chicago; I didn't know that we were going the wrong way." I want to laugh at myself now. Surely Dr. Coughlin will find this story entertaining. "I think we stayed in Gary for a few days. I remember playing for hours in a park there." I paused. "Hmph. I don't know why. And then, we got back on another train and continued on to Wisconsin and Minnesota and all the way to Fargo, North Dakota where we turned around again!" I shook my head and grinned at Dr. Coughlin.

"You see, traveling with my mother was unpredictable like that, all the while we were on the train. We went west, then east, then west again. My mother would tell one person one thing and she would tell someone else something different. It was a game. And I was Watson." It feels so good to laugh out loud now. I laugh harder and harder. I feel as if I am glowing. "I was with my mother and that's all that was important anyhow." I beam at the young doctor. I feel rather proud of myself for remembering so much for him today.

"Caroline, I see that this is humorous to remember now. When you were seven, did you know why you and your mother were going west? Away from your home by the ocean?"

"Home? You know, that's odd, I suppose. We never called that big house "home." It was "Grandmother's house" or the "castle." It was never home. So the two of us went on a grand adventure, just my mother and I, didn't we? We must have been very fortunate to have had enough money to travel back then. I know that my mother was so much happier after we had our own home in Minnesota. And I was too." I want to close my eyes to remember how happy we really were. What a wonderful memory!

"And where did you make your first home in Minnesota, Caroline? Do you remember?" Dr. Coughlin asks in a soothing voice.

"Not exactly. But it was in a city." Why can't I remember? It worries me. My heart races. I don't have a clear answer to this one simple question. What is wrong with me?

"Do you think it was Owatonna? That's not a very big city, is it?" He says this gently. His eyes are almost sorrowful.

I feel my skin burn hot. A red, itchy flush creeps up my neck to the top of my head. I crank my head to the right. Crack. To the left. It creaks. I itch so that I want to pull my hair out. Something is terribly wrong with me. Wrong. The humming. Humming grows louder. Is it jabbering? Laughing? I see Dr. Coughlin there, across the room from me. So far, far away now; I can't even reach out that far. Telescoping into the distance, smaller and smaller. His lips move but I don't hear him. What...what is he saying?

Floor slips out from beneath. Hands grasping. Hard scrapes on blades of tailbone, elbows, shoulder, head. I'm flying, dropping, shredding, knocking. Brightness falls. There's blue sunlight and screams. The yellow explodes. Tick. Tock. Tick. Tock. And then it's Red, bursting Red. It's Red and White. The Red and the White. The drowning. It's gone, all gone, ruined. And the red. NO NO *I Can't Be Alone* with the Voice. The Voice. The Voice. Tick Tock Tick Tock.

"Caroline...Caroline...do you hear me?" Someone far away is talking to me through a very long underwater tube. Talk. Talk. Tock. Tock. Tick. Tock. A hand on the back of my head and another hand puts a glass of liquid to my lips. The glass tips and some spills, but some goes into my mouth and I swallow. I take in more of the lemony-lime liquid. "Drink more, Caroline. Drink more. Come on, you can do it. A little more. Just a little more." I find that I am thirsty.

Then comes silence.

When I awake, it is Estra's face I see. She stands over me and toddles back and forth from one foot to the other, bobbing her head to music that only she can hear.

"Hi Caroline," she says. Her eyes go nearly shut with her grin. "You missed supper. Wanna know what we had? Wanna know? I'll tell you. We had creamed peas and biscuits and bologna. Uh huh. Creamed peas, biscuits and bologna. Are you hungry? Alva will come get you, if you want late supper. Late supper is better than no supper, right? Right, Caroline? That's what I say. Here she comes. She comes."

Estra backs away abruptly and Big Alva's head hovers above my bed. She has her hands on her hips and I don't like the look on her face. I know that look. It's her look that says, "You are taking up too much of my time. What am I gonna have to do for you this time?"

She clears her throat and begins. "What am I gonna have to do for you, Caroline? Do you want supper? It's gone cold but I suppose they can heat up something for you, if you're hungry that is. Sometimes patients feel like vomiting after they have lithiated soda,[xii] so then it's better not to eat, if that's the case. I wouldn't be surprised. Since this was your first time." Alva's head moved back and forth. Then leaned down close to me and whispered. "So, is this your answer, then? Nothing? That's fine with me. Breakfast will come before you know it."

As she turns her back to me to walk away, I glance at Lois' bed. Empty. "Is Lois okay?" I call after her.

Without turning around, she waves a hand and says, "No need for you to worry about Lois. You better get some rest now."

The next day, the story of Lois' death spreads across the ward. Most women didn't know her. They said, "Was that the Indian woman? She didn't speak English, right?" The few that did know who she was had this to say, "It's a cryin' shame they let her seize to death."

Yes, it's a very great shame.

19

SOMEDAY

Caroline
July 1949

Foggy, indistinct, fuzzy voices slide over me. So groggy. Barely conscious. Blurry orange light glows through closed eyelids. Random sounds echo and then suddenly, one voice is clear.

"Hi—just wanted to stop in for a short chat, Doctor. We're nearly at the end of her insulin therapy now, aren't we." Dr. Coughlin is talking to someone.

Papers rustle and pages flip back and forth, again and again. "Hmmm, yes," the other voice speaks. "Well, the record shows that we have four sessions to reach the sixty. And I *am* considering adding another ten. There's no use in rushing away from a treatment that may very well produce the best outcome we might see." That voice makes me wince. It's Dr. Reynolds, so self-assured, so pompous. *Why can't he go away? Leave me alone.*

Dr. Coughlin answers quietly. "I want you to know that Caroline is doing quite well in her work with me. She's remembering more and more and putting the broken pieces together. I have confidence that she will be able to go on from here without—"

"Without what?" Reynolds' voice is harsher now. Like a growl.

"Well, I, for one, would be comfortable with ending her insulin therapy as of today even, if you would agree, of course. She is working hard with me. I don't think we could ask any more of her."

"And if she declines after the insulin therapy ceases? Then what?" It's that haughty, smug voice again.

"I will take full responsibility if that should occur, Dr. Reynolds. The patient desperately wants to be done with this part of her treatment. Frankly, she is terrified each time she comes down here. Her sleep is adversely affected by her anxiety which I would say is growing as we near the end. She worries that the next coma will be the one from which she doesn't recover. In my opinion, she will do better after the conclusion of insulin therapy, with the removal of this anxiety."

A pause. There's a buzzing in my ear. A throat clearing. "Your opinion is appreciated, as you must know by now. You've become quite an asset to our work here, but..." Dr. Reynolds exhales loudly. "It behooves you to use caution when promoting curtailment of a treatment that has been shown to produce such positive results in this population."

"Yes, certainly. I would not want to jeopardize her treatment. Nor that of any of our pa—"

"Look, I gave you carte blanche to proceed with the talking therapy with this patient. Let's not get ahead of ourselves by altering other aspects of treatment prematurely."

Darkness and silence crashes over me again.

Late in the afternoon, I meet with Doctor Coughlin. He tells me that I have only four more coma therapy sessions. "Dr. Reynolds has agreed to hold to just the sixty insulin treatments, Caroline. You're almost there," he adds with a hint of an encouraging smile.

"Each day that I come out of the coma alive, with my senses intact...I think is a miracle." I have to try to explain once again just how much I fret about each time I go into a coma. "But that last hour, while I wait for my tongue to work properly, for my eyes to open and to focus, to think; it's pure hell! What if the next time is the one time that I don't come back from the coma?" I wring my hands in my lap.

"Caroline, Dr. Reynolds is confident that nothing bad will happen to you. We're going to have to trust him on this. He's gotten you this far." Dr. Coughlin looks at me with what looks like an apology.

I search his face. "I think I overheard you arguing on my behalf, against further insulin therapy. Did that really happen this morning?"

He looks down quickly and then up at me before answering, "You may have heard me discussing your progress with Dr. Reynolds, yes."

"Thank you," is all I can say. Four comas to go. God help me.

After every insulin-induced coma, Marilyn, Celia and I tell our nurses that we don't want to be a bother; we're each willing to lie restrained on our respective gurneys until all three of us are ready to leave the Insulin Therapy room, together. Our nurses are nice enough to allow us to do just that. We each have one day of the week when we are insulin-free. My day is Sunday. Marilyn has Tuesdays and Celia has Fridays off.

Therefore, some combination of two out of the three of us eats a late dinner together daily. Four days out of the week, all three of us eat together, supervised only by whatever noisy kitchen helper is left behind for that purpose. We eat as slowly as we can. No one bothers us as long as we are still eating.

Yesterday during dinner, I told Marilyn and Celia that there's a chance I may be able to go home again, maybe by winter.

"Really?" Marilyn says, clearly surprised. She swallows hard. "That's wonderful news." She stops chewing to smile at me a little. I nod my head, immediately sorry that I announced this possibility already. This is the first time any of us have brought up the possibility of leaving the hospital. I wish now that I wasn't the first one to bring it up, but it's too late to take it back. It feels like a betrayal to consider leaving them behind. Am I twisting the knife by talking about leaving, when I have no idea what their prospects might be? I should have waited for at least another month to bring it up.

"I'm happy for you," Celia says. Her lips are smiling but she can't camouflage her eyes. They're devastated. She clears her throat. "When do you think you'll know for sure?" she asks in a measured tone.

"Dr. Coughlin says that when I remember more, when I... well, after that happens, then he says we'll talk more seriously about it. He doesn't want me to fight the memories. So, I've been trying not to. But you know...maybe I never will leave either."

"You're afraid of the memories, yes?" Marilyn says quietly, looking down at her food.

"Yes, and I...I'm surprised by how they come at me." I say. "I might be doing something like teaching Estra a new nursery rhyme and then suddenly, out of the blue something will pop into my head. I never know when that's going to happen, when something is just going to shake loose in me." I try to smile but it feels wobbly.

"Some memories are better not remembered," Marilyn offers. "There are things I wish I didn't remember—but if it's going to get you home again, well, then it's worth it, right?" She pauses a moment, to brighten her face, while trying to read mine. There's a long silence. Then, "I will miss you, Caroline." She smiles at me with that sadness in her eyes.

"She can stop back in to visit us," Celia blurts out brightly, and then rolls her eyes, laughing giddily behind her hand. Celia's gotten her second wind, it seems. That happens unexpectedly for her sometimes. She guffaws. "Ya, right, nobody is gonna come back here to visit us. I was just funnin' you." Celia pats my hand. "When you're gone from here, you stay gone, my friend."

"No, I *could* come visit you if you were still here. Of *course,* I could, but maybe you'll have gone home too...by then." I feel desperate to convince them that there will be a happy ending to our three stories. But now I see that I've only made myself totter upon a tightrope. My friends *want* me to be able to go home. And they *want* to be happy for me. At the same time, I've reminded them of whatever brought them to this place, the weight of their pasts and their futures.

Is it a form of cruelty that I force upon them to say I may go home? If once freed from this place, should I return here only so they can see me looking well-fed and happy, wearing a nice dress from the outside and make-up and a stylish haircut?

What would the three of us talk about when I visit? Would I talk about how wonderful it is to be back home? No. I certainly will not twist that knife. Maybe I'd ask, what are you doing in Rag Shop these days? Pfft. Any suicides since I saw you last? Oh, God. What to talk about? Should I encourage them to believe they will leave here too? How insensitive would that be for me to do?

I have no right to force them to rise up to meet a visitor's empty platitudes of hope, even if that visitor is me. I love them too much for that torture. Shall I rip away that scab over and over again? No. When one of us leaves the others behind, this three-legged stool that makes up the "We three friends" will never be again.

The air between us is heavy now that I've brought up the possibility of leaving, though it's months away, if it even happens. I look at each of them in turn. Neither offers any word about their own futures, nor have they ever said how they came to be here, in the state hospital. I haven't told them my story but then, I really can't remember it. And if I did, those are the most private of our stories.

"I can come visit you where you live, *after* you leave here, too. What about that?" I throw this out into the silence between us like a poorly tossed softball, hoping one of them will reach out to catch it.

"Oh, that would be great. It would, wouldn't it, Celia?" Marilyn straightens her back a little and with a timid smile rearranges the carrots on her plate so that they lie tidily to one side.

"Ya! Would it ever?" Celia tries another big smile but it's wooden. "I don't know that I'll ever...get out of here, though," she says dully, followed by a misplaced laugh. "But I would certainly tell you if I do. And I'd invite you to come to Red Wing to see me, or...or I'd come to visit you."

"And I would do the same," Marilyn says gamely. "If my husband would let me of course, back in Wabasha." She then mumbles, "That's hard to... say." A cloud passes over her face and she looks across the hall and through the great window there.

"Look, I shouldn't have said anything about this right now. I'm sorry I brought it up. I don't know why I did. It's not a sure thing. Who knows if I'll ever leave?"

I hear only the sound of our spoons on the metal plates. I push around what looks like a beef stroganoff, but none like any dish I've had outside this place. My mother learned to make a beef stroganoff when I was little. And just that quickly, I am seven years old again.

Spring 1933

Cynthia Lee and I are so happy when Mommy says, "We're not going to ride the trains anymore, Caroline. We're going to stay right here." She puts our bags down and takes a deep, satisfied breath.

She points first in one direction, then another. "See how the Mississippi goes right through the city? And over there are waterfalls and parks. There are even lakes nearby! The state capitol is that way over the bridge. Yes, I think this will be a good place for us to live." She smiles broadly.

"We'll be happy here." She looks so pleased. "But first things first," she says, and we get into a car.

Mommy has the car bring us to a place that she says is a nunnery. It has high brick walls that circle a block of buildings. The rooms inside aren't much to look at but oh, the gardens! They remind me a little of the gardens at the castle by the ocean but they're even better because these gardens have lots of women in black and white robes working in the dirt. Some of the women sing while they work. I want to sing like that, too.

We watch the women working in the garden for a bit and then Mommy takes one of the women aside. She wears a shorter black dress than the others. In a few minutes, Mommy says to me, "This is Sister Mary Frances Robert and I've asked her to look after you outside while I go inside to talk to the Mother Superior." A mother that is superior must be really something to see! But I doubt she could be better than mine.

"But you'll be right back again, right?" I question Mommy. I feel uneasy about her leaving me outside with this stranger, even though the lady has a nice smile.

"I will absolutely be right back. I need to talk alone inside for a bit is all," she says. I watch her walk away. My tummy hurts a little to see her back getting smaller and smaller.

Then the most amazing thing happens. Sister Mary Frances Robert asks me if I want to work in the dirt right alongside her! I like that idea just fine. I take off my nice shoes, so they don't get dirty. Cynthia Lee watches.

Before too long, Mommy comes back outside, and she can't possibly miss seeing how dirty I've become. But she's smiling at me anyhow, and she says she's happy because the Superior Mother will let us stay for a while.

Mommy bends down to me and says, "I am going to go to cooking school here at the nunnery. Come. Let me show you the kitchen." The kitchen is the biggest I've ever seen! Even bigger than the one at the castle! Mommy is smiling. "You may come here to see me anytime you want, Caroline, but I must be a good student and work hard. Do you understand, my Sweet Pea?"

"Yes, I do." Soon I am spending most every day of that summer tagging along with Sister Mary Frances Robert while Mommy goes to cooking school.

Sister Mary Frances Robert never scolds me when I get dirty, unlike Grandmother who scolded me whenever she got a chance. Sister Mary Frances Robert likes how my green beans grow in a row that is mostly straight. I learn some of the songs from her that I heard the Sisters singing the first day we came. When we're not in the garden, Sister Mary Frances Robert shows me how to use a needle and thread, which is much, much harder than it looks. Cynthia Lee is very proud of the little patchwork quilt that I make for her, but I have to remind her that pride is a sin.

Sometimes, when Sister Mary Frances Robert has time, she shows me how to play the old piano in the back room. I don't play very well yet, but maybe someday.

Every day but Sunday, Mommy works in the kitchen alongside the Sisters. Early in the morning she mixes up bread while I stay asleep in the bed we share. By noon, she has made a soup and baked the bread. By supper time she's made fried chicken or meatballs and gravy with mashed potatoes or maybe meatloaf. She learns to make beef stroganoff, too, which is one of my very favorites. On Sundays after what they call "the Mass," Mommy and I go out exploring the city.

"Will you learn to make Red Velvet Cake, too?" I ask her one day.

She smiles and says, "Maybe later. Right now, it's the meat and vegetables that are most important."

Before the leaves turn color in the fall, Mommy has one of the Sisters go with her to find us a place to live. It's upstairs in a big house. It's not nearly as big as the house on Long Island, of course, but still, it's plenty big. And here is the biggest surprise of all. When we take the rooms, Mommy tells them that her name is Victoria, and that my name is Carol! And instead of Mommy's parents' name, D' Bouvier, we go by the name "Bovary." Mommy says that "Bovary" is easier to spell, plus it sounds a little more like a Minnesota name. I don't mind. I like being a detective again.

We each have our own bedroom and there is a kitchen and a butler's pantry, but no butler. We have a dining room, a music parlor with a piano, a pretty sitting room and a water closet with a pull-chain and a giant tub. There's a park with huge trees just across the street and a lake nearby called Loring. Cynthia Lee likes picnics by the lake.

Mommy enrolls me in school for the first time ever. I like going to school more than having the tutor come to the house, like on Long Island. I get to start right out in the second grade because I can already read and write and add two plus two. I make lots of new friends. Mommy tells them at school that my father died of consump—something and that we left Milwaukee to live close to Mommy's family in Minneapolis. I overhear her telling them, "It would be kind of you to refrain from asking Carol about Milwaukee. It was such a very sad time in her life."

I'd have liked it if Mommy's parents did live nearby. I miss Grandpapa and Grandmama. My grandmama made little dresses for Cynthia Lee and she brought me special treats when they came to visit us. I don't know when we'll see them again. Mommy said she doesn't know either.

We get to clean our own home in Minneapolis! It isn't hard to do, after all. "Of course, we don't have things that need polishing. That makes a difference," Mommy says. But we do have large rugs that we roll up and slide down the stairs. The nice man, Mr. Timmes, with the family downstairs helps us to hang the rugs on the clothesline. Mommy doesn't like beating on the rugs quite as much as I do. I can hit really hard! And then I sneeze, and I make Mommy laugh.

I go with Mommy to the market sometimes, to buy milk, eggs, flour and whatever else we want to eat. There are foods there that I've never seen before. Big barrels of what they call "lutefisk" sit outside the markets. The barrels smell just awful! When I see a dog peeing on a barrel, I laugh out loud, but Mommy tells me to hush. She whispers, "We should be thankful we don't have to eat that."

I hadn't thought about that. "Some people have to eat lutefisk, I guess. Oh, what an awful thing." Mommy nodded.

Before we go shopping, Mommy takes money from a drawer in her bedroom and tucks it into her handbag. I ask her, "Will all the money be gone soon?" We are learning to count money in my second grade class.

She smiles and reassures me, "Oh, don't worry about that one bit. We have our bank account with us. We have enough to last us for years and years."

"What's a bank account?"

She puts her finger in front of her lips, like she does when she's telling me, "Shhh" and she takes out a purple velvety bag that makes just a little noise when she lays it on the table. She pulls open the strings on the bag and empties it out. Tumbling out are all the necklaces and brooches and bracelets that Mommy wore when we lived on Long Island. My eyes grow big!

"This is just for you and me to know. Do you understand?" she asks in her serious voice.

"Yes, I do. Good detectives keep secrets." I wink at her. I remember how to be Watson to her Sherlock. I recognize the deep red jewels on a brooch, the pretty blue stones on a necklace, the strings of pearls and the brooch that looks like a hummingbird. My favorite is the long gold necklace with the glittery stones, each tucked in a gold half-shell.

Mommy puts my favorite over my head, and I look at myself in the mirror. "Look at me, Mommy. I'm a princess," I turn to her, glowing.

"Yes, you are my little princess, Sweet Pea," Mommy tickles me and holds me close.

The best thing about living here? There is never any screaming. No loud banging, or things breaking or thuds that make Mommy cry. I don't hear her cry ever anymore. We are happy in Minneapolis.

Late July 1949

Forward and backward I go. I talk about so much with Dr. Coughlin and I tell Arvid about some of my memories too when he visits. I get stuck sometimes though. It took a long time for me to say, "it was Minneapolis where we lived, my mother and me."

It's odd how my memories go along unwinding nicely and then suddenly, it's as if they have rolled into a patch of honey and I'm stuck there. I was stuck like that before I could finally remember that it was Minneapolis where we lived. Each time I get stuck I don't really want to become unstuck. Not really. It's easier to remain in that one sweet spot where things are alright just as they are. Taking a new leap is a gargantuan thing.

I become so tired. I would like Dr. Coughlin to let me rest for a while and say that I've done quite enough remembering, but then I think of Arvid waiting for me to come home. How blue his eyes are and how brown his arms get in the summertime. His arms that hold me tenderly.

I can't talk about this with Marilyn and Celia. It doesn't seem as though they have someone at home waiting for them to return. I don't want to see how they will miss me, and how much I will miss them. But I miss Sophie even more. She is like a part of my own body, an arm or hipbone or a piece of my heart that I've left behind on Hawk Ridge. I ache without her.

If only I could go home without talking about the baby that I don't remember. That frightens me.

Early August 1949

I know what he's going to say before he says it. "Caroline, we've been putting this off for some time now. It's time to look at the photos of baby Leah," Dr. Coughlin says.

This task has been hanging over my head since April, since I first discovered that there is a second child at home. Why no one would tell me of it is still beyond my comprehension. Arvid asks me to try to trust Dr. Coughlin. The doctor has been right about so many things. And I don't have anything to do with Dr. Reynolds anymore, which is a big relief.

"But I *could* just wait until I get home to see her, couldn't I? I mean, she'll have changed by then anyway. And what if we didn't even have the photos? I would *have* to wait until I get home." I make this one last argument to the doctor which seems very rational and reasonable to my way of thinking.

"Those things are true, Caroline. But I have to wonder what makes you want to avoid the photos. That, in itself, concerns me. Your avoidance of them, I think, tells us how important it is to face them now, while you are here in this safe place."

"Alright, I'll look at them, if it's so important to you." My voice comes out harsher than I intended. I have no reason to be angry with Dr. Coughlin.

The doctor pulls out a folder that I recognize. It holds the photos that Arvid brought us months ago, including the ones of Leah. There is a small bundle of them, maybe ten in all, just as many as all the rest of the photos combined.

"If you pull your chair up closer to the desk, I'll lay them out for you. Just two or three at a time, like we talked about, from the beginning of Leah's life." I silently nod my agreement.

The first black and white photo shows only a bundle in someone's arms, and a little face with eyes closed. The baby's hair looks to be very dark and there's lots of it! What a hairy baby, is my first thought. My second thought is, I feel dizzy. I can feel the doctor eyes watching my face.

He slowly lays a second photo on the desk. This one shows the baby with scrawny legs in knitted booties lying on a bed. She's wearing a loose shift over her diaper and she must be kicking her feet because the picture is blurred.

A third photo appears, and I am drawn to it. The baby is naked and enjoying a bath, truly enjoying herself. Her mouth is open in a big smile. She's pulled one foot toward her mouth and she's looking directly at the camera. It must be the photographer's face she smiles at.

My stomach wants to somersault. Is it nausea? All I know is that I want to be finished with all of these as quickly as possible. But I won't be allowed to go home to Arvid and Sophie until I am ready to accept Leah. I know that. "Let me see them all," I say to Dr. Coughlin. My voice sounds tinny and far away.

"Are you sure?" he asks, with a furrowed brow.

"Yes, I'm sure. Let me see them." One after another, he slowly lays the photos out on the desk before me in one long row.

The fourth photo is of Arvid holding the baby. He's holding the baby's arm out to wave at the camera while he grins broadly into it. The baby is looking back at Arvid's face, puzzled. How proudly he holds her. He looks happy. Is he like that every day when he holds the baby?

In the next picture, the baby with dark curls sits on a patchwork quilt on the kitchen floor. I recognize the baby toys on the floor, Sophie's yellow rubber duck and her little teddy bear. Of course, the picture is in black and white, but I remember that blue bear. I embroidered the eyes, nose and mouth on it. In the foreground a blurry rattle is being shaken. She looks up at it with wide, gleeful eyes and blows bubbles of delight between her lips which makes a dimple to the right of her mouth.

Another photo shows the baby, now chubby, showing off two front teeth with a grin. She stands by holding onto a chair. Her eyes look darker than before. She's wearing one of Sophie's little church dresses. I stop to stare at this photo.

"Everyone on Hawk Ridge has met this baby before I have," I remark dully.

"Do you want to continue right now? We can finish next time," the doctor offers.

I take a deep breath. I'm scared. And I want this to be over with. I look away, out the window and away from this foreign child. But I ignore the doctor's offer. I have to do this. "This baby looks nothing like Sophie. Sophie is as blonde as her daddy and she has big blue eyes. This baby's eyes are dark, aren't they?"

"It appears so, yes. Your eyes are very dark as well. Do you see a little of yourself in her?" The doctor asks me in his mildly curious voice.

For some reason, I don't want to nod in the affirmative. I pick up the photo to study it closely. "It feels so peculiar to see a baby that looks like me. Sophie was born looking just like I thought she would. It was only right that Arvid's daughter should look like him."

"Had it occurred to you that a child of yours *may* look like *you*?"

"No. I...I don't know why." I finger the photo. "Maybe I'm becoming my mother. And perhaps this one," I point at the picture in my hand, "is becoming me. We are playing our parts over again." A chill spread over me. "Maybe we'll get things right this time. Maybe that's why she looks like me?" I lay the photo down.

"Can you tell me more about what you mean by that, Caroline?"

"I know it sounds stupid. But somehow that's how I feel. I see her and it's as if the world has shifted, giving me space, the chance to make things right this time, to fix things."

"What would you like to fix, Caroline? To get right...if you were your mother, I mean?"

I blurt out the answer before it can get stuck in my throat. "I would take the two of us all the way to California, as far as the continent is wide. As far from Long Island as it's possible to get," I feel wobbly again, but I refuse to let the doctor see that. I look at the doctor's face intently.

"But I'm not saying my mother did anything wrong. No! She was a good mother to me, the best. She just didn't know..." I've said enough. My hands tremble, so I hide them.

"What didn't she know, Caroline? It's something that you learned later, isn't it? But it was too late for your mother?" His voice was soft.

"She didn't know her life would end in Minneapolis. She might have lived longer somewhere else...farther away...where it was warmer maybe."

"Hmmm, it sounds as if you're saying she became ill in the cold climate. Are you ready to talk about how your mother died, Caroline?"

"No." I snapped at him. "She just died suddenly. And then everything changed. It changed so much that it became hard to...That's all." I shake my head and work to keep my gaze steady. I tell myself to remain calm. This is just an ordinary conversation between us, nothing more. The doctor must see how well I can handle these photos.

"I think that someday, it will be important for you to talk about how your mother died, Caroline. It would have to be very important to the story of your life."

"Well, someday isn't here yet." I stand and leave, forcing myself not to run.

Late August 1949

I have looked at most of the photos of Leah now, more than once. Dr. Coughlin's determination not to send me home "until you are comfortable with the prospect of meeting your child," is palpable to me. He speaks gently, but firmly.

"It's not that you must feel the same love for her that you have for Sophie in order to go home. You haven't met her yet. But you must feel safe with her. I don't want you to feel anxiety in her presence. It's enough that you be interested in her, curious about her."

Coughlin is firm on this point, and so I will take on the most important acting role of my life. In high school, I enjoyed being in plays. There was nothing quite so freeing as to pretend to be someone else. I played a young Emily Webb in *Our Town,* and later, I was Juliet in *Romeo and Juliet.* The drama teacher said that when I cried over Romeo's body, that I brought tears to her eyes as well. Surely I can convince Dr. Coughlin that I am eager to meet my second daughter. But I will have to be someone else while I look at her photos.

Fall 1942

Janet was a year behind me in school and, like me, spent her teenage years in the orphanage. I didn't really get to know her though, until she moved into a room down the hall from me at the boarding house. When we were alone, she told me about her younger twin brother and sister. The twins were only four-years-old when they and Janet, at thirteen-years-old came to the orphanage. Within a few days, the twins were adopted by a family that lived someplace far away. "Iowa, I think," Janet said. She never saw them again.

"If you would only go to the family and explain things," Janet begged the house mistress. "It's only the three of us that's left in my family, in the whole world. Please, if you would only talk to them? They're kind people, aren't they?"

The house mistress assured her that they were. "Nothing to worry about there," she'd said.

"If you would just explain to them how important it is for the twins to have me with them. They'll miss me so much after losing their mama, too." She told me about the enthusiastic promises she'd made.

"Tell them I don't eat very much," she said, following the house mistress around the house without any response. "And...and I'm not one of those girls that just wants fancy clothes and things like that. I'm not like that. No, I'm not like those kinda girls at all. They won't have to spend hardly any money on me." The house mistress still didn't answer her.

So Janet continued, "I'm a hard worker. I *like* to work. Tell 'em that I know how to do a lot, too. I'm a real good cook already. My mama taught me. And I can manage a garden all by myself," at which the cottage manager supposedly looked at her and nodded her head, which Janet took as a good sign. "So, you'll talk to them?"

The house mistress said that she would.

She came back to Janet later, though and told her, "I'm sorry, honey. They only want the little ones. They're gone for good, Janet."

Janet talked to me a lot about her brother and sister. "I'm going to find 'em," she told me. "I need to earn a little money first and then I'm gonna find 'em."

"What will you do if you do find them, Janet?"

"*When* I find 'em, you mean. Well, I'm going to find a place to live nearby. I'll be part of their lives again. I'll know where they go to school and I'll give them birthday and Christmas gifts. I can tell them how it was when they were babies. How everybody said they were the prettiest babies they'd ever seen. I can tell 'em about how they slept in two dresser drawers; they were so little. And about how I helped mama look after them. I'm the only one that can tell 'em those stories about right after they were born." Janet's eyes were filled with excitement, anticipation.

"Edmund's first word was "truck", but it sounded like "fruck" and he called everything that moved "fruck." We all used to laugh and laugh. And Emily, my sister...her first word was "Jacha." That's how she said "Janet." Besides that they had their own special language that only they could understand. They'll be so happy to see me and to know that I didn't leave 'em. I couldn't bear it if they thought I left 'em on purpose. I can tell 'em about our real parents. No one will be able to keep us apart anymore."

Late August 1949

Janet is probably still searching for Edmund and Emily. With Janet's desire to be reunited with her brother and sister firmly planted in my mind, I will see the last photograph of Leah. I can be Janet. Leah will be Emily.

The next time I see Dr. Coughlin, Janet is ready. "Let's see the last of the photos today. I'm ready," Janet tells him with a smile. To be sure that my eyes don't get in Janet's way, they should remain looking down at the photo of the child. Janet naturally wants to study the photograph carefully.

In case my eyes should tear up, it will be because Janet longs to see Emily. Janet wonders how Emily is managing without her. She hopes that Emily is happy, and that she knows she is loved. Janet comes prepared and is not frightened by the photos.

If my head feels as if it will burst, I'll say nothing of that. I will talk of longing to see ~~Emily~~ Leah. If that boulder returns to sit squarely on my chest so that it becomes difficult to breathe, it will be for all the time that has been lost, kept away from the girl in the photograph. Yes, that is my plan.

20

THE LUCKY ONES

Caroline
Summary to Fall 1949

The rhythm of the hospital has changed without Lois here, without her grand mal seizure marking each dawn. I still glance at her bed when I awaken, as if she might still be there. But she died on April Fools' Day. The fact that someone else now sleeps in that bed does not make it anything other than "Lois' bed."

I think it's the way she repeated that same phrase over and over that twisted something deep inside me. It's been so long now since I heard her words; I can no longer repeat them. Of course, I never knew their true meaning, but I knew it was from her heart. It was her torment that she spoke of many times each day, but there was no one here to understand it. That was her hell.

Lois died too young, but how can a body continue to live being ravaged by seizures that are so violent day after day? I often think of that day, when I begged Big Alva to attend to Lois, that her seizure wasn't ending the way it had always done before. The way I see it, Big Alva killed Lois just as surely as if she'd shot her. She allowed her to seize until her brain was drained of its juice.

I see Lois in my mind's eye. She'd stopped seizing, gone silent and still, eyes frozen open, unseeing. She was gone before her heart stopped, before she stopped breathing. I wonder where Ojibwe go when they die? Is she at peace finally?

The new sister in Lois' bed invades my space at every turn. Only a few teeth remain at the back of her mouth. She is able to smack her bare gums together while at the same time click the few remaining teeth together. They say she's a biter. That's why they pulled out her teeth.

It is that new sister that now sits between Ruthie and me at mealtime. Their eating styles dovetail. After my insulin therapy ended in May, I'm back to eating at the table with Estra and Ruthie again, and Biter.

Yet, Marilyn and Celia and I find each other now and then. It's been devastating to watch Marilyn's melancholia wax and wane. In July, Dr. Reynolds starts her on a regimen of ECT (Electro Convulsive Therapy). Celia and I wait for her to return after each treatment, fearful that she won't remember what we've said to each other over the past few weeks. Will she have forgotten even more than that? Will she remember that she cares for us?

O ne Sunday afternoon in July, after Marilyn's second ECT, I am waiting for her and Celia in the solarium. We spend time together every Sunday, playing cards or some other game. Sometimes the three of us walk in the courtyard in front of the hospital buildings. We've proven that we can be trusted to stay on the grounds; we remain readily observable by the attendants. The clock on the solarium wall shows that it is going on to two o'clock, long past our time to meet after dinner. Something is wrong.

Celia and Marilyn's beds are close to one another. I know that Celia will bring Marilyn with her to the solarium. Marilyn might not remember where we are meeting, or that we are meeting at all. Maybe she won't remember that it's Sunday and that means that we have free time to spend together.

At last I see Celia's flaming red curls coming down the long hallway. Her eyes and nose seem to be as red as her hair; she's been crying. Behind her trails Marilyn. Connecting the two of them is one long piece of yarn, tied from Celia's wrist to Marilyn's wrist. My heart lurches. I move toward them, to meet them in the hall.

"Hi," I say, trying to sound cheerful, looking back and forth between them.

"Hi," Celia answers softly. She then brings me into a tight little three-person circle with her and Marilyn, but without either of us touching Marilyn. "It was a long morning," Celia mumbles.

"Let's sit down, okay?" I take Marilyn's elbow to guide her to the table I'd been holding for us. Marilyn backs away from me abruptly. She pulls her arm away, as if my hand burns her skin, her eyes frantic. These are not the soulful, wise eyes that I know so well.

Celia walks ahead, gently tugging on the yarn and says, "This way, Marilyn." Marilyn obediently follows her and sits in the chair that Celia pulls out for her.

"What's happened?" I mouth to Celia. Instead of mouthing something back to me, she turns to look at Marilyn.

"You're feeling a little bit better this afternoon, aren't you Marilyn?" Celia glances nervously at me.

"Yeah." Marilyn whispers to the table. Then she squints at me, "Who are you?"

The wind is knocked out of me as if I'd fallen from a great height. "I'm Caroline." I orchestrate my mouth into a smile. Marilyn should see friendly faces after ECT.

"I thought so," she says, but she looks skeptical. She glances around the room at the women gathered at various tables.

There are women playing "Crazy Eights" and "Whist" and a group at the far end of the room plays "Pig." Uproarious laughter comes from that end of the room. A few loners play solitaire, and others look out the windows rocking from side to side. One woman is undressing in the middle of the room. A nurse will come soon, no doubt; the woman is known as "the Stripper."

"I don't like this place," Marilyn says glumly.

"Caroline, let's you and I play something easy. Umm...Go Fish?" Celia raises her eyebrows at me, a signal of sorts, but one which I don't quite understand.

"Okay," I say. I leave the table, shaky, to get a deck of cards from the Games Closet Lady.

"What's going on with her?" the Games Closet Lady whispers to me when I ask her for the deck of playing cards. She directs her gaze toward Marilyn.

"She had ECT yesterday," I say. I bite my lip and try to release the pressure that is building up behind my eyes.

"Be careful, alright? She hasn't settled yet." I glance at her and back at Marilyn.

"What does that mean?" I whisper back to the Lady.

"She's still agitated. She'll be better later on, more like herself. Just gotta get through until then." She holds onto the cards until she conveys that bit of information and then pushes them toward me. I nod as if I understand very well what she is talking about.

Celia and I play "Go Fish" while Marilyn watches through a stranger's eyes for the next hour or more. The real Marilyn is somewhere else. Celia and I play as if we are having a lark, as if there is nothing amiss. I don't know what else to do. We just have to get through until she "settles."

There is never another day quite like that one after Marilyn's second ECT. That evening before bed, Celia and I wash up next to one another. We look into each other's eyes reflecting back at us from the shiny metal "looking glass." We know what the other is hoping and praying. Tomorrow, we'll get our Marilyn back again.

In the morning, Marilyn does seem more like herself. She doesn't remember the solarium from the day before, doesn't remember that she had ECT the day before that, nor events of the previous week or more. At least, as far as we can tell, it's time lost to her.

Celia and I nurture her as best we can after each ECT treatment. We tell Marilyn stories about things we've laughed about together. We remind her of how much we admire her kindness, what a good listener she is. She allows us to hold her hand and we tell her that we will always be good friends. At times, she appears a little surprised but pleased. By the time it seems that she is more or less herself again, that is, she's the Marilyn that is comfortable around us, she is also growing sadder day by day. She weeps at the smallest thing. Then they take her for another ECT treatment. Celia and I weep together and begin anew, our efforts to bring her back to us.

Marilyn and Celia and I talk about my leaving now and then. I hate to make Celia sad with this talk. If Marilyn continues the ECT after I'm gone, she may not remember me. And Celia will be even more alone. With the conclusion of insulin therapy also came the end of our private threesome dinners together. Now we see each other only briefly during the week, when our activity schedules overlap, and on Sunday afternoons when we meet in the solarium to play games or cards. I hate to leave the two of them here, the dearest friends I've had in years. I tell them what frightens me about going home.

There is a panic that is like being crushed. Breathe deeply, I tell myself. In and out. In and out. It comes when I think of the baby. Arvid brought a more recent photo to the hospital last time. He caught me off-guard by showing it to me directly instead of giving it to Dr. Coughlin for me to see. The doctor had told him that I handle seeing photographs of Leah quite well now. Because of that, he handed it to me and I had no time to prepare to be 'Janet.'

The stranger child is nearly fifteen months old now. She has dark curls and very dark eyes, "like her mommy," Arvid tells me with what I think is pride. In the latest picture, she stands on the front porch of the house next to Sophie in Sunday dresses that I don't recognize. Marit has sewn new dresses for them. It's obvious that Sophie was given the job of keeping the little one in place for the picture. How Sophie has grown! It takes my breath away. She's three and a half years old. Oh, she is a beauty. Such a sweet smile. I'll bet she's a good big sister.

The hand that Sophie holds onto, however, belongs to a child that doesn't look very happy about the picture or the porch or anything. She wears a pout that I've seen before, in my own mirror. Of course, we're not allowed real mirrors here, too dangerous, so I haven't seen a good reflection in a while, but I remember what my own pout looks like. I used it in the orphanage as needed. The dark-haired child is looking down so that I can see her long back eyelashes lying over her chubby cheeks.

I panic because I have no feelings for that baby. I don't know if I can ever be her mother. Will Arvid understand that? Will he grow to hate me for it? She's already had her first birthday and she's never even seen me. I've never seen her. In the pictures of her, she does resemble me. It's an eerie resemblance somehow. It's better that I don't remember touching her before they brought me here. Why, I don't know, but I know it's better that way.

I saw Dr. Coughlin yesterday. "Do you feel like you'll be ready to go home soon?"

I inhale deeply and blow the air out again. "Am I ready?" I say. "I haven't been in charge of anything for the past fifteen months. Other people decide *what* I do, *where* I go, *when* I will do anything, even *why*, and with *whom*. And now I am to make decisions for myself?"

"What frightens you the most?" he asks gently.

He waits for me to say, "the baby, Leah." But I won't say that. "Many things...will Sophie remember me? At all? If she doesn't even remember me, if she doesn't want me to touch her...if she's afraid of me? I don't know if I'll be able to handle that." Tears are at the ready. I hold them off.

"What else, Caroline? You said many things."

"Will Arvid be embarrassed to be seen with me? In front of his friends, I mean? It's bad enough that I've been gone so long; that I was in a mental hospital. But even people who don't know that will recognize right away that there is something "off" about me. Just look at me! My butchered hair. I'm skinny and my front tooth is broken to a sharp point.

"People used to tell me that I was beautiful. But now? Maybe he'll be ashamed to say he's my husband." I look around the room aimlessly. "It doesn't seem like he *blames* me for being here, but maybe he will later. Maybe he'll come to resent me for the burden I've been to him, to the family? The way I ruined things for us."

Dr. Coughlin has patient, gray eyes. He waits again for me to go on. "Are you afraid about baby Leah, Caroline?"

This is a conversation we've had a few times. I know where I need to go with it.

"I have to give things a chance to become what they will. I know I'm a different person now because I've experienced different things." I pause. "I can't make sense of everything all at once." I look at him for his approval to be just as I am, and he gives it without fail.

He nods and leans forward with folded hands. "We've talked about this before, but I want to say this again. Be merciful with yourself, Caroline. Think about Sophie learning to walk. She didn't learn all at once. She stood and fell. Crawled. Stood again. Fell. Two steps and plopped down again." He watches my face to be sure that I am with him in that place of understanding.

"You didn't punish her for falling down...for not getting it right the first time. Give yourself permission to fall occasionally. It is unfair to pile blame on yourself for an illness that you didn't ask for. For problems that you didn't bring on yourself. You know this."

I have written a letter to give to Dr. Coughlin for his birthday. I tell him that I write a letter because we don't meet on his birthday. The truth is that there are things I don't think I can say properly in person. Aside from Arvid, I've never known a man that is so gentle and kind. I don't understand what my feelings are toward him.

He's not a friend in the same way that Bernt is. For one thing, he's a doctor, and for another, he's married. But what I know for certain is that when I talk with him, I feel as though he can see right into my soul. The closest thing I can come up with is the way my mother was able to see immediately by the look on my face, when I was happy, or sad, or worried. The doctor has been so good to me. I feel like a naughty, deceitful child for playing the role of "Janet" when it comes to baby Leah, but it's the only way I can manage it, and I do want to go home again.

October 24, 1949
Dear Doctor Coughlin,

Happy Birthday. Nurse Connie spilled the beans about your birthday. Since I will not see you tomorrow, I send you my sincerest Birthday Wishes in advance. I can't tell you how thankful I am for all that you have done for me. I shudder to think what might have become of me if you had not been here when I first came. As you have told me many times, talking therapy is hard work. I wish there was some way to repay you. Especially for believing that I was able to get better. Perhaps that was the most helpful of all. I wish you the very happiest of birthdays. May you have a wonderful day of celebration with your wife and children on your special day.

With deepest appreciation,
Caroline Celeste D'Bouvier Fjeld

Wednesday, November 2, 1949

It's my going-home day. After breakfast and the goodbyes I wait for Arvid outside on a bench. He won't arrive until close to noon, but I just want to feel the crisp air on my skin. There are too many things going through my head to remain indoors. Out here, I am able to get up and pace around now and then.

I've said my goodbyes on the ward and to Dr. Coughlin. I said goodbye to Ruthie first. It was the easiest of the goodbyes for me because it will be a relief to be away from her. Shame on me for saying that; the harelip is not her fault. The only good news for Ruthie is that she now has a table partner that suits her. The Biter is at least as repulsive as Ruthie when she eats. They are perfect table partners. Perhaps that's the best that could be hoped for. I have prayed for God's forgiveness again and again, for being put off by the two of them eating.

I know that Estra will never leave here. Unlike Estra's family, mine doesn't have to fear that I'll kill myself by overeating. With Estra, that is a legitimate danger. But Estra is not distressed by her hospitalization. Somehow she finds pleasure in the simplest things. Estra says goodbye to me with one of the dozen nursery rhymes I've taught her. She cinched her arms tightly around my middle until my breath was all but gone. "I'll say my favorite rhyme for you," she said. "My very favorite!"

I've come to understand that Estra's favorite changes daily. Today it was this, and she stepped back to recite it with relish. "Humpty Dumpty sat on a wall. Humpty Dumpty had a great fall. All the Kings' horses and all the Kings' men couldn't put Humpty together again." She looked up at me, her head cocked to one side and grinned.

"I love you, Caroline. I love you *so* much. *So so* much! Don't you fall like Humpty Dumpty and don't you break into pieces so nobody can put you back together again. But if you do fall, if you *do*... you just come right back here, and *we'll* put you back together again. Put you *ba-a-ack* together." Estra giggled heartily, then she chose a new grip and with her head jammed under my breasts, she squeezed me again, finishing with a loud, "Mmm Mmm Mmm."

Estra's suggestion that I could come back here in order to be put back together again gave me a start. I shrugged it off and told her, "Be good, Estra. You are the alliteration queen and don't forget it."

The hardest goodbyes were to Marilyn and Celia. I fear for them. I dread to think how my leaving will affect them. My heart aches to think that they may spend their lives here, grow old and die in this place. If we do see each other again, things between us will never be as they were only yesterday when we knew that each of us would be waking up in that same dormitory room, sharing the same plight.

Celia goes into high speed at times and that's a problem for her here. It would be an even bigger problem for her on the outside.

There are periods when she stays awake for days at a time and busies herself at all hours. It's surprising what she can find to do in this austere environment: rearranging chairs in the solarium, cleaning everything, making the beds of those sisters that she says were poorly made. That gets her into trouble with some of them. In the Rag Shop, she organizes the cloths by color, then by pattern. During these high speed times, she's not interested in food or drink. Her laugh becomes high-pitched and maniacal and only my company or that of Marilyn seems to help her calm a little. Celia has become so terribly thin. Will she fade into nothingness?

Marilyn's melancholia plagues her more and more of late. She attempted to take her life before she came here; it was in fact, the very reason she was sent here. Only two days ago, when the two of us were alone, she told me that she wanted to confide in me about something. "Since you're leaving, Caroline, I can tell you. I just couldn't before, but you must promise not to tell Celia. Do you promise?" She looked at me with pleading in her eyes.

"Yes. I can keep a secret. Anything told to me in confidence will remain right here." I placed my hand over my heart. "What is it, Marilyn. You look so upset."

"Alright." She sighed and wrung her hands. "I had it all planned out and it would have worked perfectly too, but for a smashed finger. You see, I mixed some rat poison in with a bit of leftover hotdish, to make it easier for me to get the poison down. My children were in school and my husband was at work, roofing.

"As I was finishing what was to have been my last meal, my husband came charging through the door. He'd smashed a finger at work and was sent home because he couldn't hold a hammer. I left the table and got up to find the bandaging for him. While my back was turned, my husband dug into the rest of that poisoned hotdish. By the time I got back with the bandages, he'd eaten plenty.

"Oh, Caroline. Why did it have to be that day, of all days, that he smashed his finger?" Marilyn sobbed. "So I told him to stop eating, that it was bad food, but he said it tasted just fine.

"'You just want to save it for yourself, for your dinner tomorrow,' he said. 'Well, I didn't get to eat at the work site, so I'm hungry and I'm eating it.' He used that nasty tone that he often took with me and he kept on eating.

"It's obvious that we didn't have much of a marriage. It wasn't unusual for him to ignore me or ignore things that I said. So I had to tell him about the rat poison because he needed to get his stomach pumped. I couldn't leave my children with no mother *and* no father. I just hoped it was already too late for me to be saved. But my husband dragged me with him to the doctor, of course, and explained what I'd done, that I'd poisoned both of us.

"After we'd had our stomachs pumped and after I was very sick for a time, the police came to see me. I was arrested for attempted murder! My husband said that I would never be allowed in our house again, that I was crazy. And he said that I could never be around our children again. And I never did see them again, Caroline." She burst into frank weeping. "From the jail, they brought me here. The judge said that I was insane."

Marilyn looked at me with pleading eyes. "I wanted to tell you because...I want someone to know that I'm not a murderer. I just wanted to get out of living that life. Do you see?"

"Yes, of course. Oh, Marilyn." I hugged her tightly while she wept. "You wouldn't hurt anyone else. How could anyone think that you wanted to murder your husband? You told him about the poison so that he could go to the doctor. You saved him, Marilyn."

"I haven't told anyone else about this. The doctors knew about me before I got here, but no one else. I'm not a murderer but everyone back home thinks that I am. I can never go back there, even if I do get out of here someday."

"Oh, Marilyn, I am so sorry. I am so so very sorry." While she wept, I rocked her in my arms, saying, "Shhh now. You are a good and kind person. You would never hurt another human being. Shhh now."

I have to get up now to pace around for a bit in front of the hospital buildings.

The last time Arvid was here, he was so cheerful about bringing me home. He told me about the goings-on at Hawk Ridge. One of the Hedland's sons added another baby to their family. Five children now, all under seven years old! And the Hedlands bought more farmland when the Svehaugens sold out.

The biggest news for me, though, and the most surprising news was about Arvid's best friend, Bernt. Last summer, he took in that young girl, Inga to work on the farm with him and her little boy too, of course, Matthias. Arvid told me that Inga and Bear have gotten married, and Bear is adopting Matthias. Amazing! I guess I'll be getting used to having Inga around.

I wonder what Marit thinks of Inga. Then I remember that Marit thinks well of almost everyone, no matter what. I smile to think of how nearly everyone is "good" in Marit's eyes.

Will I still be "good" in Marit's eyes, too?

I have other worries, too. Will Arvid love me the way he once did? Will he always be worrying that I'm going to go crazy again? Like Estra says, "How crazy in the head can a person get?" I sit down on the bench again.

I see Arvid's car come down the drive and onto the grounds of the hospital. For a fleeting moment, I recall thinking that this place was a nunnery, or a prison. Arvid pulls the car up close to where I sit on the bench. Here I am, wearing this old coat over the dress that they say I was wearing when I came here. In my satchel I have only a very few personal belongings and a little bag that I made in the Rag Shop to hold a few things I am bringing home for Sophie. Just a few trifling gifts.

Arvid steps out of the car slowly, one foot on the ground and then the other before turning to look at me over the top of the car.

"Caroline." He says my name like it's a prayer. Beautiful! My eyes pulse with silent, grateful tears. He walks to me without breaking eye contact. "Let's go home," he says. His eyes are moist, too.

"Yes, let's go home." I answer, longing to drown in his blue eyes.

He helps me into the car. It's a newer car, one that I've never seen before. A dark blue sedan, another Ford. "So, Nellie finally gave up the ghost?" I ask him.

"Yup, she lived a good long life. It's time to start fresh. Don't you think?"

"Yes, it is," I answer. He puts the car in gear, and we drive away from those hulking brick monstrosities.

I want to just watch him as he drives. The reality of him is so...close. Magical. I long to touch him but somehow fear that if I touch him, he might disappear...poof. I'm having a good dream. I don't want to ruin it, nor wake up. His beard is nicely trimmed. He wears the blue shirt that he keeps for good, and a pair of dark pants I've never seen. "You look so nice," I say softly.

He reaches out to take my hand. He holds it so gently between us on the seat. We drive in silence for a time.

I have to let him know I am worried. Not the paranoid kind of worried. Will he understand the difference? "I don't know if I'll be able to manage that big house, Arvid. I haven't been in charge of anything for so long. I haven't even cooked for myself." A knot catches in my throat.

He squeezes my hand and says, "You don't have to worry about that. Grandma Marit will help you, for as long as you want her to." He emphasizes the "you" and looks at me with warm eyes. The way he refers to his own mother as "grandma" seems to put Marit right here in the car with us. And I hear in his voice, a man who is proud to be a father.

Marit has taken care of my Sophie for me all this time. Been there for her night and day. Given her all the love she had to give. Probably all that Sophie ever needed. I should be so thankful to her. And I am. But what if I'm simply not needed anymore?

Suddenly these thoughts make a knotted rope climb its way up my throat. It tries to choke me. "She knows she has to give Sophie back, right?" I look over at him, pleading for the answer I want to hear.

He knows what I mean. "Of course, she does. You are Sophie's mommy. No one can replace you."

Tears spill over silently for some time, tears of relief. Arvid just squeezes my hand now and then, gently. There are so many things I feel nervous about. When the tears have stopped, I must ask, "What have people told their children about me on the Ridge, Arvid, about the crazy lady that's coming home...about why I went away?

What has Sophie heard about me? Will everyone be afraid of me now?"

Arvid bit the edge of his lip. "Our friends know that you have been ill. That you needed help that I couldn't give. They'll welcome you home." He looked at me then. "I swear they will. And the whole congregation has been praying for your return." He seemed to grit his teeth when he added that last.

"I need to thank your mom for taking care of everything. What would have become of us without all that she has done?" I feel panicked again. It's hard to breathe. There's not enough air in the car.

Arvid looks at me with his kind blue eyes and squeezes my hand again. "She's not lookin' to be thanked, Caroline. She's just glad you're coming home."

We drive in silence for a while. My emotions are riding an unbroken bronco. Up, down, sideways, rolling. "Yesterday, Dr. Reynolds stopped by to tell me that I am one of the lucky ones." My voice becomes husky. "I never ever felt lucky around him. I felt as though I was his science project." I look at Arvid. "I never believed a thing he told me, Arvid."

"That's okay," my husband says softly, a hint of a smile.

"But I did believe Dr. Coughlin." I say. "And I could say what I thought was the truth with him. It is frightening to think how things might have gone for me if he hadn't been there." More miles pass. "It's strange to hear myself say his name out loud now that I've gone. That part of my life is truly over."

Arvid speaks slowly, thoughtfully. "You trusted him to help you. I trusted him too, a lot." Arvid squeezed my hand as he looked into my eyes. "He's been important to both of us. I'm thankful that he was there."

"Sometimes I am confused about who I am." I must get to the part that terrifies me. I prepare myself for something very hard to say. "Arvid, I know I can't expect that you will love me the same way that you did before. I've thought about that and," the pitch of my voice is rising, "and it's okay. I'm prepared. After I've been gone so long. And I left you and your mother to handle...everything. I understand how you must feel. You mustn't feel badly about it—"

"Caroline! Stop it! No, that isn't the way our marriage goes from here. Do you hear me? For richer for poorer. In sickness and in health. Do you remember those words? I've never forgotten them. I made a promise to you. You said that you believed the doctor. You trusted him. Now it's me that you must trust. I love you. Yesterday, today, tomorrow and forever. Do you hear me?"

"Yes," is all that I can say. I take a few deep breaths, and with them the pressure builds behind my eyes yet again. "Yes, I will trust you, Arvid, my dear husband."

In a little while, I pull my hand away from his and look out the window. I recognize the high ridgeline we're traveling on; it extends for miles between Preston and Harmony. I can see for miles in every direction. Shorn rolling fields where corn, oats and alfalfa once stood. Even now, after harvest, in the cold of November each crop has left behind its own muted fall color, stripe by graceful stripe. The stripes hug the shape of each roller coaster hill until they descend to the forested valley below. Then the graceful stripes march quietly up the hills again.

Hill after hill romps into the distance. But the harvested fields are tired. Used up. Thankful for winter when nothing more is asked of them. Everything around me, everything I see is suddenly evidence of the life, the lives, the seasons that continued on without me present.

I wasn't needed for any of it.

I wasn't going to say any more to torture Arvid. I don't want to make this harder for him, but it comes without my bidding anyway. "Look at all that I've missed. Do you see? Here it is, the fall again. Why should I be needed now? For *this* fall? For the *next* season?" I sob into my hands.

Arvid pulls the car over then, onto an entrance to a farmer's field. He leaves the car running, for the heater. He slides over toward me where I have shrunk against the door. "Shhh, now, my love. My Caroline. Shhh, you are needed. You will always be needed." He gives me his white hanky and then holds out his hand for me to take again, in my own time. I give him my hand and then stare at the two hands, holding onto one another, one of them so brown, calloused and strong, while the other is white, soft and thin. Yet each of them clings so tightly, as if saving one another from falling.

"I have never stopped loving you, Caroline. I will never stop loving you. Needing you. I know that you are suffering. Please... allow me to suffer alongside you. To understand how it is to come back again. Help me understand."

Who am I, how am I, to be the wife of this dear man? We hold each other tightly until there are no more tears to be cried. Then Arvid drives us home, my hand in his.

21

PIE 'N COFFEE

Caroline
November 1949

Walking back into the farmhouse for the first time after being away for so long feels like a dream. My legs move as if stiff and wooden. It's hard to believe I'm really here. If I fall asleep will I wake up back at the State Hospital again? Find out that this is only a dream? Inside the kitchen is a world that is at once familiar and yet foreign. A faint aroma of bacon from breakfast is nearly hidden by the smell of gingerbread in the oven. The kitchen is bright and cheerful, unlike any room I've seen in so very long, with shiny cupboards painted a creamy white and crisp curtains!

Marit holds me at arms' length and looks into my eyes. "Can I give you a hug, my daughter?" she asks with moist eyes.

I have to clear my throat to speak. "Yes...yes."

Over Marit's shoulder I see Sophie, shyly and slowly shifting from one foot to the other, side to side. She plays with her fingers, forming a steeple, then knitting and twisting the fingers together and apart again. She looks away when I catch her eye. Sophie has grown taller! She's three and a bit now. Marit has braided her hair in two long braids with a pink ribbon at the bottom of each.

When Marit releases me, I kneel on the cold floor, and wait, hopeful that my daughter might approach me. Arvid and Marit gently speak at the same time. "Mommy's home, Sophie."

I open the small cotton bag I made in the Rag Shop which serves as a purse, of sorts. I pull out a ball that I made in the Crafts Shop. The ball is of polished pine at its center and then it's wrapped snugly with thin strips of leather, stitched and steamed to tighten everything together. I toss the ball from one hand to the other and then roll the ball across the floor to Sophie. She watches the ball approach her feet, her blue eyes wide, as if the ball were a miraculous thing.

She bends down to pick it up, then sits down on the floor opposite me with her feet in front of her, an open "V." She rolls the ball back. "Hi, Sophie," I finally say softly to my stranger daughter. "I'm so happy to see you. I've missed you so much," I say with moist eyes. I don't want this moment to become blubbery, so I stop talking,

223

smile and roll the ball back to her. Then in a most unladylike fashion, I copy her seated "V."

"Will it bounce?" Sophie asks. "And what happened to your tooth?"

"It will bounce a little, but not indoors, okay?" Pause. "I fell down and broke my tooth. It makes me look a little scary, huh?" I try not to look sad when I say that.

"Mmm, maybe a little bit," Sophie answers. "But what happened to your pretty hair, Mommy?"

It is the first time I have heard Sophie call me "Mommy" in fifteen months. I beam, though tears threaten again.

"Oh, I had it cut really short, to see how I'd like it, but I think I'll let it grow out again. What do you think?"

Sophie cocks her head to one side thoughtfully and rolls the ball back again. "Mmm, it's okay I guess." She looks at me sideways. "But I like it the other way best."

"Me, too." We share a smile.

"What else do you have in that bag, Mommy?"

"Do you want to see? Come sit by me." When my fingers touch Sophie's skin for the first time, I have to take a deep breath. Her little hand is the softest thing I can imagine...reaching into my bag to see what else she might find. First she pulls out a small rag doll with yellow yarn hair that's braided much like hers, and, finally, she pulls out another dress for the doll and a small doll's quilt.

Arvid and Marit tiptoe out of the kitchen, leaving us alone to talk until Sophie jumps up and runs onto the back porch. "Mommy, Mommy, look what Daddy made for me."

I follow her through the front room and through the door out onto the screen porch. It seems more spacious here than I remember.

On the floor are stacks of blocks from various wood scraps. Some are square blocks, but most of them are random sizes and shapes. Each has been sanded smoothly, a labor of love from Arvid. He has followed us onto the porch and leans against the door frame, watching our daughter with pride.

Sophie stands tall in the midst of her creations and points them out. "This is my barn and my hog house and my outhouse. And this is my windmill. Daddy got me a pinwheel to put in the middle!" Sophie flicks the pinwheel sticking out the top of a stack of blocks and it spins wildly. She giggles and beams at me.

"Oh, Sophie! These are just wonderful! You built these all by yourself?" I clasp my hands to my chest, one over the other in awe of my brilliant daughter. For a brief moment, I remember the boxes of wood scraps at the hospital carpentry building.

Two things suddenly barge into my mind at the same time. Sophie doesn't lisp anymore. And the porch is bigger because the old iron bed is gone.

"Oh, you decided to remove the bed from the back porch!" I remark casually to Arvid. I puzzle for a moment over why the bed was removed. "I like it. Now Sophie has more room to play out here." I look at Arvid and smile.

"Yes. It's a good place for rainy days especially, spring through fall," he says with relief. "She needs a warm sweater out here at this time of the year, of course, but that hasn't stopped her yet. It does make kind of a special area for the girls to play."

The girls. Plural. I take a long deep breath. "The baby must be sleeping, I guess?" I look up at Arvid, apprehension forming on my forehead.

"She's been going down for an afternoon nap about one o'clock every day." Then he calls out to the kitchen with, "Is that about when she went down today, Mom? One o'clock?"

"Ya, ya," Marit calls back from the kitchen. She is giving Arvid and I space, some privacy, to knit our little family back together without her interference. I love her for it.

"Would you like to go up and look in on her, Caroline, while she's asleep?"

"I guess so," and I hesitate while I chew the corner of my lip. "I'll see her first while she's still asleep and...get her face fixed in my mind."

Arvid holds my hand as we climb the stairs. "Oh, her crib is in your mother's room!" I whisper, surprised. "Oh, but of course." I am actually relieved to see Leah's crib in her grandma's room. I'd been anxious that the crib would be in our bedroom, next to our bed. I realize now that I didn't want it to be there.

"Yes, Mom's been a godsend. She's taken such good care of..." He doesn't finish the sentence but looks at me cautiously.

"Thank God she was here," I say, to agree as quickly as possible. I don't want to hear that anxiety in Arvid's voice. "What would we have done without her?" I add. I don't want Arvid to walk on eggshells around me, wondering what's okay to say or not.

I creep further into Marit's room to see the second of Arvid's daughters. Those are the words that I hear in my head..." Arvid's daughters." I can find no memory of ever seeing this child. I peer over the crib railing at her, and gasp. Quickly, I back away from the crib.

"What's wrong, Caroline? I mean, she's changed so much, fifteen months old...it must be startling." There is pleading in his voice. I am frightening him though I don't want to.

"I feel like I've jumped out of an airplane, Arvid, and I'm waiting to crash to the ground." I step back out of the room and Arvid follows me. I whisper, "I don't *know* that baby. She doesn't know me. Arvid, I don't remember anything about her. Is she really ours? Did we bring her home from the hospital with us? You've told me we did, but I really don't remember.

"Arvid, I'm *afraid* to remember. I don't think I *should* remember it. I don't know why that is, but I don't. I can't. Do you understand? *Now* what do I do?" A tear forms and spills onto my cheek. Arvid gives me his white hanky, for the second time that day. The action serves to open a spigot for me.

Arvid folds me in his arms while I weep. Long, rasping, drawn-out waves of sobbing. He leads me into our bedroom, and we sit side-by-side on our bed while I gasp for air between each successive wail and torrent. There is no stopping the rush now. The dam broke with only one glance at this foreign child, Leah.

My husband tenderly covers me with a blanket and leaves my thin, exhausted frame lying on our bed where I finally fall asleep. Before I drift off, I hear him creep back downstairs.

The next morning I stand at the kitchen window, drinking in the last of the fall colors spread across the bluffs when a car drives into the farmyard. Marit quickly opens the door to Bear and Inga. Bear says, "We wanted to be the first neighbors to welcome you home." He speaks directly to me, and smiles with tender, unassuming eyes.

Inga grins up at him and nods at me. "Yes, we did." On her small hip rides Matt, a handsome chubby toddler. The three of them liven up the kitchen in such a way that my breath is stopped for a moment. For friends to just appear whenever they want to, without first seeking permission to come or go, it's a beautiful thing out here in the world!

I feel awkward at first. I hang back because of my brutal haircut and my pointed tooth. I am so thin. But he comes forward as if nothing has changed, and a lump forms in my throat.

"May I give you a welcome home hug?" he asks me with open arms and a small smile.

"Yes," I say. I smile tentatively and sigh my relief. "I owe you congratulations, the both of you," I say first to Bear and then to Inga after the hug. "Actually, all three of you. You're a family now. I am so happy for *all* of you!" Bernt looks healthy and happy, and there's adorable little Matt looking up at him.

"Daddy?" he says, reaching for Bernt. My heart wants to burst. Matt is a fortunate child. And Inga? There's a part of me that envies her bright, contented face. Bernt accepts my congratulations for all three of them.

As our visit ends, Inga pulls Marit aside in the kitchen. They talk in whispers.

The next morning, Inga shows up with Matt around nine o'clock in the morning and says, "I'm here to take care of the three little ones while you two," and she points at Marit and me with a broad grin, "go out and get Caroline's hair fixed nice. Now, get goin'." She fairly rushes us out the door. Sophie runs to hug Inga, and Leah goes easily into Inga's arms.

Oh, yes! Maybe someone can fix this awful hair. I am dizzy with excitement.

"Thank you Inga. I can't thank you enough," I say to her and I mean it.

Marit drives us down into the valley and on to Houston, ten miles away. I am wearing what was once my favorite Sunday dress with the navy polka dots.

Marit offers, "I don't want you to feel like a fish in a bowl right away, so, let's go someplace we don't know people."

"Do you know a hairdresser in Houston, Marit?" I ask as we head down the narrow, winding road to the valley floor.

"I have my sources," Marit is uncharacteristically smug. "And you know what else? While we're there, I thought we'd stop and have ourselves a little-lunch, like de town ladies out for de day. At least have some pie n' coffee or something. What do you think about dat?"

"That sounds wonderful," I breathe a contented sigh.

"And den, I thought we'd go look at de store. See if we can't find something dat would make a nice new dress for you. Maybe two of 'em. Look at some new patterns, and see if something catches your eye?"

"Oh, Marit. You are so good to me. You've always been better to me than anyone in my life, besides my own mother, of course. And Arvid." I feel something like an unexpected giddiness that wants to bubble up inside of me. "Thank you."

"Ya, well, Arvid thought it was a good idea to go today, too. You need to get out and about a little bit. But de whole thing was Inga's idea, really. And once she said it, I thought, well, why didn't *I* think of dat?"

"You know her pretty well now, don't you?" I feel uneasy asking about Marit's relationship with Inga. It's obvious that she's been around the Fjeld household, given how familiar the children are with her.

227

"Oh ya. Ya know at first I wondered, what in de world is dat going to be like for Bernt? Him married to such a young girl! And such a plucky one, too, ya know. But den, Arvid and I talked some and we thought, well, Bernt is happy. De little boy is happy. And after being around Inga a little more, I can see dat she is happy, too. And she's one hard worker, too, oh my goodness! Well, anyway, what else do you want in a family? Besides love and hard work?" Marit warms me with a smile.

I smile in return.

"Ya, Inga's been over to de house many times, now. We help each other pretty often. She's a good person, Caroline. Those parents of hers are not good people though. Dat is yust too bad when you come across something like dat. Oh my." She shook her head and stopped herself short and glanced at me. "Oh, I am sorry." Marit said softly.

"Why are you sorry to me?" I ask her, puzzled.

"Oh, ah," she hesitates. "I don't want to remind you of anything you don't want to remember."

"Marit, you can say anything at all to me. Don't worry about that." An apology for reminding me of unwanted memories takes me by surprise. I've never talked much about my early years with Arvid and certainly not with Marit. What does she think she knows? Maybe in time, I will tell them more.

In the hair salon, we look at the photos of movie stars' haircuts. Swing music is playing on the radio. When I get into the chair, I show the hairdresser the picture and tell her, "I'd like my hair cut like Beatrice Pearson, in *Force of Evil*."

"Hmmm, now, say, that would like *real* nice on you! Your hair ain't quite that long yet, though. How about like Jane Greer in *Dick Tracy*?" The woman points her long pink fingernail at the photo of Jane Greer. She's a beauty, ain't she?" The hairdresser marks time by humming in between thoughts. "You know, you could pass for her, or her sister at the very least."

I feel like there's hope of looking rather ordinary again, maybe even attractive, if I keep my lips closed. "I like that," I tell her. "Yes, let's do it. Jane Greer first, then Beatrice Pearson." I look at myself in the mirror and relax into the chair.

The woman starts combing through my thick hair. "Say, this is quite the cut you got here. I hope nobody *I* know gave it to ya." She snorted. "I sure don't wanna be rude, or nothin' like that, but whoever cut your hair didn't do you no favors. Lordy, I sure hope you didn't give 'em a tip."

"No. No I didn't, as a matter of fact." I smile without showing my tooth. I'd like to listen to the radio.

Maybe she's done talking now. I can hope. She hums a tuneless melody.

"Say, there's gonna be some big doin's in town here this weekend. A meatball and lutefisk supper and the high school is doin' *H.M.S. Pinafore.* I've been hearin' the kids 'r real good in it, too. It's real funny. Are you gonna go?"

"No, we've made some other plans but thank you for mentioning it."

Then, as if a lightbulb has come on, she stops humming and says, "Say, you're not related to that Fjeld family up near Spring Grove are ya? That family where the wife got shipped off to the funny farm last year? Man, what a story that was!"

The hairdresser keeps cutting. Snip, snip, snip. "Oh, mercy. That must've been an awful hard pill to swallow for that family. I heard she left two little ones behind, too and one was a newborn. Can you hold your head up just a little bit more, honey? Shoot...somethin' like that? It makes you wonder why those kinda things happen, huh?"

"Bad genes is what my friend says. B-a-a-d genes. A person can't do anything about that, can ya? But...I don't know. Maybe it's somethin' else." Snip, snip, snip.

"Maybe it's payback for somethin'. Y' know...like in the Bible, where it says somethin kinda like visiting the sins upon the third and fourth generations? But maybe it's just b-a-a-d parenting. I saw this thing in a women's magazine. It was a quote from a lady writer, Beryl Brinder—Brainbow—er' somethin' like that." She shook her head and waved her hand.

"Now, I don't know her from Adam, but what she said made sense to me." The hairdresser stopped cutting. "She said, 'Everything else you grow out of, but you never recover from childhood.' I think that's probably a true thing, right there. What d'you think? Can I ask you to hold up your head a little bit more, please?"

I finally speak up. "I'm sorry. I'm not feeling very well, I guess. Um, can I just sit quietly—"

"Ah, Mrs. Svenson," Marit pokes her head around the corner. "I heard dat you do a really good yob with cutting hair, but they didn't tell me dat you were such a big yakker. Tell you what...I can't speak for her," she tips her head toward me, "but *I* don't tip a hairdresser dat can't keep her mouth shut for a nice relaxing sit in de chair." Marit's head disappears behind the corner again.

"Well...I never..." the hairdresser clucks.

My eyes have grown huge—Marit telling a perfect stranger to be quiet? What's more, she made it sound like she goes to the hairdresser on a regular basis, and that she knows all about tipping. Pffft. Marit wears her hair wrapped around her head in a thick gray braid. As far as I know, she's *never* been to a hairdresser.

Marit pays the woman for me, "De tip coulda been yust a little bit more but, well, you know..." she tips her head to one side, and then she and I walk out the door.

"I'm so sorry for dat, Caroline. I wasn't listening to her at first."

"Marit, I've never seen you talk to anyone like that before! I didn't know you even knew *how* to shut someone up like that!" I smile at her as we climb into the car.

She smiled warmly in return. "Dat cut looks *so* nice on you, Caroline, my dear." She looks at me approvingly. "Oh, ya. You *do* look like a movie star now. Yust wait till Arvid sees dat new do."

I roll my eyes. "Oh, my heavens!" I give her a little squeeze on her arm and grin.

"Now, it's time for a little-lunch," she announces. "We can always eat what's good for us at suppertime. Let's have ourselves a little treat."

She drives us to a restaurant down the street. A business-like waitress appears with her pad almost immediately. "D'ya know what you're gonna have today, ladies?"

"Pie 'n coffee. What kinda pie do you have back there?" Marit asks.

As we drink our coffee, I wonder aloud. "Does that happen a lot, Marit? Like what that hairdresser said?" I can't meet her eyes.

"Oh, you know, now and den it does, when they don't know who we are, or they don't know dat we are standing nearby. People get to talking. Sometimes folks don't think before they talk. But not so much in Spring Grove because everybody there knows us." She pauses and sips her coffee. "Hmmm...ya, for dat reason, maybe we should have yust gone to Spring Grove for de haircut. I didn't think about dat part."

"No, I knew I'd run into this. My story makes for juicy gossip. Maybe it's better I hear right away what people are saying. I have to figure out how to react."

The first piece of lemon meringue pie I've seen in well over a year is placed before me along with a folded cloth napkin and the kind of silverware that Marit calls "the good silver." My hand goes to my throat. Such an appetizing sight! Tart lemon tickles my nose and light-as-air meringue stands as tall as my little finger is long. I gaze in near amazement at the dessert.

I must say one thing before I can take a bite. "But you know the part that was the worst?" I say softly. "That quote about childhood. Maybe I've given Sophie bad genes?"

"Oh, say now Caroline. Don't you give dat another thought. There is nothing to dat business about de yenes. Children need love and she is doing yust fine. Of course, she *missed* her mama, but she is a happy child. Don't even give dat a thought." Marit pauses for a moment, then adds quietly, "There's Leah, too, of course. I'm sure you think about her welfare, too, but don't you worry about dat now either."

"Oh, well, yes...but...she's just a baby. She had you and Arvid. She didn't know me." I take a tentative bite of the tart pie. "I can't worry about Leah, too, right now. It's too much all at once. *You* saved our family. And I can never thank you enough for all you've done." I look at her. The emotions well up again. Enough. Enough. Let it go, I tell myself.

I catch a glimpse of Marit's face showing mild disapproval. It's an unfamiliar face to me and I am surprised. I eat the remainder of my pie slowly, savoring each bite.

By mid-afternoon, we are back home again. In a paper bag, I'm carrying a dress pattern and fabrics for two new dresses. Marit assures me that I'll have plenty of time to sew myself the new dresses since she can help out as long as I want.

When Arvid comes in for supper, I see a sweet smile begin to form within that blond beard. Still wearing his barn coat and boots, he glances at his mother and says, "Mom, who is this beautiful young woman that you've brought home with you?" He makes an exaggerated show of bowing deeply, takes my hand in his and kisses it. "Forgive me, Miss, for being so bold, but may I have this dance?"

22

LOST

May 1951

Caroline had been home for nearly two years, and they were years of one momentous change after another on the farm. Power lines had run north out of Spring Grove early that spring until finally all the farms on Hawk Ridge and beyond were electrified. The farmhouse, barns, hog house, and granary all had electric lights that turned on with the flick of a switch. Every farm throughout the county had its own tall yard light too. No more would lanterns be needed to walk to the barn in the dark.

One evening in May, after Caroline turned out the kitchen lights, Arvid caught her hand and whispered, "Can I take you for a little walk, my dear? I wanna show you somethin'." The children were asleep and Marit had said goodnight and gone upstairs, too.

"Where are we going in the dark, Arvid?" she asked him, puzzled.

"You'll see," he said mysteriously.

Arvid quietly closed the kitchen screen door behind them and they stepped onto the dewy grass. He led his wife away from the house and continued beyond the circle of light cast by the yard light. Their eyes adjusted to the darkness as they walked to the top of the rise midway between the farmhouse and Marit's old cabin.

At last Arvid spoke. "You know, I kinda miss looking out the window at home and seeing a pretty moonlit night. It's beautiful out here. The crickets are so much louder away from the house and look at all the fireflies. I've gotta show the girls how to catch fireflies."

"Hmmm...it *is* beautiful...just look at that Milky Way," Caroline agreed. She lay her head against Arvid's shoulder and gazed into the vast night sky sprayed with twinkling points of light.

"Come here," Arvid gently pulled his wife in front of him, her back against his chest, and wrapped his left arm around her thin waist. He tucked his chin alongside her hair as black as velvet in the darkness and pointed to the horizon over her shoulder.

"I can tell you who lives under every one of those yard lights between here and Spring Grove lookin' south and between us and Caledonia lookin' east," he said with little-boy awe. He pointed to lights that were quite close and said, "There's the Trønby place where Martin lives."

Arvid shifted his feet and Caroline melted into him so that they turned as a unit until they were facing east. "The Kapperuds yard light is that glow shining up from the valley just below us. Hokah is that way and the Mississippi beyond, all along there," he added, drawing a large arc with his arm.

He continued the counter-clockwise pivot. "That next light nearly hidden behind the trees is the Kjelles. And those three lights," he said, pointing north, "are the Hedland farmhouses atop Twin Ridge.

"But just look how close we are to our friends," he whispered, turning to the west. "Bear and Inga's place is right there. If you walked in a straight line from here to that yard light, I'll bet it's less than a quarter-mile. And on the other side, just about the same distance from here, there's Rolf and Anna's house."

Arvid relished in a satisfied smile. "When Inga and Anna's boys are just a little bit older, they'll be cuttin' across the fields between these farms just like Bear and I did as kids. Matt and Jon will come over 'n play with our girls all by themselves. Following the road, it's a bit of a walk, but in the darkness, you can see how close we really are."

"Yes," Caroline murmured, "Looking out our windows at home, we can't see anyone's house. But we're not as alone out here as a person might think."

Arvid allowed a moment of silence to consider her observation. He wrapped both arms tenderly around her slight frame, and whispered, "Have you often felt like you were all alone living out here, my love? This is quite a different life from the city. From where you grew up." Caroline's hair was long enough to wear it up again, and the tendrils that escaped tickled his nose.

"Oh, now and then I suppose I have, but with your mother to keep me company all the time, and Sophie...and Leah. No, I don't feel alone."

Arvid registered that Leah's name might have been added as an afterthought, and it made his heart drop a beat. *I can't make her feel the same about Leah as she does Sophie. Leave it alone,* he told himself. *She needs time...how much more time?* He shook his head to clear the questions away.

"How are you feeling about having my mother here with us, Caroline? She's only here as long as you want her here, remember? It's up to you." She didn't answer immediately, so he continued, "I mean, I know she loves being here with the girls every day, but she'd be contented to go back to the cabin too. She's always been clear about wanting you to know that you're the lady of the house, now."

Caroline pulled away and turned to see Arvid's face in the moonlight. "I still *need* her here, Arvid. I didn't think I would feel like that this long, but I do. Do you mind?"

"No, no. Not at all. There's nothing wrong with that," he answered breezily. "You know, my grandma lived with us when I was little, up until she died." He gave her a squeeze. "I like having my four favorite girls in the house. Plus Mom is a big help to *me* too, now and then."

Caroline sighed. "And I've never been any good to you that way. I see how Inga...how she does so much to help on their farm," the pitch of her voice rising as she spoke, "and I don't know why I can't—why I can't just get comfortable—"

"Hey now, shhh shhh. I didn't marry you so I could turn you into a farm girl." He held her shoulders so she would know that he wanted to look into her eyes. "I know you're leery around the animals. I understand that. You didn't grow up around them. Anyway, the most important job that you have is taking care of our home and our daughters."

Caroline nodded her head, with barely a smile. Arvid kissed his wife under the light of the half-moon and when he drew his head back, was unsettled by the emptiness in her eyes.

May was exceptionally busy. An electric wringer washing machine replaced the pair of wash bins on the back porch. There was no electric clothes dryer yet, but Arvid could envision the day when they would have one. A few of the neighbors did.

Electricity also brought the means to freeze all the beef, pork, chicken and venison they would eat throughout the year. No longer would the women need to spend day after day in the hot, steamy summer kitchen cooking and canning all the meat. The first appliances Arvid purchased were the refrigerator followed by a chest freezer that was carefully slid to its new home below the kitchen by way of the outside cellar doors. He was aided by Bear and Martin and one of the Hedland brothers with promises of Marit's special coffee cake. The freezer would be full of meat by late fall.

Arvid caught his mother peeking in the new refrigerator several times those first couple of weeks. But he didn't see her removing anything from it. It seemed like she was opening the door simply to see the light come on and then to check if it went off again just before the door closed. At least, that's what Arvid had decided she was doing. He got a kick out of seeing her so delighted, like a little kid with a new toy. Until one morning after breakfast, she turned around just in time to see the playful smile on his lips.

Arvid also saw that his mother had caught him in the act. He was leaning toward Caroline, and nudging her elbow. His intent was clear. It was a silent signal, "Look. Quick. Mom's doing it again." Caroline, however, showed little interest in the exchange.

"What?" Marit asked, wide-eyed, a hint of pink rising to her cheeks.

He raised his eyebrows innocently and shook his head. "What? Me? I didn't say anything. Not a word," and he tried unsuccessfully to tamp down the smile.

Marit walked away but paused and turned around again when she reached the stairway. "It's yust dat it's so nice and tidy in dis new icebox," she said with a self-conscious smile.

He nodded with exaggerated thoughtfulness, "So you think we oughtta keep it then?" and stirred a little more cream in his coffee.

With a smirk, Marit returned to the table and lightly tapped Arvid's shoulder with her fingertips. It was something she did when her sons were small, to get them to behave in church. "Now don't you be teasing your old mother. Dat refriyerator is happy right where she sits. Don't you think so, Caroline?"

"Hmmm?" Caroline answered.

Arvid's stomach turned cold at his wife's distance from this bit of fun in a kitchen that had seemed so cheerful, only moments before.

In the front room stood a new radio that was plugged into an electric outlet. The old battery-operated radio was hauled out to one of the sheds to be stored until it was decided what to do with it. It just didn't seem right to discard a perfectly good radio into the sinkhole. Maybe somebody somewhere might need that very thing...though that was hard to imagine. Seemed like electricity was everywhere now.

A second-hand radio was plugged into an outlet in the cow barn. Arvid made a little shelf for it up and out of the way of wet tails. The weather report and the news were broadcast while he milked in the morning, and during the evening milking he listened to the waltzes, polkas and schottisches. The radio made his time in the barn go faster.

After evening chores, the family sat down to listen to *The Life of Riley* and *Gunsmoke* on the radio in the front room. Arvid appreciated the radio shows for the entertainment, of course, but perhaps more for the time they afforded him to sit quietly and hold one or both of his girls in his lap while they listened. Sometimes both Sophie and Leah crawled all over him in his overstuffed chair, giggling and trying to tickle each other while Caroline watched with a smile.

When it was Leah that he lifted onto his lap first, his wife then invited Sophie into her lap. But when it was Sophie that he pulled onto his lap first, Caroline didn't invite Leah into hers. It seemed that then she preferred to sit alone while she listened to the radio program. Leah didn't look twice at her mother. She immediately crawled into her grandma's lap and made herself comfortable.

When anyone on Hawk Ridge bought a television set, the topic of "Television" was revived again after church services on Sunday morning. Rolf and Anna were some of the first on Hawk Ridge to have a television. They often invited Anna's sister, Inga and her husband to come over with little Matt so that he could play with their son, Jon only two months older.

Before long, the Fjeld family was invited too, to watch *The George Burns and Gracie Allen Show* or the *Ed Sullivan Show*. The Flagstad's front room was full; every seat was occupied, and children were sprawled on the floor. Every time they stepped out of the car at the Flagstads on television night, Arvid announced that he smelled popcorn and, indeed, Anna's dishpan full of buttered popcorn became part of the television night routine as well.

"Eat a light supper so you have room for popcorn," Arvid reminded the family with a sparkle in his eye, when they sat down to supper on television night, though he knew the reminder was unnecessary.

 One of the very best improvements on the farm, if anyone asked for Arvid's opinion that summer, was the plumbing that provided running water to the barn. No more would Arvid have to turn the cows out twice each day throughout the winter to be watered at the stock tank. Nor would he have to hand carry water to them on those days when it was too bitterly cold for the cows to be turned out. The cows were able to water themselves whenever they wished, with the drinking cup mounted at each stanchion. It would save him hours out of each day when winter came.

The greatest revelry for Inga and the "little kids," as Sophie, Jon, Matthias and Leah were now being called among their three families, came about after the purchase of the tractors. Arvid bought the first one, used, and then Bear followed suit. Matt and Jon were especially enthralled with how loud the tractors were. They worked at mimicking the deep-throated rhythmic "Chuff Chuff Chuff" of an idling tractor. Arvid smirked to see how the boys' eyes grew bigger when he drove it into the farmyard, reducing speed. The way the tractor spit out those high-pitched "**POP**—Pop—*pop*" like gunshots as the engine slowed seemed to invigorate them.

But for Inga, it wasn't about how loud the tractor was. At least that's what she claimed when the three couples compared notes about the tractors. It was no secret that Inga was itching to drive the thing, to get out in the field with it and see what it could do. Bear was reluctant to put her on it. "Her legs are short, maybe too short for the clutch and brakes," he mused to Arvid in front of the others. Inga responded with rolling her eyes and shaking her head.

"You just wait and see. There'll come a day when you want me on that tractor, helping with fieldwork. If I can drive a team of horses, I can sure as hell drive a tractor," she said emphatically and yet with a knowing smile at her husband.

Marit had gone inside to check on something, and so didn't hear Inga's curse. Inga didn't use rough words like "hell" and "damn it all" when Marit was within earshot, though Arvid had heard them used enough times. Arvid caught the others offering a noncommittal shrug in response to Bear and Inga's conversation. But Caroline looked away. The issue under discussion was something to be settled between a husband and wife, no doubt, but she had absented herself from the conversation entirely. It was as if she were somewhere far away.

Arvid had noticed recently, that a shadow would pass over his wife's face whenever she heard Inga talking about her farm work. When Arvid glanced at Caroline now, there it was again, that darkness. Furthermore, she'd withdrawn physically, veritably shrinking into her chair while she glared in the direction of the tractor standing near the gate. *Is she even more frightened of the tractor than she is of the horses?*

As the summer wore on, Arvid found himself monitoring Caroline's reactions in social situations. He told himself that was what loving husbands did. Hadn't he always done that, without naming what he did as monitoring? *Husbands pay attention to their wives' moods, don't they? Nothing odd about that,* he counseled himself.

June 1951

Those Sunday afternoons while the grown-ups visited on the front porch, the little kids were free to roam the farm, within reason, of course. There were some rules that Arvid laid down outright.

"No gettin' near the bull, no climbing the windmill and nobody, and I mean NOBODY goes near the pond." Other rules could come later as the occasion warranted. From the front porch, the grown-ups could hear children's giggles and hoots coming from many directions. Arvid grew up on this farm and he and Bear had played here together. They could guess pretty well what kinds of things the little ones were likely doing.

There was hide-n-seek to be played in the loose hay of the loft. There were chipmunks that burrowed behind the crumbling stone wall in the barnyard to be tamed. There was a fox and her kits to spy on; they lived in the embankment by the pond. Sometimes shrieks of laughter came from the woods below the barn. They might be playing follow-the-leader, building forts out of sticks and climbing the easiest of the trees, an ancient box elder with a trunk that was so gnarly it provided "steps" up its trunk.

Unless it was raining so that they were stuck inside, the little kids ignored the new indoor water closets. Nearly every household on the Ridge by that time had installed them but they held little appeal to children outdoors at play. Arvid understood that instinctively and left the two-holer where it stood.

From the Fjeld's front porch the grown-ups occasionally heard one of their children in the near distance calling out. It might be Sophie's voice, "Jon!" The shout broadcast impatience. "Hurry up. We're gonna play now."

Then another child, much closer to the porch but hidden from it by the summer kitchen could be heard howling back in excitement. "Just a minute." It was followed by the sound of the outhouse door banging shut, and a little pair of feet racing away with a final announcement, "I'm coming. Wait for me."

The three men on the porch recalled this same exchange from their childhoods together on Hawk Ridge and passed a smile between them while Anna and Inga shared a knowing look. Only Caroline was oblivious to the nostalgia about the two-holer.

Arvid perceived Matt as the more adventurous of the four children and when a new antic was tried, he figured it was likely Matt's idea; dumping a cat on top of a cow lying in the pasture, for example, to see how that would go over with the cow. *Probably about as well as Matt might have guessed,* he smirked. Matt was the one that dared Sophie to catch a chicken by its feet. Her attempts produced a cacophony of squawking in the chicken coop yard, followed by the rapid appearance of a parental overseer with a new rule, "No pestering the hens. They've got jobs to do."

The rule-of-thumb that developed without discussion was that each of the six parents took turns at checking on what the children were up to over those few hours. Marit was lovingly exempted, "You should get to rest at least one day of the week, Mom," Arvid told her.

So, over the course of a Sunday afternoon, while they talked or played cards, each of the six parents went for a little walk to "go, check on the kids," at least once, sometimes twice. There was no planned order about who was going first or second; one of them just volunteered every little while, saying, "Okay, it's my turn to go. You play the next hand without me."

"Caroline, you've gone twice already this afternoon. *I'll* go this time," Anna said when Caroline got up for the third time one afternoon.

"Oh, but I don't mind. Really I don't," she answered without emotion.

"Is it okay if I go with?" Anna offered with a lop-sided smile. "I want to spy on them a little." She giggled, glancing back at her sister adding, "See what they're up to when they don't know parents are watching."

"Oh...well. Alright then. We can both go," Caroline said haltingly. It was hard to read her face. Arvid wondered, *is she disappointed at not going alone? Miffed? How odd.* Caroline turned and walked quickly down the steps leaving Anna to catch up.

The three men looked at one another uncomfortably, then into the distance. Arvid finally broke the silence. "Would anyone like something cold to drink?"

"No, I'm good. I'm good," Bear and Rolf mumbled in unison.

Another pregnant pause followed.

"Well, holy Christmas—" Inga was wide-eyed and exhaled loudly in frustration. "Men! Sometimes you just wanna shake 'em to get 'em to say what they mean." She took a deep breath and shook her head in mock despair at Bear and her brother-in-law, Rolf. "D'ya suppose one o' the two o' ya could ask Arvid what you wanna ask him? No. Ya leave it to a woman." Inga turned toward Arvid and in a softer voice asked, "Arvid, how is Caroline doin'? She doesn't seem like herself lately."

Arvid looked like he'd been punched in the gut. "Oh," he answered. He let his head drop, and leaned forward, his elbows resting on his spread knees. "I don't know what to say." He sighed and looked up at the three solemn faces, eyebrows knitting themselves together.

"She used to be so lively, so good with people. Wasn't she, Bear? When she came back, wasn't she so good to be around?"

"Yes, she was, Arvid. She really was," Bear answered him quietly.

"And now..." he blew out a breath and paused for all the silent sentences to spill onto the floor, the ones he couldn't find the words to say.

The door opened then and Marit stepped out. "Oh, so Caroline and Anna went together to check on de little kids, den?" She was wiping her hands on her apron and smiling but stopped when she saw the four somber faces. "Oh, what is it? Has something happened?"

Arvid could feel Inga studying him. He didn't want to open this for further discussion when Caroline and Anna would likely be returning in just a few minutes. And maybe his mother hadn't noticed any change in Caroline. She hadn't said she had.

When the moment had opened wide enough, Inga stepped into it. "No, nothin's happened. Just talkin'," she answered Marit for them, and leaned back in her chair with a smile. "You were gone a while. Whatcha got goin' inside?" And just that quickly, the time for talking about how Caroline was not like herself, had passed.

Mid June 1951

Later in June, Marit developed a sore on the side of her foot. It wasn't particularly large at first, but it didn't want to heal and then the skin around it turned red. Arvid discovered it only when he noticed his mother limping. He insisted on seeing the bum foot and then immediately put her in the car and drove her to the doctor in Caledonia. He wanted to hear for himself, what the doctor had to say.

Arvid's confidence in his mother's attention to her own health had waned in the last few years. To the surprise of both Arvid and Marit, the doctor hospitalized her that same day.

"Mrs. Fjeld, you have developed a nasty infection which needs to be treated with IV antibiotics." And then the second surprise, "Have you been told that you have diabetes? You've had it for a long time already, I see."

The old white-haired doctor had retired and this new, young doctor, Dr. Moore said things that Arvid knew his mother didn't want to hear. "Your blood sugars are wildly high," Dr. Moore said. "You are going to need to learn new ways to eat." The doctor talked to her in a no-nonsense tone of voice which Arvid knew his mother didn't believe should be used with one's elders, of which she was one. Dr. Moore also asked if she'd noticed problems with her vision. "Oh, ya, a little bit," she said. "I'm getting older you know." Dr. Moore didn't seem to put much stock in that answer.

"Age is not the reason for your worsening eyesight, Mrs. Fjeld. It's the diabetes."

"Oh?" she answered, her eyes widening. "Well, whaddaya you know about dat?" Arvid recognized his mother's way of expressing astonishment at someone who seemed rather remarkable to her. After all, this doctor was so young, but he talked like he had experience. His mother would be apt to think about his proclamation in that way.

Unfortunately, Dr. Moore didn't catch Marit's meaning. "Well, I actually know a fair bit about that, Mrs. Fjeld. The unmanaged diabetes is causing damage to your vision. It is imperative that we get control of your blood sugars immediately, before your vision worsens further."

The doctor also examined her extremities. He looked seriously into her eyes and asked, "Have you noticed that you don't have as much sensation, as much feeling in your toes, in your feet as you once did?"

"I guess so, but I don't let dat worry me too much. I yust keep going. I am so busy every day, ya know."

In point of fact, Arvid supposed that the doctor could *not* have known just how busy his new patient, a grandmother, really was. "I don't like your blood pressures, Mrs. Fjeld. I have to warn you, that you are at risk for stroke and heart attack. Diabetes is nothing to fool around with."

Arvid figured that Dr. Moore was more than likely trying *not* to become exasperated with his new patient, but Arvid also knew just how exasperating his mother could be at times.

"She's a stubborn one, isn't she?" he said to the doctor after they'd departed his mother's hospital room.

"Every bit as stubborn as some of those high-powered executives in the Twin Cities (Minneapolis/St. Paul)." Dr. Moore slowly nodded his head. "I'd been hoping that the rural community would have become more open to modern medicine these days, but I can see that I may have been wrong." He smiled and shook his head.

"I think you'll find the younger ones a little more willing to listen," Arvid offered with a smile. "I'm glad to meet you finally, Doctor. We certainly need you here. We've all depended upon the old doc for so long. It was hard to imagine getting along without him."

"I know it's going to take a long time for me to fill those big shoes he left behind. I have no doubt about that," the doctor said cordially.

"Doctor, I wonder if you might have just a couple more minutes? Since you're going to have my mother's company for a few days, I'd like to tell you something about our family situation."

Just then, a nurse stopped Dr. Moore in the hallway for a brief update. He turned back to Arvid. "I've got a few minutes. My next scheduled patient didn't show. Do you want to sit down for a bit?"

"Thank you, yes. I'll try not to take up too much time." The two men ducked into the doctor's office to sit.

"You haven't met my wife, Caroline yet, but maybe the old doc reviewed her record with you before he retired?" Arvid left that question hanging for a beat. Perhaps this could be a much briefer conversation if Dr. Moore already knew about Caroline's fifteen-month hospital stay in Rochester for schizophrenia.

Dr. Moore nodded and said, "A little, yes. We reviewed her file but tell me more."

"Caroline came home before Christmas in '49 after being gone for fifteen months. My mother took care of our two daughters the whole time that Caroline was away. She was a godsend to our family. After Caroline came home, she was to tell us when she felt capable of managing the household and looking after the girls all on her own again. The plan was that my mother would then return to living on our second place; it's a little cabin down the lane from the farmhouse."

Arvid paused to take a deep breath and a small frown followed. "But Caroline has never gotten to that point. When my mother tells you that she's terribly busy, that's no exaggeration.

"I appreciate my mother's help so much; I can't even tell you. I don't know what I'd have done without her there. At the same time, obviously I don't want her to sacrifice her own health to take care of my girls. She's stubborn enough to do just that. She sees how much the girls need her. Especially my youngest, Leah.

"I hate to say this but..." Arvid exhaled a heavy breath, "...my wife has never really...um...never really *taken* to our second daughter. She was a newborn when my wife was hospitalized and um..." Arvid squinted as if his words had made the room too bright. "Leah, our three-year-old, depends upon her grandma for everything. Always has."

Arvid had come to the doctor hoping he might find someone he could confide in and collaborate with. He'd considered that a day might come when his family would be struggling, if his mother became ill for example, or if Caroline declined again, god forbid. He hadn't expected that such a day was going to come this soon, but apparently, it had arrived. The person that Leah looked to as her mother-figure wasn't going to be coming home today. Caroline was going to be on her own.

"I see," Dr. Moore responded. "So, your wife is back home now?" Arvid nodded. "Does it look like she'll be able to make it at home? I'd sure like to see your mother take better care of herself."

Arvid felt a jolt at this. How could he have thought the doctor would have some magic answer for their family. "I certainly hope she will," he answered.

"The nurses will teach your mother about healthy eating to address the diabetes and also her high cholesterol. These are serious matters, Mr. Fjeld. This wouldn't be the first time my advice has been ignored since coming to Caledonia. But I do hope your mother will heed my warning. She needs to watch her diet and get more rest."

"Yes, I understand." Arvid soberly nodded.

Without Marit, Caroline had no compass. The structure for each weekday had long been established. Regardless of that routine, she easily lost track of it.

Monday was laundry day, unless it was raining and then it was Wednesday, Tuesday was bread-baking day, Wednesday was for mending and sewing, Thursday was for yard and garden tending, and on Friday the women cleaned the house, from top to bottom. On Saturday, there was a lot of food preparation for the following week.

There might be need for a cake when Marit's or Caroline's Sewing Circle served at a funeral. They might need two pies for the Ice Cream Social at church, a pan of bars for the ladies at Bible Study and dozens of cookies for the family and unexpected company. Finally a hotdish or two would be made up in advance, so that Sunday might be a day of rest.

Marit went to the hospital mid-day on a Monday. Most of the laundry was already hanging out to dry. Late that afternoon, Caroline took the dry clothes down off the line and carried them upstairs. That evening, after supper, Arvid was sitting in his overstuffed chair in the front room, waiting for Caroline to join him. He sent Sophie to find her, "Tell Mommy that the radio show comes on in just a few minutes, okay?"

Sophie returned in short order saying, "Mommy says she's not coming down. She has too much to do." So Arvid and the girls listened to the radio without her and she eventually came down when it was the girls' bedtime.

"I got everything put away," she told Arvid and she looked quite fatigued.

"Did you have some trouble upstairs?" Arvid asked her.

"Not exactly, but your mother has taken her clothing out of that old wardrobe in her bedroom. I can't imagine why. It was confusing at first, but I took care of it."

That evening when they went up to bed, Arvid noticed that all of the clothing in their own wardrobe had been rearranged. He was curious and peaked into the wardrobe in his mother's room, and hers likewise looked as though everything had been moved around. His mother was usually more tidy.

The next day, when Arvid came in for his dinner, there were no loaves of bread rising in their bread tins on the counter. "Oh, did you decide not to make bread today?"

"Oh, the bread!" Caroline looked stunned, as if she were blinded by headlights.

"Umm...what's going on?" Arvid queried as he sat down to the table with his dinner of fried hamburger patties, green beans and boiled potatoes with butter.

"Oh, I'd better get started on it right away." Instead of sitting to eat, Caroline pushed her chair under the table and went to the cupboard. She got out the flour and salt and the largest crockery mixing bowl.

"Sweetheart, you can surely eat first, can't you? It's a long afternoon without dinner," Arvid coaxed.

"No, I'm not hungry anyway. I've got to get going on it." She proceeded to measure out the warmed water from the teakettle and crumbled her cake yeast into it while Arvid and the girls ate their dinner.

The next day, Arvid packed himself a cold dinner to eat out in the field. He rarely did that, but he thought if he got a start on cultivating in the morning, he might be able to finish the field on the back twenty before the rain came. He could smell it in the air. The skies were gray and breezy. He harnessed Babe and Bess and was in the field riding on the cultivator by ten o'clock.

He drove the team into the farmyard after cultivating that afternoon just as the first drops were falling. He found his two little girls eating bread and jam on the front porch. "You girls having a little-lunch?" he called to his daughters with a grin. He waved and took the team on through to the barn where he unharnessed the horses.

"Sophie made us dinner, Daddy," Leah said, looking proudly at her older sister, when Arvid returned to the front porch. She was wearing a deep burgundy blackberry jam stain all around her mouth.

"Oh?" Arvid used his "Daddy" voice, with a quizzical look that asked for more detail.

Sophie was quiet, pulling her dress over her knees. Leah continued glibly, "We ate here cuz we like it outside on the big porch." Leah's pronunciation of the "ch" in "porch" made the word sound juicy.

"Oh, I see," Arvid said, but Sophie's quick glance confirmed what he suspected. Sophie was not telling him something. He sat on the top step next to them. "What's Mommy doing today?" he asked amiably.

Leah was clearly enjoying the responsibility of answering her daddy's questions. "I don't know, Daddy. I think she's sleeping." She licked jam from one finger after another.

"Oh," he answered. "She must be very tired today, hmm?" And then he got up, slapped the dust off his pants and went around to the side kitchen door.

Arvid stood inside the door, taking in the kitchen. There was no sign of any dinner having been served at noon. No dishes in the drainer. No smells from cooking in the kitchen and it was after three o'clock in the afternoon.

He could not have missed the puddle of spilled milk and the glob of blackberry jam on the floor. Sophie followed him inside, apparently remembering the mess. As usual, Leah followed closely behind. There was a jagged loaf of bread on the table and then Arvid saw the bread knife on the floor. *Is that blood on the serrated blade?* There was a red tinge on the loaf as well. He spun around.

"Sophie! Did you cut yourself?"

"Just a little Daddy. It hardly hurts at all," and she lifted the hem of her dress so that he could see where the knife had caught her dirty knee. A thin trail of dried blood went down her leg, and the cut itself was scabbed over.

He put the pieces of the story together without further explanation. On this very spot, his five-year-old daughter had knelt on the floor with a loaf of bread and a bread knife. One of the times when she drew the blade back, it sliced into the skin of her right knee. Despite that, she had continued with her enterprise until she had achieved dinner for herself and her sister. She had cut at least two slices of bread, buttered them and spread jam on them. She then put each on a small plate and the girls had gone out to enjoy their jam sandwiches and milk on the front porch steps.

Arvid took Sophie with him into the bathroom and cleaned her knee. When it appeared to be as clean as it could be, he put a bit of mercurochrome on the cut and then wrapped a bandage around the whole leg in order to keep it in place.

"Oh Daddy, I'm sorry about the mess," Sophie began. "I was gonna clean up the milk but then I forgot about it. I'll clean it up."

"No," Arvid stayed her from stepping too close to the mess. "No, that's okay, Sophie. Mommy and I can clean it up, lickety split. You just bring in your dishes and glasses, and then you can go back out and play, okay?"

"Okay, Daddy," Sophie twirled her little dress around and skipped out the door with Leah in her shadow. When the girls returned to the kitchen, Arvid knelt on a clean spot and pulled the girls close. He put a smile on his face, "You know what? There's a new litter of kittens in the haymow. They were born last week. I think they're old enough to have visitors now. Don't move them, though. They need to stay by their mommy."

Leah shrieked. "Kitties!"

Sophie answered with a grin, "Okay, Daddy. Let's go, Leah." They spun around and were gone in a moment, the screen door slamming behind them.

Arvid gazed after them tenderly. Two little pair of dusty, bare feet racing out the door. Neither would pay any mind to the raindrops coming down.

When they'd gone, Arvid slowly climbed the stairs, frustrated, dirty and tired from a hot dusty day in the field. He sharply chastised himself for leaving his daughters alone all day with their mother. He was relieved that Sophie's cut was not worse than it was. And that neither of the girls, as far as he could tell, had fallen from the counter.

In a way, he was glad that Caroline hadn't come downstairs while the girls were making that mess. He wasn't at all sure how she would have reacted. Two years ago, he'd have known. When she first returned from the hospital, she was gentle and kind. But in the last couple of months she'd become distant, unknowable. She'd forgotten who she was.

Things just weren't making sense to Caroline anymore. She was distracted, disorganized, disturbed. She hadn't washed her hair in many days. She wasn't sleeping well. He'd woken in the night to find her standing at the window, looking between drawn curtains as if afraid to be seen by "something" out there.

He hated to think what he was thinking; that this was how her mental illness looked now. She wasn't like she was three years ago, but her behavior certainly wasn't normal—a mother not feeding her own children?

"Caroline?" he knocked on the door. No answer. He twisted the doorknob. It was locked. "I need you to open this door. I need to talk to you face to face." Silence.

"I am serious. If you don't unlock the door, I'll have to take the door off its hinges. I have to be sure you're alright in there."

"Wait," he heard through the door. When the door opened, Caroline's face was flushed and feverish. Her dress hung crookedly; the buttons misaligned by one hole. The room was hot, curtains drawn, and windows closed. There was no water glass by the bed. She'd aged a year since he last saw her at breakfast.

"Caroline!" He examined her in shock. "Why is it so hot in here?" He went to the two windows on adjoining walls and raised the sashes on both of them. A breeze wafted in with the smell of freshly cut hay from a neighbor's field.

Caroline sat back down on the bed.

"Come downstairs with me, Caroline. I need your help to clean up a mess on the kitchen floor." Arvid waited until she finally stood, than took her hand and led her downstairs.

"Oh, what happened?" she asked, clearly surprised.

"Our girls made themselves something to eat. Apparently there was no dinner made today." He measured his words carefully, intending to state a fact as opposed to casting a judgment.

"What a mess!" She stood and stared at the floor.

Arvid finally sighed, "It won't clean itself up. Let's do it together, Caroline."

"Okay," she agreed, still standing, unmoving. Arvid's veins jumped with electricity. *She's not doing anything without prodding!*

"I want you to fill this pail with water. Here at the sink." He set the pail in the sink and started the water running into it. She didn't move. He took her hand and pulled her closer to the sink, placing her hand by the spigot. "Shut it off for me when it's full."

Arvid took a wet, soapy dishcloth and wiped down the tabletop, the two chairs and the counter where Sophie had been climbing up and down. He could hear the telltale sound of a pail that was nearly full of water and he watched to see whether Caroline would shut the water off. He waited. When the water was at the very rim, she finally did. She took her hand away and stared at it, as if she'd never seen it before.

"Okay, I'm gonna wash the floor now." Arvid lifted the bucket down and mopped up the milk and jam on the floor while Caroline watched with detachment. Arvid took a long, deep breath. Caroline obviously wasn't going to be making supper for them. There was no meat thawing on the counter.

"I have an idea. Mom's tuna noodle hotdish recipe is tacked on the refrigerator. She must have been planning on making that the day I took her to the doctor. How about if I throw that together for supper while you rest?"

"Oh...yes." She finally answered and remained standing, a lost soul in her own kitchen.

Marit was muttering in Norwegian from the moment Arvid entered her hospital room. By the time they were in the car heading home, she'd worked herself into a lather. Arvid had rarely seen her with this level of ire. Speaking in her first language, she was able to express her feelings much faster than she could in English. Arvid knew, however, that she wasn't talking to him so much as she was ranting directly to God.

God, of course, understood Norwegian perfectly, whereas Arvid had to translate her words into English for himself to catch the entire meaning. He listened closely while Marit told God just what she thought of the newly prescribed diet.

"They tell me I'm supposed to cut down on de sweets. *Jeg kan ikke ha kake og kaker med kaffen min. Hva slags lunsj er det? Alle tingene jeg liker å spise mest: ost, iskrem, krem i kaffen min, rømmegrøt–å selvfølgelig kan jeg ikke ha det. Og smør. Bare litt smør on brød! Herregud!*

And only two pieces of *brød* each day! Well, I can cut *my brød* however thick I want it. Pfft. You could yust as well put me in de ground right now, Arvid."

Arvid knew that she wouldn't expect him to answer her in Norwegian, but his eyes told her that he'd caught the gist of the rant. For his mother to be told to avoid cake and cookies was a blow; Marit's delicious baked goods were known around the area and she loved baking.

And then to be told to cut back on dairy, too? There was nothing she liked better than cheeses, ice cream, having thick cream in her coffee, rømmegrøt (cream porridge) for dessert and butter on her bread. She'd actually taken God's name in vain. "Good God." His eyes had opened wide at that; it was a rare thing to hear an expletive from his mother. Arvid knew better than to say anything and simply shook his head in sympathy.

23

HORSES AND PICNICS

Saturday, July 7, 1951

Unfortunately, Marit was hospitalized a second time that summer. When Arvid brought her to see Dr. Moore two weeks after her discharge, hoping to see that she was managing her diabetes well, the news wasn't good. But maybe his mother was at least beginning to understand the seriousness of her disease.

Arvid returned home that day to find Caroline standing motionless at the kitchen sink, staring out the window and whispering to herself. There were a few clean dishes drying in the drainer, but she'd apparently then lost interest in the task.

"Caroline," he said, when he walked through the screen door. He waited for her to turn to look at him. "I'm home."

"Oh," she said. "Where's Marit?"

He shook his head slowly. "She has to stay in the hospital for a few days."

"Oh." Caroline's eyes appeared worried, uncertain.

Arvid recognized immediately that he would be both father and mother to Sophie and Leah until his mother returned from the hospital. He didn't trust Caroline to keep an eye on them while he went about his farm work.

"I want you both to come out to the barn with me," he told his daughters after they'd eaten leftovers for supper. "You can help the new calf learn how to drink from a bucket. Put your rubber boots on though. The calf could accidentally step on your bare feet."

Wearing matching red rubber boots and sturdy little dresses made from pretty flour sacks, the two girls, one as blonde as the other was dark, gleefully skipped down the hill to the barn in front of Arvid. Teddy led the way. Teddy wagged his tail like he knew perfectly well that he was the good dog that Arvid always said he was. Then he lay down in his usual spot just outside the front barn door while the three of them went inside.

"Why can't Teddy come in with us too, Daddy?" Leah wanted to know.

"The cows would get jumpy with him in the barn because they know he means business. That wouldn't be good. The cows might not let down their milk. No, his job is to wait patiently outside in case he should be needed. He's keeping an eye out for anything that doesn't belong in the barnyard. He'll bark if someone comes."

Arvid made his statement with a neighbor in mind, or perhaps a stranger that might drive into the farmyard, but when it was out of his mouth, he realized that Teddy might very well think Caroline didn't "belong" either. She never came down to the barn, forever wary of big animals. If she did, Teddy might announce her presence with a bark, too. Thankfully, neither Sophie nor Leah had their mother's anxiety about animals.

Illustration 11: Gonna feed the calves

Arvid mixed the flour-like calf milk replacer powder into a bucket of water and carried it to the youngest calf penned in the barn. The bull calf was only two days old. The girls joined him in the pen, and immediately knelt to pet the new calf on his long forehead where he lay, placidly watching his new guests, from beneath his long black eyelashes.

"This little guy doesn't know how to drink out of a bucket yet." Arvid began. "We're going to teach him. We start like this. I let him suck on my fingers." He got down on his haunches and the calf latched on to his forefinger and middle finger. When Arvid got up and moved toward the bucket, the calf got up on four wobbly legs to follow Arvid's fingers.

"When he's got a good hold of my fingers, I slowly put my hand down into the bucket, so he can get a taste of the milk." He demonstrated. "Be sure to hang on to the bucket too, so he doesn't knock it over. That's happened a time or two." The calf stuck his nose into the bucket briefly and then withdrew it when Arvid removed his fingers. The bull calf shook his head, not convinced, still interested in Arvid's fingers.

"Now, you try it, Sophie. Let him suck on your hand. He doesn't have his baby teeth yet." Sophie put her hand out and the calf took it into his mouth.

"He's got a really scratchy tongue, doesn't he Daddy?" Sophie was wide-eyed. At five years of age, most of her little hand was in the calf's mouth.

"Yes, he does. Kind of like sandpaper. That's so he can hang on good to suck. Okay, now pull your hand slowly down into the bucket. If the calf lets go, you just give him your fingers again and lead his head down into the bucket. I'll bet before I'm finished with the milking tonight, he'll have learned how to drink from the bucket without your fingers in his mouth."

While Arvid milked one cow after another, Sophie and Leah focused their attention on the calf until the bucket was finally empty. The girls ran down the aisle between the two rows of stanchions chirping out the little calf's success with drinking from the bucket. Arvid was crouched against a cow's side, milking her. When the girls ran past, he paused to squirt a few streams of milk from the cow's teats toward the girls' dirty little boots as they skipped past. They squealed in delight and then he suggested they go to the haymow to check on the new kittens again.

The next morning, Arvid woke Sophie and Leah very early and took them to the barn with him again while he milked. For a while, the girls sleepily lay on the pile of straw under the chute and talked while he milked. However, before all the cows had been milked, Sophie and Leah had once again helped the bull calf to drink his breakfast out of the bucket.

After milking was done, Arvid turned the cows out to pasture, and brought the girls into the house with him, where he made bacon and eggs for breakfast. He brought Caroline downstairs to eat with them. She looked no more interested in the goings-on of the household than she had the day before and she hadn't bothered to change out of her nightgown.

"Mommy, are you sick?" Sophie asked her cautiously at the breakfast table.

Caroline looked at her as if Sophie's presence was a surprise. "Am I sick." Caroline frowned, as if unsure how to answer such a difficult question. "No, I'm..." She looked at Sophie and cocked her head. A long pause followed. "I'm...What did you want to know? It's not like—" Her voice trailed off as she gazed out the window, her food hardly touched.

Arvid hoped that his mother would be discharged from the hospital that day. When he called the nurse's station at the hospital after breakfast, however, he heard, "No, I'm sorry; she's not ready for discharge yet."

It was a beautifully warm day with a sky so blue that it made his fingers itch to get back at his fieldwork. Of course, the most important thing he had to do was to look after Sophie and Leah but, still, it was hard to sacrifice a perfectly good day of work in the field at this busy time of year. The last twenty acres of his corn crop needed to be cultivated. If the fields were cleared of most weeds now while the corn was small, then the growing cornstalks would themselves shade out new weeds. He struck on an idea.

Arvid prepared to tackle his fieldwork with a three and a five-year-old in tow. It was something he'd never done before, but he was confident that it would work. And if he made the call later that it wasn't safe to have Sophie and Leah along with him, he'd just head back home again.

He brought Sophie and Leah with him back down to the barn to watch him harness up the horses. He led Babe in harness out of the barn followed by Bess, and then he linked the harnesses so that the two walked as one close unit. He walked them to the top of the barnyard, halting the team in front of the closed gate. He walked around in front of the horses holding Sophie's and Leah's hands.

"Here we go. Leah, you stand right here," he placed her below Bess's big head, "and Sophie, you are going to let Babe get acquainted with you. When you pet their noses, keep your hand open and flat like this, so you don't get a finger nipped. They'll want to smell your hand."

Sophie stood beneath Babe's head and looked up at the horse's big teeth inside those tender, loose lips. Meanwhile, Arvid talked soothingly to the horses, as he always did, and he pet their broad necks. He knew that Babe and Bess trusted him. He'd worked with them for close to twenty years, starting as a nine-year-old when his dad was running the farm. The horses were closing in on their thirtieth birthdays.

"You don't ever wanna sneak up on an animal or surprise them. Always let the animal know where you are. They don't *want* to step on you," Arvid had taught his daughters from their first visits to the barn.

There were, however, two exceptions to the rule about how the girls should behave with the animals. Arvid took care that the girls knew what those were. One exception was the bull and the other exception was the boar.

"Bulls are unpredictable. You can't trust 'em," Arvid had told them more than once. "My father was tossed around by a bull when he was a young man. He'd been in the pen with that old bull to feed him, many, many times without any problem. And then one day, for no reason that anybody could figure, the bull got it in his head that he didn't like my dad in his pen with him.

The bull caught him with his horns and rolled him around on the ground. My father was saved by his father. My grandpa came running and pulled my dad out of the bull's pen. He had to go to the hospital for a while after that. So, Sophie and Leah...don't you *ever* go tryin' to pet the bull even when he's alone in his pen, even if he looks calm. Okay?"

"Okay, Daddy," they answered.

"And boars can be nasty and ornery," he told the girls. "Actually, all the big sows can be dangerous too. It's not that they would *want* to hurt you. They're just not very mmm—let's say, careful about where and when they lay down. A hog might flop herself down most anywhere that strikes her fancy. She'll figure it's your job to get out of her way when she does." The girls nodded their heads in unison, eyebrows knitted in understanding. This was grown-up information. It was proof that Daddy trusted them to listen.

While the horses were getting acquainted with Sophie and Leah, Arvid watched the silent ritual communication between Teddy and the workhorses that was taking place at the same time. It brought a smirk to his lips. Babe and Bess had no need of a herding dog to keep them in line.

Teddy knew he had no job to do where the workhorses were concerned. Before the team would leave the barnyard, however, Teddy would make his routine show of prancing proudly below and in front of the horses noses with his ears up and his thick, tail curled over his back. In turn, the pair of horses would lower their big heads down to the dog, allowing his tail to tickle their noses. When Teddy reversed direction, crossing in front of them a second time, they'd each give him a sniff and a playful nibble on the long hair of his raised tail. The horses would then shake their heads as if laughing at the dog's pretense at importance. Once they left the barnyard, the horses were all business, ignoring Teddy entirely.

Sophie and Leah stood quietly before the horses. Their soft noses smelled sweet. "We're just going to give Bess and Babe time to smell you and see what you're all about," Arvid said to the girls. "They want to know who you are. They'll like having you around."

Sophie held her hands up in the air, palms toward Babe's enormous teeth. Babe gently moved her soft lips over her palms and then bent her head down further to smell her hair, her dress and her legs. "She's tickling me, Daddy," Sophie giggled.

Leah wanted to be tickled by Bess as well. So, she closed her eyes tightly and turned her face upward to meet Bess' nose. The big animal gently moved her tender lips along the outline of Leah's face, sniffing as she went. Then she blew into Leah's face, "Blphphphphp."

Leah laughed. "She blew raspberries at me, Daddy."

"See, they both like you two, don't they? They'll be glad to have you with them today. Who wants to go up first?"

They both grinned with an eager, "Me first, Daddy."

Arvid picked up the daughter he was standing closest to at that moment, and said to her, "Okay, Leah, I'm gonna lift you up there now." And then he immediately went around to Sophie and hoisted her up with, "Up you go. Are you two comfy up there?" he grinned up at them both, their little bare feet now even with Arvid's shoulders.

"There's so much room up here, Daddy. I can lay down!" Sophie's excitement was obvious.

"Yup, she's got a broad back, doesn't she? See this wide leather strap right here? That's the back strap. You can tuck a foot or an arm under that. And this strap down the middle here? You can hang onto that too. Just sit in the middle, like you're doing. We're never gonna go faster than a walk."

"Daddy, does Babe like me up here?" Sophie grinned as she asked.

"Yup, she'll practically forget that you're up there. You remind her now and then, by scratching her neck or petting her. She'll like that. How does it feel up there now?" Arvid asked them.

"I'm okay, Daddy," Leah sang out. "I can see so-o-o-o far up here. Can I stand up?"

"Oh, no! No, no. You're just going to sit while you're up there. Sitting only."

"I'm okay too, Daddy. I'm ready to go." Sophie's grin could not have stretched any wider.

"Alright, here we go," Arvid called out to his girls. He took note of how their little backs were so straight and how their short legs had to open wide as if performing splits across the horses' backs. How bright and cheerful his two little daughters were. He felt a pang of sorrow that Caroline was not out there alongside him to see how proudly their girls sat atop the horses.

If Marit had been home to see it, she would have fussed over how big the girls were getting to be, and how good they were with the horses. Grandma would have praised them. Maybe she would run to get the camera for a picture of them on Babe and Bess. Of course, if she had been home, it would not have been necessary to bring Sophie and Leah out to the field with him.

The girls each tucked a foot under one of the straps and then he opened the barnyard gate and drove the team through into the larger farmyard. Then they were slowly off, Arvid walking behind the team who carried his precious daughters, and on to the far end of the farm to the last of the cornfields to be cultivated. They would spend the better part of the day there.

By mid-morning, Arvid saw that Leah's head was bobbing. He stopped the team and walked up alongside Bess. He showed Leah again where to tuck her arm under the leather strap so that she could lie secure, with her head on her arm. With that, Leah lay down and fell asleep. By the time they'd gone up and back again for another pass, Sophie followed her sister's lead and lay down to nap atop Babe.

Arvid checked his pocket watch when his stomach thought it was noon and found that it was. He lifted Sophie and Leah down from the horse's backs. He unhitched the team from the cultivator and brought them to the edge of the woods where they could stand in the shade and munch the tall green grass alongside the tree line. Then Arvid made up a little picnic spot on a blanket in an adjacent bit of shade.

He'd brought their dinner with them, wrapped in a bag and slung from one of the horses' hames. He'd made sandwiches that morning; dried beef for himself and jam for the girls. Sitting on the blanket, he sliced up two Jonathan apples with the pocketknife he always carried and shared them. Lastly there were Grandma's chocolate chip cookies. A thermos of orange Kool-Aid was enough for each to have a good long drink.

"What do you think Mommy's eating for dinner, Daddy?" Sophie crunched down on a slice of apple.

"Oh, I imagine she's eating kind of like we are today," Arvid said, looking at Babe and Bess as they grazed a couple of rods away. He considered making a pretense of checking on the horses in order to end the conversation about Caroline. He didn't know what he should say to them about their mother's behavior.

"It's too bad that Mommy couldn't have dinner with us out here. She likes picnics, doesn't she, Daddy?" Sophie continued chewing the juicy apple slices.

"Yes, well, it would have been far for Mommy to walk all the way out here from the house, wouldn't it? She doesn't like to drive."

"Maybe Mommy is having a picnic by herself?" Leah cocked her head to one side thoughtfully. She'd eaten all but the crusts of her sandwich.

"What's wrong with the crusts, Leah? The crust is good for you too." Arvid coaxed her. "In fact, the crust is almost my favorite part of Grandma's bread." He hoped that by invoking the name "Grandma" that the girls would talk about her, rather than their mother.

It worked. "When is Grandma coming back, Daddy?" Sophie eyed the cookies.

"I hope she'll be back tomorrow. We miss Grandma when she's gone, don't we?"

When they returned from cultivating corn at the end of the afternoon, Arvid discovered with relief, that Caroline had made supper. He smiled at her warmly, kissing her on the cheek and told her it looked good. It was almost like normal.

It was, oddly enough, because of the milkman that Caroline had made supper, Arvid learned. "The milkman came this afternoon," Caroline told him. "And that reminded me it was time to make supper."

Sunday, July 8, 1951

The next day was Sunday. Arvid learned that his mother would not be discharged from the hospital that day either. After breakfast, the family got ready to go to church. Arvid was looking forward to a day alone with his wife and daughters.

Whatever the family wanted to do together was what Arvid had in mind. Maybe they'd fly kites or go for a Sunday drive just for fun. Maybe they'd stop over at Bear and Inga's place. Rolf and Anna were gone for the day and so the three families weren't planning to gather on the Fjeld's front porch.

As usual, Caroline had made herself ready for church first. So far so good. Her usual Sunday morning routine was underway. Considering the last couple of days had been anything but ordinary, Arvid paid attention to her movements. Arvid heard her go into the girls' bedroom to gather their Sunday clothes. Then she headed downstairs with Sophie and Leah following closely behind, clad only in their slips. The two little church dresses were draped over her arm. With the bathroom sink at hand, Caroline washed each of the girls' faces with a soapy cloth and then scrubbed their feet in the bathtub before putting on their clean socks and Sunday shoes while they sat on chairs by the kitchen table.

Arvid came downstairs tying his tie. He would recall much later that Caroline's movements had seemed somewhat stiff and stilted.

Caroline lifted Leah up to sit on the edge of the pedestal table to wait her turn for hair combing. Sophie was taller, so she stood while Caroline sat on a chair to comb her hair. It was just about time to leave for church and Caroline was hurrying. She wielded the comb on Sophie's hair as if she were holding a stick of wood that she would have preferred to toss across the room. They were exaggerated, rapid movements. As she took vigorous swipes at Sophie's long straight blonde hair, she mumbled. Maybe she was counting strokes, or snarls, Arvid guessed.

"Ouch," Sophie yelped. Six. Seven. Eight. More snarls. "Ouch," she said again when her mother made a part in her hair and another "Ouch!" when Caroline shoved a barrette onto the right side of her blonde head. Nine. Ten. Eleven.

"There," Caroline pronounced Sophie's hair to be properly combed. She slipped Sophie's dress over her head and buttoned it down the back. "Done," she added and gave her a little pat on her bottom, a common signal that Sophie was ready to get in the car. But Grandma Marit had always been the one to get Leah cleaned up and dressed for church so that both girls were more or less ready to go at the same time.

Arvid walked past to check his tie in the bathroom mirror.

Caroline was still mumbling, "*Two* little girls, *two* little girls with dirty feet and thick hair to get ready for church."

Arvid walked back out of the bathroom. His tie was fine. He noticed that the sewing shears, pincushion and thread were still lying on the table. Caroline was usually fastidious about putting things away after using them, but the hour was getting late. He hoped she'd leave those things where they lay. He cautioned his wife, "We don't want to be late for church."

"Be still," Caroline ordered Leah. Before Arvid could react, Caroline's hand moved with a silver flash. A chunk of dark hair fell from one side of Leah's head, revealing an ear. Caroline spun Leah on her bottom and with another swipe of the shears, another hunk of thick, dark hair dropped and fell to the floor. With one more snip across the back of her head, all of Leah's glorious hair lay around her on the table and floor.

Leah had a most peculiar wide-eyed look of puzzlement on her face; she looked around herself at all the hair that was somehow no longer attached to her head and tentatively reached up to touch her head. She screamed! And screamed! And screamed again!

Arvid's numb shock dissolved with her screams. He grabbed the shears out of Caroline's hands and said, "What have you done?"

He scooped up Leah off the kitchen table where she was still screaming, her face red. Her eyes squeezed shut tight with tears escaping onto her cheeks. Arvid walked out through the kitchen door carrying Leah with her tattered head of hair. Her screams became jagged sobs as she melted into his suit jacketed shoulder and threw her arms around his neck.

Only moments later, Arvid turned on his heel and returned to the kitchen where Caroline and Sophie still stared after him. Sophie's mouth turned down at the corners and her lower lip trembled. He grabbed Leah's Sunday dress from the chair where it lay, took Sophie's hand and spoke between gritted teeth, "We three are going for a drive. There will be no church today."

Arvid and his daughters went outside where he slipped Leah's dress over her ravaged head. Then he gently tucked the girls into the front seat to be next to him, and they set off, without Arvid having any clue as to where they were going to go.

When the car reached the barbed wire gate across the driveway, he hopped out, jerked the gate open and threw it aside in anger. Caroline had stepped outside onto the kitchen stoop and Teddy stood alongside her, his ears forward and ready for action.

Caroline looked as if she might start down the road after the car. Arvid motioned to her with his hand, "Stay," as if she and Teddy were both dogs. He was later ashamed of himself for it.

After the gate was shut behind them, he heard a quiet little voice, "Where… where are we going, Daddy?" Sophie's voice was wobbly, and he knew without looking away from the road into her face, that she was crying as well. Leah still sobbed desperately and now Sophie was crying silently, too. He reached over and touched the top of Sophie's head. And then turned the car sharply to go down into the narrow cut between the bluffs and on to the valley below.

As he drove, he felt himself growing even more frightened thinking about what Caroline had done with the shears. *What else might have happened had he not been there? What would come next?*

Arvid's tears flowed at these thoughts, along with those of Leah and Sophie. Arvid's tears frightened Sophie even more than she already was. He saw it in her eyes when he glanced over.

"Oh Sophie, I am sorry to cry like this. Daddy is feeling sad about the loss of Leah's beautiful hair, but it will grow back, won't it? Yes, it will. It will be okay again. And I'm sad that she is so upset. I wish I had prevented that. And now I'm sad that I have frightened you too."

Arvid shuffled through his memories for somewhere to go… *where can we go for a few hours?* The picnic in the field the day before glowed in his mind. "Here is what we are going to do today instead of going to church. We are going to have a picnic," he said. He had something like a plan in mind.

"But we don't have our picnic basket, Daddy. We left it at home."

"No, but that is alright because I have another plan. A different kind of picnic." And he thought very hard about what that could possibly be. "We are going to drive for a little while first. You'll see when we get there. We will have a nice picnic, just the three of us. Next time, maybe Mommy can come too, but not today. I don't get to have much time alone with my girls just for fun.

"Now, let's look for interesting things while we drive, okay? Things that aren't what they usually are, like a cow on the wrong side of the fence, or a car with a flat tire, or like a fox with a rabbit in his mouth."

The bumpy car ride lulled the girls to sleep and that gave him time to think. He drove them through Hokah and across the Root River. He woke them up when they reached the Mississippi River.

Arvid told the girls about the mighty Mississippi and he told them about their special picnic plan. They crossed over the high bridge into Wisconsin, which was exciting in and of itself. Then, he drove to a grocery store that he had noticed previously while in La Crosse.

They went in together. He bought them three small cartons of chocolate milk, three large donuts with cream filling, a bag of salted-in-the-shell peanuts, an apple and a small hunk of cheese to share.

Next, Arvid drove them to Myrick Park on the north side of La Crosse. It was close to the Black River and the wetlands alongside it. Arvid remembered his parents taking him there a few times when he was a boy. Myrick Park was like a miniature zoo plus a carnival and playground all rolled into one.

Myrick Park was dense with trees and toward the far north side was an area that people called "Monkey Island." The girls had never seen monkeys before. That would be a special thing for them. Perhaps seeing the monkeys would somewhat dull their other memories of this awful day.

There were almost too many monkeys to count. All of them were busy doing monkey things. A few studiously groomed each other. A mother monkey carried a baby clinging to her chest. A group of adolescent trouble-maker monkeys chased each other up and down the trees inside the tall fence. They slung themselves across a set of ladders and swung from one arm on the monkey bars until without warning, they'd launch themselves high and into a trampoline net. Once in a while one of them dropped into the little pond below and complained loudly. The other monkeys seemed to laugh uproariously.

Then a couple of the other monkeys surrounded the wet monkey as he leapt out of the water and patted him on the back. Then with no apparent forethought, the chase would start all over again, accompanied by much shrieking and what sounded like monkey laughter.

"That one looks crabby," Sophie said, pointing to one.

Leah pointed from one monkey to another. "Look at that one...Oh, look over there! Did you see what that one did?" Much laughter.

It is so good to hear Leah laugh. "Yes, I see. Isn't he funny? I bet I could do that."

"Oh, Daddy, you silly, you cannot do what a monkey can do." Sophie giggled at the thought.

"Daddy, play like a monkey," Leah grinned.

Arvid obliged with a "Hoo Hoo Hoo" while pretending to scratch himself. The girls laughed hysterically.

Arvid and the girls sat on a bench near the monkeys and ate their picnic lunch. There was more than they could eat. Daddy told them that the peanuts were actually for feeding the monkeys.

Both Sophie and Leah started by throwing one peanut at a time in through the wire fencing surrounding the monkeys. In time, they held a peanut in their fingers and put it through the fencing for the monkey to take from their hands. The monkey fingers were so much like the fingers of a person that the girls squealed with delight.

"This is the best day ever, Daddy," Sophie gushed and hugged his suit-pants legs before carrying another peanut over to hand between the fencing to another monkey. Leah's eyes were glowing by the time Arvid drove them home.

Time to return to the girls' mother. Hopefully Caroline had not made any other poorly considered decisions and acted upon them in their absence.

He'd never before felt the need to get away from his wife. Upon entering the kitchen, Arvid found that the hair had been cleaned up and there was supper already on the table, waiting for them. There was nothing more said about the haircut.

Arvid had never found his way back to God after Caroline's hospitalization. At one time, the comfort he'd found in faith in a loving God had come so easily. But even after she'd been discharged home, the anger still burned within him– what kind of loving God would torment his innocent family? Today the smoldering coals of Arvid's anger at God were fanned into flames once again. Still, at that moment, with nowhere else to turn, he dug deep enough to find one short desperate prayer. *Please God, send my mother home tomorrow.* Even as it left his lips, he feared his was only a fickle prayer.

24

LIKE RED VELVET CAKE

Caroline
Monday, July 9, 1951

I can't get things to feel quite...right. Maybe it's the way I catch Leah looking at me out of the corner of my eye. Those big dark eyes rimmed in black lashes are afraid of me. If I look in the mirror as she passes behind me so that I see both her face and mine at the same time, I am struck dumb with confusion. Can it be that I see Caroline the child and the other grown-up Caroline, both at the same time? Is that why I am frightened of her? Is it something more?

She reminds me of something. What is it? Darkness. Fear. Trapped in the blackest of holes. Falling, falling, falling. Will my bones break at the bottom? When I look at her I want to fly. Fly away. Far, far away. My feet have become trapped, entangled in the roots of the earth. The rich loamy smell of a deep hole, a hole with rising water.

Where is Marit? Doesn't she know I crumble away when she's not here? The water rises faster and faster. It bubbles and gurgles, air bubbles popping at the surface. Sliding down the drain and away. Leaving this world. Taking me with it. Terrified.

Marit. Marit! I scream the name inside my head. Without her, what do I do? What to do? Where to go? Do I stand here? Stand there? Without her to begin something for me to follow, I am shrinking, disappearing. No one points me where to go.

Everything threatens to stop. Short. "Never to go again, when the o-o-old ma-a-n died," I hum it softly.

A song we sang in the orphanage spins in my head over and over...I sing a few lines quietly, under my breath.

"My grandfather's clock was too tall for the shelf so it stood ninety years on the floor. It was taller by half than the old man himself, though it weighed not a penny-weight more. It was bought on the morn of the day that he was born. And was always his treasure and pride. But it stopped. Short. Never to go again when the o-o-old ma-a n died."

I press my hands to my temples. *Stop. Stop. Stop. Stop.* Top. Top. Top. Top. *Stop. Stop. Stop. Stop.* Top. Top. Top. Top. *Pop. Pop.*

Pop. Pop....over and over it goes while I rock back and forth. A hive of bees encircles my brain, chews at my thoughts, makes them bleed.

The buzzing bees grow louder and louder until the tick tock is drowned. So, I put my dark-eyed replica, or is it the child version of Caroline, into the tub of water and I lock the door. "Stay there until you are squeaky clean," I say to the door and I try to move on.

The tick tock tick tock has gone away but that makes my skin crawl. Where does the tick tock tick tock go when it isn't right here? It's my job to keep track of it, isn't it? I must pay close attention. I have to listen for it everywhere, find it back again.

A Red Wing crock of cucumbers in brine is thrumming in the corner of the kitchen. I push aside the wooden cover and listen. Maybe the tick tock is beneath the cukes. I scoop out handfuls of long cucumbers, not yet pickled and spread them out on the kitchen floor. They try to tell me something, to arrange themselves to spell out something evil. But there's no tick tock tick tock inside the crock.

I pry the covers off the cannisters of flour, rolled oats, sugar, and coffee and dump everything out. I can't find it anywhere. No telltale tick tock tick tock. Nothing. Where is it?

So I hustle out to the chicken coop. Four laying hens sit on their eggs. I shoo them away and break the eggs, listening for the sound. No tick tock tick tock there either.

It's become foggy before my eyes so I must feel my way along the ground to find the summer kitchen. There sit rows of pint jars of peas that Marit canned before she went away. Maybe the tick tock is inside the jars. I open up every one of them and put my ear down to listen to the peas, but the peas are no help at all.

Where to look, where to look? Only one job to do and I can't even keep track of the tick tock tick tock. I become frantic. Panicked. What kind of person am I? But I know the answer to that...I am a bad girl, a *bad*, **bad** girl. Bad. *Bad.* **Bad.** I've lost the tick tock tick tock. What is left for me? What will become of me?

In desperation, I throw open every cupboard door and drawer in the kitchen and empty their contents on the floor. Searching. Searching. There's no tick tock but I find my knife, long and sharp. I test its sharpness by running my thumb along its edge and the line of blood proves what I know. With my bloody hand, I rest my knife on my collarbone for a long moment to think.

Where does one make an incision to remove the soul? How do I slice out the memories? Can I cut the voices out of my head? I have no answers. So, I slit the fifty-pound sack of flour slumped in the corner and then rip open the burlap bag of rice. These are the testaments to my search for the answers, do you see? Do you see how hard I search? The white on the floor is purity, now trod upon and long gone. And so, to make the truth plain to see, I dump a bowl of watery red Jell-O over the cucumbers and the flour and rice. A red and white portrait of Red Velvet Cake and spilled milk. No, it's of flesh and blood!

With my cold heart trying to push itself out of my chest, I look to the door where the tick tock tick tock must be hiding. Marit stores things inside that closet under the stairs but she calls it Sophie's "secret" hiding place. She's promised me it's a safe place for Sophie to play although I have never gone inside. If the tick tock tick tock is in the closet, then it's gone forever to me. I've let it slip through my fingers. That closet would suck my breath away. Turn me to dust. All is lost.

God help me...I've lost everything. I am nothing.

And the girls of this house: the one in the bathtub, and the other one? The other one is Sophie, who went to find her daddy in the field. The one in the tub locked in the bathroom...she cannot be my daughter. No, that little girl is me, locked away with only the cold water for company. That little girl knows what happened.

She falls...tumbling, crashing into the deep. Ricochets and collides, with bloodied head and fingers toward the suffocating blackness. Cruel fingers grasp to claim her. Pulling her down, down, down...

October 1937

*T*he Monster shouts, "Into the cupboard, Brat." He pushes me inside. Latches the small door. It's too narrow for me to sit. Too low to stand. I crouch while my leg muscles burn. I listen to the Monster talk to my mama. With one eye, I can make out movement through the slit of light around the cupboard door.

"Oh, you thought you were so fuckin' smart, didn't you? Don't you back away from me, bitch! I came here to see you."

I hear fabric tearing and my mother's gasp. But she says nothing to the Monster. That's the safest thing. "Well, look at these titties. You've been using these to get by too, no doubt. Whore!"

A loud slap and my mother's involuntary, "Aghh." Through the gap around the door, I see the back of the Monster's suit jacket, the heel of his boot.

"Don't hurt my mama," I call out, panicking, desperate. I pound on the cupboard door.

"Shut up!" I hear as the Monster's jacket sleeve comes into view. The suit back turns to me again. "Thought you fooled me, didn't you? Hmph. I've always known where you were. You whore!" The voice growls with another sharp slap.

"God, you're a pain in my ass. Pretending you're sweet little Vanessa. Slut!" He mocks with his tone and spits out her name with another slap.

Something falls against the china cupboard nearby, knocks against the wall. Glass breaks. Mama, please say what he wants. Please. I pray to whatever God hears prayers from little girls locked in cupboards.

The sound of a booted foot strikes something with a dull thud. Mama, oh Mama! I've heard thuds like that before. When I was very little.

Mama groans, "Nggghhhh."

"Where are they? Those jewels you ran off with. I'm gonna find them whether you tell me or not. Might as well make it easier on yourself." A booted foot strikes something again. A muffled crack.

"Nggghhhh! Chest...top drawer...bedroom." Her voice catches again and again. How it must hurt to talk, even to breathe.

The Monster's footsteps hurry down the hall toward Mama's bedroom. Without him in front of her, I see a bit of Mama's shoe on the floor. I hear each painful breath she takes. I hope she can hear me whisper through the cupboard door. "Mama, mama...can you get up? Can you get out the door? Please try, mama," I cry softly.

Farther away, a drawer slides open. Footsteps return from the bedroom. The scuff of the Monster's boot next to the cupboard. Jewelry is scattered onto the dining table.

I see his pantleg through the gap around the door. He mutters to himself and paws at the jewelry. "I said to myself, Al, why should you suffer when you know where these jewels are." Suddenly he sounds pleased. "Hah! The wedding ring's still here! Now I don't have to buy another one for the old widow." The Monster snickers and lets out a self-satisfied sigh of relief. Then, the faint jumble of jewels being scooped back into the velvet bag.

"You know, Vanessa, you could've avoided some painful lessons I gave you on Long Island. But you didn't want to play by the rules, did you?"

There's a scrabbling on the floor; maybe he's picking up my broken mama? "There, now you can see me better. Look at me," he sneers. The chair squeaks.

"Nggghhhh," is all I hear.

"I've got one more lesson for you." He snickers, cruelly. "See if you're still as tight as you were at fifteen. How about that?" A pause. Mama struggles to breathe.

"What do you say to that, Vanessa?" He spits her name out with cruelty. I know what he's talking about. I have to vomit. I can't move and it goes onto my right shoulder.

"I...I..." Her broken voice is painful to my ears.

"Oh God. What's that stink?" The Monster's voice aims toward the cupboard. "Goddamn. You lose your breakfast in there, Brat? God almighty. Now I have to clean you up before I have a go at you, too. You two are more trouble than you're worth."

Then the telltale squeak of weight shifted from the chair. The chair legs scrape back from the table. The Monster's suit moves across my sightline. He's moving down the hallway carrying Mama. "Well, this shouldn't take too long. You better remember how I like it." The Monster's voice and boots are moving farther away. He pants like a hungry dog.

I cover my mouth after I throw up, to prevent the sound of crying from escaping the cupboard. Now with the Monster moving farther away from me, I let a sob escape. Just one sob.

The Monster used to slap me after beating my mother. He'd say, "What do you have to cry about? You're nothing but a spoiled brat. You're not even my brat." I wished that was true.

There are sounds from Mama's bedroom at the end of the hall. Bed springs squeaking. Headboard banging against the wall. The Monster's grunting. Mama's ribs are broken. How can he hurt her even more? He'll come to hurt me next. How I hate him! I hate him! I hate him!

He's a Monster. Evil Monster!

It seems like a long time before I hear the Monster's footsteps come back from the bedroom. The latch on the cupboard door is undone. "Get out," the Monster growls. His clothes are rumpled, and his hands smeared with red.

He grabs my arm and pulls me from the cupboard. Red fingerprints mark my sleeve. I crumple from my half-crouch onto the floor.

"Get up!" he growls. Followed immediately by, "Quiet!" the Monster whispers loudly at me and claps his hand over my mouth. I hear sounds of movement below us. Doors opening and closing. The people that live downstairs have come home!

Feet are starting up the stairs.

"Is everything alright up there?" It's Mr. Timmes voice. A brief pause on the stairs. "Mrs. Bovary?" The Monster's hand still covers my mouth. "Mrs. Bovary?" The feet continue climbing the stairs in haste.

The Monster wrenches my head to look at him. "You don't know me," he hissed. "Never seen me before in your life." He waits for my eyes to register his words. Then he runs to Mama's bedroom.

I scramble up. "Help us, please." I unlock the door.

"What's going on up here?" Mr. Timmes from downstairs says, then sees my face, the vomit on my dress and red sleeve. Then there is silence around us.

"My mama's hurt in the bedroom." I whisper loudly, hysterical. "He's in there." I point. "He might have a knife."

"Stay here," he says quietly to me and crosses the dining room to the kitchen where he takes a carving knife from the counter. He comes out of the kitchen and looks at me with a finger to his lips in a "Shhh" signal. He tiptoes toward Mama's bedroom.

It's much too quiet. I wait, but I don't hear fighting or anything at all. This doesn't seem right. Mr. Timmes comes out of the bedroom again, the knife hanging from a limp hand. He looks like he's seen a ghost.

266

I run down the hall to find my mother. "Mama, Mama," I cry. Mr. Timmes catches me with one arm to hold me back, to keep me from the bedroom.

"Honey, you don't wanna go in there."

"Yes, I do." He holds me tight and pulls me toward the door to the stairs.

"Eleanor," he calls down the stairs.

"Yes? Henry?" The short little lady from downstairs starts up the stairs when she sees us looking down at her. "The police are on the way," Eleanor reports with fright.

I struggle to get free. "Where's the Monster?" There is something terribly wrong about this.

"He's gone, little one," the man says so Eleanor and I can both hear.

"Let me see my mother!" I scream again and I bite the single, kind hand that holds me back. I've surprised him. He loses his hold on me. I wriggle free. "Mama!" I shout. "Mama!"

I catch just a glimpse of her body there on the blood-soaked bed and the curtains fluttering at the open window. Her body and the bed beneath her are shades of white and red. Red Velvet Cake and spilled milk comes to mind. Her clothing torn. Head and neck at an unnatural angle. My beautiful mother. My beautiful, good mother. I can't move. I can't speak. The only sound I hear is the 'tick tock tick tock tick tock' of the grandfather clock, standing on the floor outside her bedroom door.

I was told that I didn't speak again for days. I don't remember any of that. Neither could I sleep. They told me that the only food to pass my lips was broth. Why should I continue to eat when it only made me want to vomit? The only thing left for me was fear. I was eleven-years-old. With nothing and nobody to count on. I had nothing but my fear that the Monster would come back for me.

Sometime later, days or weeks...when I talk again, there are interviews. The police detectives come to the orphanage to talk to me. They get nothing from me about where we'd lived before we came to Minneapolis. Did I recognize the man I called the "Monster?" Did I know who he was? I can't tell. They would send me to live with my mother's parents in Brooklyn. What if they sent me to Long Island? I can't go back to Long Island.

Even Mama's parents can't protect me from the Monster. What if the other grandmother insists on taking me home with her? To the Monster? Nobody denies the grandmother anything she wants.

The detectives ask me so many questions. Finally, they ask me, "Don't you want the man who killed your mother to be caught and punished? If you do, you must help us by telling us about him. Anything at all. You're the only one who saw him."

Of course, I want him punished. I want him dead! But how can I be sure of that? That Evil Man. Yes, I know who he is, what he looks like. Only my eyes have seen him. My eyes know too much. He'll want to take my eyes at the very least. Only I know his name and where he lives. I can never tell anyone that the Monster is my father.

Within the deepest and darkest of places, the eyes of my husband seek me. He holds my head in his lap, smoothing my hair. The voice I have loved calls to me to come back from the place where I have fallen away. The knife is pried from my hand and tossed away.

"Darling. Caroline, my darling. Look at me. Can you talk to me?" I lie on the kitchen floor, amidst the flour and oatmeal and red Jell-O.

Sophie stands behind him, her face smeared with snot and tears, holding a towel around little Leah, who quivers with cold...or fear? Their small faces appear gaunt, hollow. What have I done to them? To all three of them?

Where has the Monster gone?

July 10, 1951

When I finally arrive at Rochester State Hospital, they say that it is Tuesday morning. "It's Dr. Coughlin's day off today. He won't be coming in," the woman in a white dress and cap says.

So, I say, "I'll wait for him."

I wait and I wait. They put me in the dormitory and assign me a bed. I pace the length of the long room. I pace without ceasing. They want to cut my hair. And so, with a short blunt haircut, I wait.

People remember me of course. Estra finds me pacing. She follows in my wake. She talks, incessantly talks. Recites some of her nursery rhymes while I pace.

Marilyn and Celia see me as they are herded past to the washroom to wash up before dinner. They're part of a work crew and they are not allowed to linger with me.

"You're here!" They utter in synchrony, wide-eyed. They will stop back briefly after they've eaten.

"Caroline, you're not here just to visit us, are you?" I feel as though Marilyn can see all that I have gone through in the last two years, that she knows it all.

"No, no, I have something I have to do. Something very important I must do. We will find each other later, alright?" I hug each of them in turn. Marilyn's grip is tenuous at first, sad. I pull away to look into her eyes. "I've missed you so much, Marilyn. I think about you all the time. Wondering how you are. Whether you're still here."

At that, Marilyn's hug becomes strong, as if she will never let me go. "And I have missed you, but I was so glad for you to get out of here. I should be sorry that you're back, but instead I'm happy to see you. Does that make me a terrible friend?"

"No, I think that means you like my company," and I give her a wobbly smile.

I turn to Celia, "let me see you." I hold her at arm's length. "Something is different about you, but I can't place what it is." In another moment, I can see it. She's turned a pale shade of yellow. Her fair skin with the red hair was always such a striking contrast along with the freckles that lightly peppered her face and shoulders. But now, her freckles have all but disappeared into the yellowish cast of her skin. She's sick.

"Celia, what's wrong? Your skin is so yellow. Your eyes too."

"I'm sick. Something with my liver, they say." She's going to be herded out to the gardens in a moment. Time is running out. "Let me hug you for a minute before you go." I hold her fast. She won't be allowed to dally here much longer. The trustee is gathering their group together. The gardens must be weeded. And then they are gone.

I scratch at my arms. I scratch at my scalp until it is raw and red. I chew my nails down to the quick. Some of the cuticles bleed. No matter. Before the afternoon is over, Dr. Coughlin comes. He had called to the hospital to check on a patient and that's when the nurse told him, "Caroline Fjeld has returned."

When I see him, I say the only two words I need to say to make him understand my presence here.

"I remember."

PART IV

SOLID GROUND

"I am learning what I choose is the real me."

Anonymous

"For most of history, Anonymous was a woman."

Virginia Woolf (1882 – 1941)
Modernist 20th Century English Novelist

25

UNFORGETTING

Caroline
Tuesday July 10, 1951

I remember all of it. The castle on Long Island. The ocean. The grandmother that ruled everything and everyone, except for her son that no one could control. He was the one that my mother and I called "the Monster," not to his face, of course. That would have been suicidal. But she never spoke his name if she could help it. And I did not call him "father." Ever.

Illustration 12: Long Island "Castle"

I stare at the concrete floor. A gray painted floor, with a web of cracks that bleed out from the center. When I look up, Dr. Coughlin is waiting. And the memories come hurtling out.

"For days at a time, the Monster ignored my mother and me except that he would appear dressed for cocktails and dinner each evening. His mother expected it. I was happy when he was gone all day. My mother and I walked in the gardens and visited the horse barn. We played hide and seek, and Cook packed us a little picnic basket to have on the grass or down by the shore.

"I loved to lie back on the ground to look at the sky. We'd find animals and other things in the clouds. One time I saw a ship in the clouds, and I asked my mother where she would go if she could go anywhere in the world on that ship. She didn't say anything at first and I thought she was just thinking, but when I looked, she had tears in her eyes.

"'Mama, what's wrong?' I asked her. 'Why are you crying?'

"And she said, 'Oh, there are just so many wonderful places I would love to go.' She named some of them. I remember she said, 'Italy and Greece and Egypt and Brazil.' I laughed because I thought Brazil was a make-believe place.

"'And would you take me with you, Mama?' I asked her. Of course, I already knew the answer. She pulled me close and said, 'I will never go anywhere without my Carolina Baby. You are the most precious thing in the whole world to me.' I lay on her arm watching the clouds and she twirled a lock of my hair, like she did sometimes when we were alone and quiet."

I stop and look up at Dr. Coughlin. "That may have been the happiest moment in my life until then."

I look away from him because I cannot "see" what comes next properly with his kind eyes before me. And it *is* time that I "see" the thing that is dark and evil. "When my mother and I were alone with the Monster in our private chambers, he rarely smiled. But when he did, it was a terrible thing. He smiled because he had something planned for my mother and for me, too." I swallow hard.

"He kept a fancy wooden box under his bed that unlocked with a tiny key. He wore that around his neck. From time to time, he brought out the box and opened it to show us. There were three wicked-looking hunting knives inside. Each had an ivory handle that was beautifully carved to look as though a wild animal was hidden inside the handle.

"The first time I saw them, he asked me which one I thought was the prettiest. And I said, 'I don't know. I like *all* the animals.'

"But he said, 'No, I want you to pick one. Which one do you really like the best of the three?' I was afraid of him and didn't want to answer.

"My mother said to him, 'Alistair, please. She doesn't have a favorite.'

"He turned on her then so fast and he pushed her so that she fell onto the floor. 'I'm not talking to you. Stay out of it,' he said. 'She's old enough to pick a favorite.' He turned back to me and said again, 'Pick one. Which is the very best?'

"I looked at my mama on the floor. Her eyes were wild. She looked back and forth between the Monster and me. At first I thought it looked like she was afraid of the Monster and me. But then she settled her eyes on me and she said calmly, 'It's okay to pick one, Caroline. I'm okay.'

"I still didn't want to, but I would do whatever my mother told me to do, so I did pick one. 'This one,' I said. 'The one with the elephants.'

"'Ah, yes that is quite exquisite, isn't it. Now pick it up,' he said to me. I hesitated. I wasn't allowed to touch the sharp knives in Cook's kitchen. The Monster *ordered* me then, loudly, 'Pick it up!' So I did. I remember how small my hand was, holding that big ivory handle. 'Are you quite sure that's the best one?' he asked me again. I was afraid again. I wondered if I'd chosen the wrong knife. Maybe he wanted me to choose a different one, the one *he* thought was the nicest.

"So I said, 'I think...I think...maybe. I think...'" I looked frantically at him and at mama on the floor. What was the right answer? I started to put the knife back in the box.

"He said, 'No, you picked. You have to stick with your decision. Now, show your mother the knife you picked.' I was terrified by then. I didn't understand what was going on, but it felt so wrong. It made my stomach turn around. I felt sick. I tried not to, but I couldn't help myself. I threw up. Grandmother called what I had a 'nervous stomach.' I threw up a lot when I was a kid. When I was worried or really frightened about what was coming next...and it always had to do with the Monster.

"'God Almighty!' he yelled at me. 'You stink. You'll clean that up in a minute. But right now? Show. Your. Mother. That Goddamn. Knife.'

"So I went to kneel beside her with the knife I'd chosen. Somehow she understood that she wasn't to get up from the floor. I said, 'Here it is, Mama. It has elephants on it.'

"And she said, 'Yes, that is very beautifully carved. You chose well.'

"Then the Monster grabbed the knife from my hand and said, 'let's see if it's sharp enough.' And he took one of my long locks and cut it off and held it up for me to see. I shrieked. 'I like to keep my knives good and sharp,' he said, smiling. 'Be careful that you don't trip or fall on a knife, Caroline. That would be a bloody mess, wouldn't it?'

"He stood admiring his knife. Wiped the blade on his pantleg while I hunkered there next to my mother. We said nothing. I think he showed the knives to us to remind us that he could use them if he wanted and no one could stop him. I can still see that box in my mind.

"When my grandmother was away, the Monster did things to us. He made my mother hold her breath. Held a pillow over her face and counted to twenty, slowly. Told her, 'If you can hold your breath without fighting me, I won't have to hurt the brat here.'

"He smiled at me. It was more like a sneer really, and he said, 'If you make even one sound, I'll have to start counting all over again.' So, it would be my fault if my mother passed out, which happened more than once. It would be my fault if she died. All my fault!" I am breathing much too fast. My heart pounds.

"Caroline, breathe with me. In...and out...and in...and out. You are hyperventilating. It will pass. In...and out...and in...and out...there." Moments pass. "There. You are safe here." The doctor holds my gaze and breathes with me, my silence taut like a rubber band. Relearning how to breathe. Looking for my voice.

At last, I find my voice. "He'd say, 'You nearly killed your mother! You worthless thing. Maybe you don't love your mother after all. Maybe you *want* your mother to die. Can you believe that, Vanessa?' He'd turn to ask her that and then he'd smile while she pleaded with him to leave me out of this, whatever 'this' was.

"'It's really my fault,' my mother might say. 'I didn't lie still enough,' even though I knew that she hadn't moved a muscle. My mother had courage to say the things she did to try to protect me. She was younger then than I am now! Just a child herself." Tears leak from my eyes.

I pause. I feel that same old childhood fear that something horrible is about to happen. I remember how I would vomit. I feel as if I am only six-years-old again. But I have to go on.

So I close my eyes tightly and whisper as I rock myself on my chair, "He pushed things inside of her." To hear myself say this out loud makes me gasp. My veins are electrified. "How do I know? Because he kept me in the room with them and he locked the door. Told me that if I cried out, he would push the thing in harder. But I couldn't keep from crying; I just couldn't. Finally, he locked me inside a wardrobe cupboard so that I could only hear him." Silent tears slide down my face to remember.

"I'm here, Caroline. I'm not going anywhere," I hear Dr. Coughlin's voice as if from a great distance.

After a long minute, I begin again. "He chose times when his mother was out of the house to torture us. When the grandmother was home, though, he was charming. He pretended to be so nice to everyone when she was around.

"One time the grandmother was gone for a week, maybe longer. She took the train to Pittsburgh to visit her sister. When she returned, my mother was ill in bed. The grandmother called the doctor. It's the only time I saw her truly angry at her son...that he hadn't called the doctor earlier. I should have known why my mother was sick, but I was too little to make sense of it.

"While his mother was away, he brought things into the house to use." I look at Dr. Coughlin intently. "Do you understand what I am saying? He brought things to use on her, *in* her, into my mother's bedroom."

I am sick to my stomach now. Holding myself tightly and rocking. Roiling, guts heaving to escape. The words I've said are so horrific; did that really happen? I want to push the words back into my mouth, but they are too sharp, too deadly. They're too big to fit.

"Caroline, do you need to stop for a few minutes? I'll wait."

I smell the fear on myself. It is the stench of secrets kept hidden, rotting. "I *want* to stop," I say, "but I'm afraid that if I do, it will take me years to return to this same point. I can't risk it."

A picture of Dr. Coughlin and his wife sits on the desk. They look so normal. Ordinary.

My dark story has to come now, in pieces, if necessary, or not at all. I continue. "I hid in the wardrobe cupboard when the doctor came. I heard him ask her where she hurt, but it only took a moment for him to know. When he touched her, she moaned like an animal crying. There was quiet for a moment.

"Then I heard him ask her in a hushed voice, 'My God, Mrs. Westerham...what have you done to yourself?'

"I couldn't hear what she answered. Her voice was so soft. But I know she didn't tell him the truth. The Monster already owned her silence with his threats to hurt me.

"The doctor said, 'I fear that it may be a form of madness.' That's what he said to the grandmother and the Monster. 'To think that a young woman would harm herself in such ways, it is beyond comprehension.'

"The doctor put her on bedrest for weeks. And he said that someone must remain with her at all times, to ensure she wouldn't harm herself further. He also told the Monster that my mother was 'too...damaged to have...marital relations.' My mother had always had her own private rooms at the castle. The doctor probably thought he was doing all he could to protect my mother from herself.

"Grandmother took charge then. She forbade my mother visitors, including her own son. No, wait...but she did allow my mother's parents to visit. She assigned some of the house staff, the women staff, to sit with her all through the days and nights. To read to her, do needlework with her, or play cards if she was up to it.

"I think the grandmother was afraid my mother might have been dying. Only much later did I understand how close to death she likely was." I am speaking to the floor again.

"I can't help but think that the grandmother knew that there was something very wrong between my mother and the Monster. But I never heard her say so. She did send him away on a trip to Philadelphia, though, while my mother was so ill. When he returned two weeks later, my mother was starting to feel better." Now I lift my eyes to look at Dr. Coughlin. "And she did nothing further to protect either of us. Not really. I can never forgive her for that." I stare hard out the window then. Jaw set like a tightened bolt.

"And my grandfather. There's little to say about him. I might have loved him a little. He was good to me when he was home, but... he stayed away for months at a time...in Europe, the Orient, India. He owned ships. He taught me about things like the stars, ships' affairs and nautical dawn. Ships were was his only real love." My breath collapses then in deep sadness, to find that I can still mourn that grandfather I barely knew.

"The house staff were afraid of the Monster too. I knew lots of hiding places, in cupboards and other places so that I could listen to them whispering about his threats. He knew where their families lived and worked. 'Bad things happen to people who spread lies,' he told them.

"Some of them wanted to go elsewhere to work, but the others said that Alistair had promised them that he would make sure they received bad references from the Westerham house, so that they'd never be able to work anywhere on Long Island, ever again." I lay my head in my hands. I am exhausted, but I cannot stop.

"I'll tell you why we left when we did. At least, I think this is why. It was because the Monster decided to pay more attention to me. He wanted to tuck me in at night, by himself. From as far back as I can remember, he'd said that children are dirty, nasty things. He told my mother to keep me away from him. But then, he began to pull me up to sit on his lap.

"He'd never wanted to hold me before that. I didn't want to sit on his lap. His hands were always touching me, patting me. Under my dress, even, when he thought no one was looking. But my mother saw. I think that is when she decided we had to escape."

I talk until I am nearly hoarse that first day back at the hospital. Dr. Coughlin has been sitting beside me since he came in on his day off. I am spent. Night fell long ago. Perhaps it's midnight by now. The words pour from me like water from a spout. They have to come out. They gush from my lips. "If I don't get them out of my mouth, I will choke on them. I think they will poison me." My mouth is dry like I'm chewing on chalk.

Dr. Coughlin said, "Caroline, these memories *have* been poisoning you all these years. It has required every bit of your being to keep them at bay. You have feared a nameless devil rather than this real flesh and bone devil that brutally tortured your mother, and you. Now that you have named him, you can begin to take that power away from him. I will help you do that, Caroline."

We sit quietly for a time, while I think. I am drained, wrung dry like a dishrag. I'm not yet ready to be entirely alone with my thoughts. These memories that exploded into the air now surround me as fragile panes of glass, ready to shatter and pierce my skin when I glance back at them. I'm afraid of them wandering outside of my head, beyond my control.

I begin to pace, like a caged badger. Somehow Dr. Coughlin knows that I am not safe to be left alone like this. Even though it's late and he should have gone home to his family hours ago, he gets me a fresh pitcher of water and he continues, calmly, quietly.

"A person who finds pleasure in hurting others needs to be locked away, Caroline. This is a man who thinks only of himself, who lies and pretends to be something he is not. He is a person without conscience—that is true Evil."

He pauses. I stop pacing for a moment to look into his face, asking him without words to finish the job of putting these memories into some sort of order that I can live with.

"We don't like to believe that such evil exists in the world. Some might say that they simply can't believe it. It's too awful. A person that is not capable of loving others, not even their own parents, spouses, children? These are people that we don't want to believe walk on the same earth that we do." The doctor's words encourage me. To understand that the man who fathered me is the skin and bones Evil. And finally I can stop pacing. I can sit.

"It hasn't been that long since Hitler, Caroline, a man who authorized the deaths of countless people." The doctor speaks cautiously, carefully. I know that he is reading my face to decide how much to say. "People feared him and I believe that was the admiration he wanted. He only wanted to feed his ego. I contend that the Monster is much like that dictator."

I am able to continue to talk at last, "I am desperate to know what I should do with all of this." I clench my fists, and my teeth. "How do I go on?" I pace, again.

"I know," he answers evenly. "Allow me to help you, Caroline. Together we'll figure it out."

Caroline
September 1951

I have invited Arvid and Marit to come to the hospital for a family conference. A *real* family conference. It is only the three of us Fjelds, Dr. Coughlin and a new nurse, Fern Odegaard, who is younger and much kinder than Sister Alva had ever been. I am going to tell the truth that I have hidden even from myself. To the degree that I am able.

I am astonished at first, and angry, to learn that Dr. Coughlin, Arvid and Marit all know of the Westerham family on Long Island. And that they know about my D' Bouvier grandparents in Brooklyn.

"But you don't know the whole story," I begin. "Only that my mother and I escaped." I fix my gaze on Arvid and Marit. "I understand that you did not tell me what you knew, in order to protect me from something I wasn't ready to remember. I must thank you, all of you, for that."

Dr. Coughlin first lays the ground rules, "Caroline has worked incredibly hard the past two weeks. She has remembered...so very much. She has decided that the time has come to tell you about something that she has kept hidden, forgotten even, for most of her life. I wouldn't be surprised if you find yourself wishing she would stop, that her story is too sad to hear from someone you love. But *our* job now, and it is an important job, is to allow her to tell it. What she needs from you now is to be strong enough to endure hearing her story." He looks at Arvid and Marit carefully. "Do you have questions for me before we begin?"

Arvid and Marit look at me tenderly. Marit already has tears in her eyes. Almost as one, they take in a deep breath and release it. They shake their heads no. Arvid scoots his chair an inch closer to me.

I look squarely at Arvid as I begin. Then at Marit. "I want to tell you both about this because I want you to know what has made me ill in my mind. I love you so much, Arvid, and still I wasn't able to put this behind me. And Marit, you are as a mother to me, and yet I've been unable to speak of this. I blame this story for keeping me at a distance from you both, and from Leah." I look to Arvid at this last statement.

Marit's silent tears fall. Arvid knits his eyebrows and listens intently.

I take a deep breath and try to smile. "I've never told you much about my mother. She was a very special person. She was a beautiful person inside and out and I loved her so much. I was born when she was just sixteen years old." Marit releases a small sound from her throat.

"My mother's husband was, well, we called him The Monster when she and I were alone. He did have another name of course." I snort as I say this. "He was christened Alistair Westerham III. He was vain...just a vain, pretty man." I grimace to say it. "He was so proud of himself, his handsome face and all his fancy clothes and cars and those fancy names.

"He was a spoiled child that never grew up. I want to tell you that he was raised almost entirely by his mother, alone. His father, Alistair, Sr. stayed away from home for months at a time. Anyway, I'm just saying that maybe it wasn't his father's fault, the way he was, I mean.

"My mother first heard the name of Alistair Westerham at the age of fifteen years. She and her friend, Sylvia, just fifteen-year-old girls, were out walking between the shops in Brooklyn, having a nice afternoon together when there was a freak accident. Someone had a horse in town, there among all those cars! The horse got loose and ran down the street. My mother's friend was injured crossing the street. Alistair was the first to reach the girls. He would have loved playing the "hero." It was like him to put on a show. Make himself look better than he was. He scooped up the injured girl and put her into his car. My mother got in the car to accompany her friend who was hysterical. They went to the hospital." Arvid and Marit listen in silence, their hearts on their faces.

"After the friend was delivered to the hospital, Alistair said that he would notify the girls' parents and he asked my mother to accompany him. My mother wanted to stay at the hospital with her distraught friend, but she could hardly refuse to report back to Sylvia's parents, so she went with him. Afterward, he brought her home and that's how Alistair learned where my mother lived and that's when he introduced himself to my mother's parents.

"My mother said that he was very much the gentleman that day. He was so handsome, like an actor in the theatre. He complimented my mother's parents and said, 'What a devoted friend your daughter has shown herself to be today.' He told my grandfather that he could tell that he was a man of integrity by his firm handshake.' Pfft. As if he would have known anything about integrity." I scoff and squint my eyes to recall my mother's voice telling me these words.

"My mother's parents were not gullible people. My grandfather must have figured that Alistair was massaging his ego to get close to his daughter, so he told Alistair right off that Vanessa was only fifteen years old, still attending school and that she had not received her parents' permission to be courted. As if that would have mattered to Alistair.

"On the following Monday, he drove his car slowly alongside my mother while she walked the few blocks to school. He offered to tutor her in Latin. Within a fortnight, Alistair had skillfully wooed my mother, without ever proclaiming his intention to court her. And all without her parent's awareness.

"Of course, my mother was impressed by the handsome young man. Such a gentleman, so courteous and so wealthy. It must have been very thrilling to have this man interested in her. She told me that she thought she was falling in love. My mother had two exciting weeks of surreptitious meetings with Alistair.

"The day that Alistair stole her virginity from her started out like any other." I pause for another drink of water while Arvid and Marit's faces register shock. Marit sucks in her breath. I look squarely at them. "You probably wonder why a mother would tell her young daughter such an awful story?" I snort with derision and close my eyes for a moment. "You will understand very soon."

"After two or more agonizing months a bulge grew on my mother's tummy, and she finally went to her mother. She showed her mother the bulge that was me. She said, 'I must be with child, Mama.

I'm so sorry.' She cried and cried in her mother's arms. They both cried.

"'It belongs to that man that brought you home that day,' her father said to her after he'd struck the wood mantel with his hand. He paced around and then he said to her. 'I cannot believe that you disobeyed me in this way, Vanessa. This is not the way that we raised you. This is not the future that your mother and I wanted for you.' When he looked up at her, my mother saw tears in his eyes.

"My mother could barely speak. She told herself that it was her own stupidity that put her in the car with Alistair that day when he took her to an isolated place. A cemetery crypt. She blamed herself entirely. She could have refused. She should have been wary. She questioned why would he want her, anyway? So, you see she didn't think there was any point in explaining that the man forced himself on her. Not after she'd been sneaking around for two weeks to be tutored in Latin by him. She didn't even try to explain what happened. 'Will you send me away, Papa? To where girls like me go?' she asked him."

Arvid has leaned forward now, his forearms resting on his knees. His face spells out a deep sorrow. It becomes hard to look at so much sorrow, so I look away. "My mother's father, my grandfather, was thinking differently though. He said that it was the man's responsibility to marry her and raise the child. Said that an honorable man will accept the burden of an unplanned marriage as his duty. He said he would accept nothing less from that Mr. Westerham.

"Well, my mother was devastated, of course, and frightened. She told her father that she didn't care for that man, that he wasn't a good man.

"But my grandfather said to her, 'You should have thought about that before you lay with him.' My mother said that his words cut her to the quick. She felt she had no choice but to go along with whatever her father arranged for her." Marit clapped a hand over her mouth at this and shook her head, though it was barely noticeable. Her hanky had long since become wet.

"My grandfather hired a car to bring him to the Westerham mansion out on Long Island. I can imagine how cowed he would have been when he first saw that immense house and the fenced grounds surrounding it. His car would have been kept waiting at the gates, while the gateman sent a small boy to the house with his name and to ask if guests were being received.

"Mrs. Westerham met my grandfather in the receiving room, her nose in the air no doubt. She told my grandfather that her husband was not at home. 'He is likely in Singapore by now.'

"My grandfather demanded the presence of her son before he continued. So a servant was sent to find Alistair and when he finally swaggered into the room, my grandfather did not accept his handshake.

"He said, 'No, sir. I will not shake the hand of the man that stole my daughter's innocence. You have fathered a child with my fifteen-year-old daughter, Vanessa, and it is now your duty to do right by her, to marry her. My grandchild will not be a bastard.'"

I glance back at Arvid to explain, "My mother, you see, overheard her father relay this story to her mother after the fact. Alistair had protested, denying the baby was his. That's just the way he was. But suddenly my pompous grandmother interrupted and out of the blue, she asked my grandfather D' Bouvier to tell her something about himself. He turned to her, indignant, I suppose, and he asked her, 'Why in the world, madam, does my life story have any bearing on the facts before us?'

"She answered him just as innocently as if they were talking about which tree it was that stood outside the window. As if it was nothing. She said, 'If we are to be relations, Mr. D' Bouvier, I'd like to know a little something about you.' My mother said that both of her parents were completely astonished by Alistair's mother. How she immediately took over."

Although our family conference has stretched on longer than planned, Dr. Coughlin subtly encourages me to continue until I tell them this last bit...how the Monster treated my mother and me. I look at Dr. Coughlin and see his slight nod, a signal for me to tell more.

"I don't need you to know *all* of the ways in which the Monster hurt us," I say. "But, I want you to understand that he *was* a very brutal man. He never loved my mother or me. He didn't know how. I spent my earliest years terrified of him."

I look directly at Arvid now. "Do you remember when you told me the story about how Teddy's mother defended him with her life? And how I cried to hear it?" It is the first question I've asked of my family.

The room is absolutely silent, but for his soft, "Yes."

"Teddy isn't the first dog in my life. On my sixth birthday, the Monster came home with a puppy for me. It was a fat white puppy with curly hair and floppy ears. I was thrilled." My sudden half-smile is sad, I know, and I can feel tears pooling. "I'd never dreamed I could have a puppy in the house.

"I couldn't remember any other times that he'd given me a gift and I suppose I should have found it odd, but it *was* my birthday, and I was so delighted to have the puppy. I even gave the Monster a hug." My tears fall now as I speak. "I named the puppy Murphy and I took him everywhere with me. He even slept on my bed with me. I loved that little dog.

"And then one day, my mother and I came home from the dress-maker's and Murphy didn't come to greet me like he always did. I looked all over. I went outside and searched over the grounds for him, calling him. I went to the horse barn, the carriage house and the car shed. I knocked on the gardener's cottage. I even went down to the beach, afraid that he'd gotten outside the fence." There's a catch in my throat.

"I cried about Murphy at dinner that night, that he must have gotten out and become lost. The grandmother said, 'Hmph, well I think that's probably just about enough fuss about that now, don't you think, Vanessa? It's just a dog.' The Monster smiled at me at that, an odd sort of smile.

"Later, that evening when I went up to our private chambers, I found Murphy. Lying in a pool of blood on the water closet floor, his head nearly separated from his body." I gasp as I utter this last and put my hands over my mouth.

Illustration 13: Girl With Puppy

Arvid moves to me, places a hand on my back. I look directly into his eyes and it feels in this moment as if we two are alone in the room. I whisper only to him now. "I screamed and I screamed, you know? I was only six years old, Arvid. Barely older than Sophie is now."

"I know, I know." Arvid whispers to me and pulls me close. "You were just a little girl. I am so sorry...so sorry...you were an innocent little girl. What a horrible, cruel thing to do to a little girl, my love." With a hand resting on my back, Arvid cries along with me.

"My mother took me to bed, and she lay beside me, trying to comfort me." A moment passes. "Eventually, the Monster came upstairs and saw us lying on my bed. He came close and looked down at us. He was smiling." I cock my head to one side, as if perplexed. "Can you imagine? Smiling at Sophie while she cries her heart out?"

Arvid hangs his head and shakes it slowly, somberly. "No, no, I can't...no..."

"He said only these few words. He said, 'That damn dog chewed on my slipper. I won't have a dog in the house that chews on shoes.' I was still sobbing but he was pleased with himself. He said, 'That favorite knife of yours with the elephant carving is really sharp. Like cutting through butter.' And then, Arvid, he winked at me."

26

A TIME TO HEAL

Caroline
Winter 1951-1952

The hospital feels different this time because I understand the work I have to do and because Big Alva is gone. The story that circulates among those of us who remember her and are able to form intelligible sentences is that she was discharged after a pattern of substandard care. I'd like to believe that her neglect of Lois was found out and that she was punished for it. I take relief especially in this one change in protocol, that the women are no longer required to call each other "sister."

Dr. Reynolds has retired. Good riddance. I've seen the new Chief of Psychiatry, at least I know his face, but I don't go to any treatments with him. I see only Dr. Coughlin. I am assigned a bed near Marilyn and Celia and so I am allowed to eat with them too. In a very poignant way, this feels almost like a homecoming.

There's a rumor that Marilyn may be sent away for a lobotomy. The three of us hold fast to one another, terror stricken by this possibility. But Celia says that Marilyn seems better now that I've come. I'm hopeful.

Celia has been sent over to the world-famous Mayo Clinic here in Rochester to see about her yellow skin. She says that she *might* get better.

Some days feel rudderless. On others, my stomach burns with purpose. I hunger for justice for my mother. Dr. Coughlin listens.

Eventually we talk about what it would be like if the Monster were on trial for the murder of my mother. What if I were to testify? He helps me find the questions he believes I will be asked if that day ever comes. We write them down, to inure me to the sting of hearing the questions from a defense attorney. His attorneys will ask about schizophrenia and my hospitalizations to make me look as though I can't be believed.

"After going through all that you have, Caroline, we cannot allow the schizophrenia to take away anything from the truth," Dr. Coughlin tells me.

After some months I begin to envision myself differently. The questions I've written down and my answers to them are a rainstorm pounding on the tin roof over the kitchen stoop at home. It's loud and startling, yes, but the words can't hurt me. The Monster's words and his torture are like so much noise. If a trial ever comes, I'll be ready.

It is Dr. Coughlin's suggestion that it's time I give my story to the Minneapolis Police Dept. I'm sitting across from him when he calls Arvid.

"Arvid, I think that it's time for Caroline to bring the name of the murderer to the Minneapolis Police Department in-person. We'll call it a therapeutic outing. I'd like her to have the continued structure and support of this place for his arrest. I suppose rather, I should say, we *hope* he will be arrested and extradited from the State of New York after her report."

"That is an excellent idea," Arvid says. "And you, Dr. Coughlin should drive her to the Police Department." A silence hangs in the air. I know immediately that it isn't just that Arvid knows it would be a very long day for him on the road, maybe an overnight stay in Minneapolis to bring me to the police station, himself. It's also that he knows that with Dr. Coughlin beside me, I am stronger.

Dr. Coughlin laughs. "Ahh...such a thing would be highly irregular." But he doesn't say 'no' and so Arvid persists.

"My mother could accompany the two of you," Arvid says. "That would prevent any notion of impropriety, wouldn't it?" When the doctor hesitates, Arvid must figure that he has a foot in the door. "I'll pay for the gas," he suggests. "I'll pay you for your time to take her," he adds. I can hear Arvid's brain scramble to sweeten the pot a little more. "My mother will drive the three of you there."

"Has your mother ever driven in the Twin Cities?" Dr. Coughlin looks worried, and incredulous.

"Well, no, she hasn't, but she's a conscientious driver," Arvid persists, although he admits to me later, that he was counting on losing that point in the negotiation. He was fairly certain that his mother would be too terrified to drive in the Twin Cities.

"Okay, enough of this nonsense," Dr. Coughlin says with a deep sigh. "I'll drive. My car. I'll invite my wife to go with us to Minneapolis for the day. We'll have lunch while we're there. The three of us. I won't charge you for my time. I'd be too embarrassed to tell you what the hospital pays me for an hour of my time. But, so as not to appear overly invested in this one patient, I will allow you to pay for gas and lunch for our therapeutic outing. How does that sound to you?"

"Wonderful. I'm all for it, Doctor." Arvid's voice now comes through the phone more loudly. "Caroline, are you there?"

"Yes, I'm here." I call out.

"What do you think?" He wants to know my opinion.

I smile inside. I warm through and through. "I think it's just the thing. The right thing...all of it." A three-person telephone conversation. How odd.

After Dr. Coughlin hangs up the phone, there is definitely a smirk on his lips. "So, it's going to be you and me and my wife, Lorraine. I think you'll like her. Saturday. Let's say eight o'clock." He pursed his lips and gave one short nod of his head. As if to say, 'well, that's settled.'

Dr. Coughlin and I arrive at the Minneapolis Police Department on Saturday morning around eleven o'clock. Lorraine was left to shop on Hennepin Ave. We'll meet her for a late lunch, Dr. Coughlin says, between one and two o'clock.

"We need to see someone in the Homicide Dept," Dr. Coughlin tells the man at the desk. We wait in uncomfortable chairs for someone to come for us.

"I'm Detective Haugen," a voice booms at us after a long wait. "You have something to report?"

It's my turn to talk. "I am here to tell you who murdered my mother."

"Whoa, whoa now. Is this an open investigation, Mrs...?"

"I don't know if it's open. But no one was ever charged that I know of. She was murdered in 1937."

"Come this way." Detective Haugen takes us to a room with only one table and four metal chairs. When I see that the table is bolted to the floor, I begin to hyperventilate. Is this the room where they bring the people that have lost their minds? Does he see something unusual about me? My blunt haircut? The broken tooth?

Dr. Coughlin says quietly, "Slowly, Caroline. Think one one-thousand, two one-thousand." He counts slowly, calmly until I am breathing evenly again.

I can feel the detective watching me, evaluating me. He wonders if there's something the matter with me. I sit up straighter and look the detective squarely in the eye. "I'm fine now, I say." And I follow with one long, slow exhalation.

Detective Haugen pulls the cover from his ink pen. "Alright, let's start at the beginning, shall we? What is your name, ma'am?"

"My name is Caroline Fjeld. My mother and I lived here in Minneapolis. Actually, we were hiding here in Minneapolis. Hiding from the Monster that tracked her here and killed her."

For a moment I allow myself to remember Minneapolis as it was when we lived here. It was where my mother and I had four lovely years of ordinary life. Dinners by ourselves with chatter and laughter. I told her stories I heard in school. My mother learned to make Red Velvet Cake for my birthday. There were bedtime stories with happy endings. Wonderful Christmas mornings. Skating on small lakes in the winter. Visiting the zoo. Exploring St. Paul and

Minneapolis without looking behind us at every turn. Years without pain, shouting or crying or fear. But I skip all of that to get to the day of my mother's murder.

"It was a Saturday morning in the fall, October I think. I don't know the exact date. I remember yellow and red leaves falling from the trees outside the window that day. There was a knock on the door. We rarely had visitors. My mother was in the kitchen, making pancakes. I was in the sixth grade and I thought I was so grown-up when I went to see who was at the door. When I unlocked it, it was pushed open so forcefully that I was knocked down and I screamed. It was the Monster."

"You knew who the man was?"

"Yes, of course," I say.

"How did you know him?"

I hate answering that question more than any other. "My mother and I called him 'Monster' since I learned to talk. His name is Alistair Charlton L. something Westerham, III. He lives in what I knew as the 'castle' on Long Island, New York. At least, that's where he lived when I was little, when my mother and I lived there too."

The detective asks us to wait while he goes out to invite another officer into the room with us. They want to start all over again. The detectives seem taken aback to discover that the man accompanying me is not my husband. "I'm Dr. Henry Coughlin, psychiatrist with Rochester State Hospital." He pulls out his identification badge from the hospital.

The two detectives lay their pens down upon hearing that. The one sits back in his chair and runs his hand over the thinning hair on the top of his head. "Oh." he says, clearing his throat, looking at us both. The detectives look at each other.

"She is as sane as I am, Detective. I will swear to that. And she's not under commitment."

"As of when?" the detective raises his left eyebrow.

"She was under commitment in 1948 until her discharge in 1949. She's not been under commitment this hospitalization, beginning August 1951."

There's a knock on the door and another man enters the room and whispers to the detectives. Detective Haugen looks up sharply and asks me, "What did you say your mother's name was?

"Vanessa D' Bouvier."

"Look, Miss. We don't find any record of the murder of a Vanessa D' Bouvier in 1937 or in any year, for that matter.

"Oh!" And then I realize. "Of course. How dumb of me. We changed our names when we moved here. My mother went by Victoria Bovary. I went by Carol. My mother thought that that way he wouldn't find us. We never told anyone in Minnesota what our real names were. If you would look for the name, Victoria Bovary, I think you'll find it."

"Alright, I'll be right back. I hope. If the records are all organized as they should be down in storage." The detective is gone for some time. The other detective leaves us alone in the room. Later, a woman comes in to give us glasses of water. I'm glad because I'm so nervous that my mouth has gone bone dry.

At last both detectives return. "We found the file! Indeed, it was under Victoria Bovary. 'Call received on Saturday, October 9th, 1937 from an Eleanor Timmes, requesting police assistance. Caller believes that something bad may have happened to the neighbors living upstairs. Victim discovered on bed at that address.' Says here that there was a little girl in the house that was mute. In shock most likely, one would imagine. That was you?" Det. Haugen looks up at me.

"Yes, that was me. I didn't speak for days afterward. Maybe weeks, I don't know how long it was. I just know that I was at the orphanage when I did."

"The record states that there were no leads in the case. There was an open window found in the victim's bedroom. Presumption was that the killer escaped through that. No footprints were found in the dry leaves on the ground. The neighborhood was canvassed for anyone who saw anything out of the ordinary. Nobody did. There were no witnesses, except for the little girl."

He continued reading the police report. "'Seeking an unknown person, presumed to be male in reasonably good physical condition to escape out the window.' The Timmes were both interviewed. The girl's school was contacted. There were no emergency contacts listed aside from the victim, herself. Carol's teacher reported that the teachers were asked by the mother to not ask Carol about where they'd lived in Milwaukee. Too much sadness. Said they'd moved to Minneapolis to be near the victim's family. But no family of the victim was ever found in Minneapolis. They asked Milwaukee P.D. to search for anyone by the name Bovary in Milwaukee. Dead end."

The detective stared at me hard for a minute. "You and your mother seem to have appeared in Minneapolis out of thin air."

"Yes, I'm sure that's what my mother wanted."

"There was no paperwork to speak of found in the home. No letters, no bank statement. No contracts with the exception of the rental agreement and a bill from the telephone company. No birth certificates, marriage license, no Last Will and Testament or any other legal document. The detective stood and paced a bit. "Tell me Mrs. Fjeld. How do I know that you are who you say you are?"

"How could I make up such a story? And why, for goodness sake?" I am taken aback. It had not occurred to me that I would have to prove that I am my mother's daughter.

"Caroline," Dr. Coughlin interjected. "I should have thought of this beforehand. We could have asked Arvid to bring your birth certificate to the hospital at his last visit."

"How do you know about my birth certificate?" My mouth drops open. I don't remember ever telling him about that.

"Arvid told us about your little carved box in our first conference with him. Told us about the photograph of you with your mother and the birth certificate folded up small."

"Yes! I have my birth certificate," I say defiantly to the detectives. "I can bring it to you. I don't know when, but I will." My voice seems to be reaching for a higher octave. Tight. "But it will take at least a couple of weeks before that could happen. Please, I've been preparing for this day for months. And now, for you not to believe me? To have to prove who I am?" I am afraid I will become hysterical in front of these men. The last thing I want to happen. "Do I have to show it to you before you can reopen the investigation of her murder? I want to see justice done for my mother."

The detectives look at each other. It seems to me that they have some sort of silent language between them. One raises an eyebrow. The other pulls on an ear. Finally, somehow, they seem to have come to an understanding. "We believe that you are who you say you are, Mrs. Fjeld. Bring us the birth certificate when you can, but that's no reason to hold up reopening the investigation."

The other detective concurs with a frank nod.

"Alright then. Did you see your father murder your—"

"I would prefer that you not refer to him in that way, please. Call him Mr. Westerham, or Alistair, or the Monster, or anything else you choose to call him but not my father. I never called him 'father.' No, I did not see him cut her with a knife or whatever sharp thing he used to kill her." I swallow to continue.

"I heard the whole thing through a cupboard door. I was a child, Detective. Eleven-years-old. I spent the next decade of my life trying not to remember what he did to her, what I saw when I got past the man, Mr. Timmes who came to help us that day."

It's well past our late lunch time but still the detectives have questions for me. Dr. Coughlin goes out to buy us both plates of meatloaf dinner from a cafe nearby.

After we eat, the four of us go for a ride in the detective's car so that I can direct him to the house where my mother and I lived, the house where the murder took place. I don't remember the street address, but I am able to find the house using the lake at Loring Park as my starting point.

I knock on the downstairs door of the house. I am met by a small gray-haired woman who comes up no higher than my shoulder. I recognize her. She helped me that awful day. She tried to comfort me after I saw the image that could only be unseen by remembering nothing of that day.

"Carol?" she asks, eyes huge.

"Yes, it's me." How did she remember my name? "It's Caroline, actually."

"I never thought I'd see you again after they took you away. They said you would go to an orphanage. I asked." She cleared her throat. "I asked them if you might want to stay with us instead."

"I never knew that." I answer her. "Yes, I did go to the orphanage in Owatonna. I have finally come back to see that my mother's killer is punished for what he did."

"Thank God, Caroline. I haven't had a good night's sleep since that day." She takes my hands in hers and offers a tremulous smile.

Before we leave, I write a detailed statement for the record. Detective Haugen and his partner confirm to us the reopening of the investigation into the murder of Vanessa D' Bouvier, PKA Victoria Bovary. I write a detailed statement for the record. I describe the castle and grounds on Long Island, for lack of a street address. And I can describe an approximate distance from it to the train station. The detectives ask me to include the names of any other family relations. "Who else knew your mother?"

"Her parents," I tell them. "But I haven't had any contact with them since before we escaped from the castle. I was seven years old. They don't know their daughter has been murdered. They don't know any of this."

"Well, Mrs. Fjeld. I believe that it's time the Minneapolis Homicide Department notified the D' Bouvier's of their daughter's death. We'll find them. Brooklyn P.D. will help us.

Fall 1952

At discharge, Dr. Coughlin asks me to consider forgiving my D' Bouvier grandparents, my mother's parents. "What if Sophie disappeared from your life one day? Wouldn't you be thankful if someone came forward to tell you where she was? What happened to her?"

Arvid agrees that I should attempt to meet them. If they will see me, Marit will continue taking care of Sophie and Leah as she has been doing, during yet another of my absences. Arvid calls the Doucette Portrait Studio in Brooklyn, and Mr. Doucette is pleased to act as a conduit to exchange addresses with my grandparents.

The first contacts between us are by letter. An envelope arrives for me, containing two letters, one written by each grandparent. I realize with a start that I never knew their first names. How odd it is to see their signatures. My grandfather's letter is signed in a stiff script, "Most sincerely, Francois." And at the bottom of my grandmother's letter, in a sweeping but shaky hand is, "Warmest regards, Your grandmama, Genevieve."

I write back to them. I tell them about my husband, my children, our farm. I tell them that I lived in an orphanage from age eleven through seventeen.

I tell them that I have tried to be a good person, like my mother was. She was not bitter or angry. I tell them that my mother didn't blame her parents for the way things turned out for us, running away to another state and all of that. I suppose that I don't really *know* that for a fact, but I *am* certain that she wouldn't have wanted to hurt them unnecessarily. I choose to assume that they have been suffering for many years until I learn something to the contrary. I will wait until I meet them in-person to tell them about her life in Minnesota and her death. And I will tell them about the schizophrenia when I can see their faces. I need to see their reactions.

27

THERE BE JUSTICE

Caroline
1953

At last a plan is agreed upon. I will go to Brooklyn to meet my D' Bouvier grandparents for a few weeks in the fall. My grandparents send a cab to pick me up me at the Amtrak train station. The driver is a young man that regularly drives for them. He speaks warmly of Francois and Genevieve.

When I knock, the door opens immediately and there they both stand, waiting for me. One silver-haired gentleman with a receding hairline and one gray-haired woman, both with moist eyes. Genevieve, with a hand on her chest and surprise on her face. Francois with a cane in his left hand and reaching out to take my hand with his right.

"You look so much like Vanessa," they say together. They look at each other, awestruck, I suppose, to find standing before them, a similar version of their daughter.

Genevieve says, "I must sit down...oh, my. Please sit with us." And she turns with vigor toward the parlor.

"Yes, do, come sit with us...Caroline?" Francois' voice is nice. He speaks my name with a question mark attached. Perhaps confirming permission to use it? He continues to hold my hand until I break the fragile thread of the moment.

"I need to bring my suitcase into the house. Excuse me."

I return with my bag in time to hear Genevieve remarking quietly to her husband, who waits for me in the foyer. "She even sounds like Vanessa. Oh, Frank. It's as if our Vanessa has come home to us again."

"Where would you like me to put my things?" Suddenly I need a job for my hands. This was my mother's home. My mother's parents. Their warmly furnished home. So unlike the castle on Long Island. This is the house she returned to after she'd been raped by the Monster, afraid to tell anyone. She hid here for months while I grew in her womb. "Shall I carry them upstairs?" I have an urge to run back out the door. The room feels close.

"Oh, no. Please, do come and sit." Genevieve rings a little brass bell which calls a pleasantly ample woman in a starched apron to bustle into the large room. "This is our dear helper, Helen. Without her here, we would not manage in this big house." Genevieve says this with a grateful smile. "She will bring your things upstairs to your room."

Then Genevieve looks from Helen to me and back again. Time seems to stop. Is Genevieve marking this as the first time she's ever introduced me to someone? "And Helen, this...this is our granddaughter...Caroline...come all the way from Minnesota to see us."

The cinnamon-haired Helen curtsies and smiles. I grin in return. "How do you do." I haven't seen anyone curtsy since my mother taught me to curtsy for the grandmother at the castle. I suddenly "hear" my mother's voice mimic the authoritarian grandmother's voice.

She would say, "I require proper ladylike comportment in this house," and as quickly as that, I am seven-years-old again. My mother and I are giggling, and I laugh out loud to recall it. And then I laugh more, but with tears filling my eyes.

"Please forgive me," I begin. "I suddenly remembered my mother teaching me to curtsy. I haven't thought of it for years and...it made me...I don't know..."

I burst into frank tears but yet I am smiling. Both Francois and Genevieve are crying too. Even Helen has tears in her eyes, although she quickly excuses herself from the room. Francois gently leads me to sit next to Genevieve on the divan and he sits opposite me. Three weeping D' Bouviers, I think, blinded by common tears for all that had been lost to the years.

The next day, Francois asks if I will tell them how their daughter died. "I will, but I'm not quite ready yet, if you don't mind. I want to know you as you are now, first for a bit. Maybe that doesn't make any sense."

"I think I understand. We'll wait until you're ready."

It takes me another two days to be ready to tell them how my mother died. I don't want them to have the image in their minds that I have carried for so long, but it is their right to know. "I'm ready to tell you now," I begin after we've had our nice dinner that day.

Francois gets up and comes around to my side of the table, pulling out my chair. "Let's first retire to the parlor, alright? I expect we may have need of comfortable chairs."

When we are settled in the parlor, Francois says, "We want to know the truth about how Vanessa died. I have, for years, had the feeling that she was gone. There's no way I could have known such a thing, but yet I just sensed it. I am ready. Genevieve, are you ready?"

"Yes," is her only reply.

I take a deep breath. "My mother stole away with me well before dawn, on a train heading west. I was seven years old. We took what belongings we could carry, and my mother also took with her the pieces of jewelry that had been gifted to her during her marriage. She didn't steal anything that was not already hers. I want you to know that. She called the jewels our "bank account."

"Mama was very clever. We got on and off the train a few times. She told *some* people that we were going to San Francisco, and *others* she told we were going to Milwaukee. Finally, we got off the train to stay in Minneapolis. We went to a nunnery first and they helped us for a while. Mama learned to cook and some other practical things. Things which she was not allowed to do in the castle on Long Island.

"After a while, she found a suite of rooms for us upstairs in a grand old house. We lived quite happily there for nearly four years, in hiding. We used different names while we were there. I was called Carol and my mother was Victoria Bovary.

"And then, one morning while my mother was making us pancakes there was a knock on the door. I thought I was so grown-up...answering the door. But it was the Monster. That was what we always called him."

"That was Alistair?" my grandfather whispers.

"Yes, it was. He barged in, loud and full of himself. The first thing he did was to lock me in a cupboard. I heard everything that followed from there." My grandmother's eyes are already grief-stricken. She knows what's coming.

"He wanted the jewels didn't he?" Genevieve says. "It was in the newspapers, front page, that the Westerhams lost everything in the Depression. Alistair's father suicided in Japan and his mother died just a few years ago.

"Yes, he got the jewels and then he tortured her. And then...he took her life."

A gasp from the two pleasantly lined faces. I look frantically between them. Two heads framed in gray and silver that should have been allowed to spend the remainder of their lives reflecting upon the good life they've lived, not the murder of a daughter they loved and lost.

"And he got away somehow...out a window. I don't know how." I finish, feeling the story is so inadequate for the weight of it.

My mother's parents have lived the last eighteen years wondering what happened to their daughter, Vanessa. When I see their grief for myself, I, at last, forgive them for pushing my mother into that horrible marriage. I tell them about some of the good memories. "Much of our short time together was happy. Some of it so terribly sad. My mother loved me. That will always be the most precious thing I have to remember."

At last I explain the last awful piece to Francois and Genevieve. "There's one more thing you need to know about me." I've waited until the week before Thanksgiving to confess. It's evening and the room is warmly lit by the fire in the fireplace. They sit close together by the fire.

"What is it, Caroline?" Genevieve asks.

"Please don't be afraid to tell us anything." Francois says when I hesitate.

"I have been hospitalized...in a Minnesota State Hospital." Pause. "Twice," I add. "A total of twenty-seven months." They seem to look puzzled. "A hospital for mentally ill people, you see."

Why don't they ask me something? "I have or *have* had schizophrenia. The kind of illness that made me afraid of...some people. Paranoia, is what they call it." I look back and forth between them. Waiting. "I'm good now, though. No voices calling me names anymore." I try to smile and look hopeful. And then I see that their eyes are filled with tears. Silent tears.

Genevieve speaks first, "I'll bet that you have been afraid to tell us that. And I am so sorry that you were. And that I was not there to comfort you." She gets up from the chair and sits next to me on the divan. She takes my hand.

"Caroline, you must have been so frightened in the hospital. I've been to places like that. Bellevue and such here in New York. And here we were, oblivious. We did nothing for you." Francois speaks so softly.

"There's more," I say.

"Go on," Francois says.

"It was my own baby daughter, Leah, that I was afraid of. When she was born, I thought she was..." my voice catches in my throat, and in one long single gasp I finish, "the *devil*...come to *get* me."

My head is in a faraway place. How can I have been that person? I croon in agony in front of these two people that I only met three weeks ago. I lay out this dirtiness of my life for them to see.

My grandparents may have pushed a sixteen-year-old daughter into a bad marriage, but what I did was so much worse. I saw my own daughter as "evil" and I thought to destroy her before she destroyed me. I can leave first thing in the morning, I think. My thoughts run rampant. Like a cougar with his tail caught in a trap, looking for a way out. I'd gnaw off my own tail now to get away from my shame displayed in front of these two souls.

Francois arises and comes to sit at my other side. The two of them then, Francois and Genevieve together hold me between them in a pact of love and forgiveness. The three of us hold each other and weep until the fire has turned to coals. And kind Helen comes to collect us and lead us to bed.

When the murder trial is about to begin, my grandparents decide they will undertake the tiring journey to Minnesota to be there with me throughout. They bring Helen along to assist them. I live with my white-haired grandparents and Helen in a rented apartment just off Hennepin Avenue in Minneapolis.

I testify, of course. When my eyes fall upon the Monster in the courtroom for the first time in fourteen years, I see that he is afraid of me. I couldn't have wished for anything better. During my testimony I can hear the man's voice in my head, but I know whose voice it is. It's not the devil and it never was. It was this evil man.

Dr. Coughlin is in the courtroom when I testify. I also give credit to him, Henry, as I am now asked to address him, and his wife, Lorraine, as well. She is there for me two of the days when I testify. We become friends. Arvid and I are invited to Rochester next summer to visit Henry and Lorraine for a Sunday afternoon of croquet. Their little girls will play with ours. How very ordinary and wonderful!

I learn during the trial that the Monster's second wife, the woman whose fortune sustained him for a time, died mysteriously some years earlier. While I am on the witness stand, my testimony is interrupted by the sound of tortured wailing. The wailing does not stop despite the judge's command for order in the court and a woman is removed from the courtroom.

The noisemaker, I soon learn, is the daughter of that second wife. I meet her later that day, face-to-face outside the courtroom. I hear in her a familiar accent like that of my grandparents'. She catches my arm as I descend the marble steps. "Please, may I speak to you for a moment? My name is Penelope."

The young woman's eyes are filled with a deep sadness and yet, a longing. Before my grandparents and I can take a step further, she says, "My mother was abused by him, too, as was I, before and after her death." Her voice broke. "I believe that he killed my mother, too."

I grasp her arm and say, "We were just going to eat at the restaurant across the way. Will you join us?"

"Yes, thank you. I am alone here in the city. I couldn't stay away." It is the first of many meals together and the four of us sit together in the courtroom for the duration of the trial. We weep together, laugh in relief, and weep again after the guilty verdict is read. We clap when the Monster is removed from the courtroom to be transferred to Stillwater State Prison, where he will live out his days.

28

SUMMERTIME

Caroline
1954

Spring has come and gone, those bright days of hope and promise. It was a spring with good rains. The seedlings of corn have raised their heads in tidy rows and the oats are a sea of bright green grass. It's already time to hay the first crop of alfalfa. At least two more alfalfa crops will be cut before fall. Arvid says the Farmers' Almanac predicts a good growing season.

When Arvid comes in from the fields, his skin is burnished and warm and he smells of freshly cut alfalfa. His eyes dance though I know that he is tired. I welcome him with a hug and a kiss. He still catches me to dance around the kitchen floor now and then, especially when we are happy or excited about something, which happens more than I'd have thought possible. When we hear *The Tennessee Waltz* on the radio, we *must* dance. It is our favorite. It reminds us of when we met at my friend, Eileen's wedding, the first time our hands touched.

The girls have grown so much in the last three years. Sophie will be eight soon, a slender Nordic beauty with her shiny blonde locks and clear blue eyes. She has a graceful way of carrying herself, as if she cannot bring herself to step too harshly on any one piece of the earth. It makes her appear more mature than she is. Sophie makes friends so easily. Oh, to be a child that is never left out. What must that feel like?

Leah will be six the end of July and is eager to start first grade at our little country school. She can already read Dick and Jane books and print her full name. When she walks it is with purpose, as if she can barely wait to get where she is going. Leah looks like me. She is as dark as her sister is fair, with skin that browns quickly in the sun and knees that are even darker from kneeling in the dirt so often. Leah was born a farmer.

Leah is too absorbed in chattering about the new ponies to be bothered when her thick hair falls forward over her dinner plate. She is like an encyclopedia of all that happens on the farm. Without seeming to notice, she allows me to catch her hair and tie it back so that it does not fall into her food. She continues on about the ponies without interruption.

When I left the hospital two years ago, I was assigned a task that I continue to this day. Dr. Coughlin told me, "Caroline, your second daughter was born at the worst possible time in your life. Because of what her birth signified to you then, it has been exceptionally difficult for you to be her mother in here," he placed his hand over his heart, "in the same way that you are to Sophie.

"By the time Leah was born, your world had changed. You were not the same person. The illness removed the memories around her birth. That by itself, might have been remedied, but the illness also colored your understanding of who and what she was. She represented what it was to live inside the hellish years of your childhood, a tortured and terrified little girl."

But the doctor assured me that love can be learned a little at a time, just as a child learns to walk, and so that is my job: to learn who Leah is. She is not me. So I've done as he prescribed. Every day I write something I've learned about my daughter: what she dreams, what she likes and doesn't, what makes her laugh and what makes her sad. I've learned that she is unique and interesting and strong-willed. Arvid says she is a lot like her mother.

I am not to judge myself as inadequate for wanting Marit to live with us, but as wise for preserving that safety net for Leah. After all, Marit was her first "mother." So I am learning, and I am building my connection to Leah bit by bit. It is not forced. It is natural. And I have a small stack of notebooks now that attest to my growing love for Leah.

My face has at last filled in a little. I am no longer so thin that my jaw and cheekbones look sharp and unforgiving. Neither do my ribs or hip bones protrude. Arvid sent me to a dentist that repaired my broken tooth. I am contented. What a miraculous thing for me to say!

There are times when I fear that the schizophrenia will come back, just as it did after my first hospitalization. Dr. Coughlin has always been truthful with me so when he told me that such a thing cannot be predicted with certainty, I must believe him and live with that possibility.

But he also has told me that I am a woman with great strength. That what I have already lived through has shown that. Because of my strength and the love of my family, there is no need for me to waste even one more single, precious day living in fear about what might happen.

Before my daughters go to sleep tonight, I will tell them a bedtime story that my mother told me when I was Sophie's age. It was a favorite of mine.

It is bedtime, although the sun is still in the sky. "Are you ready for your bedtime story?"

"Yup, I'm ready, Mommy." Sophie is always the first to answer.

"Me, too. What story are you telling tonight, Mommy? Are there animals in it?" Leah prefers stories with animals to all others. *Bambi* made her sad, but she loved it anyway. *Dumbo the Elephant* was a favorite. Since recovering more memories of the years alone with my mother in Minneapolis, I have a whole library's worth of children's stories in my head to tell them.

"No, Sweet Pea. It's not a story about animals. Well, wait... there are a few horses in the story. How's that?"

"That's good. I'll stay awake for that." Leah smiles at me.

"The girl's name in this story is Ella. She doesn't have any brothers or sisters, but she has two wonderful parents who love her so very much, and because they had plenty of money, they give her every material thing a little girl could possibly want. Lots of clothes and toys—"

"No brothers or sisters?" Leah interrupts. "Well, that wouldn't be much fun. Did she have a pony at least?"

"Nope, no pony either." I touch the tip of her nose with my finger and smile. "Your mommy didn't have brothers or sisters either, but like Ella, I did have a mother who was very good to me and she was good at imagining things with me. But this story is about Ella. I'm telling it the way my mother told me.

"Ella loves her beautiful mother very much. The mother has so many wonderful dreams for her daughter, and she tells Ella all the happy things she sees in her daughter's future."

"Like ponies?" Leah interjects.

"Shhh now, Leah. Let Mommy tell the story." Sophie is serious about rules.

"One very sad day, Ella's mother dies." Both Sophie and Leah's eyes grow wide. "Ella and her father are so sad and lonely. They miss her so much. Ella's father is a kind man and he wants his daughter to have playmates, so he marries again, a woman with two daughters of her own that are just about Ella's age. But the poor father was tricked by the woman, because the stepmother doesn't show her true colors until one day when Ella's kind father dies too.

"Even kind people can be fooled by those who are hiding who they truly are. His beloved daughter, Ella, was only eleven years old."

"That's how old you were when your mama died, isn't it, Mommy?" Sophie whispers.

"Yes, it is. The stepmother favors her own ugly and mean daughters, Drucilla and Esmerelda, over the beautiful little Ella at every turn. The stepmother is jealous of Ella's beauty, so she makes her a servant in the household. Ella is allowed to wear only the oldest raggedy cast-off clothing of her stepsisters.

"The stepsisters give Ella a cruel nickname. They call her *Cinder* Ella because she sleeps on the floor near the cinders at the hearth in order to stay warm. CinderElla works hard to do as she's told by the stepmother and her stepsisters even though they are wicked. They laugh at her and tell her that no one wants her for a friend. They tell her to hide herself when anyone comes to the house because she is ugly. The truth is that they don't want anyone to see how beautiful she is. She's forbidden from even leaving the yard. Despite that, CinderElla remains good and kind.

"But CinderElla has one friend. Surrounding the house stands a tall stone wall. On the other side lives an elderly woman. When CinderElla works in the garden, the woman talks to her through one of the little notches in the wall. CinderElla can only see the woman's kind face. CinderElla confides in her, although she tries not to say anything unkind about the stepmother and stepsisters—"

"Well, *I* wouldn't do that. That stepmother is very wicked. I would tell the neighbor lady the truth about them. Maybe she could help her somehow." Leah wears a small pout. She doesn't like anyone to get away with being mean to the characters in her stories. I can see that she'll look out for anyone that is treated unfairly.

"Leah! Shhh...I wanna hear Mommy's story," Sophie hushes her sister.

"The elderly woman tells CinderElla that she may call her "Grandmama," if she would like to. She knows that CinderElla has no one to love her. Well, that makes CinderElla very happy. They talk together for a little while every day, and CinderElla quickly grows to love her.

"Without her Grandmama, CinderElla would surely have lost all hope. She may have become bitter and hard and vengeful, but she doesn't. The Grandmama promises CinderElla that one day, something wonderful will happen. As the years go by, Ella becomes more and more beautiful and so the stepmother tries to ensure that no one will ever see her, and she makes her work even harder.

"One day, there is a small party of men on horseback—"

"There ARE horses in the story." Leah covers her mouth with her hand immediately while Sophie gives her "the look."

"CinderElla is working in the garden when she hears men talking outside the gate. One of the men says, 'He is too ill to ride any farther. I'll see if anyone in this house can help us. Meanwhile, Geoffrey, I want you to ride on ahead and have the steward send a carriage to bring him home.'

"CinderElla hears the hoofbeats galloping off. Suddenly, a very handsome man dressed in fine clothing calls to Ella through the garden gate. 'Good Lady, might I entreat you to allow us into your garden to rest? One of my attendants has fallen quite ill and I'm afraid he cannot ride the rest of the way. If you would allow us in so that he may lie down in the shade while we await a carriage, I would be in your debt.'

"CinderElla says, 'Yes, of course.' She opens the gate for the men and their horses, although she's been warned by the stepmother not to ever open it for anyone. But the stepmother and stepsisters are gone for the day and she can see that the man is very ill. She invites them in to rest beneath the shade trees.

"CinderElla brings her own sleeping mat outside for the sick man to rest upon. She draws cool water from the well for the men to drink and lays a moist cloth on the sick man's forehead. Before long, an elegant carriage arrives to collect the sick man.

"The handsome man in fine clothing takes CinderElla's hand and bows to kiss it. He says, 'Thank you most kindly, Good Lady. I must find some way to repay you your kindness.'

"CinderElla curtsies and says to him, 'You are most kindly welcome, Good Sir.'

"It is then that he realizes that CinderElla doesn't recognize him, for he is none other than the King's only son, Prince Edward. He smiles warmly to have seen her true nature."

Both Sophie and Leah's eyelids flutter, unable to stay awake. The rest of the story of CinderElla will have to wait until tomorrow night. Tomorrow night, my girls will learn that the elderly woman next door, the one CinderElla calls Grandmama, is actually her fairy godmother. I'll bet that my precious daughters will see their dear Grandma Marit when they imagine the face of the fairy godmother.

I have pledged myself to a sacred path, to earn a place on that chain of brave women that fiercely love and protect their children above all else.

This I do to honor Marit and my mother, for it is they and others like them that pull us back when we creep too close to the edge. When we've lost sight of who we are and why we are, they hold us tightly, so that the best of what we are will be remembered and loved.

THE END

Postscript

During the earlier days of mental health treatment, asylums often restrained people who had mental illnesses with iron chains and shackles around their ankles and wrists. With better understanding and treatments, this cruel practice eventually stopped.

In the early 1950s, an organization called Mental Health America issued a call to asylums across the country for their discarded chains and shackles. On April 13, 1953, at the McShane Bell Foundry in Baltimore, Md., Mental Health America melted down these inhumane bindings and recast them into a sign of hope, the Mental Health Bell.

The inscription on the **Mental Health Bell** reads:

"Cast from shackles which bound them, this bell shall ring out hope for the mentally ill and victory over mental illness."

Illustration 14: Plaque marking the Rochester State Hospital Cemetery, Rochester, Minnesota. Photo credit: C.E. Lafler

Illustration 15: All orphans were referred to as "State Schoolers." 10,635 orphaned, abused or abandoned children were sent to the Owatonna orphanage.

Illustration 16: More than 300 children died in State guardianship at the State School; the majority of deaths were among the youngest.

Illustration 17: Harvey Ronglien lived as a state schooler for eleven years. His words are inscribed above.

Perhaps Alfred Adler, Austrian psychiatrist and psychotherapist said it best:

"Even in a model orphanage, the children live

like inmates. Emotional starvation is

inseparable from institutional life."

Alfred Adler 1870 – 1937

Glossary

Norwegian-American English

å selvfølgelig	Oh, of course
Alle tingene jeg liker mest	All the things I like the most
Bare bra, takk!	Great, thanks!
Bare litt	Only a little
En liten lunsj	A little-lunch
Gå legg deg	Go lay down! (to a dog)
God dag!	Hello (Good day)
Ha det (informal)	Bye
Herregud!	Good God!
Hva slags lunsj er det?	What kind of a lunch is that?
Hvordan har du det?	How are you?
Jeg kan ikke ha dett	I can't have that
Ja, litt	Yes, a little
*Jeg er bestemoren din	I'm your grandma
Kake og kaker	Cake and cookies
Mange tusen takk	Many thousand thanks
Nei, nei	No, no
På ettermiddagen	In the afternoon
**Sitte deg god	Get comfortable
Skål	Toast (to your health)
Skaut	Headscarf
Smør, ost, iskrem og kaffe	Butter, cheese, ice cream and coffee
Takk for hjelpen!	Thanks for helping!
Takk for maten	Thanks for the food
Vær så god!	You're welcome
***Uff or Uff da nei	Oh no! Funny

*This is a shortened version from that said in Norway.

**A phrase learned from my mother. This is not proper Norwegian and would not be said in Norway today.

***In Minnesota, "Uff" and "Uff da" have taken on a broader meaning from that in Norway. In Minnesota, the expression may be used in response to an event or idea that is unexpected, humorous, embarrassing. silly, unfortunate or surprising. In Norway, the tone of voice used with "Uff " signifies the meaning. In a grave voice, it conveys disapproval or disgust.

Selected References

Anderson, Philip, and Dag Blanck, eds. *Norwegians and Swedes in the United States*. St. Paul: Minnesota Historical Society Press, 2012.

Belofsky, Nathan. *Strange Medicine: A Shocking History of Real Medical Practices Through the Ages*. TarcherPerigee, Pub. and Imprint of Penguin Group (USA) ; 1st Edition, 2013

https://www.bemidjistate.edu/airc/community-resources/anishinaabe-timeline/

https://cvltnation.com/horrifying-psychiatric-treatments-from-the-age-of-reason/

https://edsitement.neh.gov/lesson-plans/anishinabeojibwechippewa-culture-indian-nation

Gjerde, Jon, and Carlton Qualey. *Norwegians in Minnesota: The People of Minnesota*. St. Paul: Minnesota Historical Society Press, 2002.

Gordon, Heidi M. and Deborah A. Connelly. *Failing to report details of an event: A review of the directed forgetting procedure and applications to reports of childhood sexual abuse*

https://www.tandfonline.com/doi/full/10.1080/0965821090313077 2. Journal, Memory, Vol 18, 2010

Holmquist, June. *They Chose Minnesota: A Survey of the State's Ethnic Groups*. St. Paul: Minnesota Historical Society Press, 1981.

Mental Health America MHA.https://www.mhanational.org/our-history. Founder Clifford W. Beers. Alexandria, Virginia. EPub. Upd. 2020

https://www.mnhs.org/fortsnelling/learn/native-americans/ojibwe-people

https://mnprairieroots.com/2012/01/18/inside-the-owatonna-orphanage-museum-heartbreaking-stories-and-photos/

Neumann, Aurore et al. *Specificity deficit in the recollection of emotional memories in schizophrenia*. National Library of Medicine https://pubmed.ncbi.nlm.nih.gov/16901720/ 2007

Olson, Daron. *Vikings Across the Atlantic: Emigration of A Greater Norway, 1860–1915*. Minneapolis: University of Minnesota Press, 2013

http://orphanagemuseum.com/Purse, Marcia. Reviewed by Gans, Steven. *The Discovery and History of Lithium as a Mood Stabilizer*. VeryWell Mind, partner of Cleveland Clinic, Epub. Upd. 2020

Razor, Peter. While the Locust Slept. Minnesota Historical Society Press, 2011.

Resman, Michael. *The Mailmen of Elmwood*. St. Cloud, Minnesota. North Star Press of St. Cloud, Inc., 2013

Rochester State Hospital. https://libguides.mnhs.org/institutions/sh St. Paul: Minnesota History Center. Gale Family Library, Minnesota Historical Society.

Sar, Vedet, et al. *Childhood trauma and dissociation in schizophrenia*. National Library of Medicine. https://pubmed.ncbi.nlm.nih.gov/19893342/ E pub. 2009

Tustin, Karen & Harlene Hayne. *Recollection improves with age: children's and adults' accounts of their childhood experiences.* Journal, Memory, Vol 27, 2019 https://www.tandfonline.com/doi/full/10.1080/09658211.2018.143 2661

Ulvestad, Martin. *Norwegians in America, Their History and Record*. Translated by Olaf Kringhaug and Odd-Steinar Raneng. Waukon: My Astri Publishing, 2010

Index of Place Names

Illustration Index

Reflections on Norwegian Heard in Childhood

The Norwegian I heard spoken in my hometown of Spring Grove, Minnesota when I was a child, in the 1960's and 70's, is remembered fondly as language with a musical lilt. Norwegian was my mother's first language and throughout her lifetime, she welcomed opportunities to "talk Norwegian" with anyone that was interested. After a chat with visitors who wanted to talk Norwegian, she offered this observation to my father, "Ya, they had de right words, but you got to have de right sling to it, too."

Over the years, as English was spoken alongside various Norwegian dialects (i.e. Hallingdal, Hadeland, Gudbransdalen, Telemark, to name some,) a few small tweaks in the Norwegian language spoken in Minnesota may very well have arisen. A new way of expressing an idea or action would become useful when it was easily understood by both Norwegian and English speakers.

One of my earliest memories of the Norwegian language is as a child playing on the floor at my mother's feet as her sewing machine hummed along. There, my imagination conjured up fantastic things using my mother's jars of buttons. It was there, as well, that I pestered her to teach me some of her mysterious Norwegian words as she sewed. I would be pleased, if today, I could hear her say that I give them the "sling" they are due.

Ardys Brevig Richards

About the Author

Ardys (Brevig) Richards was born in 1956 and grew up in the Driftless Area of southeastern Minnesota, the site of the first Norwegian settlement in the state. The community was ultimately named Spring Grove. She milked Brown Swiss cows on the family dairy farm along with her six older siblings and was one of eleven students to attend the last one-room country schoolhouse in Minnesota. She graduated from Rutgers–The State University of New Jersey in 1982 with a Master's in Social Work and worked for thirty-two years as a Licensed Independent Clinical Social Worker (LICSW) in Iowa, Wisconsin, and Minnesota. She retired in 2015 to sail the East Coast and Caribbean with her husband of twenty-one years on a forty-three foot sailboat. The couple has four children between them. Ardys and her husband now make their home in Memphis, Tennessee.

http://www.ArdysBrevigRichards.blogspot.com

Endnotes

i **Driftless Area.** An area of 16,000 sq. miles which includes southeastern Minnesota, southwestern Wisconsin, northeastern Iowa and northwestern Illinois. The topography is of steeply carved creek valleys and forested bluffs, caves and thousands of sinkholes. Unlike the surrounding area, the glaciers of the last ice age did not scour this region. Archaeological evidence of the native peoples that once inhabited the area remains: burial mounds in effigy and cave paintings.
https://driftlessareamag.com/index.cfm?fuseaction=page.display&page_id=38

ii A **Chivaree** is a noisy serenade which includes shouting, singing, and banging on pots and pans outside the home of newlyweds. Chivarees were popular in southeastern Minnesota at least until the start of WWII.

iii Sometimes older children at the Owatonna orphanage, (AKA **Minnesota State Public School for Dependent and Neglected Children**) were sent to labor on farms under the terms of a contract established between the orphanage and the family. The family was obligated to provide the child with room and board and a change of clothing. A limited payment went to the orphanage in return for the child's farm labor.

iv Estra has a genetic disorder which today is known as **Prader-Willi Syndrome (PWS)**. It had not been identified or named as of 1948. In newborns, symptoms include weak muscles, poor feeding, and slow development. Other physical characteristics are almond-shaped crossed eyes, narrow forehead at the temples, very fair hair color, skin and eyes and small hands and feet. By the toddler years, children with PWS become hungry constantly, often leading to morbid obesity, type 2 diabetes and lowered life expectancy. There is no relationship between Prader-Willi and mental illness. Like many others, she may have been placed at the asylum for lack of a more socially appropriate option.

Endnotes

v   **Harelip** refers to a congenital malformation of lip and/or palate. Going back to the 1500's the term was used to liken one's appearance to that of a "hare." Today "harelip" is considered an insulting term. The terms **"cleft palate" and "cleft lip"** are now used in its place. Most children living in first world countries have surgical repair early in life. Children with cleft palate and/or cleft lip are frequently prone to ear infections and hearing loss. Feeding can be problematic, and food may come out the nose. Speech may sound nasal. Some children are cruelly teased. There is no association between cleft palate and/or cleft lip and mental illness. Ruth's placement at the asylum may have come about because of behaviors that developed following a childhood of social ostracism.

vi   **Ojibwe**. or "Chippewa" is the name by which white colonists called the tribe that is now the largest population of Native Americans in North America. In Canada, they still refer to themselves as Ojibwe. In Minnesota, however, they call themselves **Anishinaabe** (aNAHSH'nAH'bay) which means "the original people." Anishinaabemowin is the native language. Today Anishinaabeg occupy land around the entire Great Lakes region. There are seven Anishinaabe/Ojibwe reservations in Minnesota alone: Bois Forte (Nett Lake), Fond du Lac, Grand Portage, Leech Lake, Mille Lacs, White Earth, and Red Lake. Anishinaabemowin is taught at Bemidji State University in Bemidji, MN as well as in Bemidji Middle School and other sites in Minnesota. There are some 20,000 Ojibwe who speak the language in Canada. https://www.mnopedia.org/ojibwe-our-historical-role-influencing-contemporary-minnesota

vii   **Seizures**: Were commonly known as "convulsions" or "fits" for centuries. Neurologists now understand seizures much better than they did in 1948 and are able to treat most seizure disorders with medication. Seizures are caused by some type of injury to the brain whether occurring as an anomaly in brain development, trauma during the birth process, or at any time in life after birth. Many types of trauma to the brain can cause seizures.

Endnotes

The same injury that produces the seizure (or seizure types) is often responsible for any cognitive delays, although many people with seizures have no recognizable cognitive delays. The type of seizure that our character, Lois, has was called a **Grand Mal** seizure in 1948. In more modern times, her seizure would be referred to as a **GTC (Generalized Tonic-Clonic) seizure**. A GTC is a seizure which starts in one place in the brain and very rapidly involves the entire brain, so that all of the brain's synopses are firing producing repetitive contractions. The individual is unconscious during a GTC and has no memory of it. The seizure itself is very exhausting, and the patient may need to rest for some time afterward.

Historically, those with seizures were considered possessed by demons or mentally ill. Sometimes people like Lois were hospitalized in asylums for lack of a more appropriate option, much the same as her sisters Ruth and Estra experienced.

It is improper/rude to refer to a person with chronic seizures or epilepsy as "an epileptic." It is socially appropriate, instead, to refer to the individual as a "person with epilepsy."

viii **Hydrotherapy,** was a practice that continued well into the 20th century. Patients might be mummified in wet cloths or sprayed with water from high-pressure hoses. With a continuous bath, the patient was strapped into a large tub, with a canvas sheet covering the bathtub that left only their head to be exposed. Such a bath could last for several hours to several days. It was most often used to treat insomnia, depression and suicidal thoughts.

ix **Insulin Coma (or Shock) Therapy** was developed by Manfred Sakel, MD, from Vienna. He was treating a diabetic actress with an opiate addiction in 1927 when he accidentally put her into a mild insulin coma. He discovered that this reduced her craving for opiates. He reasoned that an insulin coma could have beneficial application for people with schizophrenia. Improvement in psychotic symptoms was seen, although the benefits often "wore off" over time. It fell out of favor because it was dangerous, permanent results were lacking and because the first truly effective antipsychotic medication was invented, chlorpromazine.

Endnotes

x **Electroconvulsive Therapy (ECT)** was invented in Italy in the 1930s and was physically dangerous when first developed. Current practice, however, is known as modified ECT in that muscle relaxants are used to ameliorate the physical dangers of a seizure and anesthesia is used to avoid pain from the electricity. There is little doubt that many patients have had therapeutic results from this therapy. The fact that ECT has shown efficacy also helped to support the understanding of schizophrenia as a biological phenomenon. Within only a few years of its invention, ECT was used in mental hospitals all over the world. Estimates are that at least 100,000 patients worldwide have used ECT.

There is also evidence, however, that in the 1950's, ECT, and the threat of it, were used in mental hospitals to control difficult patients and to maintain order on wards. ECT use declined in the '60s and '70s, but its use was revived in the early 1980s.

ECT is known to cause some memory loss, particularly of events around the time of the treatment. Those memories often return, however. Many patients say they have little, if any, permanent memory loss. Permanent long-term memory loss has been documented, however, and it is unknown how common that is. Many clinicians believe it is very rare, based on their experience.

xi **Paul Bunyan** is an gargantuan lumberjack in American folklore. He and his equally giant companion, Babe the Blue Ox stand as statues in Bemidji, Minnesota. https://learningenglish.voanews.com/a/paul-bunyan-folk-tale-american-stories/2628785.html

xii **Lithiated soda** is lithium in powder form. "Bib-Label Lithiated Lemon-Lime Soda" ——later called 7-Up.U.S. beverage makers were to remove lithium from beverages in 1948 due to serious side effects. Toxicity symptoms were diarrhea, vomiting and sleepiness. Not all complied. John Cade, MD of Australia was beginning to use it as a treatment for mental disorders by 1948.

Made in the USA
Columbia, SC
28 December 2021

52883423R00183